The King
Must Die

Also by N. Gemini Sasson:

The Crown in the Heather (The Bruce Trilogy: Book I)

Worth Dying For (The Bruce Trilogy: Book II)

The Honor Due a King (The Bruce Trilogy: Book III)

*Isabeau, A Novel of Queen Isabella
and Sir Roger Mortimer*

The King Must Die

Murder and revenge in the time of Edward III

N. GEMINI SASSON

cader idris
press

To my lovely in-laws Pat and Milt Brickson -

For your excellent company and your endless support.

PART I:

The King must die, or Mortimer goes down;
The commons now begin to pity him.

Roger Mortimer
from Christopher Marlowe's *Edward II*

1

Isabella:

Wallingford — December, 1326

THE ANGLED RAYS OF a low winter sun glinted silver off the Thames, its mirrored surface broken only by the rippling wake of a small boat. On the riverbank below the southern gate of Walling-ford Castle, frost glimmered on the branches of an alder where a flock of starlings congregated. Their cackles rose to a cacophony as the vessel slid in to shore and its passengers disembarked.

A dozen men climbed the banks, their hushed voices carrying on the brittle winter air. Above them a cloud of blue-black wings erupted from the trees and swarmed across the river to settle on the decaying thatched roof of a barn.

Tugging the fur of my mantle up higher around my ears, I leaned wearily against the stones of the merlon. The clack of footsteps rang out on the wall-walk behind me.

"You did not sleep last night, my queen?"

1

I turned to gaze upon Sir Roger Mortimer. Hands clasped behind his back, he glided closer. He stopped an arm's reach away and tilted his head in question.

The yearning to burrow beneath his cloak and envelop myself in his warmth rushed through me. Then, a sentry on the curtain wall moved to study the new arrivals as they made their way toward the gatehouse. Achingly aware of Mortimer's nearness, I cast a furtive glance along the wall-walk and lowered my voice. "Given the day, it is a wonder I am not curled up in a corner, babbling like a madwoman."

"Ah yes, the council."

I pressed my back to the rugged stones. The icy cloud of my breath hung in the air, filled with words too fragile to be spoken. "I do not think I want to hear what they will say."

"And what, precisely, is it that you fear?"

"All of it. Anything. Whether they will seek my husband's death . . . or let him live."

He nodded pensively and moved to peer through the crenel. "It would bode ill for your son and every ruler after him if they called for the execution of Edward of Caernarvon, don't you think?"

"But it's possible."

"It's possible they could not only restore your husband to the throne, but pardon him for every wrong ever done to England and throw a feast in his honor; it is, however, very unlikely. They might wish him dead out of convenience, but no one wants to stain their conscience by ending his life." An unruly lock of hair fell across his brow, giving him the mischievous look of one far fewer in years than his forty. "Isabeau, have you abandoned your faith in me already?"

"Never, Roger. You know that."

"Then why are you so sure of our doom? I've been calling up old favors since long before we were dashed upon England's shores with our disparate army."

"It's not our end I fear, Roger. That comes for us all, eventually, doesn't it? It's what will happen if they make me go back to him. I could lose you, forever, and I can't —"

He pressed two fingers to my lips, and then quickly dropped his hand back to his side. His eyes narrowed. "Five hundred days."

I shook my head, not understanding.

"That is how long I spent in the Tower before my escape," he said. "I counted the days not by the rising of the sun, but by the changing of guards outside my door. Much of my time was squandered on thoughts of revenge: the many ways I would watch Hugh Despenser die . . . and how to bring a king to his knees when I had failed so dismally at that before. But it was also the thought of being with you, Isabeau, that kept me from giving up."

"But we never spoke in that time."

"Ah, but we did, we did. You came to visit me in the Tower, remember? It was the second time you spared my life. You would not have done that unless you had a purpose for me and . . . and perhaps an interest that was somewhat . . . *personal?*" The subtle curve of his lips shot a ripple of desire through me. Last night he had kissed me in ways, touched me in places, that had left my flesh tingling long after he slipped from my bed to return to his own. Even now I could recall the impression of his fingertips as they slid around my waist to the small of my back, then downward to grasp my buttocks as he eased me over him. His dark eyes settled on my hips, as though he, too, was thinking of last night.

The conversation of the new arrivals rose up from the barbican. I stepped closer to Mortimer to look down at them. For days now, more people had been coming than going. The members of the council, a handful of lords and bishops I had summoned, were even now convening in the great hall to set the course of Edward of Caernarvon's fate—and my own. Less than a month from now, Parliament would convene at Westminster. If they recommended I return to him, live beside him as his wife . . .

A shiver began at the nape of my neck and trickled downward, spreading from spine to ribs, my heart constricting with dread. I drew a deep breath, filling my lungs with crisp air, and then exhaled slowly. "So much depends on this day, Roger. I cannot face them without you there."

"This once, Isabeau." He turned his head to look at me, his bearded chin tucked down in a way that conveyed his reluctance. "But I'll attend only because Leicester . . . or Lancaster, whatever he calls himself now, is still in Kenilworth watching over the king. Otherwise, I would not agree. Already I'm the cause of mistrust and jealousy. I'll not give anyone further reason to come against me in the future."

"Then speak only on my behalf, not your own."

"Even that, I think, would raise just as many suspicions as if I asked for the crown for myself. Some think I mean to make myself king, did you know?"

Perhaps, I mused, *that is because you share the queen's bed?*

Suddenly, he waved to the men in the barbican below, who had recently been joined by Mortimer's longtime friend, Sir John Maltravers. "Thomas! Good morn!"

The young nobleman he had addressed, fair-haired and so long of limb he stepped like a deer, raised his head and cupped a hand to his brow. He waved back. "My lord! Margaret sends her well wishes."

"You did not bring her? When am I ever to see my daughter again? There had better be a good reason, Thomas."

"There may be, there well may be. I shall know more a month from now."

"A month? Ah, I see. Then you wasted no time. Am I to expect my first grandchild before the year is out?"

"God willing, my lord."

"That is most excellent news. A moment and we will join you."

4

Then Mortimer said aside to me, "No man could wish for a better son-in-law than Lord Thomas of Berkeley. Even when he was young I knew he had great promise. I vow he'll serve you well, Isabeau."

"So Margaret and Thomas have set up their household already, I take it. What of your other children?" Mortimer's wife, the heiress Joan de Genville, had given him a large brood of children—twelve in all, Margaret being his oldest and so far only married daughter.

He offered his arm. "My two eldest, Roger and Edmund, are seeing to all that. Even with Despenser dead and the king unable to raise objections, it will take some time to restore all that was taken from me."

As we began down the stairway to the barbican, I slowed my steps. "And your wife?"

"Already at Wigmore," he said casually, making no attempt to keep his voice hushed. "No doubt clucking orders like a frenzied hen and bemoaning the loss of her tapestries and wardrobe." After a long pause, he added, "She wrote."

"Oh," I said, unsure how to respond or why I had even asked about her. While my marriage with Edward had been fraught with complex troubles from the very beginning, Mortimer's relationship with his wife had been at worst mundane. He did not often speak of her, not even to complain. "What did she say?"

"She asked me to come home to help put affairs in order there." He gave me a sidelong glance and stroked the back of my hand. "I told her I couldn't, not soon, anyway. That there were too many urgent, important matters to attend to right now."

I wondered if he had told her that the queen would not allow him to leave her side, but I kept the thought to myself. I could not nurse my jealousy forever. How often did I need to hear him say that it was me he loved, not her? Eventually though, he would need to return to his estates, either because of business or family, and he would come face to face with his wife and . . . Oh, I did not want to think of it. Would not.

But even more, I did not want to think of the matter that was sure to arise at council: The state of my marriage to Edward of Caernarvon, still King of England.

Discreetly, I slipped my hand from Mortimer's elbow as we exited the stairway. We turned to our left to walk beneath the raised portcullis of the inner gate and out into the bailey. Cloaked in the cold shadows cast by the outer wall, we stood side by side as Mortimer's son-in-law approached, head bent. Behind him, Maltravers was issuing orders to Berkeley's servants as to where to take his few belongings.

"My lady, you remember Lord Thomas Berkeley?" Mortimer swept his hand from his torso.

"Indeed, I do." I extended my hand and Berkeley took it in his as he bowed, grazing my knuckles with a kiss.

"Your servant, my lady," he murmured. The tightly fitted sleeves of his dark blue robe were buttoned from wrist to elbow. Over that, he wore a quintise of scarlet as further protection against the winter cold, the edges dagged and trimmed in brighter blue cording.

"But," I began, "I seem to recall you were a great deal more unkempt—and nearly starved—when we returned to England three months ago."

Berkeley lowered his eyes. "Four years confined to one room, with neither sunshine nor sport, tends to compromise one's vigor. Since then, I've compensated overmuch, I confess." He patted his belly, indicating he had eaten well lately, although he was still remarkably thin. "Margaret seems to have fared better at Shouldham Priory, though."

"You've taken her on to Berkeley Castle?" Mortimer asked.

Berkeley nodded, his chin-length fair hair bobbing as he did so. Blinking, he looked at me nervously with pale blue eyes and pressed his rigid mouth into something of a smile, but very quickly he returned his gaze to Mortimer. "I came as soon as I could, although Margaret was reluctant to let me go after so long a time apart."

"Understandable," Mortimer said. "Maltravers will show you to your chambers, where you can rest up from your journey. We will speak more, later. For now, I must escort the queen to council." He laid both hands lightly on Berkeley's shoulders. "I'm happy to see you free, Thomas."

"And I you, my lord," Berkeley returned.

Maltravers hooked his half hand in the air, gesturing for the new arrivals to follow him. Lord Berkeley loped along at his heels, face upturned and eyes bright as he twisted one way and then the other to survey his surroundings.

The knight who had been standing behind him moments before flashed a yellow-toothed smile at me and ducked his head in a bow: Sir Thomas Gurney. "My lady."

Beside Gurney, a slightly built man squatted. His thin fingers cradled a scalp of stringy hair. He coughed violently, cleared his throat and spat a glob of phlegm between his feet. "God help me," he moaned, "I'm going to die."

Gurney swung an arm to cuff him on the shoulder. The man toppled over onto his side, his elbow smashing into the cobbles.

"On your feet, Ockle. Pay some respect to our queen here."

Ah yes, William Ockle. He and Gurney had found my daughters in the church when the siege of Bristol broke. A dubious pair of heroes—but who was I to question fate or chance?

Gulping air, Ockle rolled over onto to his knees. A sneer curled his thin lips into a ragged line. With an indrawn wheeze, he staggered to his feet. He peeked at me beneath oily hanks of hair, then lowered his eyes and dipped his torso in a bow. Another cough threatened to split his ribs.

"Will you be all right?" I asked.

"He'll live," Gurney answered for him, then hooked a hand

gruffly beneath Ockle's armpit to pull him away. Ockle stumbled alongside him, muttering curses. In response, Gurney yanked harder. Ten crooked strides later, they were at Lord Berkeley's heels.

A chill whispered across my cheek and I raised a hand as if to brush it away. But as I did so, fine pellets of sleet stung at my knuckles. I looked heavenward. The sun had retreated behind a dense veil of clouds. Wind swooped over the outer walls to descend into the openness of the bailey. Even the birds were huddled in the sheltered places. With stiff fingers, I clutched at the edges of my mantle, pulling it tight around me like a cocoon in which I could withdraw from the world. A hand alighted on the small of my back and I startled, gasping.

"It's time," Mortimer said.

ALREADY A DIMINUTIVE MAN, Walter Reynolds, Archbishop of Canterbury, sank to his knees before me in the middle of the great hall of Wallingford, which served for now as my council chamber. From this distance, if not for the vestments of his office, I might have mistaken him for a child.

"Rise, Your Grace," I said. The echo of my voice died away to mingle with the whisper of silk robes and the groan of leather sword belts, as twenty bodies shifted on their benches. Weak morning sunlight passed through widely spaced windows, the dusty wooden panels of the wainscoting and soot-stained, busily painted walls making the room seem even darker. The glow of the hearth did little but cast shadows. I strained to focus my eyes. To my immediate right sat Adam Orleton, Bishop of Hereford, and John de Stratford, Bishop of Winchester. To the left were my brothers-in-law Edmund, Earl of Kent, and Thomas, Earl of Norfolk. Even they had abandoned their own brother, the king, in his direst hour.

Although all had come here willingly, I was not yet sure who to trust and who to regard with caution. Unseating a king by invasion with mercenary forces was not a matter blindly supported by everyone, not even his opponents. Criticism would not die away even now that it was done. Soon, the struggle for power would begin. Likely, it would begin this very day.

Head bowed and shoulders stooped, Archbishop Reynolds tottered to his feet on stiff knees and came forward until he stood before the dais. "My lady, before these peace-loving witnesses and merciful God, I do meekly submit to you and offer my allegiance."

"Your letter to such effect was received, Your Grace, and my protection given." I longed to remind him of certain things, but now was not the time to scour open wounds with vinegar. The archbishop had been an adamant supporter of Edward's until the very last. Not until Despenser was dead and the king in custody did he see it prudent to change allegiances. Perhaps he feared for his freedom—or his station? No matter, he was harmless enough and there were greater matters at hand. I sat forward in my chair, the joints of the wooden frame creaking loudly. "Your humility, I might add, is to be admired. In these uncertain times, difficult choices must be made for the good of all England, not only for the here and now, but for —"

The door at the hall's end swung open, hinges groaning. A rush of winter air billowed in. Goose flesh prickled my arms and neck. I gripped my knees, fingernails curled into claws, prepared to admonish the person who had so rudely arrived late to interrupt. And then, Henry, Earl of Leicester and Lancaster, blustered into the hall.

My stomach lurched. No, he was supposed to still be at Kenilworth, where the king was being held. Mortimer's eyes flicked to me. If both men did not temper their tongues, this day could end badly. I cautioned Mortimer with a glance, but his sights were already fixed on the earl. The porter, his head dipped contritely, scuttled forth to latch onto the door's edge and yank it shut.

Stomping, Lancaster braced his feet wide. He glared down the length of each row of benches, his mouth curving into a smug smile, and rested the heel of his hand on his sword pommel. "Your pardon, my queen. I trust I have not missed anything?"

Archbishop Reynolds's head swiveled, his mitre tipping precariously to one side. His lip twitched as he reached up with both hands and repositioned it. With an audible exhalation, he spun around and drew his shoulders up so that his embroidered amice bunched in folds at his neck. Then, his fingers teasing at the tasseled ends of his stole, he looked at me again. "My lady, you were saying?"

I peered past him to Lancaster. The last time the earl had made such a brazen appearance, he had presented me with Bishop Stapledon's head in a basket. This time, thanks be to God, he was without any such gruesome gift.

"All is forgiven, Your Grace." My gaze swept over the faces lining the hall to remind myself I had many supporters here. Kent's eyes met mine and he smiled. I looked to the other side and there Bishop Orleton nodded sagely. "Let us begin. Please, be seated."

The archbishop went to the nearest bench, the other bishops scooting aside to make room. Lancaster stepped to his right, but no one moved. Then he swung an arm to his left, as if clearing the way, and proceeded to the very middle bench where, although there was no apparent gap, he managed to wedge himself in, unresponsive to the grumbling of those around him. Nearly unseated himself, Lord Berkeley, at the very end, relinquished his spot and went to stand next to a column behind Lancaster. The earl, stretching his meaty legs before him and rubbing at his knees, took no notice of the young lord's servile gesture.

Words stuck at the back of my throat. Having overcome so much these past few years, I would have thought myself inherently braver, but even now it was as if the demons of my fears never stopped pursuing me. I cleared my throat, clasped my hands to my belly and spoke with as much authority as I could summon.

"Welcome, my lords. You have been called here because I value your counsel. I thank you for your haste, for we must act with both swiftness and resolve. I will not belabor past events. Suffice it to say it was not lightly that I undertook drastic measures to bring about change. Even so, the weight upon my soul has at times been so heavy that if not for a handful of honorable and courageous men, I might not . . . no, *could* not have gone forward." Sir John of Hainault, Count William's brother, raised his chin proudly as I glanced his way.

"Thus, it was with immeasurable relief that I and my son found ourselves welcomed upon our return when we landed on Suffolk's shores. That alone revealed in whom England's people have chosen to entrust their future and extend their loyalty—as have all of you by coming here."

Archbishop Reynolds tucked his chin down, as if aware that others there yet doubted him. Around him, a few heads bobbed subtly in agreement and I continued. "My husband's misjudgments led this kingdom down a path of destruction and immorality. It began with Piers Gaveston—gifts of land, titles, countless favors—and did not end until Gaveston's death. The story was much the same with Hugh Despenser, but it was at Lord Despenser's hands that I was made to suffer. Edward's kingship suffered as well, and with it England's people. And so the people chose to end Despenser's life at Hereford. Two favorites dead. Will there be another? I pray not, with all my heart. But prayer alone is not enough. We must decide wisely and we must act.

"Repeatedly, the king has defied Parliament, flouted the Lords Ordainers, ruled by whim and acted out of contempt. He has failed his people by refusing to keep his word and so lost their faith. He has flagrantly disregarded the duties of his birthright and put his own egregious interests, his own . . . *perversions* above all else. If any among you denies this was so, I beg you, speak here and now."

"No one denies it, my lady," Kent said, "not even me. As his

11

brother, I have witnessed firsthand how he has both abused his power and neglected his kingdom, and made a mockery of the Magna Carta and the Ordinances, both of which he swore to uphold."

I nodded to him, and then let my gaze sweep over every face there. "I ask you all—shall Edward retain his crown?"

Murmurs and whispers rippled through the hall, yet no one spoke aloud.

Finally, Lancaster stood, arms flung wide, imploring. "Can any man rule an entire kingdom when he cannot choose wisely for himself, my lords? I say nay. Strip him of his crown. Let him wear a noose instead."

"Hanging is a traitor's death," Henry Burghersh, the Bishop of Lincoln, said. "And a man, any man, cannot be convicted of treason without a trial. Besides, how can a king commit treason against himself?"

"It is not against himself," said Lancaster, "but against the Crown."

John de Stratford, the Bishop of Winchester, rose abruptly. "You speak in contradictions, my lord. He *is* the Crown. King Edward is God's anointed."

"But so was Harold Godwinson," someone at the far end added.

"A conquest," Mortimer countered, thrusting a finger in the air. "William of Normandy claimed his lawful right to the throne and brought King Harold to battle. God decided whose claim was the rightful one."

"Then what is your claim, Sir Roger?" In four thunderous strides, Lancaster planted himself in the center of the hall to face Mortimer. A wicked smirk teased at the corners of his mouth.

"He makes no claim, Lord Henry," I said, before he could add one more dry twig to already sparking tinder. "Both he and Sir John of Hainault organized and led the forces I requested on behalf of my son. But let us return to our reason for assembling today, shall we?"

What is to be done with the king? A trial alone is a mess that I daresay we would all like to avoid. So what then?"

"Remove him from the throne," Sir John said, the crease of his bulging forehead deepening as his eyes flicked to Mortimer.

Bishop Orleton scratched at his temple, his voice leveled in a cautious tone. "He would have to be kept under guard . . . indefinitely."

Lancaster scoffed loudly. "Ah, yes! Let him live and how long will it be before some other sympathizer tries to prop him back up on the throne?"

Yes, I had considered that, too. But what allure was there to free an unpopular, even loathed, king?

"If given unto your care, Lord Henry," I said, "I doubt that would ever happen. I agree with Sir John and Bishop Orleton: King Edward should not only be stripped of his crown, but remain in custody for the rest of his natural life."

Bishop Stratford spread his arms wide, palms upturned in question. "But if he will not voluntarily abdicate in favor of his son, what then?"

Mortimer leaned forward, one elbow resting on his knee. "There is no other way. We cannot return to things as they were before. His son must take his place, so that England can heal its wounds and once again know peace and prosperity."

"Then I assign you, Your Grace," I said to Bishop Stratford, "to go to him and plead with him."

He tilted his head in thought, hesitating long before he spoke again. "If Bishop Burghersh and Bishop Orleton will assist me— although I question how much good it will do, given his defiance thus far."

"Your Grace?" I addressed Bishop Orleton. Without hesitation, he nodded in agreement. "Good, return before Parliament with his answer."

Kent stood, fingers laced together before him. "One question remains, my queen. What of your . . ."—he cast his eyes downward, giving pause to frame his question more delicately—"living arrangements? Whether king or not, in God's eyes Edward of Caernarvon is still your husband."

My smile faded to a frown. I, too, looked down. "I would fear for my life."

"How so?" Lancaster said, stifling a laugh. "The king hasn't one whit of his father's brutality. The man's a coward."

A bolt of fear shot through my spine. "Do not underestimate him, Henry. He is a man whose dearest 'friend' has been put to death. A coward deprived of his crown. By me. I think I have reason to fear."

He arched a russet eyebrow at me. "Reason—or is it simply guilt gnawing at your insides?"

How was I to respond to that? It could mean so many things.

Bishop Orleton, always my savior, answered him. "When he learned that the queen and her army had landed at the mouth of the River Orwell, King Edward was heard to utter, *'I vow, if I so much as lay eyes upon that she-wolf, I will plunge my dagger into her heart up to its hilt. Her blood will soak the ground so heavily that every tree sprung from England's soil will bear the fruits of her betrayal.'*"

I shuddered to hear it. Although Bishop Orleton had told me Edward had spoken threats, he had never said until just then how grave those threats were.

"And you were there to hear these words?" Lancaster questioned.

"Not I," Bishop Orleton said, "but Archbishop Reynolds."

Archbishop Reynolds nodded emphatically. "It's true."

For those simple words, I could not have been more grateful. Although his threat was but a fraction of the horrors I had endured for years, now they would all understand what my life with Edward

14

had been like. And then, how could anyone blame me for what I had already done, or what must yet be done?

2

Young Edward:

Wallingford – Christmas, 1326

DEATH, ODDLY, IS SOMETIMES a cause for celebration.

When in November of 1326 the townsfolk of Hereford put an end to Lord Hugh Despenser the Younger, my mother the queen had watched the spectacle from the castle walls with Sir Roger Mortimer at her side, their expressions intensely observant, almost serene. They had planned that day for a very long time. Indeed, I had looked forward to it myself. Lord Despenser had stood between me and my destiny far too long.

The gallows had been built high, so that all could see. The stack of wood before the scaffold was heaped with dry tinder. First, they hung him. Then while Despenser was still alive, uttering unintelligible words that for all I know may have been a final plea for mercy to the Lord, the townsfolk took him down, cut off his genitals, pulled out his entrails, removed his heart, and flung them all on the fire. His cries of agony were so drowned out by the cheers and jeers of the crowd that it was impossible to tell precisely when he ceased to breathe. The atmosphere was quite festive.

A fitting end for a man who believed himself the king's equal and above the law. Myself, I would not have let him get so close to unconsciousness before plunging the knife into his wicked flesh. The man ought to have suffered more than he did.

All the blessed way to Wallingford then, my younger sisters had sung as if they thought themselves angels—Eleanor to regale the coming day of Christ's birth and Joanna simply to test the strength of her own voice. Tested my tolerance, as well. To escape their cater-wauling, I rode at the head of our procession most often with my mother and sometimes toward the rear with Sir Roger Mortimer, a man whose purpose seemed dependent on reprisal.

I wondered where Mortimer would set his sights now that Lord Despenser was burning in hell and my father was powerless and iso-lated at Kenilworth. Without Mortimer, though, my mother would still be in France and me—I would not be poised to take the throne so soon. Still, my role in all this was not yet entirely clear. I only knew that to be a king meant to command and to conquer, both of which my father had failed dismally at. Surely, as Mother suggested, the king would pass his crown willingly to me. One day, I could be king not only of England, but France, as well. Only a matter of time.

As we rode across the West Country, the land rimed in frost and tendrils of wood smoke curling lazily above rooftops, the people spilled from their houses to line the roads and hail us. I imagined myself as Alexander the Great, leading my troops across Persia into the wilderness. Or Hannibal defeating the Romans at Cannae.

Then, Christmas feast at Wallingford—how grand! Although on-ly eight years old, my sister Eleanor wore a gown of brightest blue sindon, a miniature version of Mother's. Joanna, the youngest of my siblings at five, squealed and clapped her hands as servants scurried about the hall carrying platters heaped with food: capon filled with sage and rosemary and stewed in wine, its broth mixed with currants and spices; venison, hare and goose; apples and pears smothered in sauces and spit-roasted dates and almonds. I stuffed my belly near to bursting. Danced with thirty maidens, some even pretty. Made them all swoon and not from dizziness.

When the musicians broke from their revelry, I returned to the high table. A half-eaten pork tart lay cooling on my plate. I picked out a plump raisin oozing from beneath the golden crust and stuffed it in my mouth.

"Which do you like?" my brother John asked. He had joined us from London just four days ago. In that time, he must have asked four hundred questions.

I poked my fingers in the tart and scooped out two more raisins. "The food? All of it, really. But I do favor the puddings, especially the —"

"No, no." He jabbed an elbow at my ribs and hitched a shoulder toward a whispering clump of maidens. "Them. Which of *them* do you like?"

"You mean the braying donkeys there?" A senseless question. Not one of them had half Philippa's wit, my betrothed who I had left behind in Hainault three long months past. I shrugged. "None."

It had been wicked fun to make the maidens blush, whether I fancied any or not—a game at which I could always win. Their attention was flattering, but their inane chatter was enough to bore me to a stupor. I preferred a girl who would be more a match of wits at the supper table. Philippa would have stuck her tongue out at me and then asked about my hounds or who I favored in the next jousting tournament.

"None, truly?" John gawped at me. "But if you're going to be king, you'll need a queen."

"For what? Besides, Father is still king. I have plenty of time before I take a wife."

I lied, simply because I had wearied of his incessant questions. John was not yet ten. He had no inkling what girls were really for. In another four years when he turned my age, he might figure it out. I had.

One bright summer day when I was out riding with Philippa in the countryside beyond Valenciennes, we had raced through a field of haystacks and on ahead into a dense coppice of woods, our escorts briefly lost in the confusion. We dropped from our saddles and hid behind a dilapidated woodsman's shed, stifling giggles beneath our hands as our escorts streamed past us not fifty feet away. She shoved me playfully on the chest. I caught her wrists and pulled her close, wasting no time as I kissed her full on the lips. Several breaths passed before she stepped away and scolded me for my presumptuousness—but not without a flicker of a smile on her plump, inviting mouth. I was about to kiss her again when Will Montagu came tromping through the thicket and lashed me in the rump with the flat of his sword blade. As if he had never done more himself. One tankard of ale and he was overflowing with stories of his own debauchery.

John's mouth twisted in frustration at my lack of agreement. "What about the King of Spain's daughter?"

"What of her? What if she looks like a sow? What if she's no more than an infant, drooling in her cradle? Or some lackwit? What sort of a queen would any of those be to me?" The names of my prospective brides had been discussed for as long as I could remember. A wife, they told me, would be useful for forging alliances as well as begetting heirs. But producing children meant coupling, of that much I was aware. For most of my life, it had little meaning to me and held even less interest. Until I went to France to pay homage to my uncle, King Charles. Things changed then. I saw girls . . . differently—thanks to Will and his boastful talk. The women, I

19

noticed, admired and fawned over him and followed him about. The next time a kitchen maid glanced at me, blushing, I invited her into the empty pantry—a bumbling incident during which, for the most part, we simply discovered each other's body parts. Poor John, though, was not as advanced for his age or as bold as I was. It would be years before he would learn of such things.

Our uncle Edmund, the Earl of Kent, raised his wine goblet in greeting from across the hall and made his way toward us, weaving through the mill of servants. He bounded up onto the dais and leaned over, resting on a forearm. "You're coming to Westminster, I trust?"

Although the question was addressed to me, my brother squirmed beside me, eyes wide in horror. "Westminster? London? Oh, no," John said. "The people there are *mad*, Uncle Edmund. They sawed off Bishop Stapledon's head with a butcher's knife!"

So they had. The bishop may have been a sanctimonious goat and a spy, but his end was an undeservedly brutal one. While his maggot-infested head was hurried westward to be presented to my mother by the Earl of Lancaster, his naked corpse had lain rotting in a pile of refuse in London's streets.

Kent, always the doting uncle, smiled reassuringly and tipped his head at John. "You had no cause for worry, nephew. Sir John kept you safe behind a hedge of Flemish spears."

With the tip of his knife, John chased a pea around his plate, at last flicking it across the floor. "Then why did Mother not come to London?"

I punched him in the leg to shush him. "Maybe she had better things to do than coddle a frightened, little slobber-ruffed pup like you?"

"I wasn't frightened, not really. It's just that they would have killed *anybody*. Did you not hear the stories—how they clubbed people to death with the spokes of cart wheels or gouged out their eyes

20

with chisels? You would not have left the Tower, either." His face by then was red with fury at my insult. He clenched a chubby-knuckled fist around his knife and waved it in the air. "One day I'll be a soldier. A brave one, you'll see, Ned. I'll fight the Scots and I'll beat them."

"Of course you will, John," Kent said, as he reached out and ruffled his hair. "When you're old enough."

John slouched back in his chair, a scowl firmly imprinted on his puckered mouth, his breath forced out through flaring nostrils.

A blast of trumpets rent the air. Kent looked to the rear of the hall. "Ah! The mummers are here at last. Your pardon, young lords. My wife was casting urgent glances my way not long ago. I do believe she was hinting for my company. Enjoy the merrymaking whilst you can—especially you, Young Edward. Parliament is bound to be restive and no doubt they'll call on you to make an appearance as their next king."

My mouth hung open. Parliament was less than a month away. Father had not abdicated yet. What good would it do to call on me when there was so much still unresolved? Before I could ask Kent anything, he had dropped from the edge of the dais and left.

Again, the trumpets blared. A ragged line of grotesquely masked men poured into the hall through the outer doors. Clasping small hands over her mouth, Joanna tumbled from her seat at the end of the table and ran, yellow curls bouncing at her shoulders, around behind me to leap into our nursemaid Ida's arms. Eleanor shook her head and we shared a glance of contempt. Such children!

"Watch the girl—there, with the veils." I pointed to a lithe beauty, copper-skinned and hair as black as a starless night. "I hear she hails from Crete."

"Where is Crete?" John pulled his legs underneath himself to sit higher in his chair.

"Far away," I said, knowing it would take too much effort to explain and it would probably end in futility anyway.

21

"How long would it take to get there?"

"I don't know."

"Who is she supposed to be?"

"Salome, you custard-brained toad. Now stop asking questions and watch, or else you'll miss it."

He planted his elbows on the table and watched, grinning in delight as the tabor beat out a frenetic rhythm. 'Salome' bowed to us with a flourish of her hands, one bare, brown foot pointed forward, her skirts barely grazing her ankles. Gossamer veils of saffron, scarlet and emerald swayed from the silken sash at her hips, and with every nimble movement the little bells adorning the corded belt tinkled in unison. Arms snaking above her head, she arched her back, folding in half, until her palms met the floor. With a kick, she sprang backward. The very moment she landed on the balls of her feet, her body snapped back again and she somersaulted in the air thrice more in succession. This time, her hands did not touch the floor at all.

John thrust his fists into the air and shook them. "More, more!"

"You like her?"

"Yes! I was expecting carols. I hate to sing. And I'm bored of jugglers and little dogs dancing on their hind legs, aren't you, Ned?"

Palms beat on drums like the low rumble of distant thunder. Salome's arms flowed about her body like a rippling mountain stream. Her hips undulated in a languid circle and then began to move faster and tighter as she spun around the open space, small feet moving to the ever-increasing cadence of the music. Legs outspread, she sank to the ground. Then, rolling forward, she tucked her knees beneath her and knelt, head bowed, toward the rear of the hall.

Several mummers came forward, bearing two litters upon which sat a pair of robed figures, a man and a woman, each wearing a gold-faced mask and jeweled crown.

"On the left would be Herod Antipas, Salome's uncle . . . who is *also* her stepfather." I clapped him on the shoulder. "That is her mother, Queen Herodius, next to him."

Salome danced on, teasing away her many colored veils one by one to entertain the mummer-king and queen. Whenever she paused in her movements, fingers fluttering over her scant clothing, the crowd banged cups and spoons on the tables. Then she would strip another veil free and, stretching its edge from hand to hand, glide on graceful feet in a circle around the thrones, the cloth billowing out behind her like a sail catching the wind.

Fascinated, my eyes followed her every movement, studied the shape and flow of her body, the smoothness of the skin exposed on her arms, shoulders, belly and legs. Never before had I seen a woman so barely clad and so *exciting* to watch.

The mummer-king clapped his hands in the air and the drums banged louder in response. Another mummer burst into the room's center, his mask painted in grim lines, his costume nothing but loose breeches and a tunic of hemp. In his arms, he bore a platter.

"There, see,"—I shook John's forearm—"a slave comes bearing the head of John the Baptist."

"But that's a boar's head," he objected, yanking his arm away, "not a man's."

"Did you think they would put the head of a real man on a platter during Christmas dinner? You *are* daft."

"But why did they cut off *his* head? I thought John the Baptist was a good man, not like the bishop. Nobody liked Bishop Stapledon—except Father."

"John the Baptist did not think they should marry."

"Why not?"

"Because they were both already married—to other people." John flashed a quizzical look at me, but too entranced by the play, he quickly returned his attentions to it. If the distance to Crete baffled him, incestuous adultery would have made even less sense.

The slave hefted the platter to his shoulder and turned round to display the token. I searched the room, lowering my voice. "As for that being a boar's head, I doubt the priests here will take kindly to that mockery of John the Baptist, but —"

My words died abruptly as my sight came to rest on an empty chair. My mother's seat at the high table was vacant. Had I been so besotted by the attentions of giddy maidens I hadn't even noticed her leaving? And earlier, at the opposite end from John and me, Sir Roger Mortimer had been seated next to Bishop Orleton, but now some unfamiliar abbot sat in his place.

I looked again at the mummer-king, his face concealed behind a garishly painted mask. A circlet of silver was perched snugly on his nearly black, wavy crown of hair. When he turned his head my way, as if he sensed my scrutiny, I knew the incisive darkness in the eyes. Knew the hunger and the doggedness behind them. They were Mortimer's eyes. Eyes I had looked into a thousand times in the past year: in France, on the voyage home, and during the many miles I had ridden abreast of him as he spoke of how we would win England back in the name of its people and he would deliver the crown to me.

His hand crept over that of Queen Herodius's—my mother's.

If Mortimer smiled, it was hidden behind the oversized, false mouth of madder red. But as the slave hoisted the platter above his head with both hands and strode past all the tables, pausing every few strides to turn to the crowd so they could enjoy the spectacle, I detected the flash of a smile in the crinkling of Mortimer's eyes and the glint of unabashed mockery.

Joanna peeked through Ida's fingers, splayed protectively over her face, and began to wail. Ida hobbled away to carry her to safety, huffing as Joanna squirmed in her sagging arms.

The boar's features had been unnaturally distorted by the cook's embellishments: a gleaming red apple shoved deep between too-small jaws, so that its mouth had been split at the corners and sewn back together; charred tusks painted white and adorned with sugar to glitter in the torchlight like curved icicles; and the flesh so discolored from the heat of the flames that it looked strikingly like the bruise-mottled head of the dead Bishop Stapledon.

The twisting and fluttering notes of the reed pipe pitched to a frenzy. Salome leapt up and twirled across the floor on the balls of her bare feet, the last veil whipping around her in a swirl of palest amethyst. Delighted, the crowd applauded her fluid dance. Some of the men even called out ribald suggestions, so bewitching was her beauty. She turned back to Mortimer, dipped to her knees, and then lowered onto to her belly again, crawling to him.

The veil became entangled around her foot and when she tried to extend her leg to advance, her body jerked to a halt. Kent, who was passing before the nearest table, stooped to help her. He reached out to unravel the cloth from just above her bare ankle, his fingers tugging nervously at the delicate material as though he were afraid of both tearing the cloth and touching the woman. Then, just as he freed her and began to stand, the slave backed into him.

The platter tilted sideways, tottering in the slave's unsteady grasp. He thrust one hand up higher, trying to right it, but the movement overcompensated and the weight shifted. The boar's head rolled over the lip and struck Kent squarely on the back of the neck, knocking him to the floor, flat on his stomach. Air compressed from his lungs in an unflattering grunt. Chunks of leeks and carrots, sprinkled with a stuffing of suet and bread crumbs, spilled from the platter and poured over him. End over end, the pig's head tumbled unevenly across the floor, until at last coming to rest before Mortimer's feet. He nudged the thing once with the pointed toe of his shoe and then gave it a swift kick. It skidded on the top of its skull across the tiles, bounced off the arm of Salome and smashed into Kent's nose. Everyone laughed—except Kent.

He sputtered and batted the thing away, visibly shrinking from it. Still dazed, he staggered to his feet. Mother tore the disguise from her head, golden hair springing from its pins, and dashed to his rescue. She gathered up the end of her long sleeve and brushed at Kent's soiled clothing, sweeping bits of food to the ground.

Mortimer untied his mask and peeled it away to dab tears of laughter from his eyes.

Suddenly, the irony of it all sickened me. John clamped a hand on my wrist as I made to rise.

"Where are you going?" he said.

"To bed." I pried his fingers away. "I've seen enough."

3

Young Edward:

Westminster — January, 1327

O N THE EVE OF the new year, we left Wallingford behind and
went east. It seemed we were in a hurry to reach London.
Parliament was set to assemble at nearby Westminster. There were
matters to settle. Some of which, I sensed, involved me.

At dawn, long frozen ribbons of ice marked the ruts of wagon
wheels along the road. In the afternoon, we passed through Ludgate
into London itself. Above the jumble of rooftops, the towering spire
of St. Paul's thrust heavenward. Hour upon hour, we wended our
way through the crooked streets as the crowds thickened. Eleanor at
first shrieked her excitement, but in time her voice began to crackle,
then went hoarse and finally silent. Meanwhile, an overwrought Joanna fussed loudly, eventually falling asleep in her litter, oblivious to
the commotion.

If John had been afraid to return to London before, his fears were soon dissolved. Not hundreds, but thousands clamored to greet us. Pikes swept our way clear; otherwise we would have been stalled like merchants waiting to pay their toll at the city gates.

What a glorious day it was. Over and over, I heard my name, ringing in my ears like the peal of bells heralding some great event.

For all its wealth and wonders, though, London was still London: packed with too many people in too little space. Everywhere, a thick stench permeated the air, its components shifting with the wind and sector. The kilns of tilers and potters belched smoke. Tanneries spewed their dye waste into ditches already clogged with human waste. The stalls of fishmongers stank of herring and salmon. And the unwanted offal of butchers' shops rotted in heaps while well-fed feral cats dashed among the alleyways. In summer, the smells would have been strong enough to tinge my tongue with the sour taste of bile. When we passed the worst of places, I pinched my nose shut, John mimicking me, and held my breath as I waved.

When we at last came within sight of the double walled Tower of London, I exhaled in relief. It had been so long since I had been there. We rode through Lion Gate, over the moat's drawbridge and finally through the inner gate to dismount on Tower Green. I spun around to gaze at all the structures, trying hard to remember what was where.

As they took our horses away, John came and slipped his hand in mine. His slight body quivered, the angled bones of his shoulder digging into my chest as he leaned into me.

I rumpled his hair. "You're safe here. No more riots."

He turned wide blue eyes up at me. "Promise, Ned?"

"I'm here, aren't I? Besides, they were angry—at Bishop Stapledon, at the way things were. They're not anymore. It will be all right, I promise." I wanted to add that when I was king, the people would never be so angry with me, but it seemed premature. There was still great uncertainty and it was best not to presume too much. I nudged him away, not wanting to encourage him to cling to me like the leech he was. "Have courage, will you? I may need you to fight for me one day and I don't want a fainting lamb for a brother. I want a soldier who can charge into battle, unafraid of death. There is no glory in avoidance or surrender now, is there?"

His lips framed a question, but for once he did not give voice to his doubts. Blotting a runny nose on his sleeve, he shook his head and then darted off toward the White Tower, where the rest of our party was headed. I spotted Mother walking close to Mortimer, her head bent attentively toward him as he spoke to her. They went up the stairs together, her full skirts brushing his leg. When they reached the double doors, they paused as a porter tugged each half open.

I was unsure what to make of the man. Without him, England would have tumbled into ruin at the hands of Hugh Despenser. And I would not be poised to take the throne. Still, something about him unsettled me.

He turned to look at me then, his dark eyes commanding me to follow. I stared back, my feet firmly planted, knees locked, feeling neither the tug of admiration for him, nor the intimidating threat of his authority.

I might have remained there all day, passively defiant, had Sir William Montagu not strode before me to block my view. His cheeks were lifted in a broad, jaunty smile.

"Is there anything you need of me, my lord?"

Annoyed, I dodged to the side of him, but both Mortimer and my mother were gone from the doorway. Old Ida waddled past, Joanna propped sleepily on her broad hip and Eleanor trailing along. Ida clucked at me to come inside, out of the cold. When I didn't move, she started toward me and I sensed a sharp cuff to the ear coming if I did not follow her orders.

Will laughed as he turned to walk with me. When I left for

France, he had been tasked to serve not only as my companion, but my mentor, as well, tutoring me in the ways of warfare.

"Will?" I said, my voice low so no one would overhear me.

"Yes, my lord?"

"You'll look out for me, should I ever need it?"

"I already do that. Every day."

"I mean . . ."—swinging before him, I stopped so abruptly he nearly plowed me over—"defend me. My life, should anyone ever try to take it."

He arched a ragged eyebrow at me. "A sober request. Why the sudden concern?"

I shrugged. "No reason. Only that, being a king, which I will be one day, well . . ."

A grin flickered over his lips and he chuckled. "Oh, I think you'll do quite well for yourself. Then again, kings have so *many* things to concern themselves with. Let me assure you that your preservation is my sole purpose. You see, I have no fear of danger. I seek it out, pounce upon it and throttle it before it ever knows I'm there."

Nodding, I stepped aside.

He stood firm. "Does that put your mind at rest?"

"It will once you prove that you can do more than just speak the words."

"Ah. Well, pray it never comes to that."

I bumped him with a shoulder as I went toward the stairs. "We can pray all we want. God will test us as he sees fit, I suppose."

"God's bollocks, you're as sober as the pope on a holy day. I swear you were born forty." In a stride he was at my shoulder, matching my steps.

"Mind your tongue, Will Montagu," I warned him in the sternest voice I could muster. "'Tis your future king you're speaking to. Besides, it would serve you well to be a little more pious. Eternity is a long time to pay for such profane words."

"So the priests tell us." He gave a pert wink. "Just wait until you're of age, my lord. I'll teach you what all those holy men have been missing out on. You'll take pity on them, then."

I gave no reply. His vices would test my devoutness. I had no doubt of that. But I didn't need a saint as my guardian. I needed a man who wasn't afraid to battle the devil and court death. I needed a man precisely like Will Montagu.

THERE WAS SOME CONFUSION as to whether parliament could be held at all, given that my father would not come. Would not . . . or could not, I was never sure. Bishops Burghersh and Stratford had been sent to Kenilworth and quickly returned saying that my father had cursed their invitation to sit among his enemies.

It was not the crown he was clinging to, but stubborn pride.

In truth, my father thought kingship a burden. Always, he warred with his barons, blamed the clergy for condemning him, and was resentful that the people did not love him as they did my mother, Queen Isabella, nor fear him like they had my grandfather, the first Edward, called Longshanks by some. I had even overheard him say once that he would rather have been born a commoner. I found that hard to fathom, for it seemed not only a harsh life, but devoid of glory and purpose. Even then, as young as I was when he said the words, I felt a sense of honor to be born the heir to England's throne. To me, the promise of a crown was uplifting—a gift I embraced with every sinew and bone of my being.

Day by day, however, it was growing increasingly harder to hide my impatience. For so long, Mother had spoken to me of being king one day, not only of England, but France as well. My uncle, King Charles of France, had been married to his milk-faced bride, Jeanne of Evreux, for just over a year now. Already she had birthed one child, a girl, who died before her churching. A sad affair, but I was acutely aware that if she never bore him an heir, he might well name me as his successor.

And then, yesterday, Bishop Orleton returned from another meeting with my father, bearing a document. When he gave it to my mother, her knees swayed beneath her and she clutched it to her breast as fiercely as if it were her own infant delivered from the threshold of death by some miracle.

I knew its contents. Not the exact words, perhaps, but there could be no mistaking that the path of my destiny had finally been laid out before me. A thousand thoughts raced through my head as I lay in bed, unable to sleep, yet exhilarated. That morning I was awoken early, dressed in velvet as blue as the northern sea, my shoulders adorned with heavily linked chains of gold strung with jewels as big as coins. I was hurriedly escorted to Westminster Palace, where Parliament was convening.

Hours dragged by while I was made to wait in the King's State Bedchamber. I rested on my back with arms folded on the oversized, down-filled bed, staring up at the ceiling's painted oaken panels. One in particular drew my attention. On a field of blue, a winged seraph wore a cloak of dove-white feathers, his eyes cast heavenward. A halo illuminated the tightly sprung coils of his golden hair. My eyes flicked to the panel beside it, where a stern-faced prophet with a long flowing beard of gray gripped a scroll in both hands. It harkened back Orleton's arrival.

I sat up, too anxious to remain still any longer. Grabbing the ermine-lined cloak draped over a nearby chair, I marched past my tutor, Richard Bury, who had just entered bearing an armload of books.

"I apologize profusely, my lord," he blubbered, his fat cheeks flushed with effort, "but they did not tell me you were leaving the Tower this morning. It took some time to gather everything. Are you ready to begin your lessons?"

I lingered at the doorway only a moment, my heart racing so fast I thought it might burst inside my chest if I didn't do *something*. "Not today, Richard. I've too much on my mind."

"But your mother says —"

His voice faded to a faraway buzz as I hastened down the corridor, Will close on my heels. Two flights of stairs and several turns later, I stood in the adjoining chamber just outside the vast hall where Parliament was gathered. A row of armed soldiers flanked either side of the door, their expressions as blank as unfashioned blocks of marble. I started toward the entrance, expecting the guards closest to fling it open for me. Instead, a pair of poleaxes crossed before me, their heavy curved blades clanking as they glanced off one another.

"You are not to enter, my lord," one of the guards said flatly, "until called for."

"Called for?" I echoed peevishly. "By whom?"

"The queen, my lord."

The silken tones of Bishop Orleton's voice emanated from beyond the iron-studded doors as he delivered a long speech— or perhaps he was reading from a document. *The* document? My shoulders drew up tight toward my ears, my fingers curling and uncurling into loose fists. I lurched forward. A hand clamped onto the lean flesh of my arm and yanked me back.

"No," Will said. "Not yet. You must wait."

"Forever?" I jerked my arm from his hold. Once glimpse at the sharp blades barring my way told me my mother's orders had been firm. Whatever it was they were debating in there, I was not to be a part of it. And that both angered and deflated me.

I spun around so fast, my vision went gray. I threw my hands out to steady myself, groping nothing but air. Will's broad palm, so familiar, alighted between my shoulder blades, but I shook it off and strode forward as patches of color took shape around me. Bodies shuffled backward, clearing a path for me. It was then that I noticed how *many* people were filling the room: lesser barons and black-robed clerics, officials from various cities, and the masters of London's many guilds. As I surveyed the gathering, waiting for my world to stop spinning and my head to clear, they all bowed to me.

Beyond the outer doors, the rumble of a crowd grew louder. John's grotesque stories of a murderous rabble rushed back to me. Panicked, I hastened through the far door, bumping my shoulder hard. I raced up the stairs, three per stride. By the time I stumbled out through the tower door into the ashen light of a dying day, I had to fight the urge to run, because there was nowhere to run to.

Wind stung at my eyes. A glittering of snow frosted the stones. I perched myself in a crenel of the outer wall ringing Westminster Palace, my arms tucked around my ankles, my chin on my knees. A languishing golden sun flashed unexpectedly, stabbing its light between racing clouds far to the west. I blinked against the brief glare, then looked down below. Today it seemed half of London had invaded Thorney Island to crowd at the gates of Westminster Palace. From here, I could not make out what it was they were shouting. My name? Or were they crying for my father's freedom, for justice?

No boats coursed along the Thames. Its banks were thick with ice. Instead, they were all moored at river's edge, waiting for the weather to break.

Occasionally, Will peered at me from the shadows of the tower door. Each time, I chased him away with a scowl. We had an under-standing, Will and I. I may have been his to guard, but that duty did not grant him rights to my every thought and the company of my every moment.

For the first time in a long while, I felt a pang deep in my gut—a twinge of sympathy for my father. One day he had been king of all England. The next, he was running in fright. Now, he sat alone, shut up at Kenilworth, his future in doubt. They said he was a bad king. Accused him not only of crimes, but unspeakable sins. If they . . .

No, I could not question the events—or the people—that had brought me to this day. It was my fate.

The sun retreated to the earth's underside, yielding its heavenly throne to the pale glimmer of countless stars. Bitter wind drove winter's bite deep into my bones. I shivered so hard my teeth were rattling my skull. But I would not go inside. Not until they came to get me.

A roar erupted from the crowd below, but I neither looked nor moved from my eyrie.

My stomach growled. My eyelids drifted lower. My fingers were stiff with cold, my toes so frozen I could no longer feel them. I closed my fur-lined cloak tight around me and rested my forehead on my knees.

The clack of boots startled me from my uneasy slumber. Will approached at a brisk clip along the wall-walk, defiant in the face of my most threatening glare.

I pulled my fingers into fists. "Sending me to bed now, are you?"

"Too early for that, isn't it?" He flung his cloak back over his shoulders and drummed his gloved fingers on his hips. "But you'll be interested to hear that Bishop Orleton has emerged from the assembly. Looking rather smug, I'd say. He asked where you were."

I swung my legs toward him, gripping the edge of the stones as a jolt of excitement flashed through my veins. "And?"

He cupped a rough-whiskered chin in one hand thoughtfully. "Perhaps I shouldn't say anything. I heard only bits, after all. I'm sure your mother will have you retrieved short—"

"Will!" My lip twitched with a snarl. "Tell me. I command you."

"Do you?" he teased.

"Just tell me, please. I've waited *all* day. I know it's my father they've been talking about. What's to become of him?" I smacked the stones with the heels of my hands and stood. "I need to know . . . before they come."

He tossed a look over his shoulder and then nodded. "Very well. I suppose you should be prepared." He clenched my shoulder so hard I feared tomorrow would find a bruise there with the imprint of his fingers.

"Is he still king?"

The wind tore at his hair, tossing it across his face. His grip lightened. He shook his head. "They say he gave up the crown willingly, my lord."

"Willingly?"

With a shrug, he let go of me. "Even if his hand was forced, it's for the best, don't you think?"

The onus of kingship struck me like a hammer blow to my breastbone. I slumped down on the stones, the air whooshing out of my lungs so fast and completely I had to gulp air to speak. "What does this mean? What of me?"

He crouched down before me, his eyes sparkling with an un-daunted confidence that I could but hope to emulate. "You, Ned? You were born to this. You'll be king—and a fierce one at that."

He made it sound so simple, as if I should never question the auspices of my birth. Like it was a cloak I could don at will to be-come the king of England's calling. But for the first time in all my hopeful, eager days, I felt a flutter of doubt. The uncertainty that I could be all things to all people. The terrible knowledge that whatever I thought was right would be wrong in someone's eyes. And if that came to pass, would they do to me what had been done to my father?

Yesterday, I had thought I would seize the crown with gleeful abandon, secure in my destiny, an answer to God's whispered breath. Could I, in clear conscience, sit upon the throne while my father yet lived?

"Edward?" a comforting voice called out.

My mother stood in the tower doorway, her pale hair reflecting the silver glow of starlight, a thin gold circlet sitting just above her smooth brow like an angel's halo. She lifted a hand, her flared sleeve falling away from her wrist to reveal delicate bones, fingers outstretched, begging me nearer.

I went and took her hand in mine. With a gentle squeeze, the warmth of her touch eased my fears. Tears were pooling in her eyes. She tried bravely to blink them away, her teeth pinching her lower lip, but in a rush they spilled onto her cheeks. Her arms went around me, so fast and tight I fought for breath, my arms clamped to my sides. A long minute later, she snuffled and loosened her embrace. "They're calling for you. They're waiting to make the proclamation."

"I'm ready," I said.

Her head tilted. Smiling, she cupped my cheek in her palm. The sweet scent of rosewater drifted off her fingers. "I know. You always were—even before England was ready for you."

4

Isabella:

Westminster — February, 1327

O N THE MORNING OF Christmas Eve, when Bishop Orleton delivered the Great Seal into my hands at Wallingford, he also gave me something else from my husband: a letter. In it, Edward spoke of hope, of receiving his children's love, and of one day returning to the throne with me at his side. But as the days and weeks passed, his penned musings turned from pleading to accusatory, forlorn and rife with resentment, laying all blame for his misfortunes at my feet. To him, I was the deceiver, the betrayer, the unfaithful one.

Oh, Edward, blame is a shield with which we deflect duty. We learn it as children when responsibility seems too great a burden to carry upon our slight shoulders. Condemn our circumstances, let loose the victim's cry and compassionate souls shall reach out to offer soothing words. Alas, pity is but a balm dabbed upon the gaping wound of our guilt.

Never. I would *never* go back to him. There could be no harmony between us. Not even polite accord, like so many mismatched husbands and wives who lived out their years, enduring one another in silent disdain.

My contempt dwelt much deeper than mere dislike. Wed to King Edward II of England at not yet thirteen, I had thought my life would be a grand affair of ceremony and bliss. Instead, I shared him not with a mistress, nor even with the demands of war and statehood, but with a man: Piers Gaveston. Like any naïve young wife sworn to her wifely duties, I turned my face from it. In time, it was Edward's barons, not me, who brought an end to Gaveston.

In the years after Gaveston's death, Edward and I were often at Langley. In the meadows surrounding Langley, sheep meandered amid buttercups and vetch. In late spring, when the sun had chased away the rains and dried up the ubiquitous English mud, peasants tended to the fields, furrowing and sowing, so that by summer the land was striped in verdant and gilded bands. There, our family grew. We, for awhile, were content.

Hugh Despenser destroyed all that.

By then, I was wiser. I knew there was more between Edward and Despenser than mere friendship, more than the gratitude of a liege to his lord. More, even, than lust. It was not so much that Edward turned away from me and to another to sate his desires. It was that Despenser sought to sever me from my husband's life altogether, from both comfort and power, from all that I cherished. He took my money, my lands, and . . . my children. Edward did nothing to stop him.

Even with Despenser dead, Edward had still refused to give up the crown, as if someone might save him. As if I might fold with guilt simply at the volley of his unkind words and repent of my actions. Did he think the people of England so gullible—or me so weak of will? No, I was not the doe-eyed Isabella, full of airy hopes, who had stolen glances at him in Boulogne's cathedral that January day so long ago. Hugh Despenser had chased that girl forever into hiding and left in her place a woman of ruthless determination.

To do what is right and worthwhile, it is never easy. To be a woman of action is to risk judgment. But the alternative is to abandon free will—and thus to die slowly inside.

Every choice I had ever made had brought me to this day: my son's coronation. My husband had made his own choices and was now paying the price for them.

Winter light pried through the narrow paned windows of the small antechamber to fall in a broken line across square, gray flagstones. Patrice draped a long cloak over my shoulders and fastened it with a pair of bronze clasps, shaped in the form of eagles. She lifted the long, trailing hem of my gown and arranged it behind me, fussing with each fold, stretching out the wrinkles.

"Look there," she said, "a snagged thread." With a quick tug, she snapped it between her fingers.

"Juliana would have been more careful," I chided, smoothing the silk cloth against my abdomen. I stretched my arms out wide, tiny flecks in the gold threads glittering with each turn and movement. Even though I had dozens of gowns in my wardrobe, this one had been made especially for today.

Patrice's shoulders heaved in a shrug, lifting her full bosom to accentuate the cleavage revealed by her low neckline. "Juliana is not here, is she? She is in Corbeil. I hear she is pregnant . . . *again.*"

Her words were tinged with bitterness. In truth, Patrice loved Juliana, who had been one of my damsels in the years between my marriage to Edward and my return to France, but she was jealous of Juliana's good fortune—of her doting husband and growing brood of healthy children. As much as Patrice might pretend she had no liking for babes, she was the same age as me and had all but wasted her chances of ever having her own by falling in love with the handsome and dutiful Arnaud de Mone. Several years younger than

Patrice, he had married another woman at a very young age. They had a daughter soon after, but sadly the girl died in her crib. Arnaud's own mother had accused his wife of smothering the child. Mad with grief, his wife tried to hang herself. Her senses had never returned to her and Arnaud was forced to send her to a nunnery. He had never sought to have the marriage annulled, never mind that he had lain with Patrice countless times.

However, it was not my place to judge Arnaud or Patrice, or anyone, for I loved a man who was not my husband. A man who had a wife of more than twenty years. I could no more give him up than I could will the blood to stop flowing through my veins.

"My lady?"

I turned. Mortimer stood at the threshold of the doorway, resplendent in his scarlet and green. Encumbered by the almost ridiculous abundance of my skirts, I stood in place. One step without Patrice to manage the train and I would have tripped in a most ungainly fashion and been unable to right myself.

He moved forward, appraising me in a way so familiar I felt as if I were wearing nothing at all. My pulse quickened. A flush of heat fanned upward from my breast to my neck. I dabbed at beads of perspiration on my forehead, wondering if they had even been there a minute before.

"Captivating." He made a broad circle around me, careful to avoid stepping on the great swaths of cloth that surrounded me like a sea of liquid amber. "A lifetime's worth of beauty for any man to behold."

When he came around before me, he swept an arm across his torso and bowed low, his thick crown of raven-black hair glistening with a fine sheen of oil. Then he rose, offering his elbow. "The Archbishop of Canterbury awaits, my queen. The sun is strong, the people are in high spirits and your son has paced a waist-deep rut in the planks of his floor. Shall we?"

I took his arm as Patrice snatched up the embroidered hem of my train and swung around behind me. My damsels scurried out of the way, but old Ida seemed unable to move, her puckered mouth alternately smiling and quivering as she mopped away tears. Ida had been Young Edward's nursemaid since his infancy and so he was like a son to her. Finally, she hobbled to me, her bad knees making her movements jerky and unsteady.

"What is it, Ida?" I took her hands in mine, her skin dry like parchment, and squeezed lightly.

"I am so full of joy, my lady. But frightened for him, too."

"Why?"

The crease between her brows deepened. "Because of the eagle. The one that soared above Windsor the day he was born."

"Oh, that." I laughed, trying to make light of it. How many times had she spoken of the omen, declaring his birth a sign of some great war that would befall England during his lifetime? A terrible burden for any babe to bear, even one destined to be king. "Let us simply rejoice in this day, shall we, Ida?"

Then I kissed her on each cheek and took Mortimer's arm again, confident in the outcome of the day, but now sharply reminded that the future was never certain.

The archbishop led the short procession from the palace to Westminster Abbey. The crowd pressed close, waving and crying, "Glory! Glory to the king!" A robe of red samite, trimmed with gold cording, cascaded from Young Edward's narrow shoulders as he strode, step by proud step, beneath a belled canopy, the poles held aloft by a quartet of earls. Beneath his shoes flowed a river of brilliant blue silk, seducing him onward as it rippled up the cathedral steps, through the tall, arched doors and down the center of the nave.

I observed the ceremony through a veil of tears, my son posed regally on his gilt throne, a jewel-studded scepter clasped in the circle of his fingers. Archbishop Reynolds stood before him at the high altar, the crown of Edward the Confessor held high as he invoked God's blessing in Latin verse upon the reign of Edward III, King of England.

As the crown alighted on Young Edward's fair brow, a halcyon settled upon my soul. The memory of nineteen years fraught with strife and struggle flashed through my memory and was quickly replaced by the sight of this luminous moment. It was as though England had endured a long and savage storm and today was the bold breaking of dawn above the treetops: a new beginning, as pure and full or promise as the scent of rain on freshly sprung grass.

ALL THAT HAD EVER been taken from me was returned, augmented even: Sheen, Langley, Leeds and other royal residences, so that I might live in a manner befitting my station as Queen Dowager. I was also granted an annuity sufficient to reward me for England's deliverance. Two days after the crowning, a regency council of twelve was formed, headed by the Earl of Lancaster, which would remain in place until Young Edward passed his eighteenth birthday. My son would be tested in these first few years. His influences must be carefully chosen.

One month had passed since the coronation day. Since then, the arguments had been many. There were matters to be remedied, policies to be decided on, and appointments to be made. Sir John had returned to Hainault and in doing so deprived me of one of my most trusted supporters.

The regency council had just adjourned after another daylong meeting. One by one, its members slid their chairs back and departed, drifting away in clumps. Archbishop Reynolds and Bishops Melton and Stratford were discussing who to suggest for various bishoprics, while the Earl of Kent exchanged small talk with Lord Henry Percy. Lancaster and Lord Wake lingered by the table, until Lancaster's son-in-law, John de Ros, proposed they all share a drink. Lancaster clapped Ros on the back and they swaggered off, their voices raised boisterously as if they were already drunk.

Finally, there was only Bishop Orleton, Mortimer and myself remaining in the chamber. Mortimer was not a member of the council, but he had been called to sit in that day to give a report of the raid the Scots had launched on Norham on the day of Edward's coronation. Throughout the meeting, he had fidgeted in his chair impatiently, giving only the briefest account of the activities of the Bruce's furtive and ruthless commander, James Douglas.

The flames of the hearth cast an amber glow over Mortimer's features, darkening the shadows in the creases around his eyes. Leaning an elbow upon the mantel, he kicked an ember back into the fire and glanced at the door before letting his sight rest on the bishop.

"Have they found him?" Mortimer said.

Orleton closed the door and came to stand halfway between Mortimer and me. "Dunheved? No."

I turned a questioning face on Mortimer, then Orleton. "Dunheved? Who is Dunheved?"

"Stephen Dunheved." Orleton flipped the red-tasseled edges of his stole to his sides and sat back down in his chair. "A Dominican friar who once carried a message to the pope himself at the behest of Lord Despenser. You can imagine that his mission to Avignon was not in your favor, my lady. Rumors are that it was a request for an annulment. This Dunheved eventually became Sir Edward's confessor."

A flutter of worry stirred deep inside my belly. "I don't understand. Why would you be looking for Edward's confessor?"

Mortimer pushed away from the mantel. "There was a plot —"

"*Alleged* plot, Roger," Orleton corrected. "We have discussed countless times that there would be rumors in the wake of this past year's upheaval and that we could not accept each and every one as fact and condemn innocent persons."

Mortimer threw his hands wide. "How can you even *think* this is some mere rumor? I told you my sources and you still —"

"Stop!" I rushed toward the table and spread my fingers wide upon it to steady the quaking in my body. "What plot, Adam? Tell me."

Bishop Orleton drew in a breath and then released it with a weighty sigh. "A plot to free Edward of Caernarvon from Kenilworth."

"Who? And how?"

"No names of particular significance: a clerk of Despenser's, a few household servants, a lowly parson. As to how . . . that was not uncovered. Their plans were foiled well ahead of time."

A hundred more questions raced through my mind, but I refrained from asking them. "Does someone have designs on restoring him to the throne?"

Orleton and Mortimer exchanged a glance. Neither spoke for several moments, as if weighing whose place it was to put forth their theory.

Finally, Mortimer said, "I suspect the Earl of Kent may have had some vague connection to —"

"Edmund?" I rounded on him. "That is preposterous. He was with us in France. He rode beside us as we marched across England in search of Edward. He may be his brother, but I can scarcely think of anyone *less* likely to try to free him and put him back on the throne."

"Which is why," Orleton said, "we haven't drawn the Earl of Kent into the investigation, nor even told him of it."

"Yet," Mortimer added tersely. "But if we can find Dunheved, question him . . ."

I pressed the flats of my palms to my abdomen. The fluttering there had risen to a whorl of anxiety, spiraling up into my ribcage until I found it hard to even breathe.

"Rumors begin for two reasons," Mortimer said. "To stir malice and . . . because they contain a seed of truth."

"And you know this to be true?" I said. "That Edward of Caernarvon has sympathizers? Adam is right, Roger. We cannot volley accusations without proof."

"Proof? No, perhaps not. But it would serve us, and the young king, well to be conscious of the possibility—and to prepare ourselves against our enemies before they take action."

"How do we do that?"

Orleton pushed his chair back and stood. "Remove Sir Edward from Lancaster's care, to begin with."

Mortimer scratched at the scruff on his throat, his head tilted back. "There's power in keeping guard over a man born to be king. If anyone is going to turn against us, it will be Lancaster. Should he feel compelled to retaliate at any time, all he'd have to do is release Sir Edward, set him back on the throne . . . and it will be us who are put away."

"I only thought the duty of being Edward's caretaker would placate him," I said. "I never considered that he might use it against us, but I think you're both right. Better to do it now, given what almost happened. But where would we put Edward? Who's to be trusted, beyond all doubt?"

"Lord Berkeley," Mortimer said, "and Sir John Maltravers. They can both be trusted, more so than the earl, to keep your husband secure."

The reminder that I was still married to Edward of Caernarvon stung like an open cut, fresh and deep down to the vein. Except for the sharp whistling of my indrawn breath, the room was silent. Bishop Orleton must have sensed the tension between Mortimer and me, for he excused himself, closing the door firmly behind him.

I turned away to face the row of windows, the world beyond

dark with night. In moments, Mortimer's arms encircled my waist from behind, tugging me gently against him. I kept my body stiff, tempering my resolve against his nearness, but already my knees were weakening beneath me.

"Isabeau . . . sweet heaven of mine." Light fingers traced over my hips, wandering slowly up toward my ribs. His breath stirred on my neck, a fiery breeze of longing. "Let me hold you tonight, hour upon hour, until the dawn."

I shook my head, even as I felt myself wanting to yield, to abandon all. "I'm afraid, Roger."

He turned me around, his lips brushing against the crown of my hair, over my ear, the slope of my shoulder. Not until my breathing slowed and I half-closed my eyes, waiting for more, did he lift his head to speak. A smirk, hinting of something sinister, flashed across his mouth. Or perhaps I merely imagined it? His thumb stroked tenderly at my cheek, soothing away my worries. "Afraid of what—that he'll go free? You needn't worry, my love. I'll make sure he *never* has the chance."

Brixworth — April, 1327

NOT YET SUNRISE AND already the stones of Brixworth Church were awash in a rose-colored glow. Above the door by which I stood, a fanning of red tiles arched. Higher up, a robin danced on the ledge of a small, square window, a fat worm dangling from its beak as it eyed me warily. It cocked its head at me, then suddenly burst upward in a dither of feathers, dropping the worm to the ground far below. In the pale yellow glow of the tin lantern I had set on the steps, the worm wiggled inch by inch, until it at last tumbled over the edge and disappeared.

An hour ago, with no escort but Arnaud, I had set out from

Northampton where my children were staying. In a few days, we would all be in Peterborough, where the king would sign his name to the new treaty with France. Charles had been amenable to retaining the terms written down at Poissy two years ago.

Two years—so much had happened in that time. How quickly things can change; yet at other times, nothing seems to change at all. This church had stood upon this ground for hundreds of years, the workers who quarried its stones and the masons who laid course upon course were long dead, their bones now the dust of the earth. Long after I was laid in my grave, would anyone remember me or know of what I had done?

Upon my rising, Patrice had barely stirred on her pallet. I did not let her know where I was going, but told her that if anyone came looking for me to say I had risen early to walk in the orchards. Most of all, I did not want Mortimer to know where I had gone, or who I had gone to meet.

Feet scraped softly on the path behind me and I turned to see Lord Thomas Berkeley, hands clasped behind his back as he gazed up at the stones. "They say some of the bricks used to build this church were salvaged from an old Roman villa that once stood nearby. Who knows where they originally came from? I have never seen the likes of them myself."

"You came alone?" I looked past him, searching through the silver light of approaching dawn for movement. But I saw only the familiar silhouette of Arnaud de Mone, standing vigilant beneath the great oak on the hill by the road, our horses grazing lazily beside him.

"As you bade me to, my lady." He smiled warmly, dipping at the waist in a bow.

I indicated the tin lantern. He lifted it gently, so as not to disturb the flame, and then opened the door for me.

We walked silently through the arcaded nave, his steps long and floating, but his pace measured to match mine. My hand rested lightly on his arm as we made way toward the door leading to the Lady Chapel. Berkeley opened it. I went first, the darkness within causing me to go slowly until he entered with the lantern and set it upon the narrow table that served as an altar.

I sank to my knees to say a quick prayer. When I rose, I turned and looked at him. For a long while I said nothing. It was a risk, asking him here.

Last month, Mortimer had ridden to Kenilworth with an armed retinue. When he delivered the royal writ to the Earl of Lancaster, stating that Edward of Caernarvon's care was to be transferred immediately to Lord Berkeley, Lancaster had, of course, flown into a rage. Finally, he acquiesced, but swore to have the matter reversed at the next parliament. Mortimer said nothing to that. He simply rode away, his prisoner bound in ropes and surrounded by a hundred armed men.

"He is well cared for?" I asked at last, my voice barely above a whisper.

"He is."

"I mean . . ." I began, my fingers twisting the cord at my waist, "he is not mistreated in any way?"

Berkeley tilted his head inquisitively. "No, my lady. Your orders were relayed to Sir John Maltravers, and to Sir Thomas Gurney, in whose care he is sometimes left: that no harm was to come to Sir Edward. Why do you ask?"

I opened my mouth, prepared to spew out every question and concern that had lately begun to plague my mind, but stopped myself. I had known of Maltravers being appointed, but certainly nothing of Sir Thomas Gurney, of whom I knew very little, except that I did not like his gruff manners and perpetual leer. Later, I would talk to Mortimer about removing Gurney. Undoubtedly, he would defend Gurney, but I would insist. How to do so without an argument was a matter I had yet to reconcile. Simply put, I did not trust the man, even though I had no sound reason not to.

I felt pulled from two sides: one my love for Mortimer and the other for Young Edward. As much as I wanted my children's father gone from my life, I never, *never* wished him ill. If anything happened to Sir Edward, my son would likely suspect Mortimer—as would most of England. I, too, would be enveloped in a cloud of suspicion. Rather than put an end to matters, it would only make them worse.

I went to the window and gripped the edge of an unmortared stone there, the width of my outspread fingers. Back and forth I worked the stone, inching it out. Several times it caught, so tight was its fit, but I straightened it and then pulled again, until at last the stone worked free. I set it on the ledge and slid my hand into a hole beneath. A splinter pricked my fingertip and I grasped the wooden box to lift it out.

Turning about, I undid the clasp on the box. Inside lay a wad of aged cloth, its threads frayed and thin, as if it had once been torn from a garment. I peeled back the ends to reveal the object inside and laid it on my palm: a curving, thin yellowed bone.

"Swear on this relic, Lord Thomas, in the name of the Virgin Mary, that whatever words pass between us today will never be spoken of again—on your life, swear it."

His brow furrowing, he stepped back. "What . . . what is that?"

"The throat bone of St. Boniface." I moved it to my right, so that the lantern's light fell upon it more fully. "While on a mission to convert the peoples of Frisia to Christianity, Archbishop Boniface was waylaid by brigands. When his companions raised their weapons and readied to fight their attackers, he commanded them to lay down their arms, for as he said, '*Scripture tells us not to commit evil in the name of good, but to overcome evil by doing good*'. His only shield was the Holy Gospel. They slew him and —"

"My lady, why are you telling me this? I agreed to be Sir

Edward's keeper, at my father-in-law's request, and because I hope, in some small way, that doing so will allow England to correct the wrongs that were done under King . . . under *Sir* Edward's misrule. If you have no faith in me, then relieve me of the duty. There are many ways in which I can serve the young king."

"I chose this relic for a purpose, Lord Thomas, and I asked you here because you are a kind and honorable man. That alone has more value than blood or riches." I thrust my hand out, the bone quivering in my palm. I drew a long, deep breath, searching for some calmness buried deep within my soul. "Now, I cannot say a word more of 'why' until you swear, my lord. Whether you agree to my request or refuse, I will not hold it against you. But I must know, beyond a doubt, that what we share here today will never, *ever* be spoken of again—by anyone, including you or me."

Berkeley studied the relic, his expression shifting from confusion to contemplation, then to curiosity. He came closer, laid his hand firmly over mine. "I swear upon this holy relic that I will never speak of this day to anyone—not even to you."

Curling my fingers around the smooth edges of the throat bone, I drew it to my breast. "I fear that Sir Edward's life may be in danger."

"What gives you cause to believe that?"

"There are many who would wish him dead, Lord Thomas. A few in particular who might hurry it along."

He narrowed his eyes at me. "I have no doubt that is true."

"Has anyone given you orders to . . . to . . .?"

"You mean Sir Roger?"

I nodded.

"I swear to you, my lady, even if he were to suggest murder—which he has not—I would not take part in it. Neither money nor power could persuade me."

"Then I have chosen wisely in you. And I will ask of you but one oath, for I'll not have my soul bear the stain of Sir Edward's death, despite all the troubles he has brought upon England. Swear to me that you will do everything in your power to see that my husband does not leave this world until God himself calls his name. Swear it, Lord Thomas."

He extended both hands, palms down. I slipped mine beneath his, the ridge of bone clasped between us.

"I swear, in the name of God, the Virgin Mary and St. Boniface, I will do everything possible to safeguard the life of Sir Edward of Caernarvon."

The first light of day streamed through the single window in a sparkling haze of dust motes to fall upon our joined hands. A sign? No, merely an indication that it was past time to go from there. If I was not back at Northampton soon, little Joanna would fuss over my absence and that would throw Ida into a state of agitation. Eventually, Mortimer would begin to search for me. We were due in Bedford tomorrow, King's Cliffe the day after and eventually Peterborough, where we would spend Easter.

Carefully, I wrapped the bone in its tattered square of cloth and set it back in the box, which I then tucked into its hiding place.

Lord Berkeley slid the stone over it. Only a fine crack showed around its rough edge. As we moved toward the door, he said, "*Aegroto, dum anima est, spes esse dicitur.*"

Pausing in my steps, I said, "I'm sorry, but I don't know the meaning of that." It was not a phrase I had ever heard any holy man say at Mass.

"It means 'So long as he yet lives, there is hope for the sick man'."

I covered my breast with both hands, suddenly fraught with worry that Edward had been poisoned. "Is he ill?"

"Not in body,"—he tapped his fingertips first to his upper arm, then his chest—"but in heart."

"I know. He writes to me, often. He blames me, for everything."
Indeed, his letters had been heavy with sorrow, bitter with betrayal.
So persuasive were his words that at times I questioned my course of
action. Yet what else could I have done? I had far from forgotten
how I had suffered, neglected and dismissed, for so many years. With
Mortimer's help, it had seemed possible to put everything right, even
though I knew it would not be easy. Even with my son firmly on the
throne, there would be trials. Likely, it would go on for years.

"I-I-I should not tell you this," Berkeley said, his pale eyes shifting down, then back up, "but . . . he confides in me sometimes. He is
content to be relieved of his burdens. With each day that passes, he
turns more and more to God, seeking peace."

There was compassion in his tone, and in his face. I was not
convinced, however, that the Edward I once knew had changed so
drastically as to beseech God's grace.

Whether my husband was contrite or not, I could not let Mortimer put an end to him out of convenience. Nor could I allow
Edward of Caernarvon to go free. The only thing I could do was
place my trust in Lord Thomas Berkeley. Yet even though he had
sworn, on the throat bone of St. Boniface, to protect the former king,
it did little to ease my fears. So much could go so terribly wrong . . .

Distraction was in order. Young Edward could not stop asking
about his betrothed, whom he had left behind in Hainault. And in the
North, Bruce's warriors were rattling their spears.

5

Isabella:

York – June, 1327

THE REGENCY COUNCIL WAS in agreement: the king's marriage with Philippa of Hainault should move forward. Bishops Orleton and Burghersh were dispatched first to Hainault to formalize the matter and from there to the pope in Avignon to seek a dispensation on the matter of consanguinity. Philippa's grandfather, Charles of Valois, had been my uncle. He died shortly before I went to France, upon which his son-in-law, William, became Count of Hainault.

Securing matters with Hainault would prove little problem; the Holy See was a more unpredictable matter.

To the north, borderlands were still in dispute. Lancaster and the other northern barons would not relinquish their claims to lands in Scotland that had been awarded to them by Edward I; Robert the Bruce, however, would accept nothing short of total surrender of those lands. Negotiations were attempted—and failed. Neither faction would bow to compromise.

We could not afford war so soon after Young Edward's ascension. And yet, we could not avoid it.

Although we attempted further talks with the Scots, our requests were met with a resolute reply when James Douglas swooped far down into the north of England like a winged demon breathing fire and destruction. If we did not gather England's might and march north, Lancaster would go to battle himself. His defeat would leave us more vulnerable than ever. Like a ship without sail or rudder caught in a tempest, our course was determined by matters beyond our control.

The great army of England gathered for the march north. Hundreds upon hundreds of pennons rippled in a warm May breeze, each one an imitation of the other. On fields of white stood a simple red cross: the banner of St. George, patron saint of England, slayer of dragons. The column stretched from horizon to horizon, fearsome in number. Unlike the former king's call to arms less than a year ago, this one resulted in an overwhelming response, with not a single knight or baron refusing to heed it. Foot soldiers by the thousands marched in orderly rows and to the rear crept the supply wagons, laden with food and arms.

The sun's dazzling rays glinted off Young Edward's gilded breastplate. Riding at the head of the column, he sat tall and proud, a golden crown upon his helmet. His steed was caparisoned with the leopards of England, and on its headpiece, or chaufron, was a pointed spike wound with alternating spirals of gold and silver so that it resembled a unicorn's horn. Next to him rode his uncles, the Earls of Kent and Norfolk, and his cousin Henry, the Earl of Lancaster. And somewhere behind them, Roger Mortimer.

We went from London to Nottingham and from Nottingham to Doncaster. In pastures, cows nursed wobbly-kneed calves. Newly tilled fields striped the verdant hills. Along the furrows, women hunched, shuffling slowly down the rows, sacks tied to their waists as they dipped their hands inside to pull out and cast the seeds that would become that year's harvest, should God bless them with neither too much nor too little rain. Through the low-lying valleys, broad rivers threaded. Where marshes spread, herons stood hidden among the reeds, their presence revealed only when they took flight, long legs trailing through the sky. Great swaths of meadow dominated the more difficult slopes and in between lay patches of dense woods.

The orderly march brought back recollections of our return to England last September. Only this time, we were going to face an enemy far more worth reckoning with than Edward of Caernarvon. While it was reported that Robert the Bruce's health was compromised by some affliction that mottled his skin and made his joints ache, forcing him to remain bedridden for days at a time, his commanders were no less formidable than he had once proven himself to be.

My son was well aware that this was no mere parade, as last year's march had been, and yet he went forward eagerly. His eyes flashed with excitement whenever there was talk of battle and strategy, and he practiced with his weapons daily under Sir William Montagu's tutelage, until he was bruised and exhausted. It was as if he had been possessed by the martial spirit of his grandfather, the first Edward; I had never warmed to Longshanks, for his eyes had been the color of an iron blade and his soul as hard and unforgiving. I only hoped my son would prove as competent in the field, without ever relinquishing his cheerful and loving nature beyond it.

War changes men, though. It hardens them to the suffering of others and makes them blind to brutality. It gives them a thirst for power that only further conquests can sate. We laud such men, extolling their feats, praising their might, even as we preach wisdom and pray for peace.

We halted early that day, somewhere north of Doncaster, as a light rain gave over to intermittent torrents. With the hood of my mantle pulled far forward, I sat on a rock beneath the sprawling canopy of an ancient oak which stood alone on top of a knoll. Come morning, the trampled fields would be a sea of mud. Patrice was in a sour mood and muttered her complaints at the length of time it was taking for our tents to be pitched. We had been unable to make it to Lancaster's fortress of Pontefract, or even as far as Brotherton, where lodgings might have been rustic, but at least we would have had a roof and walls. If I did not order her to cease complaining, it was because I, too, was wet to the bone and exhausted from the interminable journey.

By the time my pavilion was up, a band of sunshine peeked beneath a bank of clouds to the west, its golden rays spilling over the hilltops and outlining the trees in the distance in halos of light. Mortimer walked up the slope alone, bearing a small basket.

"Tell me that isn't coarse bread and moldy cheese again," I said, the corners of my mouth turned down in a mock frown.

"For a queen, this time something special, something different." Stopping before me, he removed the little square of white cloth covering the basket. "Warmed sweet bread with butter and boiled eggs—although the cook very nearly didn't get the fire lit, what with the rain . . ." His words trailed off as he sank to his haunches, the basket cradled in his palms. "Shall I take it back, wait for him to prepare something else? I saw a few hens freshly plucked and a —"

"I'd be asleep by the time it was done and then awaken in the middle of the night with a gnawing ache in my belly. No, this will do." I tore loose a hunk of the bread, so warm to the touch that a curl of steam arose from it, and brought it to my mouth, the little crannies glistening with droplets of butter. Its sweetness dissolved on my tongue. As I reached to take another piece, I said, "But you didn't come here to bring me my supper, did you?"

His fingers, peeling away fragments of eggshell, paused. He looked up at me, his geniality replaced by solemnity. "The king tells me that Sir John of Hainault is to meet us in York."

"It was not my doing, Roger. *He* wanted him to come back. He trusts him."

"And he does not trust me?"

"That is not what he meant by asking for Sir John's aid on this campaign. Surely you understand that? The Hainaulters are seasoned soldiers who —"

Slamming the egg back into the basket, he shot to his feet. "They are *mercenaries!*"

His voice boomed across the open space all the way to the ring of tents that were forming at the base of the hill. Several of my damsels popped out through the flap of the pavilion, gazed at us, then seeing it was only Mortimer they retreated back inside. Further off, soldiers stole glances at us as they unrolled their blankets or gathered around cooking fires. With the darkening sky, they were all but shadows in the silver mist that was gathering in the valley and creeping slowly across the land.

Mortimer lowered his voice, spitting his words between clenched teeth. "Flemish mercenaries, Isabeau. *Foreigners.*"

"And did we not land at Harwich with these very same mercenaries? How is this different? As I recall, it was you who touted their worth."

"We had no choice then. There was no guarantee that your husband was not going to raise an army against us. Even so, they were resented, mistrusted, barely tolerated. Need I remind you of the fights that nearly broke out every day?"

"No," I said, "you need not." Arguing over such matters was too much effort. What I needed was something to fill my stomach and a good night's rest, not this. "But it was the king's request and it has been honored. It's too late to renege now."

He pushed a hand through his hair and eased back down beside me. Bits of eggshell began to litter the ground as he plucked them away angrily. "How many?"

"Twenty-five hundred, still only a fraction of our own numbers, but enough to make a difference. Why does this vex you so, Roger? Because he did not consult you?"

Mortimer shrugged, but the twitch in his jaw muscles conveyed something far deeper than indifference. He clutched the bare egg with a tense fist. "He should have."

"Perhaps." Mortimer was desperate to assert control over this campaign, but wisely reluctant to demand it. It didn't matter if it was the king or Lancaster or someone else making a decision, he would resent it if they did not consult and heed him. As always, it seemed my duty to create compromise wherever discord existed. "If you wish to gain his respect, don't tell him what to do. I know my son, Roger. He may need guidance, but he'll resent anything being forced upon him—the same as you would."

"But I am forty, not fourteen. Isabeau, if he refuses to seek the wise counsel of those around him, I fear what may happen when we face the Scots on the battlefield. It could end brutally, and all too soon."

I laid both my hands on his. "So do I, Roger. So do I. That is why I'm trying so hard to seek compromise, even though Lancaster protests. I have sent so many letters, pleading letters, to the Scots, that I've lost count. But they're wagering on this timing, hoping Young Edward is weak, that we lack cohesiveness and leadership. Short of giving them everything they ask for, it seems unlikely that an agreement of any sort will be reached. So when the king mentioned Sir John, there was sound reasoning behind it, don't you think? He's wise for his years, Roger. Wise enough to know that he has a lot to learn yet—and far from believing he can lead men into battle tomorrow without someone like you or Sir John beside him. He'll turn to you when he needs you. Trust him at least that much."

Drawing his hands away, he turned them over, the white egg glistening in his palm. "Trust is such a delicate thing, isn't it? So easily broken. So easily destroyed."

He curled his fingers around the egg, enclosing it. For a moment, I thought he might fling it at the ground, the tree trunk—or perhaps even me. Instead, he stuffed it in his mouth, devouring it in two hasty bites, as if it had never existed at all. Then he ripped off a hunk of the sweet bread and began to chew, a thought flickering over his pupils.

"I forgot to bring us wine to wash our meal down with," he said with an apologetic smile.

"You'll be forgiven, if you remedy your error before the sun sets. I'm afraid I'll not last much longer."

As he rose to leave, I reached out to tap him on the leg, my fingertips grazing the rough links of his chausses. "When we reach York . . ."

Beneath dark eyes, soft with yearning, he smiled. I did not need to say more. For too long, we had been surrounded by too many people. Only the promise of being with him again, wrapped in the warmth of his arms, kept me from going entirely mad. How I longed for those days in France when we had been afforded so much time alone. Longed to feel his chest pressed to my back, nothing more than a sheen of sweat between us, our lungs hungry for air as we returned to earth, deliriously spent.

It was as if there were two pairs of us: the Roger and Isabeau, who in private meshed like the hand fitted to the glove, tender words whispered over silken sheets . . . and the Sir Roger Mortimer and Queen Isabella who had sought to deliver England from tyranny, succeeded and must now forever struggle to hold onto power, lest it fall to someone else and be turned against us.

Without a word, he turned and went, striding down the hill and disappearing in a swarm of soldiers laying out their blankets and squires tending to their knights' horses. So many people. It was a wonder they could all move in one direction and arrive at the same place without disorder erupting daily.

I waited beneath the tree, red sunset fading to dusky gray, the first silver pinpricks of starlight sparkling in the east. Waited for my knight to return, bearing a flask of wine and a pair of goblets. Waited for peace, elusive and rare. The night enveloped me, sending a breath of cool air down my back. All around, the camp quieted. Even the birds went silent. Soldiers, weary from a day's march, were bedding down. I slid from the rock, mindless of the damp ground and drew my knees to my chest. My head sank down to the pillow of my forearm.

"Isabeau?"

I shook myself awake. Patrice laid a hand on my shoulder.

"Your quarters have been ready for some time now." Then she added with a smile, "Sir Roger sent a flask of French wine—and his regrets. It seems the Earl of Lancaster waylaid him and insisted on discussing strategy. Why are men so obsessed with the details of war? Can it really be so complicated?"

She helped me up. As we strolled down the hill, I hooked my arm through hers and leaned against her. "Sometimes, Patrice, I think they don't know any other way. Their pride prevents compromise."

As WE APPROACHED YORK, a soft rain yielded to cloudless skies. A merlin, perched on a distant cairn, studied our creeping horde from on high, the constant wind ruffling his feathers and scouring our faces. Far to the north of the city stretched the first hint of undulating gold-green moors. There, grouse fed among the tender spring shoots of budding heather.

My memories of York were far from being good ones. Five years ago, I had been chased from Tynemouth by James Douglas, as he and his bloodthirsty hobelars had descended upon the priory, even as lightning split the sky. After a stormy voyage aboard ship and then a pressed ride inland from Scarborough, I had stumbled sea-tossed and wind-beaten into the king's chambers at York, only to be curtly dismissed by my husband, as Hugh Despenser sat leering beside him.

Just a few days after our arrival, Sir John of Hainault led five hundred Flemish mercenaries into York. He was assigned the White-friars abbey as his headquarters, while Young Edward and I claimed residence at the house of the Blackfriars. It was Mortimer's suggestion that the Hainaulters be lodged apart from our own soldiers as much as possible. No one, not even Sir John, protested.

On a few occasions, there were slurs exchanged and taunts muttered. I could only hope that if called to pursue the Scots, a common enemy would make them forget their unfounded mistrust of one another. While little could be done to engender harmony amongst the common soldiers, I thought it wise to at least encourage familiarity between the English lords and Sir John. Thus, a feast was arranged in his honor. Come evening, full bellies and an endless stream of drink would put them all in better humor.

That afternoon, my damsels parted my hair, combed it with great care and plaited it into two halves that were brought forward to my cheekbones and then back again where it was skillfully tucked and secured with pins. My ears were carefully concealed beneath the golden weave. A silver circlet sat upon my brow, its only adornment a single ruby in the center.

Old Ida entered my chamber with Eleanor at her right, my daughter looking much older than her now nine years in a scarlet cyclas. Little Joanna clutched her sister's other hand. I rose from my stool and kissed each of the girls on top of the head in turn.

Joanna's small fingers toyed with the buttons of my tight-fitting sleeve. She pouted, her whole face twisting with impatience. "My belly's roaring."

"Then let us go, shall we?" I pinched her lightly on the cheek, turning her frown into a grin of approval.

Straightening, I tugged at the waist of my gown to readjust it. The neckline of my dark blue cotehardie dipped low from bare shoulders—a fashion which some yet considered scandalous, although I cared not, for I found it far cooler in these stifling summer months to be free of cloth which covered every inch of my body except for my face. But if my dress was a topic for wagging tongues, the gossipers forgot about me as soon as they laid eyes on Patrice, for where my bosom was modest, despite having birthed four children, hers was amply endowed. She made a point of 'arranging' herself so that the deep crease of her cleavage peeked above the jeweled rays of her brooch. We were both now thirty-two and had known each other for most of those years, yet they had been kinder to her than me. Her skin was smooth, where mine was already showing fine creases at the corners of my eyes. Her thick hair glistened like darkest midnight amidst the twisting spirals of its curls; mine was fine and straight, like stalks of ripened grain. Had I not loved her as I did, I might have been jealous of her looks and the comfortable ease with which she flaunted them.

We began down the narrow corridor, a train of chattering women behind me, all of us giddy about the night's festivities after so many weeks on the road, eating the most basic of foods, our clothing spattered with mud and our faces reddened by the sun's strong rays.

Young Edward turned a corner ahead of us as we neared the hall. Around him were brightly attired noblemen and the ever-present Will Montagu, with whom he was laughing. Upon seeing us, the king threw his arms wide and rushed toward me.

"Did you hear?!" he exclaimed.

We kissed cheeks and as we did so, I suddenly realized he had now surpassed me in height. I cupped his chin in my hand. "Hear what, my son?"

He grabbed my hand, giving it a firm squeeze. "Count William has consented to the marriage. Philippa and I are to be wed!"

"I'm happy for you, truly. But do not forget the pope has yet to agree to the dispensation."

"Mother," he said, a sneer flitting over his lips, "it *will* happen. Don't spoil my joy tonight with pessimism. Please?"

"Of course. My apologies." In truth, although I was just as hopeful as he was that all would fall into place, age and experience had made a cynic of me. I reminded myself that Young Edward's match with Philippa was one he had chosen himself. In Hainault, they had been inseparable, never at a loss for words or laughter. While the future course of his marriage couldn't be predicted, at least it would have a good beginning—unlike my own marriage, which began poorly and got nothing but worse.

Arm in arm, we proceeded to the high table. The guests rose and bowed as we entered and took our seats at the head table. Sir John was seated to the king's right, while I sat to my son's left. The hum of conversation filled the room as goblets were topped with wine. Musicians strummed a lively tune on the strings of their lutes and viols. Then, gasps of delight were heard as servants scurried forth bearing platters and dishes of stuffed duck and roasted mutton, quinces in wine sauce and custards topped with strawberries.

The first course had not yet been laid upon the king's silver plate when Sir Roger Mortimer flew through the entryway and came straight to the king, each stride urgent and agitated. The grave look on his face was warning enough that all was not well that night after all.

Mortimer bobbed his head and poured out his news before the king even acknowledged him. "Your pardon, sire. I do not mean to interrupt, but I must inform you that a fight has broken out between some of the Hainaulters and a band of English archers over a game of dice. An Englishman accused his opponent of cheating. The Hainaulter drew a knife —" He expelled a burst of air, shook his head, and stole a glance my way. "Minutes later, our archers brought out their bows. They've shot dozens of Hainaulters dead already."

Further down the table, the Earl of Lancaster jumped to his feet, his chair crashing behind him. "This is chaos!"

Murmurs of shock rippled through the high-beamed hall.

"Intolerable," the Earl of Kent remarked. He and Norfolk rose in unison.

Sir John plunked down his goblet, wine sloshing over the brim and onto his hand. "I assure you, my lord," he said to the king, "that I will punish any of my men who had a hand in this."

Young Edward nodded, his countenance remarkably devoid of panic or anger. He bent forward and scooted his chair back.

I clamped a hand on his wrist, so tight I could feel his pulse throbbing beneath my fingertips. "Where are you going?"

"To stop this."

"Stay, I beg you. Let them handle this. One stray arrow —"

"No, Mother." He peeled my fingers away and stepped back. "They'll heed me. They will. Besides . . ."—he leveled a gaze at me that was both commanding and imploring—"I cannot nestle under your wing forever."

Moments later, he was hurrying out the door with Mortimer. I heard him call for his armor and weapons, as if he were a seasoned veteran of the field and not some innocent who had yet to see even a drop of blood shed. Against every urge, I let him go.

His brother John, who had not forgotten the riots in London, quaked as the hall emptied and the noise outside rose to a terrible din. Joanna tore away from Ida and climbed into my lap, her arms tight around my neck.

My appetite was lost, my hands cold and shaking. I clamped my teeth together to swallow back the bile that burned my throat.

How can this happen? We are not even at war. Dear Father in Heaven, keep him safe! Watch over him when I cannot.

KING EDWARD RODE THROUGH the streets of York, the visor of his bascinet open so all could see his face, his empty hand upraised. Prayers tumbling over my lips, I watched, safe at my tower window. One by one, brawling soldiers paused to heed the king's pleas, abandoned their weapons, and then skulked away. Archers laid down their bows upon his passing and raised hands above their heads as they were herded into clumps to be dealt with by their superiors.

The fighting, which had begun in one quarter near where the Flemings were housed, had quickly spread to surrounding areas. Everywhere—in streets and alleyways, on rooftops, in doorways—the bodies of the fallen lay, mangled and bloodied. Within the hour, the city lay eerily still, reeking of death. Every door and shutter in York was barred and shut tight, except for those clogged with corpses.

This, I observed, is but a glimpse of war. An instant amidst the millennia. A single axe stroke in the felling of a great tree. A remembrance and a foreshadowing of every soldier who had ever fallen or is yet to fall.

In the end, more than three hundred had been killed. What chance did we stand of defeating the Scots if we could not make peace with our allies?

For a week, the soldiers were sequestered to let tempers settle. Young Edward, rather than lounge in the relative luxuries that York had to offer, wandered among them. He spoke little, but when he did he spoke of discipline and trust, his voice ringing with the youthful clarity of optimism and unmarred confidence. When they saw him again in the days following, they sank to their knees and hung their heads in shame. If anyone wondered how a king so young could say such wise words, they had but to cast a glance to the man behind him: Sir Roger Mortimer.

In this way, I could see how one complemented the other. Mortimer knew the brutal realities of war and he understood his soldiers—that to lead them into that bodily hell, you first had to promise them that immortality arose from a life lived with courage and honor. What he lacked, however, was not only Young Edward's crown, but his ease among men. After the disappointing reign that was Edward II's, my son was the embodiment of hope. He was loved and admired, if not yet wholly obeyed due to his callowness.

Mortimer had been right about inviting the Hainaulters back to England. Their skill in arms was never in question. It was the in-herent mistrust of our own against those of foreign blood. That same enmity, however, would serve them well against the Scots—a reality which arrived all too soon. On the 15th of June, the Scots crossed over the border through Kielder Gap, a hundred miles from York. Light-horsed columns, led by Thomas Randolph, now Earl of Moray, and Sir James Douglas, sped through the north of England.

Preparations were hastily finalized. While the Earls of Kent, Norfolk and Lancaster may have been the nominal leaders, all knew that it was Mortimer they would look to for guidance. None had more experience on the field of battle than him. And it was precisely for that reason that my heart grew cold with fear, for I knew he would not hesitate to rush into the confusion of killing, sword up-raised and ready, courage as his shield.

As dawn broke over the Yorkshire hills on the first day of July, the great army of England amassed outside the city gates. I rode past on my chestnut palfrey to survey the men-at-arms, archers, and ar-mored knights in their hundreds. The many-colored banners and pennons fluttered in the barest of breezes, the air already stifling in the rising heat. Patrice and a few of my damsels rode along with me, as well as several knights who would stay behind to garrison York and serve as my protectors. As much as I wanted to accompany the army on this campaign, I would go no further than York—and pray all the while that both my son and my lover would return home to me.

My chest tightened as I searched amongst the banners. Kent waved to me. "God go with you!" I called in return. I tried to smile in encouragement, but couldn't. I could only wonder how many days or weeks or even months might pass before I would see them again, before I would even know who yet lived and who had died.

Ahead, a row of archers parted suddenly, heads bowed. Young Edward galloped toward me, a cluster of knights and squires trailing in his shadow. His great warhorse, in all its fine trappings, was a spectacle to behold—and he no less, his slender frame encased in layers consisting of a padded gambeson, coat of mail, and surcoat, giving him the appearance of more girth than nature had yet seen fit to endow him with. Plates of armor, polished to blinding brilliance, further protected him from shoulder to wrist and knee to ankle. Upon his head sat a gold-crowned bascinet, which hid the downy waves of golden hair beneath it.

Not yet fifteen, and already he was more kingly than his father had ever been.

"'Tis only for show," he beamed, laying a gauntleted hand upon the gleaming mail on his courser's neck, "until we are beyond the city. Any one of my palfreys has a much smoother ride than this temperamental beast."

Black eyes wide, the steed curled a lip and neighed, then tossed its head. It stomped a hoof on the beaten grass and danced sideways a step. Young Edward laughed, pulling back gently on the reins until it settled. "See what I mean?"

But I was not so lighthearted. The king's smile faded. He moved closer to me, extended his hand. "I don't know Scripture well, I confess. Would that Bishop Orleton were here. It seems a fitting occasion to quote the Holy Gospel, does it not?"

Though I opened my mouth to speak, the words I had so carefully prepared refused my will. Grasping his fingers, I nodded and bit the inside of my lip to still its quivering.

"Should he send any word from the pope," he said, his forehead creasing solemnly, "about the dispensation . . ."

"Of course. Oh . . ." I gestured to a page behind me, seated on his hackney. He trotted forth and handed a letter directly to the king. "From Philippa. It arrived late yesterday."

For a long moment, Edward stared at the wax seal with a bewilderment that was both joyful and bittersweet. Finally, he tugged a gauntlet free and broke the seal. He scanned the letter quickly, then just as fast folded it up again and tucked it beneath his surcoat. "She says, 'Fear nothing, for I have prayed for you.'"

With a shrug he tried to dismiss the sentiment, but I could see him swallowing hard, his hand still pressed against his surcoat where the letter was concealed. I was certain the moment he was alone again he would take it out and read it once more, a dozen times perhaps, bare fingertips tracing the black swirls and slashes, as he summoned her memory and dreamt of seeing her again.

We exchanged a kiss. All I could say was: "God go with you and protect you, my son."

What else does a mother say to her firstborn son on the day she realizes he is now a man? The day she realizes she will never hold him against her breast again to comfort him? There are so many things I could say, but I won't. He is a man; I must let him live a man's life.

Heavy-hearted, I rode away, back toward the city as, far behind me, the trumpet's clarion signaled the order to march. Somehow, above the rumble of wagon wheels and pounding feet, Lancaster bellowed orders. I tried to gaze straight ahead toward York's high walls and heavy gates, but I kept turning my head to look back.

Last night, Mortimer and I had foregone parting words and probing hands, instead holding each other and talking of our future, as if it stretched open and inviting before us, no barriers in our way, no enemies to thwart our plans or quash our dreams. As I rode beneath the portcullis, I barely took note of the faces of the people who bowed to me or parted from my path.

After a brief prayer at the chapel, I returned to my chambers at the house of the Blackfriars, my bones as weary as my spirit was cheerless. In the antechamber, I bade my damsels to take their morning meal and join me later in the afternoon.

"Would you like us to bring you something to eat?" Alicia asked.

"Perhaps later," I said, one hand pressed to my churning stomach. I'd had no appetite since earlier the previous day. No wonder I was as weak as a newly weaned kitten. I started toward the door to my bedchamber.

Patrice rushed forward, grabbing the door latch. "I can help you change out of that, if —"

"No. Thank you, but no. I just need to sit awhile. Alone." All I wanted was to fall into bed, but I was sure once the door was closed, the tears would come, hard and heavy. I didn't even want Patrice there. She had no son. She might hold me, say words of comfort, but she would not understand my grief.

I slipped through the door and closed it as fast as I could. I had not made two steps toward the bed when an unexpected voice seized my heart.

"Isabeau."

Gasping, I whirled around. "W-w-why are you here?"

Drawing both hands down over a rough-whiskered face, Mortimer leaned out from his chair, hidden in a shadowy recess. "Dear God, I am so tired I can barely think straight. My head feels like it will cave in, my heart like it has leapt from my body."

With a throaty groan, he heaved his body forward, staggering forward several steps before he stopped, glared at me, then gimped toward the window, one leg dragging along the floor as he gripped a hand to his thigh.

"Roger, what's wrong? Are you hurt?"

He flipped around, casting his weight against the wall next to the window. In full light, he appeared even worse. Dark smudges hung beneath his eyes, which were rimmed in red, as if he had rubbed at his eyeballs until the blood vessels threatened to burst. He breathed in through his nose, looked toward the ceiling, and sagged. I thought he might sink to the floor, but he stayed upright, his breathing growing more ragged with each pull of air.

I went to him, touched his shoulder. "Are you hurt?"

A smirk tilted his mouth. "Nothing that will kill me. A pain in my hip. When the siege on Bristol broke, I . . . fell. Down the dungeon stairs, as I ran to see my uncle . . . but he was already dead. Not very graceful, I admit. The pain, it comes and goes. Mostly, it comes when I am robbed of sleep."

It had been nearly midnight when he left me, but he had seemed very calm then, given the circumstances. I slid my fingers up the slope of his shoulder, sensing the tautness in his muscles. His shirt was tugged to one side, crumpled. It was the same one he'd had on last night. He hadn't even bothered to don his armor. "What happened, Roger? Did Lancaster say something to you? Did the king?"

Mortimer grabbed my hand. "Gurney and Ockle arrived from Berkeley in the middle of the night. They brought news."

Berkeley—that word alone was an ill omen.

I slipped my hand from his and drew the shutters closed. "What word did they bring?"

He whispered, "Edward of Caernarvon was freed."

I had to sit down before my knees gave out. I turned away, slid onto the edge of the bed, wadding a handful of blankets in my hand to squeeze hard. "And they have not found him yet?"

71

"No, they have." A grimace flashed across his face as he hobbled across the floor. When he reached the bed, he collapsed back onto it. Hands interlocked across his chest, he looked at me. "It took them four days to find him. And the *only* reason they did was because he ran away from the people who had tried to rescue him."

"That doesn't make any sense. Why would he try to run away? Did he think they were going to harm him?"

He shrugged. "Perhaps. But nothing about Edward of Caernarvon makes much sense anymore. He talks incessantly of God, my son-in-law tells me. Says he's glad to be rid of his crown. That he wants to join the Church and be left in peace."

"That hardly sounds like Edward. Do you think he has gone mad? Or that he's simply saying such things hoping to be left in peace long enough to . . ." I shook my head. Even I was thinking in circles that didn't make sense. "Was it Dunheved, the man who tried to free him from Kenilworth earlier?"

"I don't know, but very likely it is. He and his accomplices will be hunted down and made to pay. But what matters even more is who put him up to it. Someone wants Edward of Caernarvon back on the throne—and us out of power."

I smoothed the wrinkles from my blanket. Mortimer was right. Someone wanted us deprived of our power. Wanted it for themselves. But who? Lancaster? The king's uncles? The King of Scots? It could be anyone.

I had to protect my son. I had gone through too much to bring him to the throne.

Mortimer sat up, a devilish flicker in his eyes. "But if they can't find him . . ."

"What are you talking about?"

He reached out to trail calloused fingertips over my chin and jawline, then lifted a tendril of my hair and tucked it behind my ear. "Only a passing thought. Never mind."

"Roger, swear to me you won't harm him."

"Isabeau, if you cannot trust me, then who *can* you trust?" With a weary grunt, he stood. "Now, I need to rest."

"But . . . you must go to Scotland." I followed him to the door, an even worse panic twisting my gut as I imagined my son being led into battle by the overconfident Lancaster or the inexperienced Kent. "Who will —?"

"I *will*—tomorrow. It won't take me long to catch up with that lumbering column. First, though, I need sleep." His cold lips grazed my ear. He opened the door and walked past my damsels. Although he took great pains to hide his limp, the stiffness of his gait and the scrape of his right foot were still evident to keen eyes and ears.

When he was gone, Patrice arched a questioning eyebrow at me.

"An old battle injury," I offered. "See if he requires a physician."

With that, I shut the door and buried my face in my pillow to muffle my sobs.

There are times that we contrive events in an effort to control them— and times that events control us.

I knew I must be the rock at sea's edge, immutable and impervious to the crashing of waves, but in truth that was no more than a façade, for I was the sand that shifted and flowed with the wash of the current.

6

Young Edward:

Weardale – July, 1327

EVERY DAY WHEN I awoke, I prayed to find the Scots, so we could defeat them. And every night after we failed to find them, I gave thanks that we had avoided battle.

When I left my mother at York, her apprehension had seethed through her skin and gathered in the sweat of her palm as I took her hand. What good would it have done to tell her that I, too, was afraid? None. Even as a king, I knew I was not immune to the mortal cut of a sword or the piercing of arrows, for as Will often told me when we were practicing at weapons, ''Tis the dead man who believed himself invincible.' It was only the promise of seeing Philippa again—of having her as my wife and queen—that lent me bravery.

The Hainaulters had brought something called a 'cannon', a large metal barrel which, packed with a curious powder and set afire, could shoot an iron ball far into the distance with a force so great it could fell a castle wall in one blow. Accuracy, however, was another matter. I had seen Mortimer's trebuchet at Bristol. The surprise was terror enough in itself, however. I would not have wanted to be inside Bristol's walls, wondering when or where the next stone or rotting corpse might land.

Mortimer had delayed his departure from York, claiming pain from an old injury. A feeble lie. He simply wanted to dally with my mother a day longer. By the time he arrived at our camp three days later, I saw no signs of discomfort in his stride, not even a grimace. I said nothing, lest my peevishness show, but I was also relieved to have him with us. While in France, he had told me many stories of his days in Ireland. If anyone was prepared to fight the northern heathens, I knew it was him. Certainly not Lancaster, that overblown swine. Thankfully, Lancaster headed off toward Newcastle, hoping to cut off the Scots should they take the eastern route, while the bulk of our army remained in the midlands near the River Swale, closer to Durham.

Every day scouts were dispatched in broad arcs. And every day they came back without news. Our column crept and meandered through the hills, progress hampered by the heavily laden wagons that carried our needed supplies and extra weapons.

I twisted around in my saddle to cast a look behind us. Our column trailed away for miles, its tail disappearing around a bend in the road, where a swath of marshland ran along the Swale.

"We could move faster without the wagons," I complained.

Yawning, Mortimer gazed straight ahead. He freed his feet of his stirrups and stretched his legs, then arched his back, as if he were fighting boredom and sleep. "A starving army is a weak army, my lord. Who knows how far north we'll have to go. They need their strength."

"I've heard the Scots have no wagons. That they drink from the rivers and carry only small sacks of oats tied to their saddles and make something called 'bannocks' on hot stones. And when they butcher a cow, they cook the meat in its own hide."

"They do, but they're nearly animals themselves."

"Can we beat them?"

Finally, he looked at me, his dark eyes boring through my false shield of courage. A lopsided smile broke the firm lines of his mouth. "Your grandfather did, many times. More than likely, though, we'll never encounter them. The Scots, you see, are afraid to meet us in outright battle. They are lightly armed, fewer in numbers, and fierce, though undisciplined. Face to face, we would crush them into oblivion. So they attack unprotected villages while they're beyond our reach and run before we can get to them."

"But if there is a chance of us coming upon them, why even come so far into England when it could mean their end? Why lurk and taunt? Why not just fight?"

"Because, as I said, they're animals. It's their way." He returned his insouciant gaze to the empty road ahead. "Still, never underestimate them, my lord. Night or day, always expect they're waiting around the corner just ahead, beyond the next line of hills, hidden in the forest to either side."

A shiver rippled down my back, despite the day's heat. I clenched my reins. For the next several hours, I studied the land around us, searching for shadows among the woods that stood in scattered patches all around us. At midday, a scout returned from the northern road ahead of us. Again, nothing.

The next day we arrived in Durham. But before we were settled and fed, to the southeast, beyond a stretch of hills we had passed the day before, a plume of black smoke curled upward toward snow-white clouds. *The Scots.*

At last, the rabbit is out of the hole. The hunt begins.

WE TURNED BACK THE way we had come from and then swung east through a narrow valley, the spiral of smoke beckoning. This time the scouts brought back reports of a village burned to the ground by the Black Douglas barely two days past. When we arrived there, smoke hung over the buildings like a pall of death. The army halted outside the village and I rode in with a group of thirty knights, including Mortimer. There was no danger. The Scots had been here and gone long ago.

Not a single house had been left untouched. Fire had consumed the thatched roofs and inside the walls that were no more than shells, timbers still smoldered. Barrels, baskets and emptied sacks were strewn all about. Stock pens lay in shambles; a pair of goats skittered in front of a band of riders, while a white-faced sheep bleated from behind the broken table of a potter's stall.

The cries of grieving women rent the air, their screams so raw and primeval it was like a knife shoved in the ear and twisted, its keen blade scraping away flesh and blood. As we passed the first home on the edge of the village, a little girl, no older than my sister Joanna, stood bawling. Her small face was blackened with soot. Behind her, a charred and smoking body lay beneath a collapsed doorway. It . . . *it* looked like a side of pork left on the spit too long.

I turned my head away and retched. My stomach heaved again—the convulsion so deep I thought my insides would spill out—until bile spewed over my tongue and chunks of that morning's breakfast splattered over my leg.

Will rode up beside me, offering a kerchief. I grabbed it, dragged it across my mouth, and then mopped at my chausses. I held the stinking kerchief out, to give it back to Will, but he had already ridden on. At the next house, he climbed down from his horse and circled a body sprawled in the road. The last bundle of thatch on the roof, still smoking, fell to the floor inside. A cat yowled and leapt through the window out into the road.

Will jerked at the flash of movement and drew his sword. The cat hissed at him, then scampered away, tail whipping. Will leaned down closer, poked at the body with the tip of his blade. It twitched. Cautiously, he jabbed it in the side and an arm, *half* an arm, flailed toward him. Will sidestepped the bloody stump as it flew past his knee. He kicked the dying man in the shoulder.

The man's eyes, red as the reddest harvest moon, flew open. He let out a ghoulish moan, slammed his half-arm onto the ground and tried to push himself away. It was then that I saw the hole in his gut, his entrails oozing out, and the pool of congealed blood beneath him. With cold mercy, Will plunged his sword into the man's heart, held it there, and waited for him to die.

Like that, I watched a man die. In slow, terrible agony. An Englishman. And I knew then I would see more of death and suffering, of cruelty and greed, of evil and apathy. I fought the urge to turn and ride away. Then I remembered that I was the one who insisted on coming along; no one had demanded it of me. If I ran, if I left this to others, what would they say of me?

I must be strong . . . and brave, for I am a king and kings do not cower.

I closed my eyes, gripped my knees to my mount's ribs, fighting to stay upright until my head stopped reeling and my breathing steadied.

Someone called my name. Footsteps plodded on the packed dirt of the road, coming closer. Finally, I forced my eyelids apart.

My uncle, Edmund, Earl of Kent, stood before me, head bare, his shield slung loosely over his left arm and his sword at his hip. "Everything all right, my lord?"

Drawing a lungful of smoky air, I fought back a cough, swallowed to wash back the burning taste of bile and raised my chin. "Fine. Where are they?"

"Headed"—he pointed toward a vague line of hills in the distance—"that way."

I nodded, suddenly noticing the men who were gathering around me. "Let's find them, then. Kill the bastards who did this."

FOR OVER A WEEK, we followed a trail of smoldering ashes—a trail which grew colder with each passing day. Our supply train was too slow. Paths which might have shortened our journey and put us closer to our quarry were impassable with the cumbersome wagons.

We were encamped outside the town of Bishop Auckland, awaiting the return of a scout, for another cloud of smoke had been spotted to the southwest. The division commanders were summoned to my pavilion. Impatient, I emerged from the suffocating air of the tent to wait outside. Nearby, Will Montagu cupped his hands and dipped them into a bucket of water. He dunked his face into the pool in his palms, and then scrubbed vigorously with his fingertips. I handed him a skin of wine.

"Damn cannons," Will muttered. He gulped down the drink and handed it back to me, empty. "A team of horses can barely get them up a steep hill at a crawl. And through the marshes?" He scoffed. "Useless things almost sank in one yesterday. Wasted effort to bring them all the way from Hainault."

"Hainault?" Sir John stepped through a crowd of soldiers, sweat pouring from his broad forehead. He looked questioningly at Will.

Will grinned, held open the tent flap and waved him inside. "I said it's a good thing you've come all the way from Hainault. Doubtless, once we catch up with those dastardly Scots, you'll give them a good drubbing with those cannons of yours."

Sir John laughed heartily and pounded Will on the shoulder, then ducked inside.

A sneer curled Will's lip. I flashed him a warning glare. "Need I remind you of the Count of Hainault's hospitality during the months we spent at Valenciennes?"

79

"No, my lord." With a few deft twists of his fingers, Will had un-fastened the buckles of his arm plates. "I'm not at all ungrateful. Just smart enough to know when to cut loose the stone dragging me underwater, that's all. Do us all a favor and convince them of that." He inclined his head toward Kent and Mortimer, then gathered up his weapons from the ground and left.

I went inside and a moment later Norfolk joined us. Mortimer flicked open a map and laid it on the small table in the center of the pavilion. I bent over it, studying the names of the rivers, towns and villages from Northallerton to Newcastle. By now, I had a firm idea in my head of where each was situated, sometimes even the distance between them.

"As of this morning," Mortimer said, pressing his finger on the map, the name of the fortress barely a faded scratch on the tattered parchment, "they were here—Barnard Castle."

"How many miles?" Sir John asked.

Mortimer tapped his finger on the spot, and then traced it back to our location. "Sixteen . . . by the most direct route."

"Within striking distance," Kent added. "But why haven't they gone further afield? Why loiter so close by?"

"Because," Mortimer said, looking up from the map, "Douglas is well aware of our unwieldiness. He taunts us because he can. He has no intention of ever meeting us in direct battle, even though he's brought his hobelars further into England than any Scottish army has ever been before. And he'll leave, like the coward he is, when he's tired of the sport. So let me ask you, my lords, how do we catch them and bring them to battle?"

Mortimer's gaze passed from face to face. A thick silence pervaded the space. Although he had declined command of any sort, clearly they were all looking to him for answers. Finally, his eyes met mine.

"My lord," he said, "have you any thoughts on the matter?"

Beneath my mail, an itchy rash demanded I scratch at places I could not reach. Sweat trickled from my temples, down my neck, dampening my padded gambeson. I spread my fingers on the table's edge and bent closer to the map. "Why not unload ourselves of our burdens," I offered, then quickly added, "I mean . . . since they're so close, couldn't we catch them in a day or two, if we could move more lightly—like they do?"

Stroking his stubbled chin, Mortimer eased back from the table. "Lord Edmund?"

Kent flapped his eyelids and shrugged. "I suppose we could leave the supplies and cannons here with the infantry. Take the cavalry, our best archers, some swift-footed men-at-arms as well maybe, and go after them. They'll have to cross the river somewhere. There is a ford at Corbridge, another one at Tyne."

"We'd have to march through the night," Mortimer said. "If we don't, they'll be out of reach again by tomorrow."

Norfolk nodded at their every word. He seemed unwilling to openly disagree with anything. "They'd never expect it of us."

"Do you agree, Sir John," I said, hoping this sudden shift in tactics would not erupt into a heated argument and thankful Lancaster was not with us, or else it surely would have, "that if we are to trap them along the river, we must abandon the cannons for now? We'll need your mounted knights."

Readjusting his sword belt, he nodded. "I will do as you command, my lord."

His ready obedience took me aback. I expected that one day I would hear the same words from all my lords, but not so soon. I barely knew how to block Will's blunted sword in training, let alone how to lead an army into battle.

It was not enough to be a king in name; I had to act as one, even if that meant stepping aside when those around me knew better than me how things should be done. Not doing so had been one of my father's greatest failings. I would not make the same mistakes. I would seek counsel, listen to it, learn, and when the time came that I knew, beyond all hesitation, what needed to be done, I would do it.

But today . . . today was not the day. I was not ready to carry that burden on my slight shoulders.

WE LEFT IN BLACKEST night, stars shrouded by a blanket of clouds. The infantry, the cannons, and any supplies that could not be carried on our saddles were left behind. The road to Barnard Castle twisted and turned. The miles went on and on. I was lulled by a monotony of endlessly plodding hooves, the mournful creak of leather and the sporadic jangle of bits. I closed my eyes and must have fallen asleep, for my body jerked upright as my horse skittered. A stag, its great pronged horns gleaming white in the darkness, bounded onto the path before us. It turned with a kick and crashed into a thicket of woods, branches snapping.

The jolt had more than awakened me, it set my heart racing. My thighs were cramped, my back aching from lack of rest. Again, I closed my eyes, my horse following my standard bearer before me.

From time to time, I took a glimpse around me and for hour after hour everything was black and oddly silent. I kept waiting for dawn's first light to break beyond the western hills, but the clouds remained thick, the world beneath a cavern of nothingness.

A burst of light blazed across the sky, followed by the ear-splitting crack of thunder. The shrill whinny of horses rent the air. Moments later, lightning flashed again and again, until night became day then became night again. Then, the rain began. It poured from above as if we stood beneath a mighty waterfall and could not move from it.

The sky was a watery gray, every image around me blurred by the deluge. Yet we rode on, shoulders slumped beneath the pounding rain, water leaking into the cracks of our armor, soaking our shirts beneath. Wind stirred across my face. Shivering now, I realized it must be morning, even though there was no sun to be seen.

The front line lurched to a halt at a row of pine trees spread across the top of a hill. In the valley before us lay a mud-engorged river. A stone bridge, leading to a small town, spanned its width. Surprisingly, there was no sign that the Scots had laid ruin to the town. Had they indeed run back north? Or had we passed them in the night as they watched from the forest depths, laughing? Somewhere in the branches above, an irritated '*chuck, chuck*' sounded. I glanced up to see a red squirrel grasping its pine cone, tufted ears pointed alertly forward.

Mortimer blinked against the rain pelting his face. "Haydon Bridge."

"What river is that?"

"That, my lord, is the South Tyne. But it doesn't look as if they've crossed here. We should rest a few hours, allow the men to eat."

I nodded dully. A burning cramp spread from my neck through my shoulders and upper back. I reached inside the sack slung from my saddle and groped for the loaf of bread. My fingers met a soggy lump. I pulled it out, wrinkled my nose, and tore off a piece with my teeth. Rank with mold, I spit it at the ground and then flung the entire loaf away. It smacked against a tree with a dull thud. The squirrel scampered down the pine's trunk, tail flicking wildly as it eyed the tainted food.

My stomach groaned. I unstoppered my flask of wine and took a long swallow, even though I was too wet to be thirsty and knew it would do little to fill my belly. I might have asked for a cake made of oats, but there would be no fires in this downpour. "What next then?"

Climbing down from his saddle, Mortimer glanced about. The

83

others had already staggered beneath the trees, but there was no dry shelter to be found there, and so they crumpled into sodden heaps beneath their horses' bellies, reins clutched in stiff hands, or made a tent of their cloaks barely big enough to keep the rain off their faces.

"Same as before." His voice cracked with fatigue and he sank to his haunches. "First, we must find them."

I swung a leg over my saddle and slid to the ground, clutching the cantle to keep from falling. "It seems it would be easier if they found us."

Mortimer's lip twitched, as if to answer. But instead, he flopped over on his side with a grunt and curled into a ball, pulling his wet cloak over his head.

FOR DAYS IT RAINED. Heavy, relentless rain, stabbing the misery sharply into the marrow of our bones. Food was quickly becoming scarce, for we had each packed no more than a few days' worth and much of that had been ruined by the rain and the sweat of our horses. We drank from the rivers, brown and gritty with silt, and took sleep when we could. Armor rusted, although we dared not abandon it, and leather became so rotted that straps and cinches were in danger of breaking.

Always, they were one day ahead of us, the hoofprints fresh in ankle-deep mud. Gentle valleys became seas, as streams overflowed their banks, and bogs lay all about in scattered pockets, impassable and reeking of stagnant water. The Scots' looping trail wandered up and down hills, dove deep into forests, and crossed stream after stream. Pressed hard, many a horse went lame. Daily, we left some of our men behind, some ill, some whose horses had sunk belly-deep in the muck. As we rode off, we knew there was every chance the Scots would fall upon them and murder them.

Our formation disintegrated with each passing day, until our column straggled out far behind, more a scattering of clumps than orderly lines. Those who had somehow kept up their strength forged ahead, while those whose spirits were lagging trailed behind.

One night—I don't know how many days ago it was that we had left camp, for every day seemed much the same—we bedded down in a thick woods somewhere in the valley of the River Gaunless. We knew they had been here, because villages had been ransacked and there was no shortage of victims to attest to their ruthless brutality. Still, we were in danger of losing them altogether. The trail that day had been nearly washed away, even though the rain had lightened and eventually stopped.

Someone had gathered wood and after much flint striking, a smoky fire sputtered. As tired as I was, sleeping on the hard, wet ground held no allure. Lightheaded from not eating, I stretched my palms toward the fire and dreamt of a table heaped high with food and a dry bed piled with pillows. Either we had to find them and fight—or go back home. If we left, they would run rampant and burn every town between here and Newcastle. I couldn't let that happen.

"I would grant a lifelong fortune," I thought aloud, "to the man who could track them down."

Kent and Norfolk stood on the other side of the fire, their faces sallow in the wan, amber glow. They looked at each other.

"Why not send out more scouts?" Kent said.

Clasping my hands together, I looked up, smiled. "Yes, why not?"

I offered up the challenge to any who would accept. It would only take one man to find the Scots and return with word of their whereabouts for us to succeed and end this frustration. In the end, only one man came forward: Thomas Rokeby. He rode off at dawn as the first pale slice of sunlight in what seemed like weeks beamed from the east.

The next afternoon, he stumbled horseless into our makeshift camp, his face purpled with bruises and a jagged line of blood oozing across his forehead.

Mortimer strode forward and looked him over. "I take it you found them?"

Rokeby clenched his trembling knees with filthy hands. Mud caked his legs and arms, as if he had traversed a bog and fallen more than once. "More like they found me."

My gut was grinding with emptiness, my head pounding with an ache that made it hard to think. I glanced at Mortimer, but he was intent on hearing what Rokeby had to say.

"You saw Douglas?" Mortimer said.

"Spoke to the devil himself." Rokeby's fingers probed the swollen flesh beneath his left eye. Next to it, a smear of dried blood ran from temple to jawline. Standing, he swiped a hand across his face and gazed intently at me. "Says he'll wait for you, my lord, on the banks of the River Wear."

At last!

"Show the way," I told him and went to my horse. My knees folded beneath me. I flailed a hand out, catching hold of my stirrup, and quickly righted myself. My mounting weakness made me wonder if they were as hungry as us.

Damn Douglas to hell and back. I will not let him jeer at us from across the river, then run home laughing. He will bleed his last drop of blood on England's soil—or be the death of me.

THEY WERE PERCHED, LIKE crows sunning themselves, atop a steep outcrop on the other side of a loop in the Wear. Thousands. An array of demons, with their flowing hair and naked arms. Whooping and waving their hands high in the air.

Norfolk tusked and shook his head. "Out of bowshot."

"Which is precisely why he's there," Kent added. He cinched his sword belt tighter, so it no longer drooped low on his thinning hips.

We stood in the broad plain of the river across from them, holding the reins of our horses. Without fodder and the grass gone scant because of all the mud, our beasts' ribs were showing. The journey had been as hard on them as us. My steed hung his head low between bony withers. He sniffed the grass, brown with mud where the water had flowed over it, and snorted loudly. I slipped my fingers through his silver mane to untangle the knots, but they were so many I gave up the cause. I had discarded most of his trappings days ago, not wanting to burden him to the point of lameness. Yet every night, I had slept in my armor, mindful that we were probably being watched. How else had they known where to go to stay ahead of us, always out of reach?

"My lords." Mortimer's armor, like the rest of ours, was dulled and pitted with rust. Still, he carried himself with his shoulders back, his chin thrust slightly forward and his eyes, hard as flint, taking in everything around him. His helmet was tucked beneath his arm, ready to be donned, should some stealthy Scot hiding in concealment let loose an arrow. "They'll stand there taunting us like that forever if we let them. No, they're not likely to advance. But *we* could strike."

Norfolk scoffed. "Suicide. By the time we get our horses across the bridge —"

"You're thinking like a knight eager for glory, my lord." Mortimer tried to suppress a grin. "But truly now, what is our greatest weapon, the one that will endanger neither your life nor mine?"

Kent threw a look back toward our forces, nodding thoughtfully. "We've enough archers with us . . ."

"But they're out of bowshot!" Norfolk jabbed a finger toward our foes, safely positioned. Wide-eyed at the outburst, his horse tossed its head back and pulled away. The earl yanked the reins closer, holding firm until the animal settled. "Come now, Sir Roger. You're speaking in riddles."

"Then let me speak more plainly." Mortimer turned to me. "Send a detachment of archers to the other side. If the Scots fly down from their eyrie, the archers can rain arrows on them and half will be dead before they ever come within an axe's throwing distance."

"And if the Scots flee?" Norfolk said.

"If they run, why would we let them go?" Mortimer leveled him with a gaze so stern and commanding that Norfolk cringed. "We would cross the bridge with our cavalry then and give chase. A month we've spent wandering this land, hampered by rain and mud, and they've never been as close as they are now."

As if they had heard him, a thousand voices rose as one from across the plain. They shouted insults, but their unintelligible words all tumbled together in a deafening roar. Soon, they were thrashing their swords against their small round shields in a rhythmic '*thump, thump, thump*' that pulsed across the valley and rattled the heavens. I prayed that God might reach down and flick them into the river with one angry sweep of his fist.

A hand alighted on my shoulder. Startled, I jerked my head toward the pressure. Kent leaned close, his fingers pinching harder in order to draw my attention away from the jeering horde.

"Send the archers," he said.

It was a command, not a question.

I nodded obediently. "Very well. Send them."

But even as I gave the signal, my gut tightened. I wondered if we should wait awhile before taking action, for it was an impulsive move, however logical it may have seemed. I knew enough of the Black Douglas's ways to know that he never acted without a plan. Surely, Mortimer knew that, too?

Kent and Mortimer strode off to give directions, while my uncle Thomas and I looked on.

Norfolk scratched at the scraggly beard covering his unshaven neck. "Perhaps they don't think we'll take the first move? Perhaps they're only bluffing?"

I shrugged. "Perhaps." Then, I mounted my horse and waited.

The sun was just past its peak when two hundred archers and a host of men-at-arms streamed across the narrow bridge, bows strung and ready. Had we encountered the Scots just a day ago, while the rain was still coming down, their strings would have been too wet for use. Today, for once, luck was in our favor. I scanned along the hill where the Scots stood, a hill so steep it may as well have been a cliff. My eyes paused from time to time on a figure with dark hair or a helmet that might hide Douglas's identity, but there was no clear indication who was in command of the rabble.

"What day is it?" I asked Norfolk.

"The thirtieth of July," he said, pulling the chin strap of his helmet tight. "Why?"

"I just couldn't remember how long ago we left, is all." It had been a month since we'd departed from York and I had yet to receive any word of Philippa or the dispensation. Odd how at times like these, such thoughts invaded my mind.

In disciplined precision, the archers arrayed themselves along the far bank, soldiers at their backs and waiting with swords held firm. Still, the Scots shouted their fiendish cheers. The echo of the pulsation reverberated from hill to hill, swallowing itself. The cadence of their thumping on iron-studded targes grew faster and faster, until one strike was indistinguishable from the next. The soles of my feet tingled. Soon, I felt a throbbing in my knees. The ground beneath my horse vibrated and I clamped my knees tighter to stay in my saddle.

The archers drew the first arrows from their quivers, raised their bow staves to the sky, and then took aim at the cliffs above.

Norfolk maneuvered his horse closer to mine and kicked me in the calf. He raised a gauntleted hand toward a break in the rock face of the outcropping, not a hundred strides from where our lines stood. There, on the other side of the river, a sizeable host of Scots rose in unison from a crouching mass. And among them, a knight on a dark horse, shouting orders. From beneath his helmet peeked a fringe of black hair, barely visible at the nape of his neck.

"Back!" At river's edge, Kent spurred his horse, riding fast toward the bridge, shouting over and over, "Call them back!"

Before our archers could discharge a single flight, their captain called the order to retreat. In staggers, the archers lowered their staves, looked about. The retreat began as a trickle, but in seconds they turned like a wave breaking upon the rocky shore, shoving and stumbling over the soldiers behind them, who had yet to recognize the fast-approaching threat. Swords held fast, the men-at-arms stalled in confusion. Then they, too, turned and ran.

Hundreds of Scots poured out from the gap. Their war cries cutting across the distance, shredding the air. Axes, keen for English blood, glinted in the sunshine.

My throat constricted. I couldn't breathe. I bit hard on the inside of my cheek, hoping I wouldn't pass out. My hands trembled—with fear, anger, disappointment . . . I wasn't sure. Finally, my chest heaved and I gulped a mouthful of air.

"No. No!" I pounded a fist against my thigh. "He will not do this to me!"

Hooves rumbled across the earth. Mortimer and Kent reined their horses to a halt before me.

"Send a delegation, sire," Mortimer said. "Bargain for peace."

My fingers flexed, clenching and unclenching. My breaths came in gasps so rapid, I was nearly panting.

Behind us, row upon row of mounted knights sat watching in shamed silence as the last of our soldiers, splattered with mud up to their ears, straggled across the bridge. The Scots halted partway across the marshy field and whirled their weapons above their heads. Scottish spears jabbed heavenward in triumph.

"Bring me a messenger." Blood throbbed in my temples. Fire raged in my veins. A messenger hurried forward and knelt before me. "Tell him . . . tell him to come down from his position, cross the river and when we are both arrayed on the open field, face to face, he can fight us on even ground. Neither side will strike a blow or give chase until then. He has my solemn word."

Mortimer expelled an audible breath. He steadied his voice, lowered it, as if speaking to a child. "I remind you, sire, that Bannockburn was lost, in part, because your father positioned himself with a river at his back. Douglas was there. He won't agree to —"

"My father was a fool! Now tell him what I said!"

The messenger dipped his head, nodded once, and rode off.

Neither Kent nor Norfolk spoke for a good long while. I think they dared not.

Earlier, I had done as Mortimer suggested, even though my intuition begged me otherwise. No, I would not let them—Mortimer or anyone else—lord over me again when doubts begged examination.

Kings do not cower in the face of battle. And kings do not bow to their underlings.

Half an hour later, the messenger dismounted and knelt before me, his knees squelching in the mud. He couldn't have been more than a couple of years older than me.

"His reply?"

He gazed up at me through a tangled mess of sandy locks. "Lord Douglas said: 'The king can see we are in his kingdom and have laid waste to it. We shall stay so long as it pleases us. If he likes that not, then let *him* come over here and address the matter.'"

7

Young Edward:

Stanhope Park – July, 1327

I AWOKE TO A demonic howl. A keening . . . something *otherworldly*.
Rain slapped against the low roof of my tent. The odor of
moldy rope and rotten leather invaded my nostrils. I placed a hand
on the ground to push myself up. Mud oozed between my fingers.
Forcing cramped muscles to unbend, I sat up, feeling the unwelcome
restraint of my armor—a reminder of where I was and how long we
had been here.

Breath held, I listened, waited. Except for scattered coughs or
the nickering of horses, the camp was silent. Soon, the sound came
again: a long bellow, rising in pitch. Trumpets, not demons. Then, I
heard the banging of swords on shields and shouts from the far side
of the river.

For a few hours, I had forgotten.

Nine days we had sat here—watching them watching us. And

every blessed night, they sounded those infernal horns, at intervals so erratic it was maddening. Sometimes they would blast them just once or twice, and then fall silent. An hour later, the same again. We might have slept in shifts during the day, but they were always there, mocking and shrieking as the deluge continued. Whenever the rain stopped, their cooking fires blazed high and the faint aroma of charring meat drifted across the distance to us.

The only advantage we had gained during the standoff was that the Earl of Lancaster had arrived with supplies, including my own tent so I could at last sleep someplace dry. He'd also brought along a pair of Sir John's cannons. But much of the food, like our spirits, had soured. Yesterday I had feasted on a bland stew of beef and cabbage, washed down by a horn mug of watered wine, only to have it all run clean through my innards by nightfall.

The cannons might have proven more useful, but it was impossible to ignite them in a downpour. Every day, the bastards stood on their hilltop far beyond reach, taunting us with their mere presence. Sir John insisted on firing the cannons to make a display of their power. With a thunderous belch, the iron balls arced into the air, propelled at an amazing speed, then slammed into the soggy earth with an unimpressive thud, leaving craters a hundred paces short of their mark.

I cradled my head in my hands. My skull throbbed with pain. My thoughts were muddled from lack of sleep.

The noise had stopped. So had the rain. For once, the trumpets were not bringing the sky down. Blissful quiet enveloped me. I blinked, clutched for a blanket that was not there. Like everything else, water had seeped into it and so I had tossed it in the corner, hoping to spread it under a warm sun tomorrow to let it dry. My stomach churning, I lay down and closed my eyes.

Somewhere in Hainault, my sweet Philippa was asleep, her milky limbs tucked between a down-filled mattress and a freshly laundered blanket, perhaps dreaming of me, of our life together in England.

Only . . . not *this* England.

"DOUGLAS! DOUGLAS!"

Praying it was only a nightmare, I slapped at my cheeks to bring a rush of blood to my hazy head.

Hooves clattered. More shouts. Then . . . sword clanged against sword, struck flesh. Chaos. The cries of the wounded.

My heart clogged my throat. The realization struck me with the deadly force of one of Sir John's cannons: we were under attack. Swallowing hard, I groped in the darkness for my sword. Frantic, I flailed my hand in a wider circle, my palm swatting at a mat of crushed grass. Then, my fingers smacked against my shield. My bones screamed in pain. Great, burning throbs. I pulled my hand to my chest and tried to move my fingers, but couldn't.

The sounds were coming closer, growing louder.

"Kyrie, eleison," I chanted. *"Kyrie, eleison. Kyrie —"*

A dull glint caught my eye. I flexed aching fingers, wrapped them around the hilt and pulled my sword to me. Then I grabbed at the edge of my shield, dragging it over a crumpled shirt, and slipped my left arm through the loosened straps. No time to pull them tight. Rolling over onto my knees, I scooted around the center pole toward the opening. My blade clunked against metal—my helmet. Tucking my sword on my lap, I reached out, grasped it, and settled it snugly onto my head.

The shrill neigh of a horse ripped through the night air. Hooves crashed to a halt just outside the opening of my tent. I froze.

"A Douglas!"

Sweet Jesus, if I ever had to piss it was now.

"Ave Maria," I whispered, my bare fingers worrying at the binding on my hilt, *"gratia plena, Dominus —"*

Outside, a blade hacked at ropes, over and over. The walls of my tent vibrated with each blow. One wall began to lean dangerously inward. I heard a creak and turned to peer into the darkness behind me.

A heavy object struck the back of my skull. My face slammed against the ground. Air blasted from my lungs so fast I thought my ribs were caving in. Then I realized I was cocooned in canvas, my tent collapsed on top of me.

Too stunned to move, I tried to listen, but the dull clanging in my ears made it impossible to distinguish one terrible sound from another. My sword was trapped beneath my hips, its honed edge digging into the cloth of my leggings near my loins, one short inch above the links of my chausses. If I moved . . . I didn't want to think of what I might injure.

My whole body leaden, I wrenched my shield arm free and struggled to raise myself, easing up from my blade until it shifted and fell flat beneath me. But a weight bore down on my spine. Something had pinned me down . . . *The pole.*

I couldn't expand my lungs fully. My breaths came in shallow gulps, but every time I exhaled, it became harder to breathe in again. My ribs screamed in protest, burning for air. If I didn't suffocate, I would soon be trampled under rampant hooves.

Why has no one come to my aid? Were the pickets asleep when the Scots so casually strode into our camp?

Spurs jangled as a pair of booted feet landed on soft earth close by. The horse nickered, stamped a hoof.

A quiet laugh floated to my ears as clear as if its maker and I were standing an arm's reach from one another in an empty room.

The voice was hushed, amused—and distinctly Scottish. "What have we here?"

I imagined him, the Black Douglas, looming above me, a smile of wicked glee tipping his mouth as he grasped the hilt of his sword two-handed, point down, and raised it up high.

Dear Father in Heaven . . . free me from this shroud of death. Let me wield my sword so that I may longer serve you. Do not let me die ingloriously like this. Let me fight. Please, God, let me —

"Arrrgh!"

Will! I knew the savage bellow. I had heard it a hundred times as he taught me how to fight.

Metal struck metal, again, and again, and again. My teeth rang with each bone-shattering blow.

Somehow, I found the strength to roll from beneath the pole. With a final heave and a kick, I freed my leg from the load. But the canvas still encased me, folding more tightly around my body as I squirmed and twisted in futility, encumbered by my armor shell. I could not tell which way was out. Could not find a part in the tangled layers. I began to thrash wildly at the canvas, seeking any exit through the snarled heap. Eventually, I would find the bottom edge and a way out.

Will grunted with strain as he heaved his weapon. It struck flatly on a shield.

"You'll not get out of here alive, Douglas," he swore.

"Ah, I was right, then. 'Tis your young king buried there." Douglas laughed again, this time loud and arrogant. "Well then, I'll take what I've come for, but first . . . you're in my way."

Their swords rang in unison. The crossguard of my weapon dug into my thigh. Carefully, I wedged it upward until it was clutched to my breast. With my free hand, I batted at a part in the heavy cloth, slipped my arm through a widening gap, and writhed forward, inch by onerous inch.

My hand burst through. Damp air brushed my skin.

I lifted the canvas edge in time to see that another knight was closing in on the stealthy Scot from behind. As Will and Douglas parried blows, the approaching knight craned his arm back and swung a thick piece of wood. It struck Douglas squarely in the back with a muffled thump. Douglas staggered a step, whipped his sword arm backward and, without looking, knocked the length of wood from the knight's grasp. He might have skewered the man with a single thrust, but by then he was aware of an oncoming third assailant. In an amazing leap, the Black Douglas bounded onto his saddle, his sword still clenched in his fist as he beat back the newcomers.

The figure I took in did not match the image I had harbored of him these past months. He was no taller than me. His build was lithe and lean. Certainly not the stalwart, broad-shouldered giant I had conjured in my visions. Every movement was quicker than the eye, precise and graceful, almost as if he knew ahead of time what his foe would do.

Wheeling his mount around, Douglas blocked Will's furious blow with his shield, the blade pinging as it skipped over the metal boss in the center. Then, with a sharp kick to his steed's flanks, Douglas set off at a gallop through the darkness and confusion.

Shaking his sword, Will shouted profanities after him.

Around us, I saw the Scots pulling back in waves to follow their leader. In minutes, they were completely gone. Our first encounter— and I had been trapped helplessly under my tent like a runt piglet in a sack.

I rammed my sword into the ground, pulled a knee forward. Will extended his hand to help me all the way out. Free of my tomb, I stood on shaky knees. Shame flooded my chest, sickened me. *How had this happened?*

Out of the darkness, Mortimer appeared. Along the fuller of the sword dangling from his hand ran a thin streak of crimson, a darker smear marking the tip.

As if he had read my thoughts, Mortimer answered, "They must have forded the river somewhere to the north. They killed a set of guards at the rear of the camp, broke through before the call could go up. We lost just a handful of men; a dozen more were wounded."

When I did not acknowledge Mortimer's report, Will asked, "And the Scots?"

"Five, maybe six dead. A few captured, though. If we can get them to talk . . ."

All around was the evidence of the Scots' raid: tents toppled, kettles overturned, horses running loose, a wounded man with his fist pressed to a gash in his leg, trying to stanch his own blood. Next to him lay a dead friend. Last night they had shared a meal by the fire, laughing together.

"We should have slaughtered them," I mumbled, my voice cracking through restrained tears. "*We* should have crossed the river. Attacked them."

Mortimer gave me a patronizing look. "Before you can win against any enemy, my lord, you must first know their strengths and weaknesses. You must know yourself. Douglas and Randolph are keen opponents. Do not underestimate them. They had the advantage of position."

"Advantage? The greatest advantage they had was that we took no action. They teased us like . . . like a cat toys with mice. And now we cower here humiliated. What of honor and courage? What is it that we're so afraid of?" I glared at him, resisting the urge to swipe my sword at his bare neck and watch his arrogant head tumble from his body. "We cannot win if we do not fight."

"Nor can you lose. Defeat is a bitter drink, my lord. I know as well as any. I have led men into battle when the odds were against me and paid for it in lives. I would advise you —"

"You *think* you know much!" I stomped at him, fisted him in the middle of his chest. He drew his chin back, but made no attempt to remove himself or stop me. "How to lead an army. How to rule a kingdom. Yet you refuse command and then take offense whenever your word is not heeded. How would you have it, Sir Roger?"

"I would have you alive upon the morrow . . . and for the next fifty years so you can rule as you were born to. My duty is to see that you survive to do so. Not sacrifice a thousand men for the slim chance of a single victory."

I half thought, then, that he wanted the Scots to get away. That he *allowed* them to. But why? Rage boiled in my veins. I turned away.

"They're long gone now," I said with regret, for I would have hunted them down like limping deer had my own men not been so spent and hungry. "Tomorrow, we shall make to return to York. You, Mortimer, will keep your distance from me. This won't happen again."

He remained for a few moments, as if wanting to spew out further protests, to imbue me with more of his godly wisdom, but he resisted. He would go back to my mother, complain to her of my behavior and then I would have to deal with this again. So be it. I had tired of being ordered about.

Someday, the outcome would be different. I would ride at the head of a great and mighty army and lead them to victory—over the Scots, over the French. If need be over rebels from my own land. I would not accept defeat. I would learn whatever it took to win. And my men would fight for me because they loved me. Because they believed that with me they could win any battle, beat any foe who dared to take the field against us.

8

Isabella:

York — August, 1327

ON THE DAY I rode out from York to meet Young Edward, an August sun poured into every crevice, chasing away the shadows that had lurked in my heart for more than a month. It had not rained in nearly a week. At last, the rivers were receding within the confines of their banks, the mud had dried to leave roads passable and, fed by the radiant light, the grass blanketing the hills beyond the city gleamed in shades of green more brilliant than any I had ever seen.

I paused with my riding party at the crest of a hill where the road stretched out to the north. There, we saw the first rows of the army's column, pennons bobbing rhythmically. Midday heat pressed down on us. A thread of perspiration trickled from my breastbone to my stomach, dampening my linen chemise. A hot breeze tickled my skin and I brushed a stray hair from my cheek. On my head, I wore only a caul of woven pearls. Patrice had clucked at my decision to don it that morning, insisting that the white of the pearls was indistinct against my fair hair, but the headdress had been a recent gift from my brother Charles, King of France, and I loved it for that reason alone.

"Do you wish to wait here, my lady," my squire Arnaud de Mone said, shooing a pesky fly from his horse's mane, "or ride out to meet them?"

It was his way of asking to go. Understandably, he felt fealty to both Mortimer and me. For many years he had been my loyal servant, before flying to France with Mortimer when he escaped the Tower. Upon discovering him in my brother's court, I had quickly forgiven him for abandoning my service. Patrice, who had been until then his lover, was not so indulgent of the offense. For a year, she kept him at arm's length, until we were back in England and she could no longer pretend to hold anger toward him.

"They've marched many miles," I said to Arnaud. "Let us go out to greet them and hasten our reunion. Too many days have lapsed already since I last saw my son." *And Roger*, I wanted to add. But my love for him was something I could never proclaim aloud. Too many knew of it already.

My son John eased his horse abreast of mine, his eyes bright with anticipation. "May we go now, Mother? It has been ages since I've seen Ned, too."

"Why don't you lead us, John? Your brother will be overjoyed to see you're the first to welcome him back."

With that, John spurred his horse in the flanks. I gestured for Arnaud to accompany him and together they closed the distance, small clouds of dust billowing behind them in their wake. My damsels and I, surrounded by a small collection of guards, followed at a more restrained clip. Patrice sneezed at the road dust. She hated to travel— to her, it was *always* too hot, too cold, too wet or too dry, never a comfortable in-between.

When I had received word early that morning that the king would return by afternoon, I was dressed and ready to go within the hour. So giddy I was with excitement that I could hardly refrain from riding out immediately. Yet now, as I saw Edward and John clasp hands and begin back toward us, a sense of foreboding settled on me. Just behind them rode Lancaster, Norfolk, Kent and Mortimer. None of them appeared joyful. Every mouth was downturned, their shoulders slumped with weariness.

It was Lancaster who hailed me first, urging his horse ahead of the group. As he came to a halt, he slipped his fingers beneath his collar and stretched his neck. "Bloody Scots haven't changed a whit. But at least we've run them from English soil."

"Yes," I said, "we heard of their 'tactics' at Stanhope Park. But should any of us have been surprised by their unscrupulous methods?"

"Mother?" Edward called, coming around Lancaster. He reached out to grasp my fingers, brushed stiff lips over my knuckles and dropped my hand as coldly as one greets a hated nemesis. A snarl flickered over his mouth. "I say Cousin Lancaster has grossly understated our failure. If the Scots left, it wasn't because they feared us. They left because they'd made their point—that they could kill me, given the chance. Had I been better advised, they never would have had the chance."

He flashed a smoldering look over his shoulder at Mortimer. Then with a smart slap to his mount's rump, he rode past. Lancaster, obviously not concerned that the king's comment was directed at him, was close behind. Kent and Norfolk hesitated, and then followed.

As I swung my palfrey around to ride beside Mortimer, he imparted, "I did as you asked—kept him from the certain death of battle. He doesn't, however, appear to appreciate the fact."

"No," I said, keeping my voice low, "I don't expect he would.

Perhaps now we can bargain for peace, as I intended all along?"

"You might get that for now,"—he nodded toward the king ahead of us—"but if he has his way, eventually he'll wage a war on Scotland that will eclipse his grandfather's achievements."

It vexed me to know he was right. King Edward III of England would one day pride himself on the wielding of his sword, much as I had my use of the pen. Conquest in lieu of compromise. Perhaps in arranging the invasion which had put him on the throne, I had set a poor example.

Already, I could see that my influence on my son was fading. He was far from the innocent babe who had once gazed at me with admiration and smiled at my lullabies. He was grasping at manhood, in the resolute way that kings who crave power do, and I, as his mother, would only grow less useful and more contrary to him with each passing year.

For my own preservation, it was imperative that I hold on to control—authority, lands and wealth—however I could. I had been deprived of those things once before. I would not be again.

Let men believe this is their world to conquer and rule. More women have decided the fate of kingdoms than would ever be recorded in the annals. Yet they must wield power silently, otherwise it will be taken from them.

Somerton Castle — September, 1327

AMPLY COMPENSATED FOR HIS service, Sir John returned to Hainault, the English levies dispersed homeward and Mortimer left briefly for Wales, where he now served as Justice. I made him swear to return to me with all haste in preparation for the upcoming parliament. A part of me, however, did not want him to linger so close to Ludlow, where his wife Joan resided. So far he had made no mention of doing so, but the simple fact that he would be so near to her sent waves of panic and jealousy crashing through me, even though he had held me the night before he left and professed his love a dozen times over. My bed never seemed so vast and lonely a place as when he was not there.

But there were things I could do for Mortimer that Joan could not: I could make him powerful—king in all but name. To remind him of that, I arranged to have him granted the castles of Oswestry and Denbigh. Other lands I garnered for myself. If too many of these holdings ever fell to avaricious men such as the Earl of Lancaster, those individuals might one day prove too weighty a force to reckon with. In increasing my own wealth, I was protecting my son's future, for whatever I owned would one day pass to him. In the meanwhile, if I could not command an army, I would make good use of my holdings and ensure a certain level of influence. I had seen my husband's options restricted due to lack of funds—a predicament he had brought on himself time and again by being overly generous toward his friends—thus, I was well aware that income equated to power.

A full week after the parliamentary session opened that September in Lincoln, Mortimer arrived, his spirits bold and his appetite for me renewed. On his first night, he joined me at Somerton Castle in Navenby, a swift ride through the countryside from Lincoln, but far enough removed from the city's crowded streets.

We always stole time together when we could—most often he came to me, for it would have been too easy for someone to notice when the queen was rambling about the castle after nightfall. What we suffered in lack of sleep, we made up for in the exhilaration of our lovemaking.

Once, many years ago, I had announced at the foot of this very same bed to Edward of Caernarvon that I was carrying our second child. He had seemed unimpressed by the news and all too eager to leave my presence as I swallowed back the sour taste of morning sickness and threatened to spew it on the floor. How different this place was to me now, how bright the world shone, if only because Mortimer was here with me.

Moonlight cast Mortimer's features in silvery light, accentuating every fine line of his face and each contour of his muscle-hard body. I trailed a hand over the mat of dark hair on his chest, then around the side of his ribs, my fingertips pausing at the ridge of a scar I knew well. "Did you have time to look in on your estates?"

He caught my hand, pressed my palm over his heart, held it there. "I did not see her, if that's what you want to know."

"I did not ask —"

"No, but you've been wondering ever since I left, haven't you?" He let go of my hand, slipped his fingers into the hair at the nape of my neck and pulled me close. "She was a good wife for many years, managed both brood and household well, but she is not you—certainly not as beautiful."

I rolled onto my back, my head sinking into a feathery pillow, and pulled the sheets up over my breasts, as if modesty had suddenly overtaken me. "It's me you love, then?"

"Mmm, do I love you?" He pushed himself up on an elbow, gazed into my eyes. "Isabeau, I would give my life for you."

His kisses chased away my maddening doubts, banished my jealousies like a dandelion seed dispersed with a puff of breath. Again, my passions quickened. I could no more deny the thrill of his touch than I could cease breathing. Being apart from him only intensified our encounters in ways that both intoxicated and terrified me. To what lengths would I go to save him? And what would he do for me, if I but asked or needed it of him?

In his arms, I felt safe, needed, desired beyond reason. And in moments such as these, I realized that love was more powerful than wealth or armies.

SOMERTON CASTLE COMMANDED A modest hill. Surrounding it was a moat barely wide enough to have deterred any attackers. It had once belonged to Antony Bek, the Bishop of Durham, but upon his death he left it to my husband. Edward had never favored the place, but I liked its less imposing size and bucolic environs. Often, I would stand upon the curtain wall, looking out over the green of the fields and woodlands as the wind fluttered over blades of grass and stirred the tree leaves.

I crossed the bailey and climbed the spiral stairs of the southeast tower. As I neared the top, the light from the open door poured into the narrow space. Cool air brushed my cheeks. Then, Mortimer's voice reached my ears from just beyond the door. My steps became lighter, quicker, as I yearned toward the view that I knew would refresh my tired body.

Then, I heard another voice, one only faintly familiar, but distinctly coarse. It was someone I had not heard speak for some time, months perhaps, and so I paused, not meaning to eavesdrop, but simply to ascertain whether or not I should interrupt.

"There was another plot," the other man said rapidly, "to free Sir Edward."

A sickening shock washed through me. I leaned against the wall to steady myself. It was William Ockle, one of those Mortimer had assigned to my husband's keeping. Rather than retreat, I took the last few steps, each footfall of my leather soles silent against the stones. Upon seeing them on the wall-walk, I paused in the shadows, ready to fly back down the stairs as quietly as I had come.

Mortimer grasped the front of Ockle's shirt and yanked him close. "Dunheved, again? Has he been found?"

"No, no sign of him. But it wasn't him this time. 'Twas the damned Welsh." Ockle dug a letter from beneath his grimy shirt. "Words of 'advice' from William de Shalford in Anglesey."

Mortimer snatched the letter away before Ockle could even extend it. He moved from behind the merlon so that sunlight fell across the page and read it quickly.

Ockle craned his thin neck sideways, squinting as though blinded by the day's brightness. Short in stature, he stood on his toes as he tried to read over Mortimer's shoulder. "What does he say?"

"That he suspects certain . . . *highborn* English nobles of taking part in this latest conspiracy."

"He has proof? Lancaster? Kent? Who?"

"He didn't say. But I don't doubt there's some truth to it."

Nobles plotting to overthrow the king and put his father back on the throne? But who? And why?

Mortimer's face sank with worry. He gazed out into the distance, gripping the letter in his hands murderously tight, as if he could wring the answers from the ink itself. "As far as the Welsh are concerned, if they succeed the next time, not only is my life in danger, but those in my employment"—he turned toward Ockle so fast I jerked back instinctively, afraid of being seen, and barely caught myself from tumbling backward down the stairs—"meaning you, William."

Swaying on the balls of his feet, Ockle tugged at his fingers. "What will you do, my lord?"

"Not me, William. Not me. The question is: What will *you* do?"

Head dipping between his shoulders, Ockle's lips twisted grotesquely. Slowly, his mouth warped into a heinous smile. "Yes, my lord?"

Mortimer gripped Ockle's shoulders and shook him once, hard. "Remedy the matter."

Ockle's head bobbed atop a spindly neck. Mortimer handed the letter back and said something else, but by then I had already turned to go.

I had heard more than I needed to, more than I ever wanted to.

107

SLEEP ELUDED ME. NOT because of Mortimer's visits, for they had ceased as Lincoln bustled with England's barons and talk of charters and taxes and military service consumed everyone's attentions. No, it was my conscience that haunted me. Like a winged beast from deepest hell, it sank its claws into my soul and screeched its inculpation. If I suspected a crime before it ever happened and did nothing to stop it, was *I* twice guilty?

To carry such a secret is torture. I could not share it with anyone, not even Patrice. I dared not risk putting my suspicions in a letter to Charles. Besides, he was too far away to be of any use. And Mortimer—he had sworn to me he would never harm Edward of Caernarvon. A dozen times I committed to confronting him. Yet each time I saw him, there were either others present or our time together was far too short to expend on an accusation that would certainly be followed by his adamant denial and an argument regarding trust.

At a time when I had lost all hope, Mortimer had been my salvation and my champion. To assume the worst of him was counter to all he had proven himself to be. As the days passed, I convinced myself that somehow I had heard wrongly, misinterpreted, or conjured plots out of my own irrational fancy. Doubt was a constant that I could not overcome. I did not see William Ockle at Somerton Castle or in Lincoln again. It was as though he were never there.

Then, it occurred to me the lengthy letters Edward once sent with persistent regularity had ceased entirely. At first, they had been sorrowful and full of pleas that I return to him, clearly stating his wish to again occupy the throne. In time, his messages became more vitriolic, tainted with references of *my* adultery. Given the irony, I could barely force myself to read them. I almost didn't. But by this past spring, his tone had changed entirely, the words containing a sense of serenity and acceptance, as though he had given up the fight entirely. The last one—short and consisting of little more than well wishes and references to God—had reached me in June. Since then, nothing.

While Parliament rattled on, I tried to enjoy the fading warmth of the harvest season. I sat often on the edge of a crenel atop the curtain wall, gazing out over the fields as greens turned to golds, my sight always drifting toward Lincoln.

On the 23rd of September, the parliamentary session came to a close. Young Edward was visibly relieved as he strode jauntily into the hall of Somerton that evening. He joined me at the head table, but first gave me a hearty kiss upon the cheek before seating himself. His uncles Norfolk and Kent followed him and took their places to either side of us. At the far end of the oak-beamed room, the blind harpist Einion plucked at his instrument, fingers gliding over the strings to elicit angelic tones. Servants filed in carrying platters of spit-roasted pig. A dozen other lords and a few of their wives sat at the side tables. Mortimer had declined my invitation, saying he still had matters relating to his station as Justice of Wales to address. I did not press the issue, for I wasn't sure if he and the king had resolved their differences about the Weardale campaign yet. Knowing my son would be weary after the two week assemblage, the long days filled with debates and discourse, I had arranged only a small gathering.

"As much as I loathe these tedious sessions," Kent declared, echoing my own thoughts, "I much prefer them to the futility of pursuing Scots through some godforsaken marshland in a deluge. God's teeth, I've never been so miserable in all my life." He swirled his goblet of wine, then emptied it in one greedy gulp.

Norfolk cocked an eyebrow at him and leaned away, trying to distance himself. It was a sore subject to mention in the king's presence, whose pride had been wounded in Weardale. But Mortimer, as always, had done as promised and kept him from pitched battle. I braved a look at my son. He ignored Kent's remark and busied himself by carving his pork into smaller portions.

Kent, however, had imbibed too much wine and could not guard his tongue. "Hah, even with the Bruce on his deathbed, his dogs are to be reckoned with. We may have driven them off for now, but Lancaster will want —"

Edward plunked his knife down on the table. He forced a smile and, in as congenial a tone as he could muster, said, "Some other time, perhaps?"

Kent slid his goblet forward, leaned back with a snort and shrugged. "As you wish."

Desperate to salvage the evening, I laid a hand on my son's forearm. "Bishop Orleton wrote from Avignon, recently. It seems the pope may be persuaded in your favor, after all. Count William is already making arrangements for Philippa's journey here, maybe as soon as the New Year. Of course, nothing is final yet, but I thought you might like to know."

And like that, his mood brightened, as if I had plucked the sun from the sky and given it to him on a plate of gold. The conversation soon turned to lighter topics. The king talked of jousting with Norfolk and hawking with me. Kent said no more, merely nodding his head whenever someone looked his way and spoke. An hour later, he was verging on sleep, his head propped on his fist.

Most of the guests had drifted away when Young Edward stifled his first yawn. "I think I would like to stay a few days before moving on. You mentioned plans, not long ago, to go . . ."

His words trailed away as something caught his attention at the far end of the hall. A hulking form lurked in the shadowed recess of the doorway, and then moved forward into the torchlight. There, Sir Thomas Gurney stood, a letter held loosely in his hand. His cloak was covered in road dust so thick its true color was indiscernible. He took a few tentative steps forward.

The king gestured for him to approach the head table. Gurney knelt briefly, heaved his bulk up, then extended the letter across the table and stepped back.

"I bring ill tidings, my lord . . ."

9

Young Edward:

Somerton Castle – September, 1327

THE WORDS DRIFTED TO my ears as if spoken through layers of wool:

"... of the death of your father, Sir Edward of Caernarvon, two days past at Berkeley Castle."

The letter lay in my open palm, heavy as a smith's anvil. Slowly, I drew it to me, opened it and read aloud:

"My Lord King,

It is with a heavy heart that I must inform you that the Lord has called your father, Sir Edward of Caernarvon, to Heaven. A few days ago, I withdrew to my manor at Bradley, having taken ill. Your father was, at the time, in the competent hands of William Ockle and Sir John Maltravers, who stated he was in good spirits after his evening meal. Although he seemed slightly fatigued, he did not complain or appear unwell. The next morning, they discovered him sprawled upon the floor. It is assumed he died during the night, perhaps had fallen, and did not suffer, but was quickly given unto God. Whether by accident or illness, his departure was a peaceful one, as any of us would wish for him.

Know that he departed this Earth with God in his heart and his children in his thoughts.

With deepest sorrow,
Lord Thomas Berkeley"

My mother lowered her eyes. Those other few who had remained in the hall were silent. There was neither weeping nor rejoicing. There was simply nothing. The news was unexpected, but not entirely unwelcome. It was as though a burden had been removed, like the death of a mad uncle who serves no purpose or an interminably ill child who has become a burden, but no one dared give voice to the deliverance.

What was it that I felt—this quiet beast gnawing at my insides? Sorrow? No, I neither loved nor hated the man. He had been a poor husband to my mother and an even worse king, but as a father he was never unkind to me. I had repaid him the shortcoming by occupying his throne. Was it guilt, then? No, he had foregone sound advice and squandered his kingship willfully. I would not do the same. Shock? Perhaps. He was neither old nor ill. Relief? God strike me for thinking it, but yes . . . relief. Pure and utter relief.

I lay the letter on the table and pushed it away. Like a cold, enfolding rush of winter air, darkness descended on my soul. Death was unfamiliar to me, but at that moment I realized it was more powerful than any deed of man or king.

Death is dreadful, mighty. It is final. It evokes fear and inspires faith.

And one man's death . . . can change everything.

113

GRIEF SHOULD HAVE OVERWHELMED me, but I had not seen my father for two years. Not since I left from Dover for France to swear homage to King Charles for the lands of my inheritance. I had gone in my father's stead because he would not, dared not. If he had departed from his kingdom, Hugh Despenser's life would have been in danger. Yet it all came to the same end, did it not? Despenser was brutally murdered at the hands of a Hereford mob—an inglorious, but fitting death. I had loathed the man, but not half as much as my mother must have. He had taken from her, threatened her. So when they dangled him from the gallows and then savaged his body before letting the flames consume it, both she and Mortimer had stood by mutely, witnesses to justice. My father's greatest crime had been in loving Despenser. Perhaps then, my father had died of a broken heart, bereft of his favorite, his wife and children, and his kingdom?

In comparison, I knew nothing of such grievous and utter loss. I prayed I never would.

A few days later, I departed from Lincoln for Nottingham, where I was to preside over the signing of a charter. I rarely understood what such documents were about. I was told to sign them and I did. Why question the trivialities?

My mother remained behind in Lincoln, she no more tearful than me, but as his widow the duty of arranging his funeral had fallen to her. For the place of his burial, Westminster was discussed, for it was there both my grandfather and great grandfather rested in their tombs, but it was quickly ruled out. A funeral procession of so many miles ending so near to London was considered unwise. At last, Gloucester was chosen and although St. Peter's was as grand a cathedral as any, my father's memory had clearly been relegated to that of a lesser and unloved king.

My gaze followed the length of fir skyward. The lance was taller than two men, its tip ending in a blunted coronel. Although made of the lightest and straightest wood, balancing it upright for any length of time was no small feat, especially with a restive horse beneath me, shifting his weight as he stomped a foot. Beneath us, an emerald sea of grass fluttered, its edges tipped with brown from the first frost a few days past.

"Peace, Grani," I said to the horse, a gift from the Count of Hainault. He lifted his head, ears twitching, and calmed. I had named him such because he was a spirited gray, and he would allow no one but me to ride him, just as the Norse hero Sigurd's Grani had done. Mother had protested my use of a pagan name, but none other seemed fitting.

When Will first put a full-length lance in my hand, he would not let me run at the tilt with it. I had to carry it about on foot, first lightly dressed and then in full armor. My muscles had burned fiercely that first week, its weight growing heavier with each passing minute. Today was the first day I would joust. A lesson only, Will had said repeatedly. I was ready. I had been ready for weeks.

At the far end of the tilt, he raised a hand in the air, the butt of his own lance resting easily on his thigh. I lifted my shield in answer and then snapped my visor shut. My page and armor squire scuttled backward, whooping in encouragement. The onlookers ringing the grounds whistled and clapped. Couching my lance, I dug my heels in. Grani hurled himself forward, his hard muscles rippling with each thunderous stride. I heard his breathy snorts, the jingling of his bit, the creak of the saddle as I clamped my knees hard and braced my weight.

Will flew closer, closer. My torso leaned forward, mimicking his position. He adjusted the angle of his lance, flared his elbow out slightly. Grani dipped his head. Suddenly, my balance shifted—only a hair, but it caught me off guard. The lance swerved right. I gripped it tighter, held on, and guided it in the other direction.

But in those few seconds, Will had taken perfect aim. And I had lost mine.

The coronel of his lance nicked the top of my shield and slammed into my chest plate, just below the hollow of my collarbone. I jerked backward with the force. My lance sailed from my hand. I saw sky. Clouds whirling end over end. Grani galloping away, silver fetlocks swishing as each hoof struck the ground, his tail streaming in a plume behind him.

The world went suddenly black. I lay on the ground, my lungs emptied of air. I gulped in shallow, raspy breaths, my ribs tightening with each painful draw. My head rang, as if someone had taken an iron mallet to my helmet. Muffled voices reached my ears, but I could not make out the words. Someone flipped my visor up. Sunlight blinded me. I flexed my fingers one by one, and then bent my knees. Sweet Jesus, even my teeth hurt. Feet pounded on the dusty earth. A shadow blocked the sun. Water dribbled onto my forehead from above. I sputtered and flailed an arm. Then more slowly, I rolled over and pushed myself up onto an elbow.

"Damn you, Will Montagu," I grumbled. "That was no lesson. It was a pummeling."

"Bruised, but not broken." Grinning, he offered a hand. "*That* is the best sort of lesson. You'll improve."

My squire and page hooked their hands beneath my armpits to help me up. My bones felt as jarred as if I had jumped from Dover's cliffs. I staggered to my feet ungracefully. "God's breath, I swear when I can get back on my horse, I'll return the favor. Mark my words, Will Montagu—one day, I'll batter you senseless. I swear it."

"A few years from now, perhaps you will indeed."

When I finally unbent my spine and stood straight—although every bone in my body moaned in protest—they let go. Stiff as an old man, I took a step, felt my knees fold, and stumbled into Will's steady arms.

"Perhaps you should stand here a minute?" He slipped beneath my arm to hold me up. I sagged against him, grateful for his sturdy frame. "Besides, it seems someone wants to speak to you."

I lifted my eyes. Shapes blurred and swayed before me. I had not noticed until then that some thirty or more people encircled us, their faces fixed in concern.

"Who?" I whispered to Will, unable to turn my head.

He beckoned a small man forward from the crowd. The man swept back his long, brown hood and fell to his knees, muttering.

"Speak louder, man. Who are you, anyway?"

"Eustace, my name is Eustace, sire."

"Who sent you, Eustace, and why do you seek me?"

"I was sent by the Bishop of Hereford, my lord. He has returned to England. Pope John has at last agreed to the dispensation for your marriage to Philippa of Hainault."

My heart somersaulted inside my chest. I pushed away from Will, grabbed Eustace's head between my hands and kissed his great, gleaming bald forehead. "God bless you, Eustace—you and your children and grandchildren!" Then to Will I said, "See he is given a squire's wages for every day of his journey here and home."

Will rolled his eyes. "A bit generous, don't you think, for someone merely doing their duty?"

"Do it, Will Montagu," I said, "and do it cheerfully—or else it's your wages I'll see that he gets."

"As you wish,"—Will swept an arm across his body and dipped in a mocking bow—"sire."

HOW SLOWLY THE HOURS crawled, every day longer than the day before. Both glad and beleaguered, my heart was as light as a dove's wing, my mind in a thousand scattered places. Having also heard the wondrous news, Mother joined me in Nottingham, but her insistence on immersing me in wedding plans were too often futile attempts to capture my attention. *Yes, York Minster is an agreeable place for the wedding. Yes, that lord can come. And that one. No, too unimportant, too disagreeable, too boorish. Feasts, yes. Jousts, most certainly. Music? Whatever you wish, dear Mother. No, I do not care what is served, as long as there is food to eat. Yes, yes, no and yes, ad nauseam!*

I would just as soon have left everything up to her and gone back to jousting with Will. The patronizing bastard, however, had not allowed me to joust again since knocking me flat on my back. It seemed I still walked with a limp when not concentrating on my gait. So I beat out my impatience with my blunted sword against Will's dented armor. He never tired, never gave ground and never praised me. I hated him for those things, but I was determined to one day better him because of them.

It had been over a year since I last laid eyes on Philippa. How I longed to take her hand, brush the backs of my fingers against her round cheeks and feel her lips on mine. Oh, that and more!

"If you're so eager, Ned," Will said one day, rapping his knuckles against my shield, then backing away and peering at me over the top of his, "I could . . . 'introduce' you to a maiden or two. Would you prefer her as yet unplucked, pure as an infant's first tears—or a shameless wanton who could show you the way to heaven?" He swiped his sword harmlessly above my head and then lunged to his left. His blade snapped down, glancing off my shoulder plate with a sharp click. "Fair-haired, raven-tressed or red as flames? Older, younger? English, Irish, German . . ."

It was by then afternoon, but sluggish December clouds darkened the sky and lent a chill to the air. Most of the garrison and servants were busily going about their daily tasks, but as it always was when Will and I met in the bailey to play at swords, a small crowd loitered outside the kitchen door to watch at a respectful distance.

"You talk too much of impiety, Will." I feinted to the right, then spun opposite and struck for his elbow. He jerked backward, laughing. My blade whooshed past his arm. I flicked it back and the tip skipped harmlessly off the links of mail over his hip. "What do you take me for—some worldling like yourself?"

"Ah, you speak too highly of me, my lord. I prefer 'irreverent, wine-soaked ribald', if you will." He held his hands wide, shield and sword extended outward, his unprotected chest an invitation to my temper. "Come now, you don't want to disappoint her on your wedding night, do you?"

My pride urged me to launch myself at him, thrash him soundly and leave him whimpering in a battered heap. But I knew I couldn't—and wouldn't for years, yet.

"What happens between Philippa and me is none of your concern, Will Montagu." I tossed my sword at his feet, loosened the straps of my shield and dropped it, too, to the ground. Then, I tugged my hands free of my gauntlets and flung them down. "She is to be my wife and my queen. And I will only *ever* be with her!"

I shoved my way between the stable groom and a kitchen maid, but Will clamped a hand on my upper arm. My face hot with anger, I spun around to face him, ready to spew enough admonitions to last a lifetime.

"Your pardon, my lord." He dipped his head contritely. "I shouldn't have spoken thus."

I flicked his hand away. "You shouldn't even *think* such things, let alone speak them. Like everyone else, you forget who is king."

The first drops of rain fell like cold metal against my face. By the time I had crossed the bailey, stormed up the tower stairs and into my chambers, I was soaked and shivering. Sleet now blew through the open window. I peeled the mail hood from my head, swung the shutters closed and turned to find my chair. Will stood by the door, closed it.

"I never forget who you are," he said, propping his shield and sword against the wall. He moved to the hearth, pulled off his leather gloves and stretched his palms toward the fire. "But I know what you are capable of becoming. Kings must be more than mere men. They must be fearsome and decisive, yet know when to compromise, when to retreat, when to yield."

I wanted to do none of those last few things, but damn him, he was right.

Joining him by the hearth, I sank to my haunches and cradled my head in my hands. Minutes later, the heat had warmed me. I desperately wanted to crawl out of my mail and don dry clothes, but I felt moored in place, unable to commit to the effort.

"They want to make peace with Scotland," I said.

"Your mother?"

"And Mortimer, yes."

"That is a bad thing? Do you think being king is all about waging war?"

"They want my sister Joanna wed to the Bruce's son David."

He scoffed. "That would be years from now, surely."

I gazed up at him. "I wish that were true, but King Robert's health is failing. They want it done soon. Within the year."

"Who proposed this?"

"Remarkably King Robert."

Will scratched at the scruff on his neck. "Ah, his last great act— merging his noble blood with that of England's. You must credit him with boldness, my lord. As for the queen and Mortimer, I suppose they fear if he dies David's regents may squabble and have a change of heart. Anything could happen then. Better to secure a sure thing while it's being offered, than risk losing it."

"This doesn't sit well with me, Will. She's far too young. And peace with Scotland? When has there ever been peace with Scotland?" I dug my fingers through my hair, pulling at the roots. "But after Weardale . . . No, I'm not yet ready to bring arms against them. Besides, who would I trust to lead the way? Mortimer misled me, Kent was worthless, and Lancaster was all ideas and no substance. One day, one day perhaps. When you've taught me enough. For now, what choice do I have?"

Will sat down on the floor beside me. "You're asking me for diplomatic advice?"

I rolled my eyes at him. "Much as I value you, I would never do that. You know as much of diplomacy as I do of weaving tapestries. No, I'll agree to the terms, for now. There's been too much turmoil in one year, as it is. With my father dead . . ."

My thoughts suddenly vanished, interrupted by a roiling uneasiness. I wrapped my arms around my knees, leaning closer to the fire. My father's death was a deliverance for many, and too convenient.

"Can you leave for Gloucester early with me, Will? The funeral is set to begin within a week, but there is something I need to do."

"Details of state? Again, I'm not —"

"No, something else." I rose, fumbled at the buckles of my arm plates, but gave up. "I need to see him. Need to be certain."

"See who?

"My father."

10

Young Edward:

Gloucester — December, 1327

A THOUSAND CANDLE FLAMES wavered in the vast darkness of St. Peter's Abbey, as though God had hurled the stars down from the firmaments to scatter them amongst the bulging piers of the nave, where they would forever remain trapped beneath airy vaults of stone. In the corbels and capitals of the masonry, grapevines crowned the stout faces of green men, their chins bearded with oak leaves. As I stood at the entrance, I ran my fingers over the intricate figures on the surface of the lead font, but those long forgotten kings and saints offered no guidance.

A pair of heavily armed guards had been posted at every door, as if the danger existed that someone might steal away with my father's corpse. His bier stood before the altar. There, a man had been sleeping, but my footsteps startled him into wakefulness. He cast off his blanket, revealing a sword clutched in both hands. Upon seeing the guards relaxed at their posts, he lowered his weapon, but stood his ground.

"William Beaukaire?" I called. My footsteps rang from the tiled floor to the celestial arches above, Will's echoing in unison. "I am the king."

At once, he laid his sword down and dropped to his knees. I approached my father's bier. Two days from now, it would be loaded upon a hearse and drawn by four white horses throughout the streets for the funeral procession, before being returned to the church. Here, my father would rest eternally in his alabaster tomb, his spirit no less troubled than mine.

I had left word with my mother that I had plans to visit with my cousin John de Bohune, the Earl of Hereford, before the funeral was to take place. It was a plausible excuse for leaving Nottingham a day ahead of her. Winter's first snow had fallen soft and virginal around us as we rode southward, to Coventry and Kenilworth, then to the River Avon. At Tewkesbury, Will suggested we stop for the night, but I pressed on, eager for Gloucester. A sense of urgency pulled me onward, refusing rest. Now, past midnight, I had reached my destination, road-weary and wondering why the hurry to view a man so long dead?

When I first received the news of my father's death, it was with stunned acceptance. Banished were the clouds of doubt and discord that had accompanied my crowning. But it was what Berkeley had *not* said in his letter that gave rise to suspicion. Just as a weed will sprout in fallow ground, I could not shake the question that rattled my mind: *How* had he died?

As I moved closer, something struck me as odd, out of place. It was not his body lying there in full view, waiting for the mourners to gather and pay their final respects, but a wooden effigy. The likeness was carved in painstaking detail, down to the hem of a king's robes and painted with the brilliant colors of the jewels he once wore.

Gesturing to Will to stay where he was, a dozen steps back from the coffin, I beckoned William Beaukaire closer. One shoulder hunched higher than the other, he ambled forward.

"Sire?"

"My father . . ."—I indicated the effigy covering the coffin, my sights coming to rest on the immutable face—"lies beneath?" Although recognizably my father's resemblance, it was far too peaceful to depict the expression he must have worn in his final, turbulent year.

Beaukaire's head bobbed, streaks of candlelight flashing across creviced features. His nose was crooked and the thick ridge of a scar ran where the outer half of his right eyebrow should have been. The man had survived more than a few battles, witnessed death firsthand in all its naked gore.

"And how long have you watched over . . . the body?" The last two words stumbled across my tongue. To me, yet so young, it was still strange to know that one day a person lived and breathed and the next they were but a shell, yellowed bones and decaying flesh, empty of a soul.

He pushed a tongue through a gap in his jumbled teeth, one eye squinting thoughtfully. "Since the day after Sir Edward's death."

"Ah, you were at Berkeley Castle all along, then?" Eager for details, I pressed him further. Perhaps the manner of my father's death was not important. Still, I wanted to know. "You saw my father beforehand? Spoke to him, perhaps? Was he ill or weak?"

"No, my lord. I never saw him . . . I mean not when he was alive."

"Did you see him before . . . before the embalming?"

He looked down. "No, my lord."

Disappointment welled up inside me. I had hurried here for nothing, it seemed. This Beaukaire was of no use. "Tell me, when did you first arrive at Berkeley?"

He lifted his hunched shoulder in a half-shrug. "The day before, I suppose."

I rubbed at my temple. Beaukaire was either daft or confused. Surely, he had his days mixed up? If not, it was all a strange coincidence. "By whose orders?"

"Sir Roger Mortimer's."

"Mortimer?"

"Yes, my lord."

Always Mortimer. Was there anything in England he did not seek to control? Why had I ever so blindly admired the man?

My hand drifted up toward the effigy, but the faint odor of decay wafted to my nose and I yanked it back. Summoning my courage, I laid both palms flat against the side of the coffin, pressed my forehead between them and whispered:

"When the Lord God calls thy name,
Then shall thee pass
From bed to shroud,
Shroud to bier,
Bier to grave,
And the grave will be closed up,
Bones to dust will be
But thy spirit shall roam
Forever free."

A QUARTET OF GOLDEN lions and angels playing their harps adorned my father's hearse. His funeral was as stately as any king's. So many people filled the church that one would have assumed him far more beloved than he had truly been. In the streets outside the abbey, wooden barriers had been constructed to keep the oglers from disturbing the day's solemnity. Some of them had come on foot from hundreds of miles away. Like the rest of us, they wanted to witness with their own eyes that the shambles that was King Edward II's reign was truly and finally over.

My mother appeared more agitated than grief stricken. I am certain if she had been given a choice, she would not have been there. They handed her a small silver casket containing my father's heart. Her grip on it was so tenuous, her hands trembling terribly, I feared she might drop it at her feet and the contents would spill open.

My uncles Kent and Norfolk were there, as well as half the lords and prelates of England.

Kent wrapped me in his arms, clung to me. His fingers dug into my cloak, bunching the cloth into a wad. As he detached himself and turned his head to speak to me, his tears moistened my cheek.

"So unexpected," he said, gripping my shoulders as if to steady himself. "It was by God's grace that he did not suffer. I regret . . ." He lowered his eyes, closed them so tight it looked as though his brow might collapse onto his cheekbones. His breath caught sharply. When he forced the words out, his voice was frail with grief. "I regret I did not make peace with him."

Those words cut me with guilt. Guilt that I had not been a better son. And anger that he had not been a better father or king.

"You didn't know," I said. "None of us did."

But they were words offered in comfort, not candor.

As the congregation began to filter out, I saw Mortimer among the mourners. He must have sensed my gaze, for he turned around, nodded in acknowledgment, then was lost in the crowd. I distrusted the man, but I would not bother to ask him the questions that had begun to fill my head. He wouldn't have answered truthfully anyway.

York — January, 1328

ONE MONTH LATER, I stood before another altar—this one at York Minster. Archbishop Melton presided over the wedding. My bride wore a gown of palest blue, the hue of a winter sky. Even beneath the diaphanous veil, secured by a circlet of gold and pearls, Philippa's smile was bright enough to outshine the past year's darker moments.

Through a haze of happiness, I remember uttering these words: "I take you to be my wife; and I give to you the fidelity and loyalty of my body and all my possessions. In both health and sickness, I will keep you; for neither worse nor for better will I change toward you, until the end of our days."

Somewhere in the crowd was her father, the Count of Hainault, who was given a special chair to sit in and a padded stool on which to prop his gouty foot, and with him was her uncle, Sir John. Hundreds of faces gazed on, yet I saw only Philippa and a thousand tomorrows stretching bright and boundless before us.

While a howling wind lashed the snow into knee-high drifts, we proceeded to the castle. Philippa and I rode abreast of one another, our horses caparisoned in heraldic silks, the silver bells attached to their bridles and reins tinkling gaily amid the clamor. It may well have been the coldest and snowiest day in years, but it did nothing to dampen the spirits of England's people. We dismounted before the steps to the great hall, the bells of York's churches pealing in celebration. She slipped her hand from beneath the warmth of her miniver-edged cloak. I grasped her fingers and pulled her closer.

"I regret to say," I whispered rapidly, before anyone could close in and overhear, "that my mother has raised objection to our wedding night being so close to Lent. She thinks we should forego, ah, a certain 'rite' in the hopes of receiving God's blessing upon our union."

Philippa clasped her other hand over my forearm. "I had not

thought of that. Will we not . . .?"

Casting a glance around, I guided her up the steps. A pair of porters opened the doors before us. I shrugged. "Do *you* want to?"

"I do." Lowering her chin, she shrank inside her hood to conceal her blushing. "That is, if it would not trouble *your* conscience."

"Mine? No." I scoffed. "Christ himself could not keep me from you tonight." With my thumb, I stroked the fleshy part of her palm. She shivered in response.

We entered the hall to a tide of applause. Warmth and music surrounded us, elevating our excitement.

Philippa pulled her hood back and bit her lip to suppress a giggle. "But how will you —"

I pressed a finger to my lips, as servants rushed to take our mantles. "Don't worry. It's been arranged. I will come to you later. Wait for me."

The hours passed in a dizzying blur of dance, food and drink. Congratulations were showered on us with wearisome abundance. In every touch or glance that Philippa and I shared, I both sensed her nervous anticipation for our wedding night and felt the undeniable strength of our bond. With her beside me, I knew I would never want for comfort or friendship, courage or pleasure.

SHIFTING THE LOOSE GOWN so it wasn't twisted around my middle, I glared at Will. "You didn't tell me about this part."

"How else do you think I was supposed to get you into her chamber?"

True enough. Still, I fought the urge to plow my fist into that smirk of his. After the wedding feast, several of my companions and I had escorted Philippa and her ladies to her chambers. In a glow of smoky torchlight, I had kissed her cordially on the cheek, stating that we would exchange gifts in the morning. By then, it was clear from her dubious expression that she had begun to doubt my earlier promise. Feigning a yawn, I bowed as I backed away, and then retired alone to my apartments. An hour later, Will had arrived with a drab lady's gown of dark gray and a plain white wimple for me to don as a disguise.

We turned a corner to see a pair of drunken revelers staggering at the far end of the corridor.

Will yanked me back into the shadows. I leaned away from him to peer around the edge of the wall. Laughing, the two men pushed open a door, went inside a room and slammed the door shut behind them.

"If I am discovered like this, Will, you'll —"

"It's a good thing you haven't grown a beard yet." He patted me on the cheek and then tugged at the wimple to rearrange it. "Although, you do make a fetching maiden."

I clenched his wrist, squeezing hard, but he only laughed.

"Now go, Ned." He cuffed me sharply on the arm. "Before she falls asleep."

Head down, I shuffled forward alone, trying to tread as silently as possible. A servant girl appeared ahead of me, lugging a bucket of water and an armload of rags. I stumbled as I glanced up. The front hem of the skirt was too long, so I gathered it up a few inches, but as I did so and looked down at my feet, I realized I still had my boots on. *Mother of Christ!* I lowered the hem, shortening my stride until the girl was well past me.

A dozen steps more and I found myself standing before Philippa's door. I raised my fist to rap on it, but just then Will, at the far end of the hall, cleared his throat. Reclined against the wall with arms crossed, he mouthed, *'Good luck'*.

'Go!' I mouthed back.

He slid back into the darkness, but I waited several heartbeats before raising my fist again. In truth, it was a very short time, for my heart was racing more wildly than it ever had before. For all that I had looked forward to this night, I was suddenly very unsure of myself and what I would do when the moment came: what I would say beforehand, when I would kiss her, where I would touch her, how I would —

Hinges groaned. I leapt back. The door opened, but only a crack. Pale young eyes, framed by dark lashes, peered at me questioningly. I did not recognize the woman, but Philippa had arrived with so many ladies and servants that they were all as yet unfamiliar to me.

"Who are you?" Her accent was heavy and Flemish, her tone disparaging.

"M-M-Matilda." Dear God, why couldn't I speak correctly? And I no more sounded like a woman than looked like one beneath these skirts. "Lady Matilda."

She shut the door. Someone whispered on the other side. Then I heard laughter, squeals, and the *swish-swish* of slippered feet across the tiled floor. Moments lapsed. My heartbeat slowed to a sickly plod. I knocked. Silence answered.

Splaying my fingertips on the door, I rested my forehead against it. So, she had reconsidered? I spun away, only to see Will frantically waving me back. When I looked back, Philippa was standing with one hip propped against the door frame. She wore a plain dressing gown, the front gathered tight across her breast. The young woman who had greeted me slipped past her, rushed through the corridor and threw herself into Will's waiting arms.

"Coming in . . . Lady Matilda?" Her head tilted, Philippa opened the door further.

No sooner had I stepped inside and lifted the wimple from my head, than she slid the bar across the door. A well-tended fire crackled in the hearth, its amber light flickering with every surge of flame. I took off the gown and dropped it beside me, feeling more comfortable in my tunic and leggings—and thankful we were finally alone for the first time ever.

"How did you chase away the rest of your women, my love?" Hastily, I tugged my boots off, then wrapped my arms about Philippa's waist and pulled her to me.

She touched a finger to her lips and then pressed her lips to mine.

The back of her hand grazed my abdomen. A moment later, her sash slipped away as she pulled it loose. The front of her gown gaped open. In the glimmer of firelight, I stepped back and took in the full beauty of my bride. I closed my eyes briefly, capturing the memory of that incredible sight in my mind forever. As she took my hand and led me to her bed, the gown fell back from her shoulders, white and inviting, the silken veil of her long hair cascading down her back. Before she could escape me, I caught her by the waist and laid the lightest kiss where her neck sloped into her shoulders.

"I take you to be my wife,"—I breathed her in, her hair smelling of cloves and her skin of lavender—"and I give to you the fidelity and loyalty"—I tossed my shirt off, fumbled at the laces of my hose, cursing myself for having knotted them so tightly—"of my body and all my possessions . . ." There I paused to sweep her up into my arms and laid her softly upon the bed.

"In both health and sickness," she said, lying back, holding her arms out to me, "I will keep you."

"For neither worse nor for better will I change toward you."

"Until the end of our days," we said in unison.

PART II:

Now, Mortimer, begins our tragedy.

Isabella,
from Christopher Marlowe's *Edward II*

11

Isabella:

Brixworth — April, 1328

T HEY SAID THAT MY husband Edward of Caernarvon, once king, was dead. I have seen him with my own eyes—it was him: the lifeless corpse embalmed, cocooned in a shroud of cerecloth; his long, rigid form stretched out on stone like an eyeless effigy on a tomb; his flesh shrunken to the framework of his bones; his features vaguely distorted in their tranquility, even though they were without disfigurement or blemish; his eyelids sewn eternally shut.

When I arrived at Gloucester, I had the midwife who had done the embalming brought to me. She had never seen Edward before then, could not confirm it was him, nor that it was not. She could only tell me there were no bruises or wounds on the body, nothing to indicate foul play. I paid her handsomely for her services and sent her on her way. Then, I had the coffin opened. I could not look long, but the image seared itself into my mind. I shall never be rid of it. I said a prayer, asked for God's forgiveness and fled the church.

I should have thought it a relief to be rid of him, just as it was with Hugh Despenser. Why then was I so haunted by the ghostly image of him? Because I did not know how it came to be? Because I had wished it so? Or that I did not trust my own eyes?

It began suddenly, although looking back I cannot confess it was unexpected. The first nightmare came to me when the merriment and feasting after Young Edward and Philippa's wedding was over. Until then, I had so immersed myself in the details of the wedding that I would go from dawn until midnight with barely an idle moment. I carried within me only a vague angst, a wrenching tightness in the pit of my stomach and a rapid heartbeat that I dismissed as a mother's nerves. But as soon as the urgency and chaos disappeared, the fist of anguish seized my heart and tightened around it, suffocating my spirit like a blanket thrown over my head and held tight.

Night after night, the apparition of Edward of Caernarvon hovered at the foot of my bed, dressed in tattered black rags of serge. He glided toward me, bony hands outstretched, speechless lips twitching, rats scampering about his bare, dirtied feet, beetles crawling through his hair, worms writhing from his nostrils . . . I begged him to stop, telling him that he was alive—alive! Woefully he shook his head at me, staggering closer, slowly closer, and I could not run, could not fight back. Then, his icy hands went around my neck, tightening, squeezing, strangling . . .

And all I could do was recite prayers to the Virgin Mary. As his fingers closed off the air from my lungs, I heard my own voice somehow growing louder and louder, word by word. Then, I would awaken in Mortimer's arms to the shrillness of my own terrified screams.

Lying down in bed brought a cold, raw fear, for whenever I would go to sleep the dreams were almost always there. It was not until absolute exhaustion overtook me a fortnight after the nightmares began that I found any rest at all. Still, the dark visions came and held me captive.

For several weeks I lived in some tortured, wakeful sort of death, until Mortimer suggested we go away somewhere, someplace quiet and isolated, keeping our location a secret. I refused outright, for in truth I did not want anyone to think there was anything amiss or that I had anything at all to hide. But the madness persisted.

In my heart, I believed Edward was still alive—or maybe it was only that I wanted to make myself believe it, to rid myself of this affliction—but what proof did I have? Through all of this, even as he saw how I suffered, Mortimer seemed unshaken, as if nothing macabre had happened, as if his heart guarded no secrets.

At last, in early April, I summoned Lord Thomas Berkeley to come early to Northampton, where Parliament was to convene within the month. While I awaited him, I attended a Mass at the church in Brixworth, a few miles north of Northampton. My soul was deeply troubled and the only way to achieve peace was by God's guidance and the truth that I was sure Lord Berkeley was keeping to himself.

Brixworth Church had been built in the time of the Saxons with stones recovered from nearby decaying Roman villas. In the entranceway to the nave, there was even a stone carving of an imperial Roman eagle. I paused there to gaze upon that vestige of the ancients, with its wings outstretched in a display of ascendancy and its beak agape in a voiceless cry of ages gone by. For a moment I was unaware of anything but this spiritless creature, frozen in flight, fixed in eternity.

"Shall I have your horse readied, my lady?" Arnaud had come up behind me, but between my own daydreaming and the gentle buzz of the congregation as it filtered from the nave and on outside, I had not heard him at all. Patrice was at his side, a soft smile on her mouth and her face alight.

It had taken time, nearly three years, before the rift between Patrice and Arnaud had completely mended, but with it Patrice had regained both the brightness and the fire within her. I had heard that Arnaud still visited his wife, who was by now so completely bereft of her wits and incapable of even the simplest tasks, that the nuns of Aldgate made sure she was kept watch over every waking hour. Useless as she was, they would probably have turned her out into the streets if not for Arnaud donating generous portions of what little funds he had to them. It was easy enough to tell when he was away at Aldgate, for Patrice became quite irascible. But whenever he returned, as he had only a few days ago, she was like a new bride flushed with joy. I did not need to discover them together in the stables, strewn over with strands of hay, or tucked away in the wardrobe, their clothes all disheveled, to know that they were intimate again with one another. It was easy to see in moments like this and further betrayed in the number of times Arnaud went to chapel to absolve himself. I often hoped, as I witnessed them sharing that look of deep familiarity, that Mortimer and I were never so obvious.

"The horses, my lady," he prompted again. "Shall I bring them?"

I meant to tell him 'yes', to ready for our return to Northampton, for I had much to discuss with Mortimer and the king before Parliament commenced, but I was still hoping for Lord Berkeley to meet me here. "I will take a meal first, on the hill."

Patrice arranged my short mantle over my shoulders and closed the clasp. Although the sun shone arrogantly in a cloudless sky, it was deceiving. Being only early March, there was still a biting chill in the air whenever a spring breeze picked up. It had snowed lightly not more than a week ago, but a few warmer days had painted the first tinges of green upon the land and the song of birds heralding the end of winter had brought everyone out of their shelters to absorb the rejuvenating sunlight with outstretched arms.

"Very good." He nodded to me, but then paused, catching eyes with Patrice. They looked at each other for so long that I was sure they were no longer aware of me even being there.

I jostled past them, giving one more reminder about the food, lest they wander off and lose themselves in one another to forget altogether.

No sooner had my friends left me to arrange our meal, than I found a gaggle of half a dozen highborn ladies who had attended the service closing in on me. I nodded politely, lowered my eyes and scurried away. But even as I retreated to a pretend solitude, their whispers chased after me. In my head, I imagined them speaking of the mysterious death of the old king, gossiping about private details of my affair with Mortimer and speculating of murder. The moment I turned to look at them, they smiled and waved. I turned away and again I heard the faint whispers. From the corner of my eye I saw the glances, the shaking heads.

Arnaud spread a blanket for me on the grassy hillside. While he and Patrice went to fetch a basket, I sat there alone, trying not to look at anyone, hoping they would leave me to myself and desperately wishing to get back to Northampton to close myself inside my private rooms and be with Mortimer. I was beginning to believe that he was right—that we needed to go away somewhere undisclosed, despite what anyone might think. I needed to be where I would not have to be surrounded by murmuring mobs or exposed to those I did not trust. But too soon I found myself besieged by several of the querulous ladies, wives of the local barons.

"My lady?" A tall, heavy woman, dressed in her best brocaded blue kirtle, one which had seen many wearings, waddled toward me. Her gray-streaked chestnut hair was pulled back tightly from her face in an attempt to lift her deeply sagging cheeks, which slightly resembled the jowls of a scent hound. The smoothed hair, however, had the opposite effect of accentuating her advancing years. Another lady, older perhaps, or merely more worn with troubles, straggled along beside her. Together, they dipped their heads and bent their stiff knees toward the ground.

"I am Gladys de Warley of Banbury," she huffed, struggling to rise as I motioned her up. "This is my sister, Maudeline. She hails from Dunchurch. My husband is Peter, squire to Sir Walter Barlow. Perhaps you know him?"

I nodded, wishing to hurry this strange introduction along. I had never heard of the squire and the knight's name was barely familiar. Wondering to myself if my own skin was beginning to hang loose like hers, I touched the tips of my fingers to my cheekbones and then drew them down toward the underside of my throat. If it sagged at all, at least it did not look like the stuffed cheeks of a squirrel.

"We were wondering if you had heard?" Maudeline said. Her beak-like nose was bent to one side and had several bumps along the ridge of it, as if it had been broken more than once.

"The news from France?" Gladys added. She looked at her sister and simultaneously both raised their eyebrows up and tucked their chins in, then shook their heads judgmentally.

"There is news from France all the time. I hear a great deal." I inched backward to signal my withdrawal from their petty little festival of gossip.

"Oh!" Maudeline exclaimed, slapping a hand against her breast in feigned relief. "Then you must be elated? Or perhaps not . . . considering it is not good news for the king that, well . . ."

Although I had tried to resist being dragged into it, my curiosity was piqued. "Elated? About what?"

"About the baby," Gladys offered with a shrug, as if it were known to everyone what she was talking about and I was the only ignorant one. "But of course you knew . . . did you not?"

"What baby?" I was both annoyed by their intrusion and agitated at them for dribbling morsels of information, as if they were tossing out bits of cheese to trap a rat.

THE KING MUST DIE

"Why King Charles and his queen, Jeanne, are expecting. Wonderful for them, naturally. Who would not want a child? We all do. I would give them one of my nine if I could. But after so much trouble for your dear brother—forgive me, you must feel in the middle. Dreadful. There is no chance at all now that our dear young king would be named to —"

"If it is true," I began, glaring harshly at her, "then my brother would have told me so. I would not hear such joyful news from a snake-tongued gossipmonger who takes cruel delight in others' plights."

Gladys sucked her lower jaw all the way into her throat. Maudeline's mouth gaped in shock.

Thankfully, I did not need to offer an excuse to escape that pair of carping geese, for I saw a lone rider approaching at a steady trot toward the church. Without dallying to wait for an apology, I hurried down the hill to meet Lord Thomas Berkeley at the bottom.

He dismounted and bowed before me. "I came at once, my lady. I stopped at Northampton first. Sir Roger said I would find you here. I hope you do not mind my coming. I sensed it was a matter of dire importance, although you did not say as much."

Lord Thomas had the honest face of a priest and an unassuming, polite manner that made him endearing and easily liked. His features reflected his character—ordinary, in a way, and tending toward boyish with his sun-streaked hair and a spattering of freckles across the bridge of his nose. He had served Mortimer since before the Marcher Lords had risen against Edward II in 1321 and during that time Mortimer had happily rewarded him with the hand of his eldest daughter, Margaret.

I motioned for him to follow me through the verdant meadow which flowed down the hillside and back toward the church. Since he had come alone, he had no page to tend to his horse and so he led it behind him. Most of the churchgoers were by then drifting away, but

I led him along a little used, winding footpath littered with small rocks embedded in trampled mud—away from the sneering Gladys and Maudeline, who were both still sending me unpleasant looks. They now had a growing gaggle to commiserate with over their mistreatment. The indignant buzz coming from their vituperative swarm could be heard even at this distance.

"Did Mortimer ask why I sent for you?"

Berkeley's reply was direct, like that of a schoolboy responding to his tutor's questions. "I told him you didn't give a reason. When I see him again, what shall I say?"

"Only that I was mustering support before Parliament, that is all. As for the real reason—I called you here because the relic is here, Lord Thomas. Remember?"

He looked at me blankly, befuddled at my reference. "I regret, my lady, that I don't. What relic? Every church, it seems, has one—a knuckle bone, a broken nail, a splinter from the true Cross, a bloodied thorn—but I'm not familiar with that belonging to Brixworth, or if it even has one."

"The throat bone of St. Boniface."

"St. Boniface? Ah, yes. A martyr, one of many. Now I remember. What of his relics, then? What relevance do they have?"

I stopped in mid-stride. Relevance? How could he have forgotten?

"I swore you to an oath, Lord Thomas. Not so long ago."

He shook his head and glanced around us. His horse dropped its head to nibble at the fresh spring grass. I began walking again toward the church and he yanked roughly at his horse's reins to catch up with me. "What oath?"

I gave him a quizzical look over my shoulder. Surely, he was either jesting or just playing the fool until we were alone? Arnaud exited from a recessed door near the rear of the church, where a small room served as a storeroom, and approached us, hailing

142

Berkeley. In the crook of his arm he hugged a jug of ale. I told him to take Berkeley's horse to a groom. As soon as that was taken care of we went inside, where I found Patrice sucking honey from her fingers and moaning over its sweetness. I instructed her to take the honey and bread outside and Berkeley and I would be joining her shortly. Greedily, she gathered up the pot of honey and two loaves of bread, asking with a wink if the handsome lord with me would be joining us. In spite of frequent flashes of jealousy from Arnaud, Patrice never ceased to charm men with her wiles. Once defeated by their own desire, she had confided in me, they were a constant source of information.

I led Berkeley further inside the old church to the Lady Chapel. For whom the chapel was built no one could remember, but most likely it was intended for the private prayers of some lady longing for the return of her lord. I shut the door, went to the window, grasped the ledge and wrenched free a single, unmortared stone—just far enough to wriggle my hand into a small hole beneath it and take from within the rough hewn box hidden there. Then I opened it and took out the object wrapped in a smudged remnant of linen.

I showed him the relic. "St. Boniface's throat bone. Do you remember now? You placed your hand on it and swore, on your life, an oath to me."

"And when was this?"

"September," I reminded him tersely, compressing my lips tightly together. "Before the . . . the death of Sir Edward of Caernarvon."

His voice did not waver in pitch or pace, remaining smooth. "Where did I swear this *supposed* oath?"

"Here!" I unwrapped the relic, slammed the lid shut before setting the box aside, and thrust the yellowed fragment at him. "I rode from Lincoln and you from Berkeley and we met here! It was before sunrise."

"Just you and I—here?"

143

"Yes, here. There was no one else!"

He ignored the piece of bone in my hand, turned slowly around as if to jostle his memory and shrugged again. "One thing I can swear is that I have never been in this chapel before, let alone this church, although I have often ridden past it."

By then I was shaking. My blood was afire with rage at Berkeley, maddened by his convenient loss of memory, but I was also being sucked downward by the havoc of my own memories, growing more and more disjointed with each passing day. I was no longer sure if he was lying to me . . . or if I simply remembered something that never was.

Am I indeed mad?

"Do not engage me in a game of words, Lord Thomas. We were here, you and I. I showed you this —" I shoved my fist with the relic in it at him, pounding it against his chest, "and *you* placed your hand on it and *swore* never to repeat my words again. I told you that I believed Mortimer meant to have Sir Edward murdered. I told you I wanted to spare my husband. Told you to see to it and sent you on your way. I *must* know . . . Did you do as I requested?" I clenched the bone in my hand so hard that its sharp edges bit into my fingers. I thrust it at him again. "Tell me—does Edward live?"

I did not realize I was beating on his chest until he grabbed my wrist to stop me. He peeled away my clamped fingers, one by one, took the bone and put it back in the box. Then, calmly, he slipped the box back behind its stone and wedged it back in place.

He was shaking his head with pity when he said to me, "You must stop this, my lady. It does you no good to torment yourself thus. There was a pronouncement of his death. A funeral. You saw the coffin, as did I."

I pointed a shaking finger at him. "But was it *him*? Was it his body inside?"

He studied me a long while before answering. "My queen, had I sworn you an oath, *on my life* . . . would I not keep it? But I do not recall any such oath. I wish that I could."

"You lie! You lie!" I railed at him. "I need to know if it was him. Don't you understand? I must know!" I started at him again, ready to hammer the truth from him with my bare fists, but he quickly backed away, shaking his head, and left me there.

Patrice came to me a minute later. She must have seen Berkeley rush from the chapel and take to his horse. I was lying before the altar, face down, raking at the tiles of the floor with my bare nails, trembling violently. I could not tell her my troubles. I could not tell Mortimer, either.

And Berkeley . . . he would say nothing at all—to me or anyone.

12

Isabella:

Northampton – April, 1328

I T HAD BEEN JUST a few days since my troubling meeting with Berkeley. Mortimer and I were seated across a small, square table from each other in my private chamber at Northampton taking breakfast. A letter lay on the table between us. Although I eyed it with niggling curiosity, I delayed opening it. I had not left my room since returning here, claiming a headache that would not go away and forbidding visitors. Mortimer, I sensed, was not so easily fooled by my false malaise, but he did not pry, instead tending to me delicately at brief intervals before going about his own business each day. I suspected that Berkeley had informed Mortimer of my attempt to extort the truth from him. Still, it did not make sense. If Berkeley would not admit to me he had sworn an oath, why would he tell Mortimer?

Mortimer glanced at the letter from time to time; I pretended not to as my mind wandered through a tangle of suspicions. Finally,

I stretched my fingers toward the letter and dragged it to me. Before I even opened it, I felt its sadness seep through the tips of my fingers as I touched the seal belonging to my sister-in-law Jeanne.

Dearest Sister,

It is with a sad, sad heart that I tell you your brother and my beloved husband, Charles, died while at Vincennes. His illness was sudden and swift. He did not suffer. So few were our years together, but so very, very happy. My one regret is that he will not have lived to see the birth of our child. All France awaits . . . and yet I find the impending birth, instead of joyous, a hollow event without him. Perhaps, as everyone tells me, time will heal the grievous wound in my heart, but I am not so certain. I think it will only grow greater and heavier.

With deepest sorrow,
Jeanne, Queen of France

"Charles is —" My breath caught. I could not say it. *Dead.* How? He was little more than a year older than me.

I stood, barely noticing the letter as it fell to the floor. With a hand pressed to my stomach, I went to the window. April rain had fallen lightly, but persistently for three days straight. Why did it always rain when someone died? Even beneath gray clouds, the grass had greened until it was blindingly bright to the eyes. Soon, the rain would stop, the sun would break through and daffodils and dandelions would spring forth like sun-yellow stars in an ocean of green.

At other times my heart would have lightened with the onset of spring, but today was not so. My heart was as heavy as Jeanne's, even though France now had a throne without a king to sit upon it and my own son stood staunchly in line for that throne. I could not think in that manner yet—not happily, at least. My brother, who I loved greatly, was gone.

I had seen three brothers die before me, none of them old. Was it my fate, too, never to grow old, or see my children wed, or hear the first cries of my grandchildren? Would some insidious disease quietly eat away at me from within, slowly, so that my death loomed inextricably before me, or would it take me swiftly and mercifully? Or would tragedy be my end—the axe, the gallows, a dank, stinking dungeon and long, cruel starvation?

Charles . . . dear, dear Charles. You always sought to protect me. I am grateful for that, even though I resented it at the time. I mourn for Jeanne and for your unborn child, but do not think less of me if the child is a girl and I must pursue the rights of my son. It is only right that I do so.

"So," Mortimer began, setting the letter back on the table, "do you think it possible that they would dare offer our young Edward the throne? Could it be worked?" As always, he read my thoughts— or was it that I read his?

"Jeanne is with child," I uttered despondently. Charles and Jeanne had been deeply in love. The pregnancy was a blessing she had long prayed for. In every letter she had ever written me, she had embedded the wish for a child. To her, whether it was a son or daughter did not matter, but she knew that Charles desperately needed a son. Three years had gone by fruitlessly for them and when it had finally happened—now this, his death.

Mortimer sank back in his chair. "If it is a boy —"

"If it is a girl, or if the child dies, the throne will be vacant. My cousin, Philip of Valois, will say the crown belongs to him. Roger, we *must* assert Young Edward's claim, before Jeanne's baby is born. We have very little time. We must argue for it vehemently, relentlessly, immediately." Had I not just said to myself I was too full of sorrow to think in this vein? Mortimer had a tacit way of encouraging my ambitions.

"If this happened in England, the throne might be yours."

"A pointless musing, Roger. Besides, if I were ever to rule

France, I would have to leave England. Then everything, everything we had striven for and toiled to put in place, it would all erode in the wake of our ship as we sailed away. At any rate, it is preposterous to presume France would ever allow a woman such power, but the firstborn son of the king's only daughter . . . that is a different matter. They will, however, resist the notion of an English king upon their throne. We will have to force our arguments upon them, write to the pope. First, though, we must have the support of England's lords."

"When Parliament convenes then, we shall make the French throne our cause. Whatever doubts and suspicions have been hung on us will pale in comparison to that glittering temptation." The familiar glint in his dark eyes revealed that his mind was fast at work. "We can lure them from beneath Lancaster's wing with the baubles of French lordships . . . To think, though, it all hangs on the birth of an infant—what sex it will be, boy or girl, king or nothing."

"As it so often does, Roger. I love Jeanne with all my heart, but to wish her well in this, to wish for a son to carry on Charles' line . . . it would be to deny my own son. If I cannot rule, then he shall. I will never begrudge him the advantage of his sex. Besides, ruling a kingdom is a burden I could not bear forever. I've had enough as it is. You listen to advisors, do what you think is right and there will always be someone arguing over it." I rose, went to him and placed my hands upon his shoulders from behind. "As for French lordships—how can we possibly give away what we do not have?"

"Kings of England have drawn men to fight against Scotland and Ireland for centuries with such promises. They will fight, if only for a chance at those lands. Greed drives men to seemingly impossible deeds. Do you not want this for your son? For the House of Capet?" He turned sideways in his chair and drew me into his lap, squeezing my waist in emphasis. "Think on it! He can be the greatest king in all the world. He will be remembered—like Charlemagne, like Alexander."

Why do you try so hard to convince me, Roger? I slipped from his hold and returned wearily to my chair, slumping forward on the table, overwhelmed. It was all too much. Drained of thought, I swept aside my plate and cup, put my head down on the table and muttered into my forearm, "I cannot decide this now. I need to go away, desperately. I need to think."

He rounded the table and knelt beside me. "Where to?"

"Castle Rising, I suppose." I gazed at him from the pillow of my arm. Castle Rising was as good as any place. There were few distractions there. The low, flat, wet fens stretched mile upon mile. Towns were few and people kept to themselves. There was nothing but grass and sea and sky near Castle Rising. Its only beauty was in its simplicity.

Mortimer tenderly smoothed the hair on the crown of my head. "Whatever you wish. You can stay as long as you need to. If you want to come back and speak before Parliament after you've had time to think, we'll return. If not, I'll carry whatever message you want me to. This is a grave decision."

Grave, indeed. "It could mean war, Roger."

Just as our returning to England had posed the risk of war. We had avoided it then, only because everyone had so tired of Edward and his piggish minion that they abandoned him with glee at the first favorable opportunity, but would we be so fortunate in this venture? Sooner or later, luck will turn against us. Even knowing that, why do I dare tread so dangerously beside you?

He imparted a fleeting smile, meant to reassure me. "I know, I know. Perhaps, fortune will favor us once more and all will turn out for the better? Hasn't it always?" He took me in his arms and held me in that gentle way that tamed my rampant fears. "We will have peace in the north, then, as you've wanted all along. Joanna will wed David of Scotland and one day become a queen, like you."

My littlest Joanna! Why did Mortimer remind me of that now? I do not want to think of losing a daughter so young. I do not want to think of thrones or wars or Parliament and its squabbling barons. I do not want to think of any of those things.

No matter what I do, there is neither good nor joy in it.

Castle Rising — April, 1328

WE SPOKE LITTLE OF politics in those rare, quiet weeks at Castle Rising. Somehow, in not speaking of it, it all became clearer to me: I would write to the pope, to the nobility of France, to the barons of England. I would not cajole or threaten or complain. I would study the laws, precedence, Scripture. I would speak reason and appeal to their sense of logic. I would not act out of impulse and I would not preach war. I would not lay that terrible burden at my son's feet for him to carry like a load of stones. If, in times to come, he would pursue it himself, then it would be his choice, his doing, not some debacle that I, Isabella of France, would be remembered for.

I wanted the people of England to love me again, as once they had. But I feared it would never be so again. They did not trust Mortimer, now or ever. It seemed that in England one could not say his name without saying mine in the same breath, so aligned had we been since before landing at the mouth of the River Orwell. I knew how such things went. People believed what they wanted to. I had ridden both the highs and lows of it and I was never lower than in those months following Edward's funeral. The only hope I had was in believing that it could not possibly get any worse for me.

But optimism, when frail, is a target poised to be shattered.

I lay in bed, unwilling to rise, pathetically secure in my lethargy, wrapped in my blankets like a caterpillar snug in its cocoon.

"A walk today, my love?" Mortimer brought my hand to his lips and kissed each finger in turn. Morning light shone red from behind through his dark, disheveled hair, making it look as if he wore a crown of flames. "We can ride out to the Wash, take a walk along the shore, bring something to eat. I woke up early and stared out the window for hours, waiting for you to join the living. The sun is bright. There are birds everywhere. They're singing your name, I do swear."

With tremendous effort, I rolled over onto my side toward him. He was propped up on one elbow in the bed, nothing but his braies on, smiling like a little boy possessed by the devil and wanting to play. This was the private side of him that only I knew, that he showed to no one else—the capriciousness, the lightheartedness—and I loved him all the more for it. But I had not the energy for it today. There were letters to write, important minds to influence, and little time to accomplish a monumental task in such a menial way. The couriers would have to be recklessly swift.

"I would love to, but I have work ahead this day," I said blandly. "Important matters."

Pouting, he dropped my hand and flopped onto his back. "I see. The same as yesterday? And the day before?"

"Roger, it *is* important. I cannot tarry away the day frolicking on the strand while my son's and France's futures are at stake."

For a long, plodding minute he stared at the ceiling. His breath came in loud, short bursts, like steam escaping from a covered pot. "Why did we come here, Isabeau, if not to be alone? You are troubled, I can tell. And yet you find all manner of duties with which to distract yourself. You are no more separated from the outside world here than you would have been in Northampton, with all the barons of England sitting in a room demanding your rapt attention simultaneously."

He was right. I had needed to escape, or so I thought. Instead, I was only grasping at distraction. Already, it seemed that my son, very much smitten with his new wife, was drifting away from me. Rumors were circulating among the populace of Edward's murder and the fingers were being pointed in unison at Mortimer and me, ironically by the very people who once would have loved to see Edward hanged, beheaded and eviscerated beside his coddled favorite, Hugh Despenser. Lancaster was leading the wave of dissent. And I was excruciatingly aware that I could not even trust my own memory—but to speak to that of anyone, even Mortimer, was to admit my own insanity. One prod, one more curse upon my head, and I felt like I would tumble headlong into the absolute depths of lunacy and drown there.

My only salvation was Mortimer.

I inched closer to him and placed my arm across his chest. For a while I just listened to his heartbeat, felt it, let the strength of its drumming resound through my soul and carry me on its pulsing ebb up out of my blackness.

"I wanted to be with you," I whispered. "If I could make everything go away . . . and have only you. If only I could make that happen."

He turned to me, enclosing my hands in his as we clasped them between us, and pressed his forehead to mine. "For now, this moment, I can make that happen for you. Surrender your troubles, Isabeau."

I opened myself to his kisses, let him caress me, love me, as giving as any man could, and the sweetness of it all stirred me. It was, however, as if I was not even there with him. I responded to him, did as he liked, held him as he spent himself in brief, selfish ecstasy . . . and then I felt nothing but resentment that it was not so easy for me. The hour was not even done before I felt myself slipping again back into that dark space that so terrified and paralyzed me. But sometimes, even when we are not inspired in spirit, we must attend to the motions and walk among the living.

My letters were written and dispatched to Paris and Avignon.

They had not even reached their destinations when, a day before Parliament was due to convene and Mortimer and I had returned to Northampton, we received word that Jeanne had given birth to a daughter. The peers of France had elected Philip of Valois as Charles' successor.

In the Treaty of Northampton, Parliament approved the marriage of Joanna to David of Scotland. Reluctant as I had been to put it forth, it was unavoidable. England could afford no more wars in the north. The sacrifice I had to make to guarantee that—was my own six-year old daughter.

The wedding would take place in a little over a month in Berwick. But first, there were other weddings to attend—those of Mortimer's two daughters: Joanna to James Audley and Katherine to Thomas de Beauchamp. The dual ceremony was arranged to take place in Hereford.

Mortimer's wife would be there. He had not seen her since before his imprisonment in the Tower, not even in the two years since returning to England. That alone should have been comfort to me, but it was not. He had married her when he was only fourteen— twenty-seven long years ago. She had given him twelve children. *Twelve.*

I could give him none. And I would forever remain a widow . . . for I could never marry him, so long as Joan Mortimer lived.

13

Isabella:

Hereford – May, 1328

NO ONE COULD HAVE ever questioned the paternity of any of Roger Mortimer's twelve children, several of whom had gathered at Hereford that May.

His sons were strongly handsome. Roger, his namesake and second eldest after Edmund, was heir to his father's Irish holdings. Soft-spoken John, who was the youthful image of his father, was developing a deserved reputation for his skill in the joust. Dearest among Mortimer's sons, however, was Geoffrey, who had been with relatives in France at the time of Mortimer's escape to there and thus had grown quite close to his father.

Mortimer's daughters Joanna and Katherine, however, were not so much beautiful as they were sturdy and lacking gross imperfection, like a good horse with which it matters not if it is well-marked, but more that it is reliable and healthy—not altogether undesirable traits in a young wife. Joanna was the older and stouter of the two, dour in expression, but surprisingly pleasant in private conversation. Her bridegroom was five years younger than her. The fifteen-year old Lord of Heleigh, James Audley, looked as wet behind the ears as a newly whelped pup. While Joanna was very staid about the ceremony, her bridegroom appeared so anxious as to be on the verge of illness. When the final words pronouncing them husband and wife rang out, it was Joanna who supported James by the elbow and guided him down the aisle.

Hereford had been chosen because of the size and grandiosity of its church. My old friend Adam of Orleton, the Bishop of Hereford, presided over the ceremony. He had been old already when I left for France, although of good vigor. Yet I marveled at the constancy in his appearance. His devotion, he had told me, had preserved his robust health and spirit. I had always believed that one could look upon an old face and read in its lines, or lack of, either joy or sorrow—so surely all the world could read of my troubled life in the furrows that were beginning to etch my countenance.

Not only were the king, Philippa and I in attendance, but dozens upon dozens of earls, lords, knights and their relations. The place was packed full and with the rising warmth of a late spring day, the rank scent of perspiration permeated the air, making the closeness of all those people seem even closer. My own wedding had been one of winter cold—the air like brittle glass and Edward's soul a closed door to me.

Katherine, just two years the junior of Joanna, and her husband-to-be, the young, rakish heir to the earldom of Warwick, Thomas de Beauchamp, could hardly keep their hands from one another. Never once, as he held her hand, did Beauchamp look away from his blushing bride.

The wedding was not overly long, but it may as well have gone on for days, so torturous it was to me. Two reasons: first was that in a few weeks, I would give away my own daughter Joanna, a mere child, and years might pass before I could ever see her again; second . . . was that *she* was there: Joan Mortimer.

I entered the church, but she never glanced my way. A relief that was to me, for I would have betrayed all the enmity I felt for her in a single, damning look. As her daughters were joined in matrimony, Joan wept silently, conveying a mother's love for her children and her reluctance to part from them. In that, we were alike. From the moment her daughters appeared wearing their pearl-encrusted head-dresses with starched veils and their exquisite gowns of satin, though, her eyes were as much on Mortimer as on them. He, however, did not return her gaze in the same way; he merely acknowledged her with a slight nod when he took his place next to her. Her misty gaze was one of old longing and new questions. His manner—the averted eyes and constant shifting—was one of discomfort.

That Mortimer was seated beside her—that alone made my blood boil with jealousy. But what had I expected? They were still married and this was the wedding day of two of their children. It was only for appearances that Mortimer had left my side. Soon it would be over and he would come with me to Castle Rising perhaps, or Langley, or Windsor, or any of a dozen other places. She would have to accept that. It was his duty, as my advisor, to be with me at all times. The kingdom depended on him. He could not abandon me, or Young Edward, for familial dalliances.

As the two young pairs—one all atwitter like a pair of courting robins in springtime and the other a mismatch of apprehension and somberness—left the church, my eyes locked with hers. While the sight of her torched an inferno of disdain inside me, she radiated back nothing but kindest sympathy and perhaps a twinge of pity.

During the wedding feast, a minstrel picked at his lute strings and sang, ironically, of joyous love. Joan—who had not wandered more than an arm's length from Mortimer the whole day—invited the young king and his wife to Ludlow for a short stay.

Philippa, who engaged in conversation as readily as a nightingale sang, snatched up the invitation. She ran her fingers over the buttons of the king's tight-fitting sleeve. "Can we, Edward? It's such a lovely time of year. We could go riding. It's been so long since we've done that. And I've brought my best birds."

He leaned over and kissed her on the cheek. "If it would please you, I don't see why not."

I should not have looked their way, for Philippa returned my gaze and proposed what I dreaded most.

"Will you join us, my lady . . . Mother?" Abruptly, her anticipation turned to embarrassment. "I'm sorry, Lady Joan. I did not mean to impose on your hospitality."

For the first time that day, Joan's composure showed signs of fracturing. She pinched the handle of her spoon so hard her knuckles went white. Her left eye twitched. Then, her mouth jerked into a false smile as she gazed toward me. "My husband and I would be honored to have the queen as a guest at Ludlow."

How dare she gloat at me!

I could have declined. I wanted to desperately. I no more wanted to be in the same room as Roger's smug consort for another day than I had wished to remain married to Edward of Caernarvon for the rest of my life. Mortimer was my most trusted advisor, my constant companion, and the only man I had truly ever loved, but whether he showed her any affection or not, she, as his legal wife, would always be my rival.

And that was precisely why I had to go to Ludlow—to remind her who it was that he had chosen.

THE ROYAL PARTY LEFT Hereford the very next morning in a jumbled parade of horns and banners.

Before I mounted my palfrey, Adam of Orleton embraced me long.

"My lady." He broke the embrace, his gaze one of concern and protectiveness. "I would tell you it is a mistake to go to Ludlow, but I can see what is happening."

"What do you see, Your Grace?"

"You're afraid of losing him."

"You are the one who is mistaken, then. I go because I am not afraid." Arnaud helped me onto my saddle. I reached down and clasped Orleton's hand affectionately. "I'll write—and I am certain I'll have nothing but happy things to report."

"I shall pray for you daily."

"If you're praying for my virtue, Adam," I said, winking at him, "you're too late."

The hills of the Welsh Marches were low and broad and inhabited by tenfold more sheep and cattle than people. The road north from Hereford ran beside the rushing Lugg River as far as Leominster, where we spent the first night. The next morning, where the river valley turned westward, we left the narrow plain for rolling pastures to the north. I kept close to Philippa, her congenial chatter a needed diversion.

Although Mortimer was occasionally at Young Edward's side during the journey, he also frequently went to be with his wife. It seemed they spoke of nothing but their children. She did not ask of his duties, nor he of how she spent her time of late or what she had done in those years of his absence from her.

But I saw through her courteous coyness. She was as clever as any temptress. If Mortimer had gone to Hereford with the guilt of adultery blackening his heart and expecting a brutal tongue-lashing, or at least a frigid reception, he had instead been put at ease with constant, unwarranted kindness. She had elected not to punish him or drive him away, but to coax him closer. And he, if for nothing more than the sake of appearances for their children and to preserve himself politically, was falling prey to it.

Had I been her, I would not have debased myself so. She knew of us. Everyone did. I held no delusions in that regard. Why then did she not unleash her fury on Mortimer or at least treat me with cold disregard?

When we arrived at Ludlow there was already a feast awaiting us, fit for the king himself. She had been expecting this—and Mortimer had obviously prearranged it without my knowledge or consent.

In the hour before supper was served, Joan Mortimer flitted about issuing orders and arranging details like a finch leaping from thistle-head to thistle-head, stripping the seeds away. To see her transform in so short a time from a woman of modest tranquility to such a fountainhead of energy was amazing. I no longer wondered how she had survived twelve birthings, let alone the raising of all those children or Mortimer's many travels and warring.

Mortimer disappeared briefly to see to the care of our mounts and survey his stables. He had barely set foot in the great hall when I snagged him by the sleeve. He had been headed directly toward Joan, who was making sure that the best linens, plates and knives were being brought out.

"Will you show me to my quarters?" I asked pointedly.

He indicated a large stone-framed doorway to my right. "Over there—the new addition. Spacious, lavishly furnished. Fit for a queen. The king's chambers are adjacent to yours." His announcement was succinct, rigidly formal and somewhat loud, as if he meant to be overheard.

"Your wine cellar, then? You've spoken of it proudly many times. I would like to see it." My request was met with an open stare of defiance. "You do have one, don't you—or was I mistaken?"

He could not have been more displeased with me had I asked him to fall to his hands and knees and lick the soles of my feet. I noted the flicker of a sneer on his lips. "This way."

I hooked my arm through his and let him lead me straight past Joan, who faltered momentarily in her domestic tasks to watch us leave. Mortimer called for a lantern and with it we went down the narrow stairway. The low-ceilinged cellar was stacked with barrels of French wines and English ales. The walls glistened with moldy dampness, and although cramped and dank, it was seemingly free of rats and impressively stocked. Mortimer had not been to Ludlow more than a few days total since his return to England, but he kept the place—and his wife—well provisioned.

Mortimer stood stubbornly in the doorway at the bottom of the stairs while I meandered between the rows of barrels, barely a shoulder's width apart, pretending to inspect the selection. The light was scant with only the one lantern and I stubbed my toe on a small cask on the floor before hobbling back to him.

"I have known many earls and kings who did not keep this much drink at hand," I said.

"Is there something in particular you would like?" he offered politely.

A proper and timely question, even though I knew he meant drink. I went to him, pulled him clear of the door and shut it softly behind him.

"You," I whispered. "Quickly, before someone has a reason to bother us with petty details."

He glanced back at the door and set the lantern carefully on top of an empty barrel. Then he grabbed me abruptly by both arms and backed me away from the door. His voice was low, almost growling. "Isabella . . . this is entirely awkward. I didn't want to bring you here, to Ludlow. But I could not refuse her without making a terrible scene out of it. She . . . she would not have said much, but others . . ."

"Others? What might *others* say?" I wrapped my arms about his neck and kissed his throat playfully, as he often did to me to shift my mood. "That you prefer my bed to your wife's?" I kissed his throat

161

again, his neatly trimmed beard, his lower lip. "Come to me later then—after midnight."

"Isabella, Isabella . . ." He peeled my hands from his neck, hanging on to them apologetically, and stepped back. "I don't know . . . if I can."

I tore my hands away. "Why not?"

"In her house . . . I don't know if I can . . . can be with you. She has been my wife for twenty-seven years. Please, understand that. There was never any ill will between Joan and me. We were apart for a long time. So I put her out of my mind. I had to. And then, there was you and . . ." Jaw clenched, he shut his eyes for a moment, as he fought to force the words out. "Isabella, do not question me on this. I love you and no one else—but I will not dangle you in front of her under her own roof. I beg of you, do not contest her here, not now. We—you and I—will be gone from here within the week. Can we not both endure this brief chastity for that long? We can be together again then—for as long as we wish, as often as we want."

Together, yes . . . perhaps. In the dark of night. Behind closed doors . . . or hiding in cellars like this.

I should have ordered him to leave with me then, to abandon these sloppy pretenses of being the good and faithful husband. But when was I ever one to defy this man? He had but to speak to me in that liquid tone of authority to weaken my resolve, despite whatever presentiments might have whispered within me. Had I not loved him so much, I would have hated myself for being so servile to him.

"I give you three days, Roger. Three days with her." I shoved past him, yanked open the door and took the steps two at a time, stumbling over the hem of my skirt as I reached the top when the light from the kitchen momentarily blinded me.

I did not tell him not to touch her, hold her, or be with her. I did not think I needed to. He had said that he loved me—*me*, not her— and I had made him the most powerful man in England, next to the king himself. What reasonable man would have given that up to placate a staunch and settled wife who had outgrown her usefulness and allure?

At supper, when Joan took her place beside Mortimer at the head table to the right of Edward and Philippa, with me to my son's left, I finally saw Joan as she was—a face virtually untouched by the passing years, despite all the accompanying hardships and tribulations. I hated her even more then—not because I knew her at all, or that she had ever wronged me, but because when I saw her I understood . . . I understood why he had loved her from so young an age and for so long after their wedding, and why he had kept from her since coming back to England: Joan Mortimer was *beautiful*. Exquisitely, breathtakingly beautiful, even past her fortieth year. That she had given Mortimer so many children only augmented her physical beauty with a maternal, goddess-like strength.

As plates and platters were emptied and casks drained dry, I envied her not only for her years with Mortimer before he came to me in France, but rather that all her troubles had not taken their toll on her appearance. The only wrinkles that Joan had were almost imperceptible: a faint brushing of crow's feet at the corner's of her soft, brown eyes and the small indentation of lines of laughter at the folds between her mouth and cheeks. Her hair was still a river of auburn restrained by silver combs, untouched by strands of gray. My own pale hair was twined with wisps of white here and there and beneath my eyes showed the dark circles that come with years of sleepless worry. She was ten years older than me, and yet . . . she could have passed for ten years younger.

My cheeks aching from the effort, I feigned a smile of merriment while the jugglers tossed their flaming sticks between the outspread legs of one of them who was standing upside down on his hands. I drank of Mortimer's fine imported wines as the mummers engaged in their hilarity, drank until I was light in the head and laughing at a lapdog playing the part of Philip of Valois. Then I drank some more and floated away on a cloud of melancholy while a Welsh bard, not half as mesmerizing as the blind one the former king had employed, sang in his guttural, rolling tongue and plucked plaintively at his harp. In my glum and envying mood, his singing sounded more like the torturing of a cat to me than a ballad meant for lovers.

Mortimer conversed with his sons, Geoffrey and John, then later his namesake Roger for a good long time, while Joan made a valiant attempt to become better acquainted with her new sons-in-law.

And while everyone else talked gaily and laughed on into the night, even before the drowsiness of drinking tugged at their eyelids, I claimed fatigue and stumbled to my chambers and waited . . . and waited. For Mortimer—who never came.

THREE NIGHTS I WAS spurned—left to simmer alone. I did not ask if he slept in the same bed as her. I did not want to know.

Every time I saw Joan, I seethed with murderous jealousy. When I was near Mortimer, I refused to look at him. I could not. I might not have left my chambers at all by the fourth day, but for Philippa needling me to accompany her to the mews. I had never taken much to hawking, but as most nobility does, I used it as an occasion to pass the time.

The warm day and tranquility of the hillock where we stopped to hawk were more conducive to a long nap than any serious pursuits. So we spent most of the hour lounging in the grass beneath the shade of a hornbeam tree, its trunk twisting sideways and low to the ground so that we tethered our horses to its branches.

Philippa balanced a merlin hen on her fist, admiring its brown spotted chest feathers. "Do you think she could take a lark?"

The little merlin eyed Philippa with curiosity and then stretched her neck to take the piece of raw venison gently from Philippa's gloved fingers.

"She is too young . . . and too tame," I observed. I stretched out on my side and looked out over the curving green land. Wind rippled the grass in short bursts and swept down the hillside into the valley.

"Taken from the nest? Then she will need a patient teacher." Philippa stood clear of the tree's branches, lifted her fist abruptly so the merlin felt the rush of air. The bird spread its wings and tried to lift from Philippa's hand, but the leather strap on its leg tugged it abruptly back down, leaving it out of balance and flapping in frustration. Philippa clucked at the bird to capture its attention and calm it. "In Bruges every year, they bring cages and cages of merlins, peregrines and sparrowhawks from the north countries to sell in the markets to those who will train them. The falconers from Brabant are among the best anywhere. My father employed several of them, although he never encouraged us, his daughters, to learn hawking."

"And why not?" I asked. My father had encouraged me to learn anything I expressed the slightest curiosity about, raising me more like another of my brothers than a spoiled, helpless girl-child.

"Because he thought it more important that we study books and say our prayers." She wrinkled her nose in disagreement. "But while my sisters struggled over their letters, I learned quickly, grew bored and snuck away again and again—never mind how severely I was scolded for it. I pestered the kennel keeper, the falconers, the musicians, the squires, the guards . . . anyone who could teach me anything that was not written in books."

So that was how she had impressed Young Edward over her sisters—not with discourse of scholarly matters and religious philosophy, but with talk of horses and hawks and hunting dogs? My son had chosen wisely. All kings needed a confidante—and who better to be that than one's wife, always at his pillow? Royal advisors came and went, but spouses were intended to last a lifetime.

The merlin shook its leg, tinkling the little silver bells attached

165

to its jesses. Philippa tilted her head in thought. "Do you think that Edward would appreciate a skilled Brabant falconer, my lady?"

But I was no longer listening. Instead, I was thinking of Mortimer—thinking of how long he had been married to Joan and that it was altogether possible she might outlive him . . . and that Mortimer and I would have to go on like we had been, clinging to our shameful secret forever. Or worse, that this was the beginning of our end— that he would return to her and I would never be with him again.

The summer breeze was strong, hot and horridly uncomfortable. I felt as though I were burning from the inside out. Vaguely, I was aware of petite Philippa plopping down beside me and the little merlin cocking its head from side to side.

"I do not think," she said, "that Sir Roger wants to be here now, either. He and his wife have been estranged for years, yes?"

I sat up and hugged my knees. "You know . . . of us?"

"I think most everyone does, although they do not speak of it— openly, at least." She draped her free arm over me and leaned her head on my shoulder. "You are going to Berwick soon?"

Another dagger in my heart. "Yes."

"He will go with you then—away from here. It will get easier between you, with time, I think." As she withdrew her arm from me and stood, I turned my face toward her. She undid the leash from the bird's jesses. Again she thrust her fist upward, this time encouraging it to flight with a command. The bird caught a burst of air under its wings, flailed erratically above her a moment, then alighted on the branch closest to her. "See, she does not want to leave me, even though she can."

"Come to Berwick, Philippa." I wanted her with me. Her intelligence was refreshing and her honesty invaluable. Besides, it would be terribly awkward, cuttingly painful actually, to travel so far with Mortimer alone. Patrice could not always be depended on for distraction because her attentions were too often on Arnaud. "As King of

England, Edward should be there, also."

She shook her head sadly. "I suppose he will tell you in time himself, but my husband does not approve of Joanna's marriage to David Bruce."

"Why?" He had said nothing of the like to me. "It will be an insult to the future King of Scots if he's not there."

"Because he feels it was done without his consent." Philippa glanced sideways at me. "It is not to say he won't allow it—indeed, he cannot keep it from happening, but . . . he says he will not attend the wedding. That it is a farce. The treaty with Scotland—Edward feels that Sir Roger coerced him into signing it. He does not agree entirely with the terms—particularly in regards to the marriage of Joanna and David. He feels it's giving them, the Scots, too much too soon."

"He is expected to go. His presence in Berwick is very important."

"They say King Robert is frequently ill and will likely not be there, either. Does it matter if Edward is then? After all, his attendance was not required in the treaty."

Those last words were Edward's, not Philippa's. "Still, it would be an insult—to David and to Joanna. It matters to her that he is there."

"Edward said it is being forced upon Joanna."

I almost blurted out that Joanna was only a child, but it would have only proven her point. When I was Joanna's age, my father had taken me aside and spoken to me about marriage—of which country I should like to live in and if I would like to be called a 'queen' one day. He had painted a deceptively pleasant picture of England and the mythical, handsome prince who lived there named Edward of Caernarvon. Someday, I had thought, I might like that, but not until I was much, much older. I did not know then that my father was already in negotiations with Longshanks and that documents had been shuffled back and forth, sealing my fate. Now I had done the very same thing to Joanna—telling her of the pretty jewels she would wear and how important she would be to all the people of Scotland, all the while promising to send her own set of playmates along so she would not suffer from loneliness.

"Philippa, why are you telling me this? You should not betray Edward's trust. You should have told him to come to me and tell me himself. I don't wish to hear such things from someone else."

"No, no, please . . . you don't understand. I'm telling you this, because . . . because *he* would never do so." Step by step, she had inched closer to the merlin, their gazes locked. Holding out her left arm, she removed another morsel of meat from the pouch at her belt. She clicked her tongue again. The merlin beat its wings once, and then hopped down onto the perch of her waiting arm to receive its reward. She gave it several more bits of the venison to ensure its loyalty. "He told me of Stanhope Park—the Scots, how they almost took him prisoner, or could have killed him. It was William Montagu who saved his life, but Edward feels it was Mortimer who advised him poorly and put them all in danger in the first place. Ever since then, he is not sure he can trust Sir Roger." She stroked the merlin's back as it sat sleepily on her gloved fist, secure with her soothing touch; then, she kissed the bird on its beak. "You understand now why I've told you all this?"

I did—brutally so. Edward's faith in Mortimer had been tenuous from the beginning. Still in his minority, Edward was guided by the regency council, over which Mortimer and I held considerable influence . . . but it would not be so forever. Our hold on him would one day be undone, just as the jesses on Philippa's little merlin had been untied to set it free.

If I trusted my son, if I believed in him, why did I so dread that day?

Yet the day would indeed come when Edward, the son who was

so poised and contemplative from such an early age, would be old enough to rule on his own. A day not so very far away.

14

Isabella:

Berwick – July, 1328

T HE JOURNEY TO BERWICK was the longest I had ever endured. I was giving away my youngest child, sweet little Lady Joanna, handing her into rough Scottish hands to live and grow up in that frightfully cold, wind-torn, wild and uncivilized land. The now very public objections of the young king only exacerbated the guilt that already plagued me.

Furthermore, relations between Mortimer and me had decayed into bouts of hurtful spite. Even after leaving Ludlow, we slept apart. We spoke only of political matters, and then tersely so. While I treated him with open scorn, he returned quiet contempt. We were silently at war, although what either of us was fighting to gain, I do not know. Perhaps he wished for my forgiveness. Perhaps he resented my envy and no longer loved me for that pettiness. We were both proud. Each of us blamed the other. Why is it that when we are hurting most we seek to hurt others?

Desperately, I wanted to tell Mortimer what Philippa had confided in me, but I could not, in my heart, forgive what I believed to be true—that he had lain with Joan, that he loved her still, always had . . . and that he had only used me to gain his revenge on Edward of Caernarvon and achieve his power hold on England.

Such were my preoccupations while I held Joanna's hand as she was wedded to the four-year old David of Scotland. Joanna held herself proud and tall, bejeweled and draped in shimmering cloth like a doll painted into adult clothing, well-rehearsed in the role for which she had been diligently groomed. David, however, fidgeted, whined and tugged at his leggings like a fitful infant. Next to him stood Sir James Douglas, his black radiant hair curling behind his ears and coming to rest on his slender shoulders. His ghostly pale eyes looked straight into my soul with every furtive glance.

Oh, how the very mention of his name, the 'Black Douglas', had once stricken my heart with terror! Twice, I had nearly fallen prisoner to him. More recently he had almost taken the young king at Stanhope Park. Douglas alone had virtually been the undoing of the English. Yet in spite of his fearsome reputation, James Douglas was nothing but dignified in his demeanor, his words barely above a whisper whenever he spoke. He even displayed the care of an older, concerned brother when he whisked little David aside to change the prince's soiled clothing near the ceremony's end. The prince was too young to be embarrassed by the event; others, however, would remember.

As we feasted that evening, I wore the bravest face I could, but I don't think I smiled the whole night long. When Edward and Philippa were married, it had been a joyful day—because I truly believed they loved and had chosen one another. But this day was different. It was purely political—and completely my doing. Done for England's preservation and benefit, whether Young Edward understood and approved or not.

And Joanna—she thought it only another holiday . . . that she and I would be together again soon and her older sister Eleanor would come to visit her in the summers.

The next morning, I wept as James Douglas and Thomas Randolph pried her from my arms on the road outside Berwick. Joanna flapped her tiny arm at me in a wave as they sat her on her gray pony. Long before she was out of sight, she was already talking to everyone around her in that commanding, precocious tone of hers. I stood there, the scouring grit of road dust wafting over me, choking my throat, until she was gone from sight . . . and still I stood there, waiting for the wedding party to turn around and for Joanna to come back.

"Isabella."

A finger tapped at my shoulder and I turned—reluctantly, for I thought I had seen Joanna's party crest another hill in the distance—and saw Mortimer, his mouth drawn downward in sympathy.

"It is not easy, I know," he said, his arms enfolding me, "to let a child go. But it is easier for them than us."

I sank into his comforting embrace. How I wanted to drown myself in him, if only to forget the heartache of that day.

York — September, 1328

OVER AND OVER ON the monotonous ride south from Berwick, Mortimer told me it was a small sacrifice to make in the name of peace and that thousands of lives would be spared because of Joanna. It was, of course, the logical thing to say. Why, then, did it feel as though I had swallowed my heart? Perhaps because I had given my daughter into the care of that cold-hearted James Douglas. I had seen him kill a man at Tynemouth while I barely escaped with my own life.

A queen, however . . . a queen cannot cling to such dread. A queen must do what is right for all. If only Young Edward could see the wisdom in the union, the benefits of it. He could not afford to wage the same perpetual war with Scotland that his father and grandfather had engaged in. It had to end. And the sacrifice I was willing to make was my daughter.

The days were yet warm, but the nights growing more chill, as we rode to Tynemouth, then to Durham and finally on to Pontefract. It was there that Mortimer learned that his son, Roger, had died in Ireland in a skirmish over shifting loyalties among clans. Mortimer grew quiet, but kept his composure, sorrow showing in the sunken corners of his mouth, the dark moons beneath his eyes growing heavier day by day.

Before leaving Pontefract, Mortimer made arrangements to have his Irish estates transferred from his namesake Roger to his third oldest son John on his eighteenth birthday . . . but young John, so modest and full of promise, would never be able to partake of that wealth, for when we turned back north in order to attend an important council meeting in York and were within sight of the city, a rider from Shrewsbury raced up from behind our train.

The messenger dropped from his snorting mount in a billow of dust, barely dipping his knee before he plunged into his tidings. Our procession staggered to a halt in a long line behind us.

"Your wife, Joan," the messenger breathlessly said to Mortimer, pushing the brim of his cap up from a grime-covered forehead, "who was attending the tournament at Shrewsbury five days ago, wishes to inform you of the untimely and accidental death of your son, John. He was knocked unconscious from his horse in the first pass of the jousting championship. They say he failed to raise his shield in time. His opponent's lance struck him in the forehead. Tremors gripped his body and grew worse and worse. He could not be revived. Lady Joan says that he died doing what pleased him most."

Mortimer plummeted from his saddle as abruptly as if he had been toppled by a lance himself. For a moment, he stood there, hunched over, one hand pressed against his horse's ribs to keep himself upright and one holding his head, before he sank to the ground, folding his head into his knees. Then he turned his cheek to the dirt and wept softly.

As if cued by his grief, the skies to the west blackened and the wind gained force. It was my turn, then, to be strong for Mortimer, even when I did not yet believe I could be. I knelt on the ground beside him.

"I should have told him," Mortimer said hoarsely, "never to lower his shield." He slammed a fist into the ground. "I should have told Roger, too."

"Mortimer, my dear, gentle Mortimer . . ." I stroked his back and shoulders, knowing that it was but a feeble solace to him at such an insufferable time. "I am so sorry. So terribly sorry. If there is any comfort, it was that you were able to be with John not long ago— Roger, as well."

"Do not mock me with words," he growled, clawing at the hard-packed dirt. The wind rippled across the back of his shirt and tossed dust into his face. "There is no fortune in the death of someone you love—*ever*."

He spoke no more that day. Except for my personal attendants, I ordered the remainder of our retinue to find quarters within York. Parliament was set to take place in Salisbury in a few months, but rumors about Lancaster had bade me to summon a council meeting in York beforehand to settle matters. The timing, given the morbid news of Mortimer's sons, could not have been worse.

MORTIMER AND I TOOK up residence within the King's Tower with its eagle's view above the sweeping, rock-strewn moors. For two days

174

he said very little, drifting through the daytime hours in a cloud of despondency. Meanwhile, the wind had shifted and a great, black storm thundered in from the north. Lightning flashed across the sky and cracked from dawn until noon, coming again in the evening and continuing on through the night so that it was impossible to sleep without being awoken with a jolt. A tithe barn to the west of the city caught fire and it was only the constant deluge from above that saved it from burning to the ground. Meanwhile, the wagon ruts in the roads filled up with deep mud, making them impassible. Soon, the streets of York flowed like rushing rivers.

There was nothing I could have said to Mortimer to ease his pain. He could not put his sorrow into words. He did not seem to want to. My loss of Joanna to the Scots no longer seemed a tragedy. She, if not happy, was at least alive and well. That, ironically, eased my misgivings.

Undoubtedly, the rains had delayed the arrival of Lancaster and the others. It was a small blessing the weather turned bad when it did, for Mortimer was in no state of mind for diplomacy. By our fourth evening in York, however, he gradually began to engage with the world around him. Still, he did not speak of his sons or the mortal ache in his heart.

He came to me after I had taken to bed for the night, dismissing Patrice almost insouciantly, as if his presence in my bedchamber had never ceased to be a regular occurrence. Patrice was dubious that she should abandon me, with him standing so insistently by and not altogether in his right mind, but I assured her it was all right. Ever eager to be with Arnaud, she gave no argument.

Mortimer and I had not been together intimately since before the weddings at Hereford, more than two months before. But as he stripped himself of every last thread of clothing and stood fully naked beside my bed while the silver light of a half-moon poured over him—as though his doing so was a right that had always been his—I could tell it was but a physical act to displace the anguish inside him.

He yanked aside the covers I was clutching to my breast, shoved my gown up to my midriff, and surveyed my body from foot to neck, lingering halfway . . . but he would not meet my eyes. With all the mindless ceremony with which Edward of Caernarvon had once carried out the act, Mortimer climbed onto the bed and thrust his hips at me, missing his mark the first several times. His movements were jerky, his breathing shallow and rapid. He did not kiss me or touch me tenderly or whisper of eternal love into my ear after he ended with a gasp and a shudder. He merely rolled from me onto his back, his hands clasped across his stomach and a single tear rolling silently down his cheek.

"I would rather have died first," he said, his voice so low and fragile I could barely hear it, "than to lose my sons before me."

I laid my arm across his chest and held him until the glow of moonlight yielded to the shining light of a new day.

LANCASTER NEVER ARRIVED IN York, nor did Edmund of Kent or Thomas of Norfolk. Lancaster's failure to appear was no surprise. It was, in fact, something of a relief, for even though Mortimer was coming out of his melancholy, he was commonly short on both tolerance and optimism. Had Lancaster shown up in a foul mood too soon after the deaths of Mortimer's sons, it might have come to blows between them. But the fact that the king's uncles had stayed away, as well . . . that whispered of collusion.

More unsettling news came when we heard there had been a public outcry in London that threatened to erupt into havoc. The Abbot of Westminster was preparing to return the Stone of Scone to the Scots, as had been agreed to in the Treaty of Northampton. Instead of realizing the peace with Scotland would deliver prosperity to England, the people were regarding it as an act of treason. I was

hard pressed to understand how they could view it so, but old preju-
dices are not easily shaken. In the end, the Stone stayed put and
whether or not any Scottish kings would ever again be crowned while
sitting on it remained to be seen.

Again, I sent word to the councilors to come to York and
demanded to know the reasons for their truancy. Days became weeks
as we waited to hear news from elsewhere in the kingdom. Conflict-
ing rumors reached us in waves—some whispering of rebellion and
civil war, others claiming Lancaster was ready to capitulate. Whatever
was being spoken or by whomever, returning to London forthwith
seemed unwise, given the discontent there. The rabble could descend
on us and a riled mob is a mindless monster that knows no
inhibitions. At last, Mortimer and I struck out southward, aiming
for Salisbury, but just north of Nottingham we received a summons
from Young Edward to come with all haste to Barlings Abbey in
Lincolnshire.

Lancaster had at last agreed to meet with the king.

Lincoln — September, 1328

WE KNELT IN UNISON, Patrice and I flanking the leaning altar of the
seldom used, dilapidated little church that sat on a rugged knoll not
far from Lincoln. We had risen early that morning and put two
leagues swiftly behind us before I insisted on stopping for an urgent
word with God on my son's behalf. The night before this, we had
sent word ahead to Edward's camp that we would be arriving at
noon. It was almost that now and we had over a league to go.
Lancaster, for all that we knew, might be loitering over the next hill,
waiting to pounce. Against our combined forces, Lancaster would
not have had a chance against us, but hewn in half as we yet were . . .

Father Norbert began his Latin incantations, making the sign of the cross and then uttering a prayer as he dabbed a spot of holy water on each of our foreheads. Through the small open windows of the chapel, I heard the gay chatter of sparrows gathering on the roof and in the nearby plane trees. Then there was a loud burst of protest as the sparrows took to flight. Soon, an emboldened magpie settled on the window sill to view the curious ritual within.

I had turned my head slightly to study the smug black and white bird, when the distant slap of hooves upon the dry, packed road came to my ears.

Patrice clasped her hands over mine as Father Norbert droned on. But the pace of his verse quickened and his eyes kept flitting toward the closed door. He lost his place and had to begin again.

"Sir Roger is outside," I reassured, turning my hand over and pressing the rosary into Patrice's palm.

She smiled nervously. "Or a messenger from the king, perhaps?"

There was a single rap on the door and then the blow of a shoulder being laid into it, as the old rusted hinges resisted. My heart faltered until I saw a familiar face appear.

"The king," Mortimer declared, bracing himself in the middle of the doorway.

He had barely turned to give a perfunctory greeting when Edward bounded past him into the church. Sharp on his heels, Sir William Montagu, with his long golden hair secured loosely at his neck by a leather tie, loped close behind. If there existed an English version of the furtive Black Douglas, Montagu was it. With the king he was quick-witted and easy going, but toward others he kept a stern vigil.

Edward halted stiffly before me. He was fully dressed in armor and looking short on sleep. "You must come at once," he commanded.

Slowly, I stood. What concerned me most was not Young Edward's sudden arrival, or his insistence that we go to Lincoln

178

immediately, but the way he kept looking at Mortimer. Edward's brow was drawn tight, the muscles in his face taut. It was the irascible look that a displeased father gives an unruly child who is deserving of a lashing.

"Why?" I asked. "Has Lancaster arrived already?"

"You want to know why?" Edward struggled to tame the fury rising within him, but it meant battling nature. The Plantagenet strain was renowned for its temper and he was beginning to show that the fiery blood of his forefathers originated deep in his marrow as well. I had tried so hard to blunt that edge in him, to make him use reason and to seek to understand even his enemies' causes, but I had, I began to fear, been trying to push back the mighty tide of an ocean. I could see it in the hardness of his eyes, the clenched fists. Hear it hammered in the combative cadence of his words. "Lancaster asked to meet us. I agreed. He has levied certain . . . accusations. Serious ones. And yes, he is awaiting our arrival."

"Accusations?" I had requested Lancaster to come to York to address his disagreements over the Treaty of Northampton. He had avoided the meeting without explanation, as had Kent and Norfolk. I knew I must tread carefully. There was far more to their impudence than what I had first guessed. "Tell me—what sort of accusations?"

"Oh, Mother." He shook his head sadly. "Where . . . oh, where would I begin?"

That answer alone should have warned me.

"Lancaster claims my father was murdered," he said. "That Mortimer was responsible. And you knew of it all."

Sometimes, the line between truth and rumor is blurred, like an ink stroke smeared by a falling tear.

179

15

Young Edward:

Lincoln — September, 1328

WE MET THE EARL of Lancaster on the grounds of Barlings Abbey near Lincoln. Fields of rye and barley rippled lazily beneath an amber sun. In the pastures, speckled fat sheep wore long ringlets of wool. It seemed too pastoral a place for a confrontation. But there was no castle big enough to contain Henry of Lancaster—especially when he faced us with a force large enough to wage battle.

"He means war," Mortimer said.

I turned my mount to face Mortimer squarely. "Not while I wear the crown." It may have been a bold statement coming from a king of only sixteen years, but I had sworn to myself early on that England would be strong from within and I would tolerate no insurrection.

Knights shifted their shields, checked the straps on their armor. Morning sun bounced in bold flashes of silver off helmets and breastplates. Lancaster's forces were fanned out over a low ridgeline to the south on either side of the road before us.

My mother beckoned Arnaud to her from the front line. "I will ask the earl to meet with me alone," she said.

I threw her a look of denial. "Madness!"

"He's right," Mortimer joined in. "You cannot go to him by yourself. It's you he's intent on destroying. Take Edward along. Lancaster will listen to him."

"For once we agree on something," I remarked.

"What is it," Mortimer began, his dark brow furrowing stormily, "that you so resent about me? Still in a dudgeon over Weardale? Will you ever let it go?"

"Hardly a dudgeon, Sir Roger. I was made a laughingstock. The Scots ran bloody circles around us like hungry wolves stalking a herd of sick sheep. And my life—was very nearly forfeit."

"Your life was preserved," Mortimer said.

"Because William Montagu saved me! Where were you?"

"Stop!" Mother shouted, putting a halt to our argument before something more came of it. "Edward, come with me, then, if you feel the need to, although I've no fear of that bombastic fraud. We'll put an end to these lies here and now."

Arnaud was sent forth with a request for Lancaster to join us halfway between our two forces. He sped back with a reply of consent from the earl. Mother and I rode alone across the gaping, vulnerable expanse—my eyes darting toward heaven should an arrow descend silently from there.

"Sir Roger was right in that Lancaster will hear you out," she said. "So I will bow to you and hold my tongue for as long as I can. But do as I say—I know how to deal with him. You must ask him to put forth his grievances, in full. Let him speak without interruption. He will not even begin to listen until he is heard. It may take a while. He enjoys the sound of his own voice. Knowing Lancaster, he feels what he has to say is more important and truthful than any objections or protests we might naturally have to his actions. You will express concern, ask him to elaborate and then you will repeat what he has said. This will disarm him. He will begin to see you as a benevolent negotiator, and not a potential enemy. What he thinks of me does not matter so much as how he regards you.

"Then, when he finally slackens in his complaints, you will tell him, plainly, that he has until the opening of the Salisbury parliament to collect and present the full proof of his accusations . . . and if he has none by then, he is to abandon them and give a full apology, in writing, at said gathering. Do you understand all this?"

She was beginning to sound too much like Mortimer, who had over the last couple of years meted out advice to me in a manner which conveyed the expectation of absolute obedience.

I eyed her sidelong, considering the alternatives. "I do . . . but how do we know he won't demand proof of your and Mortimer's innocence on the spot? Perhaps it is as Mortimer said—that he came eager for a fight and this talking is nothing but a ritual, a chance for him to confront you personally."

"Because I know Henry of Lancaster and I knew his brother before him . . . and I know how such men think. They think blood alone entitles them to power. Any decision that is made without them, they consider an affront, an undermining of their authority. The Earl of Lancaster did not invite us here to risk his life today. He came to prod us into some rash action so he could raise the hue and cry against us and then he can make a grab at power. His accusations are not based on truth. They are a means to assert himself. If he can thrust you in the middle of the mayhem and make you doubt me—or Mortimer—then he will have won half the battle."

Reluctantly, I nodded. Lancaster by then had broken from his ranks and ridden forward with Thomas Wake, Lord of Liddell, who had openly protested that the Treaty of Northampton would cost him his Scottish estates—lands that he had not had access to or benefit from since the Battle of Bannockburn fourteen years past. He had also been the one to take my father and Hugh Despenser into custody.

"Where is Mortimer?" Lancaster shouted out before we had even reached him.

I kicked my horse in the flanks and galloped straight up to the earl. "You will address us properly first . . . or your answer will come from there." I pointed behind me to the impressive array of knights, archers and foot soldiers.

Lancaster squinted toward my army. It was not the sun that made him squint, however, but eyesight that was slowly beginning to fail even before his fiftieth year. He shrugged. "My lord, where is Sir Mortimer? Why did he not ride forward with you?"

I lied, "Because I told him to stay where he was."

"Send for him then."

"I will not."

"This concerns him, as well as the Queen Dowager."

"It would only delay us. He has no say in any of this. I came to hear you. Now, list your grievances, Lord Henry, if you please."

Lancaster may have had it in mind to volley his complaints directly at Mortimer, but it obviously delighted him more to hear me say I wanted to listen to him. Without acknowledging my mother, he began: "The queen has amassed estates beyond her right and squandered the royal treasury. She and Mortimer have forced their influence upon you by controlling the regency council. Mortimer conspired with the Scots to allow your capture in Weardale. Furthermore, they have bartered with said traitors in marrying Joanna to David, thus forfeiting the inheritances of numerous Englishmen there. Lastly . . . our king, Edward of Caernarvon, was taken from Kenilworth, forbidden contact with the outside and then"— Lancaster finally turned his eyes on her, his lips twisting into a wolf- ish scowl, the low tenor of his voice now booming as far as he could force the words—"was heinously *murdered*. The world knows of your crime, my lady! Eternal judgment will be brought upon your pretty head."

Her hands shook violently as she held her reins. In the heavy pause that followed, she curled her fingernails deep into the palm of her hand, as if to hold back her screams.

I wrestled with the urge to leap from my saddle and strangle Lancaster before a horde of witnesses. "Murder? Is it my mother you call a murderer? Give us proof. You, my lord cousin, would not say such a thing without *very* good reason."

"Because the king—your father, I mean—" Lancaster blurted, "is dead. There was no reason for him to die."

"Men live . . . men die. It is the same for everyone: plowmen, kennel keepers, kings . . . *earls*." Pausing to give him time to think on it, I raised my brows. "Some die by the knife, some by the axe, and some from a will too weak to go on. There were no marks on his body. And there was no mischief in his death." I held Lancaster's gaze, but he was not one to concede a staring match. If anything, it only reinforced his stubbornness. Finally, I glanced back at the royal army in all its strength and readiness. My message was clear and pointed. "I'll let you leave in peace for today, but come to Salisbury and, I shall say this again, either deliver proof of what you say . . . or recant—else it will be a sentence of treason on you, Lord Henry."

The earl's forehead, cheeks and nose reddened like a scarlet mask of rage. He slammed his fists against broad thighs. "Proof? What proof do you need? They will bleed you dry from your eyeballs! Rule you like an infant in his cradle! They bartered your sister, a mere child, away. Gave her to traitors. Infant killers. Gave away our lands. Stole your money from under your runny nose. Open your eyes, boy! Before it comes to war. I'll tell you your proof, if you—"

But at the word 'boy', I had already turned my horse, grabbed my mother's bridle and was leading her back to our lines at a brisk clip. We were nearly back to the others before Lancaster's rumbling outburst faded in the distance.

"Thank you," she said, before we rejoined the others.

I said nothing to her. Too many unanswered questions had been raised, even though Lancaster had provided no proof to back up his accusations. Still, despite wanting to believe that my mother was innocent, the smallest worm of doubt had burrowed into my gut.

Mortimer, however, was entirely capable of murder.

16

Isabella:

Gloucester – September, 1328

I HAD NEVER BELIEVED in omens, but in portent the golden eagle gliding above Windsor on my son's day of birth loomed large and horrific.

When there is civil war, brother faces brother across the battle-field. Families are broken, lineages sometimes annihilated altogether. Kingdoms are destroyed from within—lands charred, farmsteads ravaged, and fortresses battered. One city is sacked, while the next one stands unscathed.

I had seen all this in the North when the Scots slipped across the border and wreaked their havoc, just as the English had done to their land. If it came to civil war, the devastation would be even greater and more widespread. A kingdom maimed is left vulnerable to invasion by foreigners, sometimes for decades.

Lancaster, who I had counted among our allies when we

returned to England from France, had to be dealt with. He had drawn Kent and Norfolk into his maelstrom of insurrection. For the present, the king's uncles were lying low, doubtless waiting to see what the prevailing wind would be when the time came to choose sides.

While Mortimer and I went with haste to Gloucester in the Welsh Marches to muster troops, the king went to London to confer with the mayor.

Bishop Orleton and I took supper with Mortimer in the great hall. Halfway through the meal, Mortimer excused himself to inspect arms and to make arrangements with the garrison's captain to receive the various barons who had begun to answer the king's summons. Orleton and I departed to the solar where we could talk in private.

I sat on the broad window ledge overlooking the road east. "This is but the residue of old grievances stirred anew, Adam."

"Doubtless it is." He stroked pensively at his smooth jaw. "One wonders, though, where and how such gossip originates. Perhaps it thrives only because mankind cannot be content with peace."

I ached to confess all to him, but reason overruled my embattled conscience. With practice, hiding the truth had become an increasingly easy habit to uphold. Each time the lie is woven and never rent apart, it becomes stronger, more real.

A company of armed riders was approaching from the east. Fixed in cold fear, I pressed my hands to the window ledge. The pale light of dusk obscured their identity from a distance. The riders paused before the gatehouse and were admitted entrance. Edward galloped into the inner bailey, his cloak flaring from his shoulders as he wheeled his horse around to hurl out orders to his men.

Orleton came to the window to stand at my shoulder. "The king? Already returned from London?"

The horses of the king's company heaved for breath. Their hides were dark with sweat. My knees shaking, I grasped the stones around the window. "Too soon."

Gently, Orleton pried my fingers from the stones. "But a good sign that he arrived here safely, is it not?"

"I am not sure what it means."

I pressed the flat of my palm to my breast, feeling the rapid flutter of my heart beneath it. I feared the worst: that Lancaster had plucked the malcontents from London, armed them with iron pokers, pointed sticks and rusty knives and was marching on us even now. Unlike his father, my son the king would bar their path, stand and fight until the brutal end. Years ago when I had toiled to correct my husband's errors, I had been the trusted one, and particularly popular among the Londoners. It was not until now, however, with matters slipping from my control, that I realized how completely opinions had changed.

"But he came here—to you." Orleton turned me by the waist and took my hand. "He doesn't believe any of Lancaster's claims. He believes you."

"I pray you are not overly ambitious in your faith of my son, Your Grace." I gripped his long-fingered hand, needing to draw on his strength. "I only want to know that all of this trouble with Lancaster will pass, that a resolution will come of it, and that in the end peace will prevail. Do I ask so much?" I let out a sigh steeped in despondency.

"What you ask is what God would have us follow always. But He also presents us with trials so we may choose either the path of righteousness or the path of worldliness. Too often, the way of the world offers temptations: dazzling jewels that cannot be resisted, empty indulgences, pleasures of the flesh, the gratification of pride, the greed for possessions. Things that feed the carnal appetites, yet leave us wanting more, never thankful of our daily sustenance, blind to the abounding gifts around us and thus slighting Our Lord's munificence. The promise of Heaven is unknown to many; the path to it easily obscured. It is there for those who seek it. The way is there."

His face had turned heavenward, eyes alight with an awe of the divine and an ecstasy that filled his being. Of all England's prelates, he seemed the most genuine in his faith. More than observant of it, he felt the hand of God on his soul, recognized God's work in every lightning-scoured branch and winter-dead wisp of grass, and patronized none who did not; instead, he shared his exultation, reminding those of us who overlooked those daily miracles and humbling us by our own awareness. I felt not so much shamed in his presence, as I felt awakened. At last, his chin dropped and his eyes misted over with sadness. He shook his head and touched clasped hands to his lips. "Yet how many of us say we walk the road to Heaven, even as we dance like heretics celebrating our sins?"

Another time I would have delved further into this discourse on God's glory and how we—me, daily, as well—fell to intemperance . . . but Young Edward had arrived. War loomed. War. All because of a horrific act which I had not stopped from happening. Did it matter that I had tried?

"Shall we see, then," I said, prompting, "what brings our young king with such haste? Perhaps the news is good?"

"Scripture says: Ye shall hear of wars and rumors of wars: be not troubled, for all these things must come to pass, but the end is not yet." The fine corners of his mouth lifted in a smile. "Come. Have strength, my child. God will guide us, if we but seek the answers. As for peace, it is always His will."

I hooked my fingers into the crook of the bishop's arm and together we descended the spiral stairs of the tower, the amber flames of the torches bowing as we passed and springing to new life in our shadows. We reached the darkened yard to find it empty but for grooms gathering up the horses and a few loitering soldiers, some guzzling from their flasks, others bent over with weariness and rubbing at stiff muscles from too many hard hours in the saddle.

At the door to the great hall, William Montagu lingered, his lithe form molded to the doorframe as he surveyed every corner of the bailey like a fox watching for the flicker of a mouse's tail in tall grass. Wherever Edward was, Montagu was always close by. I dropped my hand from the bishop's arm, lifting my skirts to consume the distance more rapidly, and bounded up the steps two at a time. At the top, I paused before Montagu to catch my breath.

He bent deeply forward, his head dipping to waist level. Golden strands dangled across his eyes, but he never took his gaze from me.

"My lady," he greeted in a bland tone. Montagu raked the hair from his eyes. They were a shocking amber—a color I had never seen on any living creature before but a cat. Not only was his burnished hair tightly tangled and knotted, but his clothes were sullied and wrinkled, revealing that he had slept in them for several days straight and, judging by the bodily stench, not had the leisure of a wash basin either.

As he moved to open the door for me, I touched his wrist to stay him. "London? How goes it there?"

"I would not know, my lady. I have not seen it recently."

I glanced back at Orleton, who by then was coming up the stairs to the hall. He gave me a questioning glance as he came abreast of me.

"As I thought. London defies the king." I nodded to Montagu to open the door. Bishop Orleton and I entered a barely lit hall. I saw only shadows thrown by scattered candlelight and stirring black shapes that floated through a gray world. The door closed behind us. My eyes could not adjust quickly enough to ascertain who was present. I could locate the long lumps of servants asleep beneath their blankets by their snoring—some near the trestle tables, others by a dead hearth smelling faintly of ashes. To our left a gruff voice cursed.

"Bloody, fucking bastard! Watch where you're going."

The gray shape swaggering above retorted, "I would not utter such curses without knowing to whom you are speaking."

I heard a swift kick and a wilting moan, then brusque muttering, something like the grunting of an angry swine. A lantern swam through the blackness, throwing long swaths of light before it and upon the king's haggard features, his appearance every bit as road-worn as Montagu's.

"Edward?" I called out. He looked at me sulkily as he undid his scabbard and dropped it carelessly beside him. I picked my way through the scattered heaps of dozing bodies. As more lights were brought forth, the hall suddenly began to bustle to life. Utterances of 'The king . . . 'tis the king' echoed forth, beginning in frail whispers and then rising to a jittery buzz. Soon there was a swarm of frenzied servants piling kindling and stout logs upon the hearth, others rushing to bring food and drink or offering clean blankets.

I reached Edward and embraced him, but immediately detected trouble in his rigid stance. "Son, what of London? Why did you not go there?" I had begged him to come with us directly to Gloucester instead, but he had insisted on going his own way, certain the city would welcome him upon his arrival.

He hurled his gauntlets at the floor in disgust. "We did not get past Cambridge, Mother." Hands braced upon his narrow hips, he scowled at his own blighted hope.

"Lancaster?"

"Approaching from the southwest with his army—and not on friendly terms. Just as bad, Mayor Bethune, whom I trusted, was ousted in favor of Hamo de Chigwell—that despicable sewer rat. So my plan to rally London—utterly pointless. It was not safe to even go near it." Chigwell had been one of those who had sentenced Mortimer to death when he was imprisoned in the Tower. His appointment boded favorably for Lancaster and ill for us. Young

Edward balled his fists and shook them in the air. "Argh! It is Lancaster's fortune that I left. I was ready to fight. I would have. I wanted to."

"But you didn't."

He brought his fists down to his sides, fingers clenched like catapult stones, ready to be hurled at a waiting target. "No, no, I didn't. Didn't because . . . because he had openly given orders that I was to be taken captive—and I could not give him that opportunity. Scouting reports said that Lancaster had a large contingent of Londoners with him." He jabbed a finger in the air behind him for emphasis. "If it comes to battle, I'll be the one to have the num-bers—and the people—on my side, not that self-serving mongrel."

Already he understood what his father never had: that kings who have the masses behind them rule long and well.

"How many?" I said. "How many Londoners did he have?"

He pushed his hands up the sides of his face, rocking his head back and forth in aggravation, trying to recall the number. "Enough . . . five, maybe six hundred."

It was then that Mortimer's voice grabbed us from behind. "That many, plus his own men?" His shadow parted from the other side of a bulging column as he drifted calmly toward us. He came into the light and stood plank still some distance away, as if the events bore no urgency of decision, but rather careful contemplation. It was a trait of Mortimer's, one which he was always trying to impress upon the young king, to keep his wits level, even in the most frantic of situations.

Young Edward threw his hands wide. "Yes, that bloody many. He taunts. He lies. He sets the snare and then would chase me straight into it. It seems I cannot avoid this fight, Sir Roger."

"And you shouldn't," Mortimer replied carefully. "At least . . . not if that is how Lancaster means to settle this. He's had his chances. Still, he rebuffs your graces."

"He has. He does. Outright rebellion, I say. As plain as the beard on your face." Edward dragged a chair close to the hearth, yanked loose some of the straps on his plate armor and slumped down, defeated by exhaustion if not dwindling options. One elbow propped on the arm of the chair, he balanced his chin thoughtfully upon the knuckles of that hand. "Before I was crowned, I swore to myself that in my reign I would never let it come to this—that I would never see civil war in my lifetime. Yet it hasn't even been a year and already . . ." He threw his head back, eyes shut tight, and then exploded in frustration, tearing at the roots of his hair. "Why?! Why, God, do you test me like this? What have I done to cause it? Was I not meant to be King of England? Did I come by it wrongfully and this . . . this is my punishment?"

I cringed at those words. He had been reluctant to take the crown, accepting it only after his father's abdication in writing had been witnessed. That tentative beginning had compromised his mettle even then.

"You have done nothing, my son," Orleton said. "And God is not the cause of it. Lord Henry of Lancaster is."

Skeptical, he opened his eyes a sliver. "Then, dear Bishop Orleton, how do I keep it from happening?"

Orleton glanced toward Mortimer, who leaned against a column, crossed his arms and kept his thoughts to himself.

The bishop went to the king and stood before him. He inclined his head in a bow of respect. "If you will permit me to speak honestly, my lord?"

Young Edward flipped his palm open. "Go on."

"The earl has raised serious . . . accusations. Levied them at those nearest you. You asked for proof. What proof has he given you?"

"None . . . yet."

"Then I would say he has none to give. My king, I am a man of

God and do not condone violence, but he has armed himself and come after you. You must stand against him . . . and you must defeat him, for if you do nothing, it will indeed be Henry of Lancaster who rules England . . . and not you."

Edward slid lower. He stared into the fire for a good long time before finally forming his thoughts into words. Like the boy-king he still was, he wriggled in his chair. "I don't always know the right thing to do. That was my father's flaw, as well, I think."

"It is to be human, my son," Orleton replied.

"But what is it to be a king? Kings command. They rule. But how?" He closed his eyes again and rubbed at his eyeballs, squirming with discomfort at his predicament. Finally, he looked squarely at Mortimer, pausing long before posing the question. "Sir Roger, tell me—what do I do, when I know not what to do?"

Mortimer's words were measured and sincere, not forceful. "Gather wisdom from those around you. Listen to reason. Weigh the risks—the cost of each possibility against the outcome. Then, take action."

"And if it does not go well?"

He shrugged. "You do differently the next time."

Young Edward dropped his hand from his chin. "Yes, if we are so fortunate . . ." The edges of his mouth curled upward in a facetious grin. His overture for Mortimer's advice had been thought through. For a boy not yet seventeen, he was exceedingly clever. I had hoped he had given up his mistrust of Mortimer and it almost appeared so. Still, there remained the underlying grievance of Weardale that the king would not let go—and he would remind Mortimer of it just often enough to keep him humble. Mortimer, however aware he was of the insinuation, seemed unfazed by it.

"Mother?" Edward turned his bleary-eyed gaze on me.

Lost in contemplation, his voice startled me. "Yes?"

"I've heard from the Bishop of Hereford and Sir Roger. What

do you say on this matter of Lancaster?"

The rising heat of the fire warmed my back, but my fingers were ice cold. I pulled my hands inside the long draping sleeves of my kirtle and moved closer to him. "I say he has made himself your enemy."

"Strong words."

"What else would you call him?"

"Hah. Not a friend by any means." He stifled a long, deep yawn and stretched his sinewy, deer-like legs. "Your advice, then?"

"Avoid Salisbury."

"Not go to Parliament?"

I nodded. "Don't go. Let Mortimer and me go in your stead. If Lancaster brings his army, then Mortimer will be the one to meet him in battle, not you. He will be defeated, without risk to your life, and peace shall at last return to England."

"But *I* want to be the one who—"

"Which is precisely what he wants. He made it well known that his mission was to take you captive—the true purpose of which was to use you against us. Do not so much as stumble within his grasp." To mark the gravity of my advice, I knelt at his feet and took his hands in mine—hands that had once barely been big enough to clutch a spoon, now big and strong enough to take off a man's arm with one swipe of his blade. I rested my head against his knuckles, my cheek soft against his calloused fingers so that he could feel the tear trickling from the corner of my eye. My voice was wispy, unveiling the fear in my heart when I had wanted to speak only wisdom. "Yes, you could . . . you could go and fight him, with or without Mortimer at your side. But if you are taken, you will be made to do and say things against your will, all at Lancaster's whim. I beg of you—go not to Salisbury. Go to Marlborough. Be with Philippa. How long has it been since you shared her bed? She worries for you. She needs you near. Let those loyal to you carry out your commands

195

and uphold your authority until Lancaster meets his senses. Then . . . then deal with him as you will—with ruthless vengeance or with gentle mercy, as suits your end."

"Mother, Mother . . . I would just as soon have his head for his treason, yet you propose that I consider mercy? Why?"

"Because those who rule by terror and practice not mercy walk a fraying rope that ultimately will give under their weight. It is to forswear the teachings of Our Lord. Forgiveness is not a weakness. It is to be God-like." Perhaps it had been my recent time with Orleton that had inspired me so, but the old ways of vengeance had not proven useful. Something had to change. Lancaster would not be the one to realize that.

I raised my face and saw in my son's furled brow and twisting scowl a mess of confusion: the affront that had wrecked his pride, the instinctive hunger for revenge, the yearning to do what was right and best, and also the hesitation that hinted at his youthful, faltering sense of confidence. He had taken the crown partly because he believed he could rule more wisely than his father before him, but now he doubted whether that was so. I trailed a finger over the cold metal plate still covering his forearm. "What better an ally than one who owes you his station, his privileges, or his life even?"

When I said those things to my son, I was not speaking solely of Lancaster, but of Mortimer, as well.

Young Edward lowered his head, his eyes transfixed on my hand. "It would please me greatly to inflict harm upon those who have threatened or endangered me, yes. Greatly. But, I understand what you have said. I do, Mother. Perhaps I haven't been generous enough to those who have already helped me. Perhaps I should make it more worthwhile to those who follow my will."

He forced his spine hard against the back of the chair to straighten himself. His gaze turned directly on Mortimer. He smiled at him—a strained, weary smile.

"I am tired, so bloody, unbelievably tired," he mumbled. Edward forced himself to his feet and staggered forward several steps before pausing to look over his shoulder. "Morning, Sir Roger. We will talk more then."

Mortimer nodded his agreement.

Then Montagu, who had appeared from seemingly nowhere, lurched forward to slip himself beneath the king's arm for support. Together, they shuffled across the great hall toward a servant, waiting to lead the king to a comfortable chamber that had been hastily prepared for him.

Bishop Orleton soon excused himself for the night. Mortimer escorted me to my chamber, where he, of course, loitered long into the night.

But we did not lie together as lovers. Instead, like conspirators invested in our own preservation, we mulled every possibility, for there were untold outcomes to consider—some foolishly optimistic, others bleak and terrifying.

"Isabella, I am curious." Mortimer sank to his haunches beside where I sat on my stool next to the fading warmth of a brazier. "I know you well enough to recognize when there is more swirling around in your head than what you give up in words. Tell me—when you go before Parliament, you mean to gain something more, don't you?"

I slid my hands down my lap and fanned my fingers over my knees. "It is time, Roger, that you were raised up."

He flicked at an ash flake that had drifted to the floor. "How so?"

"To be an earl."

"Ah, I think not. Indeed, I would balk at the offer. Too many noses would be bent if I reached to take it." He laughed lightly, and then gave it ample thought. "Earl of what?"

"Whatever you choose. But something worthy."

"Earl of Ireland, maybe? Or is that too much? Too boastful? Too much like being a king . . . Although, I've always fancied the place, heathens aside." He took the short knife from the belt at his hip and poked between the iron slits of the brazier at the lump of peat.

I humored him. "Grandiose—and too far from me."

"The Welsh Marches?"

"Hmmm, fitting." I tugged loose the pins holding back my hair, setting them in a tidy pile beside my stool. Then I separated the strands of my hair and wound it in a twisting rope of gold to loop over my shoulder. "There was a time when you did not shy from power, when you stood in the fore and seized it confidently. Why do you now hide from claiming it, even though you wield it with such skill?"

"I'm older . . . and wiser, I hope. Less arrogant than I was in my youth." He pulled the knife from the brazier and raised a brow at me. "Besides, before, I had not been declared a traitor . . . and I had not yet bedded the queen. Envy is an unforgiving demon, my love, that will tear you limb from limb."

A morbid chill gripped me. I drew my hands inside my draping sleeves to warm myself, but it did little good.

What some perceived as our chokehold on power—our interest in guiding a young, impressionable and inexperienced king, no more—was a threat to them. One in particular: Lancaster. If we faltered and fell, he would leap upon us. And when he was done there would be nothing left of us but the lurid tales of the devious queen and her avaricious lover who scraped the kingdom's coffers bare and then begged for more.

MORTIMER, ORLETON AND I went to Salisbury, where all the prelates and barons had gathered—all but Henry of Lancaster and those known to support him of late.

The townsfolk jeered when Mortimer rode into the town with an armed force. For some time now he had kept his personal Welsh guards close at hand daylong, when such assemblages of arms had been forbidden to others; but it was the king who allowed him that protection because of Lancaster's threats.

In Parliament, Mortimer juggled the dangerous accusations launched at him deftly—like a hare evading a pack of lagging hounds in a long, futile chase—particularly in regards to insinuations that he and I had forcibly overridden the rest of the king's advisory council. Mortimer argued, with overwhelming evidence, that Lancaster had absented himself from those council meetings and therefore voluntarily relinquished his influence. Gradually, Mortimer was able to turn the blame back onto Lancaster and away from himself.

The murder of Edward of Caernarvon was never mentioned, for no proof had been brought forth and no one else there would risk joining Lancaster in his blundering endeavor.

Day by day, my tensions eased, not so much because my fears did not come to pass, but because Mortimer carried himself with such tremendous dignity and courage that my apprehensions were replaced by admiration for the most scrutinized man in the kingdom—a man whom I loved beyond possibility, however privately.

As it became clear that Lancaster had retreated elsewhere for the time being, Young Edward left his beloved Philippa long enough to come to Parliament and bestow three earldoms: one upon his beloved younger brother John, who became the Earl of Cornwall; one upon his good friend James Butler, now Earl of Ormond; and lastly . . . upon Sir Roger Mortimer, who became the first ever Earl of March.

Nothing could have provoked Lancaster more severely.

What we had tried so hard to avert was now inevitable. Peace, sometimes, was not to be had without there first being a fight to reveal the weaker opponent. So it must be.

17

Isabella :

Marlborough — November, 1328

WITH LANCASTER NOW FIRMLY entrenched at Winchester, Mortimer and I left Salisbury to join Edward, who had returned to Marlborough to be with Philippa. We took the more circuitous road to the northwest, to swing further away from Winchester, should Lancaster bolt from there. Then, we would lodge overnight at my castle in Devizes before heading eastward to Marlborough.

Meanwhile, a warning was sent to Lancaster that he would be charged with treason if he did not stand down.

The single high tower of Devizes peeked above the barely leafed trees lining the road. Leaden clouds slogged above a dying landscape. The fields had already been scythed and the grain gathered and stored to be milled, leaving dun-colored bristles over a nut-brown earth.

"I don't want to see my son go to war, Roger," I said.

"Nor do I." Mortimer kneaded at his neck with one hand, his

reins held slack in the other. "I'll lead the army in the king's name—and he can stay safe from harm. He'll live to rule another fifty years and have ten sons who will fight for him."

"He is too young, Roger. Too young to fight." I took a hard jounce in my saddle as my horse leapt a muddy rut dissecting the road.

"And I . . . am too old." Mortimer gave me a sideways look, questioning what I had not said.

"I don't want you to fight Lancaster, either."

We rode silently for a long time beneath darkening skies. The chill breeze that had greeted us that morning was giving over to brutally frigid gusts, as the clouds drove down hard from the north.

Behind us trailed a formidable retinue of men-at-arms, the ranks of which would swell considerably when we joined with the king's contingent. I had never wanted to believe it would come to this, but there had been a time when I thought no further than ridding the kingdom, and myself, of Hugh Despenser. Now, I could not help but look years ahead at the consequences of every single decision I might make.

"The news from London is encouraging," I said, grasping at hope.

"But from elsewhere?" Mortimer countered, returning me to bitter reality. "Edmund of Kent, I tell you, may be an even greater problem to us than Lancaster."

"How so?"

"Lancaster is Lancaster," Mortimer remarked plainly. "But Kent . . . sometimes he is the doting uncle, sometimes the disgruntled brother of the former king, still clinging to a grudge."

"But a grudge toward Despenser, was it not?"

"Despenser then. Us now. He was snubbed before and assumes the same of us. No matter that he is not worthy of responsibility."

"Your grandson—what did they name him?" Mortimer's first

grandchild had just been born to his eldest son Edmund and his wife Elizabeth. Mortimer had shared very little about the news. I had expected a small burst of jubilation from him at the tiding, but instead he had been dour about it.

"Roger," he said with a scoff.

"A good name. You should feel honored."

"Honored?" A glint of pain flashed behind his eyes. "Edmund named the babe after his brother, not me. I am neither vain nor delusional enough to think he would honor me thus. He gave the child the name 'Roger' to gain my attention, if anything. Edmund is my oldest, more intelligent than his siblings, but a laggard and too docile for his own best interests. Not that he expects things to be given to him. He simply does not care. He learned how to use a sword out of duty." He scowled. "But that is ever a father's disappointment—that the firstborn is not always the most promising—and a harsh reality of fatherhood, I suppose. I shall hope for more from my grandson, should I live long enough to see him grown."

Fists clenched, he fell silent for awhile. Finally, he rolled his head back, his eyes fixed on the sky above him, and muttered, "Forgive my rambling."

"You speak honestly," I told him.

"And you? You are pleased with your children?"

"Yes, I am, but . . . oh, I do not know how to put this—" It was indeed a complicated matter. Young Edward was like my brother Charles in many ways, only Charles never showed flashes of anger or moodiness like my son did. I only prayed he would not become as cold and ruthless as his Plantagenet grandfather, Longshanks. If he could not comprehend the power of forgiveness, England's future would be a horribly bloody one. Robert the Bruce had understood it and because of that he had been able to unite warring chieftains against a common enemy, England, to rise above the dust and blood triumphant at Bannockburn. "Edward—he both pleases and frightens me."

"Frightens? How?"

Far to the northwest, a high, flat-topped hill broke above the gently rolling horizon. It was called Silbury Hill—named after the king, Sil, who was interred somewhere far inside its depths of chalky earth many hundreds of years ago. Such places recalled the ancient peoples of Britain, before the Romans came. They had left their marks in many places: the cairns erected from boulders so enormous that only a giant could have moved them; the bulging mounds of earth like Silbury where the bones of many corpses lay; the mystical stone circle capturing the light of the rising and setting sun on the Salisbury Plain; the great white horse of chalk on the hillside not far to the north of here, who some said was cut there to honor the horse-goddess of the ancients—but those people had followed the old ways and did not know of Our Savior Jesus Christ. They had been pagans, ignorant. Bishop Orleton once told me they had perished because of their refusal to accept the Christian ways. More likely, however, was that they had what others coveted—land—and they had been annihilated under the pretenses of a false religion. Their crude weapons had been ineffectual against the mighty fist of Rome.

"Isabella?" Mortimer sought to regain my attention. "About Edward . . . you were saying?"

"That he can sense things. Things that are not said. And . . . he is guarded, as if he does not always trust those around him. I am not always sure of his true thoughts."

But then, I believe that of you, too, my love.

Mortimer shrugged. "He is merely cautious. A wise thing to be, sometimes, especially for a king. You, my dear queen, tend to believe precisely what people tell you. You trust too easily."

And you, my gentle Mortimer, believe me to be the naïve one? Our love, sadly, is built on lies. For as much as I love you, depend on you and have achieved with you, I shall forever question the meaning and motive behind your words.

Yet even as we are . . . I would not give you up. Not for anything.

I felt the touch of ice on my wrist between my sleeve and the fur cuff of my glove. A snowflake had alighted there, sparkling white in the fractured, gray light of a fading November day.

I looked at Mortimer until he met my gaze. "If I am easily gulled," I said, "it is only because I believe there is some good in everyone. You call it a weakness. I say it is a gift."

"I say I do not like the way you look at me when you say that." He winked in jest. Then he spurred his horse into a canter and rode on ahead, toward the gatehouse of Devizes as it came into view.

OUR STAY AT DEVIZES was hurried. I could count on the fingers of my two hands the total number of times I had stayed there since first coming to England. When Hugh Despenser had been on the rise, I had given up both Devizes and Marlborough to him, falsely believing that such a gesture would engender his appreciation and loyalty. But I had been utterly foolish then. I was no more. I would give up nothing, unless willingly.

Eastward we tramped, over roads clogged with mud from melted snow, to arrive at Marlborough late the next afternoon. Philippa's influence there was immediately apparent as we walked through the great hall with its sturdy furniture from the Lowlands, each piece functional enough to serve for years to come, yet splendidly crafted to please the eye. On the walls hung the brightly dyed Flemish tapestries, all with a story to tell.

We found Edward and Philippa in a topmost tower room. In the room's center was a large round table surrounded by a dozen chairs and one particularly high-backed one. There sat Edward, elbows on the table, buried behind a wall of books with Philippa at his right side. She reached out and turned a page for him.

"Ah, come, look." Edward curled his fingers at us.

Mortimer stooped to avoid banging his forehead on the low lintel. The ceiling was barely tall enough for a grown man to stand. Every wall was stacked with burgeoning shelves of books. The room smelled of musty parchment, burnt wicks and beeswax. I turned in a circle, trying to estimate the number of books there. Indeed, I had not seen such an extensive collection anywhere, not even in a monastery, nor had I even known of this one.

Edward blinked several times as Mortimer shut the door behind us. "Bishop Orleton is not with you?"

"He has returned to Hereford temporarily," I said. "But if you wish him to —"

"No mind. Come, come look at this." He stooped over the pages, squinting as he studied them with boyish fascination. "Philippa heard there were monks in Ireland skilled in illumination and had several of them brought over to work at the scriptorium at Canterbury. She commissioned this. Have you ever seen such detail?"

"A book of prayers," Philippa announced with a cherubic smile.

I moved around the table to stand behind Edward. The work was indeed beautiful, but decidedly pagan in its embellishments, adorned with the scrolling curves similar to the jewelry worn by the warring Scots and skulking Welsh hill people. Knotted designs bordered every page, the beginning letters of each prayer were painted in bright colors and traced in gold, and everywhere were mythical creatures, some with curled and reaching claws, some fanged, others winged, embracing, hiding behind or leaping from the text, each incredible in their grotesqueness.

"There is good news from London," I beamed. "Hamo de Chigwell has been replaced."

He ignored my announcement for a while, then finally nudged the book away and peered up at me. "By whom? Bethune again?"

206

"John de Grantham. The Londoners elected him only a few days before Parliament adjourned. I'm quite certain Lancaster knows of it by now, as well." I wholly expected to see Young Edward's face alight with glee, as the news would be a sharp blow to the earl, but Edward remained sober, guarded.

"Three mayors in less than six months' time . . ." His words trailed away, as if distracted by some other, more troubling thought that he had not yet grasped fully.

"And Lancaster?" Philippa asked in anticipation. "Where is he?"

Mortimer and I exchanged a glance, each of us pondering who would shatter the superficial peace into which Edward had enclosed himself in this room full of parchment and leather. I lowered my eyes, yielding to Mortimer.

Mortimer accepted the task. "In Winchester, still. He has been warned to lay down his arms and submit to you."

"And?" Edward scratched at his temple.

"So far, he has not."

The king did not respond. He pulled the book closer again and hunched over it, one finger following intertwining threads of red and gold within the letter 'E'.

"Edward," I said, my voice shaky, "your uncles, Kent and Norfolk, they have not denounced their ties to Lancaster. Grantham says that . . . that Kent has told something to Lancaster in confidence—and that is why the earl will not remove himself from Winchester."

Without looking away from the book, Edward's lip curled ever so churlishly. "What did he say to him, Mother?"

There was more behind his words, but I deigned to leave it alone. Perhaps it was nothing more than confusion. Rumors grew in life the more often and more loudly they were repeated.

"I don't know," I said, trying to think quickly of how to divert the subject. If Edward clung to even the least suspicion about Mortimer or myself, our cause was thwarted. "He is still trying to incite London to rise against you. Still calling on your uncles to join him in arms."

Thomas of Norfolk I knew less well, for he had not often been at court in Edward of Caernarvon's day. As for Edmund of Kent, while I was indebted to him, there was always a tickle in my belly, an intuitive mistrust of him. Besides that, I had no good reason to doubt him. Because of that uncertainty, I had questioned him in France when he vowed to join us—even looked for signs that he might betray us after we landed near Walton. Edmund of Kent was a fickle opportunist, lured by intrigue and spurred by gossip—and that was the most dangerous sort to have around, for it made him unpredictable.

Edward blinked. He leaned back, threw his long legs up on the table and drummed his fingers on his knees. "We go to Winchester. With every available man riding fully armed behind us. Lancaster will bow before me and make amends . . . or he will meet his end."

Abruptly, Philippa dashed herself at his knees and buried her face in his lap. "Edward, please. Your mother is right about Lancaster. If you go, it means war."

He smoothed the errant wisps of her pale hair and touched a fingertip to her quivering lip. "Come with me, my sweet, and you can watch from a distance and see what a king's army can do. It is said my grandfather took his second wife, Queen Marguerite, on his Scottish campaigns with him so he could return to her every night. Even our good Sir Roger here took his beloved wife Joan abroad while he battled Irish pagans. Is that not so, Sir Roger? Did she ever suffer a scratch?"

Mortimer crossed his arms. "Never. But she stayed miles from any fight. Sometimes I did not see her for days."

Edward slammed the illuminated book shut and gave Mortimer an accusing look. "Help me, but I cannot recall the last time you ever left the company of my dear mother. Such loyalty is hard to come by." He flashed a sardonic smile. "There shall be no more delays in dealing with the Earl of Lancaster. We set out for Winchester in the morning. My sweet?" He traced a fingertip around the rim of Philippa's ear. She lifted her face to show him eyes that were misty with foreboding.

Philippa, above anyone, could have kept the king from going, but this time he was not swayed, nor did she persist. Instead, she bit at her lip and bobbed her head. Edward drew her up and leaned forward to give her a kiss.

"My lord," Mortimer said, "as one of your advisors, I caution you not to go."

Young Edward paused with his mouth inches from Philippa's face. "And as your king, I inform you that I *am* going. But thank you, kindly, for your concern." He kissed his wife.

"If you are taken," she protested, "or killed, then —"

Edward took Philippa by the hand and helped her up as he stood. "It is your duty, Sir Roger, to make sure that does not happen." Without further argument, his arm about his wife's shoulder, they left the room.

Before Mortimer could speak his mind, I did. "Why does he defy us?"

"Perhaps because he is a boy coming into manhood—as you once reminded me. And he will buck and rear until he breaks the tether that binds him." Mortimer came to me and swirled his fingertips along the curve from my shoulders to my neck. "Isabella, you cannot hide him behind your skirts forever. You have to let him be the king he was meant to be."

"But —"

"But . . . he is right." He cradled my face between his hands and drew me irresistibly closer. "He must do this, and you must let him. He is not yet ready to command, but he must make an appearance. He will grow more confident. He will see and he will learn—from me. Remember, it is not your son that we seek to hold sway over, but his enemies. Edward shall be our banner. I shall be his sword and shield. I will do whatever I can to protect him, as I have you. I swear it."

I buried my face against the warmth of his chest. "But I fear it may come to battle—many battles. That the next will not be the last."

"There will always be war. But Lancaster—he does not have the heart for more than one. Actually, I don't even think he has one good fight in him. Douglas and Randolph have harassed Lancashire for years and never once has the earl met up with them. He simply cries to London for help. I would not doubt that, like his blustering brother Thomas before him, he is conspiring with Scots even as we speak."

He wrapped his arms tight about me, as if he would never let go.

There are times when reassuring words and heartfelt embraces are not enough, though. I did not sleep at all that night. The next morning, Young Edward rode eagerly at the head of his army, with no intention of hiding from Lancaster. He was resplendent in his new suit of German armor—every plate polished to catch the sun's rays. His puissant warhorse sported its own mail and a chaufron of polished metal from muzzle to ears. Behind him fluttered scores of banners, flowing and rippling like a river of color across the countryside.

Next to the king rode Roger Mortimer. Even though Mortimer had counseled me to allow my son his freedom, he was constantly at the king's side, guiding him by understated suggestions or provoking a decision from him through thoughtful questioning, and only letting others have their say when it posed no threat to his judgment. It was subtly done, but it did not go unnoticed—by me or by others.

We arrived at Winchester just as the last of Lancaster's forces were fleeing the city. He would not submit, nor would he fight. For reasons not yet known, the earl was buying time.

210

Edward burned to pursue him. Philippa begged him not to and thus he yielded—no more to my matronly advice, but to the honeyed wishes of his genteel wife.

I knew in my head that Mortimer was right, that I could no longer keep my son from youth's rash follies. But it is always in a mother's heart, no matter how old or how high her child, to watch over and protect him.

A mother, however, is a woman also.

I love my son. I love Roger Mortimer, as well. If God might grant me one kindness in this cruel irony of a life that I live, it should be that I shall never have to choose between the two of them.

18

Isabella:

Kenilworth – January, 1329

A PAIR OF BUZZARDS cut across a sunless January sky on jagged wings. Close on their tail feathers, diving blackbirds cried out, their caws piercing the fragile air.

Young Edward stood apart from his army on the causeway before the gates of Kenilworth. Behind him, his caparisoned dark gray pricked its ears forward and snorted steam from flared nostrils. It pawed at the ground, feathered fetlocks swishing with each stroke of its hoof. Every time Edward boldly stepped closer to the impassable iron portcullis, the horse, curious and vigilant, followed him, even though he had dropped its reins long ago when he dismounted.

"Open, I command!" Edward's words boomed out far and high, carrying to the clouds above, which were moored in place like over-laden ships at harbor. There was no wind to push the swollen clouds along, no downy snow descending from their shapelessness to relieve them of their burden. He wrung the gauntlets from his hands and threw them onto the ground.

With every step he took, a cold river of sweat surged down my breastbone. My heart altogether stopped when I saw my son wrench the helmet from his head and toss it carelessly aside. High on the face of the nearest tower, an arrow jabbed through a slit. Edward did not hear my stifled cry of terror, so far away.

He did, however, see the face of the archer who had taken aim at him. "Let loose, base coward! Am I so far or so fast that you cannot hit me?" He threw his arms wide and waited, but nothing happened.

No arrows flew to rip through his breast. The gate did not rise. No figure appeared along the wall or from a tower window to parley with the newly fledged king. Lancaster had been here and left not long ago . . . and apparently with firm orders to refuse entrance to King Edward.

As impatient as he was foolhardy, Edward gave up, turned on his heel and strode back along the causeway, plucking up his gauntlets as he went, cramming them into his helmet and snatching at the loose reins of his mount. He arrived fuming and red-faced at the place that Mortimer and I had been waiting—well beyond arrow range—where the causeway leading away from the gatehouse at the castle's entrance became road. Sir William Montagu went dutifully to his side, taking the helmet from Edward and tucking it under his own arm.

Beneath my long flowing surcoat of blue and gold, I was encased in a suit of mail that hung so heavily from my shoulders that my neck and back burned with cramps. Upon my head I wore a mail coif with a thin twining crown of filigreed gold. The armor had been a gift from Charles before I left France for England. Although usually more lavish in his tastes, he could be practical as well.

Agitated, Edward ground the toe of his boot into the frozen earth and pounded at his thighs. He was obviously aware that all eyes were on him, waiting for him to speak. Abruptly, a change swept over his countenance. There was excitement in his eyes, but a crackle of fear in his voice. "An assault?"

Mortimer shook his head. "The causeway is too narrow. The width at the front of your column would be too few. The garrison's archers could pick them off one by one. No, an outright attack would be bold, but too costly and short lived."

Stealing a look at the ring of water encircling Kenilworth, Edward thumped the heel of his hand on his sword's hilt. "The lake?"

Montagu spoke bluntly, "Too deep to wade. Too wide to cross."

"Other options?" The king crossed his arms, looking from Mortimer, to Montagu and back to Mortimer. "A siege?"

"To what end, my lord?" Mortimer said. "If it's the castle you want, yes, you could besiege it and eventually starve it into submission, but that could take months. If it's Lancaster you want—I assure you, he's not within. You would be wasting your time and resources."

"Still, I do not like being snubbed like this. No fortress is allowed to deny me entrance. None!" Almost imperceptibly, Edward shot a sideways glance at Montagu. "Very well, then. We forget about Kenilworth, for now. In time, I shall exact payment for this offense. Sir Roger—you are to go to Leicester and take it, in my name."

"And if I am met in the same fashion as this?"

"Burn his lands—from here to there, in as wide a path as you please. If Lancaster will not meet us face to face, we will wreck everything he owns or lays claim to. That will bring him to his knees more quickly than laying siege, wouldn't you say?"

I knew the face and form that I now looked upon as my oldest son's—the very one who had balked at becoming king so long as his incompetent father still breathed. But this person before me—it was not him. The voice that emanated from my son's mouth . . . I did not

214

know it. Where was the helpless, little boy who I had cradled in my arms and sung to when he cried out in the night? Where was the young, pure-hearted man who not a year ago had blushed at the kiss of his new bride? Or only months ago had heeded to my advice and then recited it nearly word for word to his kinsman and greatest enemy? No, this was not him. Not him, but some imposter. Or the ghost of his heartless grandfather, Longshanks.

"Edward . . ." I lowered myself from my saddle as quickly and yet as cautiously as I could, trying not to topple sideways with the pitch of my added weight as I did so. "You cannot put fire to England. Not any of it. Not even a cattle byre. If you do, it is only the beginning of an endless desecration. Lancaster will retaliate. The kingdom will be toppled into despair, at your own hands, simply to have your revenge on him."

"*I* will not burn anything, Mother." He suppressed a wicked grin like a little boy wending his way out of a lie by a literal twist of words. "Sir Roger is experienced in that method of warring. Why, he burned out old women and babes from their homes in Ireland, did he not? I hear he was bloody good at it."

I rushed forward and grabbed him by the forearm. "I will take this to the regency council. They will overrule you."

One of his golden eyebrows dipped low. "Will you? Good then, I'll do as they say. Ah, but yes . . . they aren't here, are they? That will take time and by then . . . well, the deed will be done. And Lancaster, who was supposed to be one of the councilors appointed to guide me, he will no longer be able to run from rabbit hole to rabbit hole." He pried my fingers loose and stepped away from me, making it clear that he was his own man now, not the solicitous prince who had tractably stood at my side while in France, defying the angry demands of his father. "Oh, yes—Sir Roger, I don't know if it was your usual practice to burn *everything* in front of you, but spare the churches, abbeys and such, will you? I don't want to begin my kingship with a reputation for careless sacrilege."

Smug, he took back the reins of his steed from Montagu and rode off with his friend, meandering his way through the ranks as if he had not a care in the world.

I stood there flabbergasted, unable to call after him, confused and confounded. "Where is he going?" I finally said. Of all the possibilities I had envisioned for this dreaded day, Edward challenging our authority and flippantly ordering Mortimer about, and then leaving altogether, had not been among any of them.

"How am I to know?" Mortimer said tersely, the line of his lips tightening in perturbation. He stared hard at the high walls of Kenilworth, as if he could topple the stones from crenel to ground with only a black look.

"I'll summon the council."

"It will do you no good, this late. No, I will do as he says. Retaliate against Lancaster. Finish with the bastard. The king is challenging me, nothing more. And I accept, willingly."

Nothing more to say, Mortimer rode away. I had lost this argument. And I was left alone with the great, dark, glassy lake of Kenilworth at my back reflecting a gray sky—and before me the king's men-at-arms flexing their fingers on spear poles, archers gripping their longbows, and knights with shields strapped tight and ready.

Leicester — January, 1329

LIKE A STACK OF dry hay, the city of Leicester burned. A pall of black smoke obscured the sky all the way to Rockingham. Mortimer had done his work quickly and completely. His Welshmen ravaged, taking grain and livestock, axing fences and woods, draining ponds and torching every timber of every barn, building and hovel of those beholden to their lord, Henry of Lancaster.

Predictably, Lancaster reciprocated with an oath of war.

The day that Edward and I rode through the still smoldering ruins of the town of Leicester, wet cloths pressed to our mouths to keep the smoke from scouring our throats, its people emerged seemingly out of nowhere to hold out their soot-smeared hands and beg King Edward's mercy. I had thought they would curse his name and run for fear of their lives, or even join the earl in arms against the king, but none did. Edward, taken aback by their sorrowful pleas, abandoned his vengeful madness and took pity on them.

Leicester Castle swung open its gates to us without resistance and together we rode under the raised portcullis. That very day letters arrived from both Edmund of Kent and Thomas of Norfolk, forswearing any allegiance to the traitorous Henry, Earl of Leicester and Lancaster, and beseeching mercy from the king. The very act I feared might ignite public displeasure with Mortimer had in fact turned the tide of rebellion in King Edward's favor. But in its wake came another fear for me—that Edward, his confidence augmented, would turn irretrievably from my influence and that he would test and abuse Mortimer's loyalty even more.

I felt myself confined to a crevasse, too narrow before or behind me to escape, no way out, while two enormous boulders toppled from opposite summits and rolled on a collision course toward me.

Bedford — January, 1329

NOT LONG AFTERWARD, EDWARD and I left Leicester and rode to join Mortimer in Northampton. Philippa had stayed safely behind, but I was not about to remove myself from this crisis. We had no sooner arrived than we were riding south again—this time through the frozen night. At Edward's insistence—or perhaps it was Mortimer who urged it—we hastened southward, unimpeded by mud or rain or snow, pressing our soldiers at double pace long into the night. Our way lit by a crescent moon, we finally stumbled to a halt between two woods within striking distance of Bedford, where Lancaster was known to be.

Thankful for the respite, however brief, and no matter what daybreak might bring, the soldiers collapsed in their lines and bedded down on their cloaks beneath an open sky. They quickly drifted off to sleep, their weapons hugged close to their bodies in readiness. No one dared loosen a single strap of their armor—Lancaster was too close.

Edward claimed right to a small farmhouse at the edge of the woods, ejecting its confused residents to a shed, which they were forced to share with pregnant cows. When the scouting party returned, he called a council of war immediately.

"Lancaster is still encamped at Bedford," Arnaud de Mone reported, standing before us.

The night sky was aglitter with pinpricks of silver starlight. White hoarfrost shimmered on every blade of grass and tree branch. My breath hung suspended in a pillar of ice. I tried to breathe through my nose, but felt the tickling of a winter cold. With numb fingers, I tugged the edge of my cloak across my lower face and drew air in through my mouth. A lump of pain at the back of my throat the size of a small egg made swallowing difficult. The inside of my mouth was as dry as ground bones.

"How far?" Young Edward asked.

"Mere miles," Arnaud said. "Five maybe, close to six. It's hard to gage at night, especially when riding swiftly."

Mortimer gripped the hilt of his sword. "We can be upon him well before dawn if we leave now."

"Attack at night?" I said, the corners of my mouth splitting and bleeding as I did so. It was unusual to pursue battle in the winter at all, let alone in the dead of night, I knew that much. "Edward, I beg you, do not hasten to your death. Lancaster and his soldiers are rested. Yours are not. We have not —"

"Lancaster and his soldiers are asleep," Mortimer interrupted with a sharp edge to his voice. "If we hesitate, opportunity flies from our fingers."

I had thought Mortimer more prudent, but it was what I heard next that surprised me most.

"We go then. At once," Edward said.

I had begun to suspect that Edward was perhaps toying with Mortimer—letting him believe he both needed and trusted in him, simply to keep him close. And Mortimer, thriving on the compliment, would go with the opportunity for as long as he could, just as he once had with Edward of Caernarvon before he turned against him. If there was any chance that Edward's outward trust of Mortimer was only a ruse, I had to know so I could keep him from destroying Mortimer in the end.

Power and the thirst for it—it changes people, especially those bred and born to lead. It makes them forget who they once were. I understood this. I saw it happening before me, in both of them, and even so I could not stop it.

IT WAS TOO EASY. Lancaster had snapped and crumpled like a splintery piece of dry-rotted lumber. The moment the earl got word that Mortimer and the king were approaching in the night with a full and ready army, he sent a messenger bearing the promise of a full submission if the king would return leniency. Edward sent back word that he would do so, but Lancaster was to leave his retainers behind and come with no more than a dozen attendees.

Lancaster must have believed he had run out of options, for when we came upon him in a broad open field, a perfect site for a battle, he had done as requested. I recognized with him Simon Meopham, the Archbishop of Canterbury, and Lord Thomas Wake.

Daylight was but a hint in the east as Lancaster stumbled forward, alone, fell upon his stiff, old knees and bowed his thinning head of hair.

"I yield to you, my lord king."

Edward waited a moment before replying. "Hardly good enough, Cousin. What more have you to say? Do you still stand by your accusations?"

Anything less than a confession of guilt, Lancaster must have known, was to lay his head on the block and bare his neck for a sharpened blade. He trembled slightly, as if afflicted with palsy. "I retract them all, my lord king. They were said in anger . . . and stupidity. I had taken offense over small matters. I should have spoken my mind sooner."

"Speak now. What small matters, then, are you referring to?"

"It is . . . unimportant. Your uncles, Kent and Norfolk, their jealousies fed my discontent. I should not have listened. I should have come to you and told you *everything*." He lifted his head, opening his eyes wide and then squinting strangely into the half-light of pre-dawn. The folds beneath his eyes drooped heavily from years and lack of sleep. Every crevice in his countenance was cut more deeply than the last time I had seen him. He looked pale, ill with worry, and by the tremor in his voice sounded completely broken in spirit.

But Mortimer was not so easily moved to pity, nor was he convinced of Lancaster's contrition. "What if Kent and Norfolk have a different story to tell?"

Lancaster turned his head, not to look, but to listen more closely. "Your pardon? I do not understand what you're —"

"What if they say," Mortimer cut him off, raising his voice and spacing each word as if he were talking to a near-deaf invalid, "that it was *you* who incited them to rebellion?"

Lancaster's upper lip lifted in a snarl. "I would expect as much of them, given the circumstances, my lord . . . *Earl of March*, is it?"

There was no mistaking the mockery in his tone. Mortimer's arms and shoulders drew up in tension. I thought he would spring from his saddle, whip loose his sword and be done with Lancaster, but it was Edward who spared us from that ugly scene.

"You were not there, Cousin Henry," Edward said, erect and noble in his crowned helmet and fur-trimmed cloak, "when I honored him thus for his loyalty to me. You have not come to council meetings of late. But as you said, it was your own doing."

"It was," Lancaster grumbled.

Mortimer twitched and drew breath to lash back, but again Edward interceded.

"In the end, you lost far more than you gained, wouldn't you say?"

Lancaster forced a dull nod.

The king was satisfied. There would be no battle at Bedford, not today. Roger Mortimer had served his purpose. Kent and Norfolk had vowed their allegiance. Lancaster was not only subjugated, but he had been properly cowed to make an obedient vassal of him.

The Earl of Lancaster was losing his sight. Perhaps it was not so much the ravaging of his lands at Mortimer's hands and loss of his royal allies that had forced him to his knees before the king, but his disease. Thanks in part to Archbishop Meopham, who had urged him there, his life was spared and he kept his freedom. But his personal losses were to be heavy. The fine levied upon him hurled him into abject poverty. He was formally removed from the regency council and stripped of his high offices.

It should have been that the worst of our fears was blotted out—squelched like a smoking fire in a steady rain. But we do not always see the danger that lies so close, straight ahead.

19

Isabella:

Langley – February, 1329

P HILIP OF VALOIS—I refused to call him King of France—
demanded homage of Young Edward.

Envoys from France had arrived without forewarning at
Westminster, where the king was in residence. We had known that
eventually Philip would assert himself, only not as soon as this. Along
with the king, Mortimer withdrew to an urgent meeting of the
regency council, debating it well into the night. Without sleep, he left
Westminster before dawn and rode to Langley to seek my input.

A cold fog hugged the forest about Langley, reaching its white,
shifting fingers between the leafless trees and resisting the light of a
rising sun. Mortimer and I were walking along a wooded path, when
he told me of it. His voice cracked with fatigue. "The king refuses to
go. I warned him that we cannot afford war."

Is war ever well-timed? Is it the only way of settling matters that men know?

Mortimer shook his fist in frustration. "Does he seek to repeat his father's obstinate stupidity?"

"My son is not obstinate, Roger. He is determined . . . and patient enough to wait for whatever it is he wants to come to him in its own time."

"Call it want you want. This is not a waiting game. Philip *will* take action."

Frost sparkled like crushed glass on every blade and twig as morning mist drifted thick on the path before us. I could not see more than a few feet ahead—perfect cover to hide from those whom we did not wish to see us, but also a danger in treading so far from the castle alone in it. Even the tender crack of twigs beneath my own feet jolted my heart.

"Philip is not worthy to sit upon the same throne as Charles," I complained bitterly. "I should have pressed my brother to name an heir. But I believed it had to be his thinking, not mine. Why did they pick such an arrogant fop as Philip of Valois over Edward? He's naught but a faithless pretender. A sham. An idiot with the brains of a cart ox."

"Insult him if it makes you feel better, Isabella. But it changes nothing." Mortimer swung before me to block my path and seized my fur-gloved hands in his. "Besides, did you think, for even a breath, that the nobles of France would *not* want one of their own blood, born on their own soil, to rule? I refuse to believe you are *that* naïve, my love."

"I am not naïve. Nor am I disillusioned. I have studied the laws of inheritance. I know where the flaws are and the frail, disjointed reasoning they used to get around them. I also know that just arguments can be made on Edward's behalf—ones that a knowledge-able court would uphold. He is French—half so, at least. I am his mother—sister to the last three Kings of France and the daughter of a king. My son stood next in line. No other. Certainly not Philip of

Valois. But they rushed it, out of fear and prejudice, and would not even let their own courts decide the matter, as should have been done."

"It would have been a wasteful formality. You know that. They are not about to let France become a possession of England. Even so, had Edward been chosen to rule in France, what would he have done—divide himself in two?"

"He could have entrusted us, Roger. We would have taken care of things for him here."

"As we have already. And then there would have been those who would have loved us even less for it than they do now. It would have been too much, Isabella. For him . . . and for us."

I shook his hands loose and shouldered my way past him on the narrow path as branches scraped at my face and arms. My foot sank deep in a frozen pool of muck. I pulled it loose and scraped the bottom of my shoe clean on the weathered stump of a fallen tree. "It is his birthright to rule—both here and in France."

He retrieved my hand abruptly. "Yes, Isabella. But some-times . . . sometimes we have to accept that what we have is enough. France *should* have been yours, Isabeau. But the matter is dead. Do not use your son for your own vengeance."

I spun around so hard I nearly lost my balance. "Roger, you don't understand. This is not about me. It's Edward's ambition of which I speak. He tried to earn Charles' favor at every turn when we were in France, all with the same hopes that I had. And all for nothing in the end. It is not that I feel slighted for myself or my son, but that I know my son. Had Jeanne given birth to a boy, then Edward would have ceded humbly, even to an infant—but one right-ly born into its place. Philip's claim is thin. Edward is painfully aware of that. I know he will never let what he believes is his to be so easily taken from him." I felt the cold kiss of a distant sun upon my face as it broke above the mists. "You have seen it in him—at Stanhope

Park, at Kenilworth. Edward will fight. There will be war . . . one day."

"That is inevitable."

"Is it?" The mud had soaked through the loose leather sole of my shoe, squelching cold against my foot, but I turned and strode on, eager to get back to a warm fire and hungry, the gnawing in my belly reminding me I had not yet eaten that day. "He will not go to France, Roger. Tell them that."

"He will have to, or else Philip will seize —"

"I know"—I wheeled around to face him—"what will happen. I know the consequences!"

"Then if what you say about the king is true, this war will be long and hard. It will be severe. Bloody. Costing lives by the thousands. Tens of thousands, maybe. The lesson should have been learned. He must pay homage so that —"

"No! Hear me on this. I do not trust Philip of Valois, not in the same way I trusted Charles. I would fear for my son, for his life, every moment, if he were to go to France."

"Whether or not you believe in Philip's right to rule, he is not stupid enough to make such a move."

"Sometimes, Roger, I do not speak as a queen, but as a mother. I don't want any harm to come to my son."

I thought he would go on arguing, but his stance had softened. He gave me his arm. "I will tell the council you are reluctant. I'll tell them why. But they will have to give an answer to the French envoys and they will not buy a bluff so many times as his father gave. He will have to go, eventually."

We walked along the narrow path as one. "I know . . . but . . ."

I knew. Edward would have to go to France, in time. It must be done.

Wigmore — September, 1329

YOUNG EDWARD DELAYED MAGNIFICENTLY, carefully tidying his words in furls of diplomatic courtesy as three months slid by before he finally boarded ship and sailed for France, accompanied, much to my displeasure, by his uncles Norfolk and Kent. Both were in a perpetual state of groveling toward the king since disassociating themselves from Lancaster.

William Montagu, who had been made a Knight Banneret for his service to the king, was told never to let him out of his sight, on pain of death, although even saying it was superfluous. Montagu would have tossed himself into the fires of hell to spare Edward any mortal danger.

On the 6th day of June, resplendent in his yellow leopards of England flowing from the scarlet robe about his shoulders and the jeweled crown balanced perfectly on his fair head, King Edward III paid homage to Philip of Valois. They said that Philip scowled in disdain and afterwards referred to him as a precocious cockscomb. Before two days had passed, Edward fled France. Montagu had received details that Philip was poised to take the king into custody in order to charge him with a plot of usurpation and so Montagu ushered his lord from Amiens in the deepest, stillest hour of night. The king, they said, escaped from France on a nag, dressed as a nun.

By the time Young Edward rejoined us in Canterbury, there was yet more news: Robert the Bruce, traitor to England, victor of Bannockburn and acclaimed deliverer of Scotland, was dead. His heir, the whimpering David, would become king at the fragile age of five—and my Joanna his queen.

Soon after, two more of Mortimer's daughters were wed— Beatrice to Norfolk's son Thomas and Agnes to the son of the Earl of Pembroke. Prudent matches, but they only served to further incite contempt across the land toward Mortimer's deserved good fortune.

Lands and fineries that I bestowed upon him fanned even more jealousy. I would not, however, allow such pettiness to trample upon my tokens of gratitude, toward Mortimer or anyone. If my enemies ever succeeded in poisoning me, or by some other bloody act ended my life, then I would make certain that Mortimer and his heirs were properly endowed.

It was a frail thread from which we dangled, Mortimer and I. As we reveled in the ecstasy of profane pleasures, I sensed the eyes upon us becoming ever more watchful . . . and more damning day by day.

If not for Roger Mortimer, rightly Earl of March, England would have stumbled and fallen to forces from both without and within. I did not give one whit of care for those too blind with envy to see that. I kept buried the secrets of my heart, believing that if I did not admit to them, they would remain dead, just as no arrow flies from the bow that is not strung, nor music comes from the harp that is not plucked.

It was not until the tournament at Wigmore in September that the first worn threads began to fray and snap.

The pavilions stretched outward from the castle grounds and wound around the town walls, spilling out in a ramble of colors toward the woodland hunting grounds. The blast of trumpets opened the day and a herald galloped onto the tilting field with a scroll in one hand, from which he proclaimed the tournament open to all comers.

I sat in a private box in the stands, shielded from the sun by a striped awning of red and gold. Mortimer passed behind the row of empty chairs, paused at mine and leaned over me. He plucked a grape from the platter on the arm of my cushioned chair and offered it to me "Shall I be your Arthur," he whispered, a grin teasing at his lips, "or your Lancelot?"

"The latter is more fitting between us, do you not think?" I licked at the smooth flesh of the grape and then bit it in half, sucking its sweet juices dry before swallowing what was left. Roger's eyes followed my actions, knowing full well what I implied.

"Arthur was the jilted one, yes, and Lancelot—who would not argue that he was the lucky one? But I rather prefer being 'king' for once. A man can pretend, can't he?"

"Come, sit beside me." I patted the seat of the vacant chair to my right in invitation. "I will crown you 'King Arthur'. All in good-hearted play, naturally. Look over there, even Young Edward is in high spirits. He can be your Galahad, bravest of all knights of the Round Table."

He settled beside me. "Here comes Galahad now, my queen."

The king approached on a bay, wearing full armor but no helmet.

"Edward, dear,"—I beckoned him to the edge of the box—"will you take a pass or two at that upstart Sir Walter. I say his skill does not match his boasting of it. You can unseat him with a single blow—two if he's not drunk."

"With this horse, no," Edward replied with a scowl of displeasure as he slid down from his saddle. His horse was yet another gift from his father-in-law, the Count of Hainault. Evidently it was proving harder to train than he had anticipated. "No, I cannot trust him yet. He could take me to the next town faster than any steed without tiring, but he would spook at the first crash. Next time, perhaps. Or else I will turn him into a plow horse. But the foot combat, now there is where I stand to win, if I may boast this once. Will is a master of swordsmanship and as good a teacher of it, but I beat him last time handily. Gave him a good battering and the bruises and bloody lip to prove it."

I looked about—in the crowds jammed in the stands, amongst the onlookers milling curiously about higher up on the hill, in the teeming swarm of squires and knights making preparations in the closest pavilions—and nowhere did I see Sir William Montagu. "Where is he?"

"Who?" Edward asked too innocently.

Precisely then, Thomas of Norfolk, having climbed unseen and unheard to stand behind us, appeared to my right. Sweeping his arm across his waist, he bowed deeply and plopped himself down lazily in what should have been Edward's chair, however uninvited. He looked over at me, then at Mortimer, a glib smile on his crooked lips.

"My lady. My lords." Norfolk cast a swift glance down the length of the stands. "Your daughter Beatrice, Sir Roger . . . what a lively little creature. Reminds me of a sparrow—always flitting about, singing. Neither too slight, nor too plump. Pretty eyes. I am pleased for my son."

"And I for my daughter, *Lord* Thomas," Mortimer replied, but the use of Norfolk's title was meant as a reminder for others to address him likewise in the future.

A sneer flitted across Norfolk's upper lip, but he quickly pretended to yawn and covered his mouth with his hand. "I heard mention of Sir William Montagu. Did he accompany Edmund, dear nephew?"

Edward scratched at his horse's muzzle, avoiding the question. "I have no idea where Uncle Edmund disappeared to. I am disappointed not to see him here. I shall have to scold him for it later."

Norfolk scoffed. "Then it will be a good while before you can. He's in Avignon—at least that is the excuse he gave when I invited him to the wedding. He wrote me from Bristol before he left and said that Sir William was thereabout seeking passage to the south of France. I only assumed he was headed for Avignon, too . . . but, maybe I was wrong?"

"What would take Uncle Edmund to Avignon?" Edward leaned his shoulder against the low wall of the stands in repose. Slowly, he drew his sword from its scabbard and tested its weight by balancing the blade on a single finger. Very adroitly, he spun the blade upward with a turn of his thumb and caught it by the handle, blade down.

Then he slammed the point into the dusty ground between his feet. "Has he heard the call of God and gone on pilgrimage?"

Norfolk rubbed at his narrow nose. "Not any more so than Sir William, I would say."

"Since you will not let it go —" Young Edward began, glancing slyly over his shoulder at Norfolk, then back to the tournament action, which was about to commence, "I thought the pope should know that I went begrudgingly to France and bent my knee to Philip of Valois, who would have taken me prisoner had I not escaped. His 'hospitality' deserves reproach, wouldn't you say?"

"Granted," Norfolk agreed. "That was rather uncivilized of him, if indeed true."

"It is."

"By what source?"

"Does it matter? Besides, I'll not lie down and let him primp about forever with that crown on his head. It's not his." Two knights, their lances pointing up at the sky, rode across the field on their mounts, great clouds of dust billowing up around them and trailing in drifts behind. "How curious, though, that Uncle Edmund is also in Avignon." He wiped his sword clean on the corner of his royal surcoat, ironically bearing the fleur-de-lis of France, and returned it to his scabbard.

"I had heard Kent speak," Mortimer joined in, his tone purposefully bland to convey only casual interest in the topic, "of going on pilgrimage with his wife to Santiago de Compostela."

Edward smiled. "I imagine he will tell us all about his journey as soon as he returns. Chances are we will find out something about it before that, though."

Suddenly, the king's countenance brightened even more. Philippa waved to him from the adjacent side of the field to our right. "Ah, there she is—my fair queen! Perhaps she'll grant me a kiss?" Lighthearted, he rode away to collect on his lady's blessing before preparing for combat.

I glanced at Norfolk, but his expression betrayed nothing. He was an uncomplicated man. Meddlesome, perhaps, but a follower and not the opportunist his brother Kent was. Had he known more, it would have been plain.

At the trumpet's signal, the two knights spurred their horses forward on a collision course. The tall points of their lances dipped downward over the arched necks of their mounts. The rumble of hooves was lost in the rolling roar of the crowd.

They leaned hard behind their weapons, the distance closing quickly, tips bearing to the left of each knight, level and steady. But both missed their mark by a foot as the horses rumbled past without a blow being exchanged. The crowd let out a collective groan.

"I still favor Sir Walter," I said to Mortimer, leaning toward him and touching his forearm, "although I find his reputation has yet to match his prowess."

But Mortimer was staring straight forward over the heads of the crowd across the field, his eyes focused on nothing in particular, his fingers clamped over the arms of his chair possessively. I pinched the skin of his wrist. He turned his face toward me, his eyes followed, but his mind was elsewhere, preparing against troubles yet to come.

20

Isabella:

Kenilworth – Winter, 1330

W HEN I READ THE letter from Pope John, heat rose in my breast, building to an inferno with each word.

Most Devout and Beloved Queen,

> *I pray this day finds your heart overflowing with love for our Savior and reverent of his ways. I advise virtue in private matters. Yours is a delicate position . . .*

Evidently, someone had complained to the pope of my relationship with Mortimer. Did the pope before him ever chastise Edward of Caernarvon for unnatural weaknesses? No, he turned a blind eye. A woman's voice does not carry as far as a man's, it seems.

Weeks later, I was told that when Kent visited the pope in

Avignon, he told him that he knew Edward of Caernarvon to be alive. *Alive?!* Why would he say that? What proof could he possibly have? Later, Kent denied having made any such claims to the pope.

Rumors grow in malice the longer they live and yet . . . yet I have known some rumors—stories that I thought too fantastical or distorted to be real—to later prove true.

Once more, I spoke to Lord Berkeley and implored with him to break his vow of silence and reveal to me if Edward of Caernarvon had evaded death. Again, he claimed ignorance and expressed his concern for my wellbeing. I was left courting madness, isolated by my own unwillingness to beseech comfort from anyone. How desperately I wanted to give up all my secrets, thinking that if I did I would feel the weight cast off my chest. But I feared losing Mortimer, or my son . . . or worst of all that my husband might indeed be discovered alive and returned to the throne. No, it was best to bear my burden silently.

Not all the news that winter was bad. Philippa was pregnant. She grew slightly plumper around the middle, but that being her natural shape it was hard to notice the change day by day. Young Edward, meanwhile, hunted and went riding more often and treated Philippa as if she were a delicate moth whose wings might tear with a careless touch.

I remained at Kenilworth much of the winter with Philippa. Normally, I would have chafed at being fixed in one place for so long a time. The last few years of prolonged worry and, of late, gnawing suspicion and rampant rumors had driven me to a restless state. But Philippa became a pleasant diversion for me. I delighted in her optimism and truthfulness. So as we lingered at Kenilworth, she and I grew close, taking short walks through the orchard on the sunnier days or doing needlework by the hearth when the weather turned rough.

Being from the Lowlands, Philippa was skilled with a needle, although she often complained that she only partook of such domesticities to be among friends. Books were her greatest love, but it was a very solitary endeavor, she complained. And so she idled in the solar with me, Ida, who was too weak in the eyes to thread her own needle, and Patrice, who spent most of her time filling in the empty moments with a stream of gossip that delighted the younger ladies who had also joined us.

The hours went by quickly for once. Ida was the first to retire. Mortimer's daughter Beatrice was kind enough to escort her to her pallet in an adjoining room. When even Patrice began yawning, the other ladies begged their leave and she went, too—to Arnaud's bed, I was certain.

I leaned over Philippa's shoulder to admire her handiwork. "A beautiful piece."

She shifted on her stool and arched her back to stretch, eyeing the work critically. It was a small scene of sheep in a rolling pasture, dotted with fruit trees in bloom, no bigger across than the width of her palm, but painstakingly done. "My distraction shows. The stitches are uneven here and here," she grumbled, pointing, "but from arm's length, I suppose it is not obvious—not unless one knows what to look for." She stood and placed the needlework on a table nearby. Lips pursed, she finally turned to me with a questioning squint.

"Yes?" I asked.

Her brows flitted upward. "What?"

"You are about to ask me something, yes?"

She blinked and shook her head. "No, nothing, nothing at all." Her hand wandered back to the needlework, tracing the bumps of thread beneath her fingertips. "Perhaps, there is . . . something. Only that . . . I don't know how to ask, or if it's even proper to. If what is happening is normal?"

"About the baby? Your body changes when a child is growing inside. It can seem unusual and —"

"No, not that, actually." Her mouth twisted strangely and she averted her eyes, embarrassed. "H-h-he . . . he does not hold me, or reach for me in that way anymore."

"Since when?"

Philippa gave me a hurtful look. "Since I told him about the child. He was happy, so he said . . . but he hasn't been the same. And so I wonder, if . . ." Her lower lip began to quiver and a furrow shadowed the small space between her brows. "I don't like it this way. He is

not at all the same and I wonder how I have changed to appear so terrible and uncomely to him. I'm not so far along that I look like a . . ."—she struggled for the right words—"a bulging heifer in calf, am I?"

I went to her, took her hand and stroked the back of it gently. "Philippa, it will not last forever. After you have had the baby and your churching is done, he will be more amorous than ever. Trust me. There is little more a man prides himself on than his ability to put a child in you. The more the better."

"But until then? Must I suffer his neglect? Idle here as I mindlessly jab a needle—and meanwhile, he rides the forest with his hounds loping along and drinks barrels of ale long into the night, singing those bawdy songs with drunken friends?"

"He will do none of that if you tell him not to." I said that not from my own experience with Edward's father, who would not have heeded my wishes one whit, but from knowing my son, who loved his wife dearly. "As for now—doubtless some ill-informed person has told him he could 'damage' your delicate parts or the child somehow by being intimate with you. I doubt he is avoiding you out of disdain for your figure, which has yet to change at all." I embraced her and kissed her lovingly on the cheek. "He only wants to keep you safe."

She hugged me back, and then parted with a pat on my wrist. I had thought my words would soothe her and fill her with reason, but she was dubious still. Her chin brushed her shoulder as she looked toward the window. Wind gusted against the shutters and blasted through the cracks around them, sending a frigid blast of air through the room. The flames in the torches along the wall wavered.

"Perhaps it is so," she said half-heartedly, gathering up her needle and colored threads and heaping them in a basket, "but there must be something more in his head. France maybe? Trouble with Scotland? Usually, he speaks to me of such things. I cannot help but wonder . . ."

One hand buried in her basket, she paused in thought, looking at me. I had no answers for her. I simply smiled and dismissed her fears with a shrug.

She left the room, leaving me standing alone. A draft curled down the neck of my gown and blew the icy breath of suspicion down my spine. What she had said—that there was something Edward was not saying—I had felt, too. My mind leapt to the rumors I had heard of Kent's visit with the pope.

In February, Philippa was crowned Queen of England at Westminster Abbey. I did not begrudge her that privilege, although some might say I did. I loved her as much as my own daughters, born of my own womb.

More than that, I had her trust and her confidence—and because of those, I still had influence over my son.

Winchester — March, 1330

A FEW DAYS AFTER Philippa's crowning, the court moved on to Winchester. I rose early, dressed and entered the great hall, expecting to see no more than a few servants beginning their daily tasks. Tables had been moved aside for cleaning, benches resting upside down on top of them. Except for an old hound, there was no one there. The fluted columns flanking the central area stretched upward, traces of soot from a fire twenty years ago evident in the joints of the masonry. The entire central roof had been rebuilt and fresh timbers sprung from the stone arches like the ribs of a whale. The pale golden light of morning flooded through the high, traceried windows topped with quatrefoils.

I was almost at the opposite door when I saw Mortimer standing between one of the far windows and a column, a letter clutched in his palm. The brush of my footsteps on the flagstones made him look up. When I reached him, he shook his head, opened the letter and began to read in a hushed tone:

"Brother,

> *I have moved Earth to find you, knowing you were alive—somewhere. I tremble to think what they have done to you. Patience and faith, I beg you. You shall be freed. Justice will be done. Arrogance and greed will be the downfall of those who have wronged you—but all in its proper time. I must be careful and cannot misstep.*
> *The great lords of England are with me. You shall be king again.*
> *Until then, God keep you. Be strong of mind and will.*

Edmund"

Mortimer gave me the letter. "Delivered into Sir John Deveril's hands at Corfe Castle."

I read it four times before handing it back to him. In my heart, the tone rung too true. Had Berkeley carried out my wishes and then lied to me, because I made him swear on his life never to speak of it again?

"Corfe?" I uttered. "I don't understand. What is he talking

237

about?"

"Kent has been interrogating the servants there and all the near-by townspeople. He claims Edward of Caernarvon is alive and being kept at Corfe. Could he conjure a more absurd fantasy?"

My stomach turned inside out. Everything around me tossed and swirled. Colors blurred together. Edges lost their sharpness. I wanted both to run in fright and lie down and shut out the world in denial at the same time. I pressed a hand against the nearest column, leaned into it for support.

He lives, he lives, he lives . . . And now everyone shall know. My son will lose his crown. And I will lose Mortimer. I will lose—everything. Everything. I will bring down those around me because of what I have done—or what I did not do. Tumble into darkest hell.

Oh God—have gentle mercy on me and let me die rather than witness what horrors my sins shall bring.

"Isabella? Isabella? This is a lie. A great and terrible lie."

A lie? A lie? What is a lie? What is truth? What we say it is? What we pretend it to be? I do not know the difference anymore.

"You know it is a lie, Isabella!" Roger smacked the letter against his palm. "And we shall stop it from going any further. We must! Do you hear me?" He grabbed my upper arm with one hand and dug his fingers deep into my flesh.

The black look behind his eyes snatched the breath from my lungs. It was the terrified, wide-eyed look of an animal backed into a corner, bared fangs dripping with spit, ready to bite.

Does he still believe, even upon learning this, that Edward of Caernarvon is dead? He deceives himself.

"How do we stop it?" I asked in a voice so small and feeble even I barely heard it.

"A sentence of treason. An execution." He reeled me in so close the heat of his breath singed my face. "Kent will never trouble us again."

"But Roger —" I could not look at him, so possessed he seemed that I thought surely the devil would leap from his chest and devour my soul. "To accuse the king's own uncle of treason? When will it end, Roger? When?"

He pierced his fingernails even deeper into my skin. His words seared into my ears like a burst of fire from a smith's bellows. "When he draws his last breath, king's uncle or not. This letter is his condemnation, his blood in ink. I need give no more proof than that."

His fingers loosened and slipped away. My arm throbbed. I rubbed at it as Mortimer stomped about the room, grumbling on and on about Kent's falsehoods.

He doesn't know. He must not. He still thinks that Ockle carried out his orders and Maltravers and Gurney murdered Edward of Caernarvon. And I . . . Everything rests on my shoulders. Everything that is the truth. The real truth.

And the price of keeping things as they are—is Kent's life.

Kent, who opened his arms to me and helped me return to England and remove his own brother from power. Kent, who knows the truth. The truth that could take everything away from me. Everything. From me. From Roger.

From my son.

EDMUND, EARL OF KENT, sat teetering on the edge of a short bench before the appointed deputation. His hands alternately fluttered in his lap and kneaded at the tops of his kneecaps. He looked at each face in turn as he argued in defense of himself.

What look did Edward of Caernarvon wear when Lord Wake took him captive in Wales? When they demanded his abdication? When he knew that his days as king were done?

Did he look as Kent now does—his eyes sunken deep in disbelief, his mouth turned permanently downward in self-pity, his features shadowed with anger? Did he look as utterly, pitifully helpless?

My heart bled for him, but there was nothing I could do. Kent should have come to me. By secretly gathering allies, he had consigned himself to the role of traitor. Even if he truly believed Edward of Caernarvon to still be alive, what did he hope to gain by restoring him to the throne? There was only one answer: he wanted his nephew deposed and Mortimer and me ousted, as well. Such would be the path to England's demise. How could he not see that?

Only yesterday, the king had argued with me on his uncle's behalf, for he loved him and believed there must be some way to spare his life. But hours later, I eventually convinced him that Kent had tried to incite insurrection and must pay the price.

The longer the trial wore on, the more hopeless Kent appeared.

"You went to Corfe Castle yourself and asked to be taken to your brother, Sir Edward of Caernarvon," Robert Howel, the royal coroner, charged. He thumbed through a stack of documents and letters, finally pulling one aside to inspect it more closely. "When you were told he was not there, you presented Sir John Deveril with a letter—this letter." He held it up for all to see. "Who told you that you would find him there?"

Kent hunched his shoulders and shook his head, whimpering.

"Who told you? Who?" Howel's voice rose in volume and severity. "Answer!"

He flinched, then looked directly at me and shook his head again. "I cannot say his name . . . for I never knew it. A Dominican friar. That is all I know."

"A Dominican friar? One without a name?"

"He would not give it, to protect himself."

"Convenient," Mortimer mumbled.

"Did he not have a face?" Howel pressed.

"Not that I could describe to you now, no."

"Did he hide it?"

"He wore a cowl. It was dark. I could not see."

"Could not see his face. Did not know his name. Where did you meet this 'friar'? From where did he hail?"

The questions went on for another hour thusly and in the end came back to where they had begun, but Kent did not change his nameless source. He did not withdraw his claim—that what he said he believed to be true. He did beg forgiveness. All for naught.

Without Edward of Caernarvon standing before us fully fleshed, Kent stood guilty. By Mortimer's orders, Corfe Castle had been turned inside out, servants brought forth to give testimony that they had never seen the former king there, and locals questioned extensively. Yet no evidence of a living Edward of Caernarvon was found.

The only bit of rumor uncovered was that of an idiot monk, who had looked vaguely like the former king, wandering through the area the year before. Since very few from near Corfe had ever seen Edward of Caernarvon up close and of those only one or two had also seen this purported monk bearing similar features, the information was summarily dismissed as a mistaken identity and not presented.

The trial lasted half the day. Kent wilted on his rickety bench before me as Howel volleyed accusations and evidence relentlessly, occasionally backed by Mortimer. The handwriting was Kent's. The seal upon the letter, as well. During all this, Kent would stare at his lap for long, sorrowful periods of time, unresponsive, and then raise his eyes to look my way—only at me, no one else—begging tacitly with those wistful, lipid eyes for his feeble life.

As his guards drew him up roughly by the arms, he resisted, reaching his hands out to me.

"Sister! Isabella, please! I have done nothing —"

But with a cursory black glance from Mortimer, they gagged him with a dirty length of cloth, tying it snugly at the back of his head so that his tongue was crammed into the back of his throat, nearly choking him, and they bound his hands behind him. Then they shoved him toward a side door as he stumbled and went down on one knee, again looking back at me before they hoisted him to his feet and dragged him away.

My heart shriveled. I could not help him. He should have kept silent. Should not have meddled so foolishly in Mortimer's business. The guilt was one more mark of blackness upon my soul, piled high upon the mountain of secrets and lies already buried there.

Young Edward had refused to attend the trial. He was informed of the sentence: Edmund of Kent had been found guilty of treason, as charged. The punishment: death by beheading five days hence.

I thought surely the king would spare his uncle's life and send him to the Tower to live out his years alone. But he kept his silence.

Kent was marched to the scaffold in an open field outside the gates of Winchester. Feet and legs bared to the chill March day, he stood trembling upon the raised platform as a brisk wind blew his shirt stiffly from his starved body, his features as white and bloodless as winter snow.

The executioner refused to carry out his task. When they tried to assign another, none would accept the heinous duty. Edmund of Kent was not greatly adored, but he was not a hated man, nor had the masses deemed him guilty of any crime against the Crown, despite what the court had hastily decreed. Finally, a murderer— a man who had strangled his wife in a fit of rage before the very eyes of his three children—was granted pardon and gleefully took the axe in his grip.

Kent laid his head upon the dark-stained block, muttering, they said, not prayers to God to beg for his own absolution, but words of forgiveness to those who had led him there. The blade fell cleanly. His blood spattered upon the faces of those nearest. Kent's head rolled to the edge of the platform.

The executioner retrieved it and held it aloft for the crowd to see. The spectacle was met with silent revulsion.

The confessed murderer who had swung the axe walked free.

Kent was dead. His heirs were stripped of their lands and their livelihood. His wife, Margaret Wake, was also accused of conspiring to treason. One month later, she gave birth to their fourth child, John, a little boy whose only memory of his father would be a tomb at a church in Winchester, humbly marked and containing Kent's body in two disconnected pieces.

The man who came to my bed at night . . . the face I looked upon in the morning light, I did not know anymore.

He had become the very sort I had once, with his help, tried to rid myself of. But I loved him. Still. Even though I grew more and more afraid of him. And ashamed of what I had become.

21

Isabella:

Woodstock — June, 1330

THE BABE GAVE A hearty wail, displaying the back of his throat and a curving ridge of pink gums. He struggled against his swaddling until at last I freed his small, strong arms and cuddled him to my bosom. Small eyes wide and bright, he calmed and turned his mouth toward me, his tiny lips puckering for milk.

For a month now I had awaited the birth with Philippa at Woodstock. And now to finally see him, so full of life, it made me believe that the past was behind us now, that old ghosts had given way to new beginnings.

I laughed in delight, recalling the utter joy I had known when his father—oh, it was so hard to believe that this was *his* son I cradled in my arms now and not my own—had made his entrance into the world in precisely the same manner: abruptly, easily and absolutely. When Young Edward had hungered, he let the world know by gathering all the force of his lungs and caterwauling so loudly no one could have ignored him. As soon as his needs were met, his complaints turned to coos and he drifted off into blissful slumber. Later came John—the same loud wails, but most of it seemingly without reason or repair. The girls—they had been content, seldom in distress. In fact, it might have been easy to forget they needed anything at all, but Joanna had been so active that it was always necessary to keep a close eye on her, lest she wander away and drown in the fish ponds at King's Cliffe. Eleanor was never far from my side and always, always full of questions. Her incessant queries were wearisome and occasionally tinted with worry, but she was curious and attentive and the swiftest at her lessons.

The emptiness in his belly consuming him, the tiny baby in my arms began to gasp for breath, gathering effort. Then he howled mightily enough to topple the walls of Jericho single-handedly.

I didn't want to give my first and only grandson up, even with his plaintive howls piercing my ears, but at long last the old, barrel-bottomed, midwife pried him from my arms with her stubby fingers, and carried him over to a basin to wash him up. He protested the coldness of the water, but she paid no heed, rubbing him vigorously and going about her business without thought as she had a hundred times before this one. With a linen cloth, she sopped away the sticky wetness of birth and handed him to a waiting wet nurse—a tall, flaxen-haired woman, not quite twenty, with a fairy-like, delicate nose and full apple-red lips that contrasted starkly with the pearly translucency of her skin. She had been fetched from Ireland at the recommendation of Mortimer's daughter-in-law Elizabeth Badlesmere, the wife of his oldest son Edmund, for precisely this purpose. It was a high honor to be settled upon a woman of such coarse breeding, but a calling to which she seemed naturally suited. I suspected her ancestry was Norse—a theory later confirmed when she told me her name: Grimhilde.

I sat down carefully on the edge of Philippa's birthing bed. The sheets had been soaked through and already her handmaidens had peeled back a set and replaced them. They were due for another changing again. The old midwife darted about like an irritated hornet, grumbling that we were in her way as she rolled up old pieces of cloth and packed them between Philippa's legs to absorb the drainage of blood.

Patrice mopped the sweat from Philippa's forehead and cheeks. With tender fingers, she pushed the limp, wet tendrils of Philippa's hair from her face. "He is healthy . . . and strong."

Just as the baby boy gave another cry, Philippa wrinkled her nose up and mustered a wan smile. "Loud, too."

Patrice squeezed Philippa's wrist lightly. "The noise is good, I'm told. It makes him draw breath and grow even stronger."

"And when, dear Patrice, will you ever have children of your own?" she teased. "I hear you had a dozen suitors, all at the same time once."

I would not have been so bold. It was still a delicate subject, even years later, with Patrice. She might have frolicked freely in bed with many a man, but Arnaud de Mone had been her one true love and he had offended her greatly. His wife yet lived, pulling turnips and scrubbing radishes for the Poor Clares.

"A dozen? Hardly. Maybe half that." Patrice wound a ringlet of hair around one finger until she was pleased with the shape and length of the curl. "Most of them were too old, too smelly or too disagreeable to even think of punishing myself with for the rest of my life."

From behind me came the tentative steps of a concerned, young father. Young Edward stood across the room, transfixed for a long while, gazing at his own son with a look that vacillated somewhere between wonderment and disbelief.

"Come closer," Philippa murmured. She had been brave and

determined, crying out seldom during the labor which lasted the better part of a day, bearing down hard in the last hours with all the strength of a plow horse straining against its harness to break rocky soil, until at last the baby's head had crowned. With one long, last push, the infant had slid out, his cries shattering the solemnity of the wondrous spectacle before his feet were even clear of his mother's birth canal. In that moment we were all snatched from breathless silence and were immediately hurled into the mundane normality of a newborn child's primal needs.

Philippa batted her eyelashes as she fought against the draining pull of sleep. She held her hand out to her husband, beckoning him so she would not need to raise her voice. "Why so dumbstruck, my love? You look as though I have given birth to a calf, not a baby. You have a son—an heir. Does he not please you?"

Young Edward—and he seemed to me that day even younger than his seventeen years, all awash with astonishment—straggled toward the bed, pausing to look again at the babe as it burst out in a renewed fit of discontent.

"Is he . . . n-n-normal?" Edward stammered.

"Completely," Philippa assured him. She curled her fingers up around his dangling hand and tugged him to sit on the bed beside her. "There is one, very small problem, however."

Concerned, Edward shaped his lips into the question that he feared to utter. *What?*

"He is without a name," Philippa whispered.

The king slouched in relief. "Edward."

Pulled by curiosity, he went to the corner of the room where Grimhilde was reclining on a stool and cradling the sleeping prince. Carefully, he lifted his son from Grimhilde's arms. The loose swaddling fell into the wet nurse's lap to reveal a naked baby boy with perfectly shaped limbs.

"Edward," he repeated proudly, holding him aloft. "Edward!"

247

But which 'Edward' will he liken to?

The little prince yawned, stretched his chubby arms, kicked his legs and smiled in dreamy agreement.

Nottingham — September, 1330

HANDS CLUTCHING MY KNEES, I bent over beside a rose bush, abundant with blushing blooms, and vomited onto the earth beside it. Again and again I retched emptily, each wave forcing me lower until I was scooting on my hands and knees deeper between the musky scented rose bush and a waxy row of boxwood hedges. There, I hoped I would be less visible to anyone who might be wandering in the gardens of Nottingham.

I dug my fingers into the musty earth, clenching my teeth to halt the tide of yellow bile from pushing upward. Then, a hand fell lightly upon my back. Startled, I gasped, so that my mouth fell open and, once more, I felt the unstoppable, acrid swirl shoot up from the back of my throat and over my tongue.

"Ohhh, Isabeau, Isabeau," Patrice muttered. Finally, when I had ceased to spew out my insides, she knelt down on the ground beside me, mindless of the thorns that caught at her hair and snagged her pretty green gown. "You are not well. Not at all. Let me help you inside. I will have Ida fetch a physician for you." She pressed the back of her hand to my forehead. "No fever. Something you ate, perhaps, did not agree with you? You never had a delicate stomach before, Isabeau."

"Nothing I eat," I said, drawing the sleeve of my kirtle across my lips, "agrees with me lately. It all refuses to stay down, and yet . . . and yet I can hardly squeeze into the very gown I wore just last week."

She stared quizzically at me for what seemed several minutes, before the clue finally caught on. Her dark eyebrows arched upward, pleating her forehead. In astonishment, she covered her mouth with both hands. "Nooo . . ."

"I think 'yes'." Until that moment, I had refused to even believe it was possible that I was pregnant. I had been very careful, using the concoction that Patrice had taught me long ago with great diligence.

Suddenly, I felt the alarm of panic—of something wildly beyond my control. The looming shadow of disaster. The urge to run gripped me hard. My breath quickened. My heart raced so wildly that I thought it might explode inside my chest. A knot of emotions, I grabbed Patrice's hand and squeezed it tight. "I did not mean for this to happen, not in a hundred years. Believe me. I didn't, didn't . . ." I crumpled within her loving embrace.

"I know you didn't. I know." She stroked my back.

Finally, she asked the question that I knew would inevitably come. "Does he know?"

"No, I am not yet sure if I —"

"My lady?" Mortimer called out, sweeping down the grassy path toward us.

I clutched Patrice's hands between mine and whispered to her, "Say nothing. This *cannot* be."

Instead of condemning me with a look of judgment, she imparted a smile of compassion.

"Isabella?" Mortimer said. Then seeing Patrice huddled beside me, he quickly added, "My queen?"

He lent me his hand. Weakly, I rose, Patrice supporting me on one side with her hand firmly under my arm.

"My lady had some curds this morning that had gone bad. I'll tell the kitchen maids to dispose of the rest."

"Give the cook a tongue-lashing, too," Mortimer told her.

She dipped at the knee and then gave me over to him before leaving us. My knees still shaking, Mortimer and I strolled along the garden path. My skirt brushed the hedges as I staggered sideways, despite his arm about my waist. He gripped me tighter.

"The council has been waiting, but I'll tell them you are indisposed. We should get you to bed, Isa—"

"No, no . . . it will pass."

But things such as this—they do not pass. They stay with us forever. They carry on through the ages long after we are dead.

I CLAIMED A LINGERING illness, but I imagined that those surrounding me began to suspect it was my mind that was troubled and not so much my physical being. I was living each day mired in the present, in dread of the future, growing more and more regretful of the past.

Every tomorrow became bleaker than the yesterday before. With every day that passed, the hope that some other ailment had caused my cycles to stop withered. It was useless to curse the physicians who had told me long ago that I would have no more children. Useless to be angry with myself for being in this predicament. Yet I did—every moment, both awake and in my troubled dreams. Pregnancy—an event which was a blessing to Edward and Philippa and had been once to me—it was the worst of the worst. Catastrophic. And I alone shouldered the tragedy of a life growing within me.

Parliament was due to convene at Nottingham in only two weeks. Mortimer was growing increasingly paranoid over rumors that Lancaster was part of a movement to oust him—or worse to put him on trial for crimes against the kingdom. Preoccupied with my own troubles, I did not care to hear Mortimer's obsessive ramblings about plots and conspiracies, some of them involving mention of the king. It had been dealt with previously and put in its grave. I would not live my life in fear of shadows and whispers.

I was alone in my chambers, having given orders not to be disturbed, as I had often done of late. It was yet early evening, but I blew out the few candles that Patrice had lit for me and lay down upon my bed, still clothed. I could still smell the smokiness of the burnt wicks and marveled at how all my senses had gradually heightened these past three months, smells, especially. I could smell the dropped petals of a rose past its bloom a hundred feet away and the sweet pungency of cut hay in the next valley. The smell of spiced sausages, however, invoked retching. And the cravings—I had sent Patrice to the kitchen twice alone this last week in the dead of night to fetch me almonds and fruit. She had not been pleased to be roused thus and after the second time decided to keep a supply at hand on a side table.

My hands wandered over my lower belly, cupping the growing roundness there. I thought I felt . . .

Yes, there it is—a stirring. A movement. Life.

"Isabella?"

My heart stopped. It was Mortimer. My breath was trapped in my lungs.

How do I tell him? Should I? I do not even know what to do—to let it live or to let it go. I have waited too long already for the latter. By not deciding, I have decided.

But I can't . . . It cannot be. Too much shame. Too many lives to be wrecked.

He came toward me through the darkness without stumbling, sensing where I was by my breathing alone. Then his sudden weight upon the bed made me roll on my side toward him, my hand still on my belly.

"Isabella, are you ill again?" He reached out, swept my hair from my cheeks with a tender caress, and bent to kiss my ear.

"I am well . . . well enough. You needn't worry. It's just that . . . I have felt better. It comes and goes."

Stroking the curve of my neck, he lay down beside me. The scent of leather and horse hide lingered around him. "Lancaster took up residence within the town. I do not trust him, Isabella. I never

251

will."

"What would you have me do about it? He is here, like everyone else, at the king's command, fulfilling his duty."

"I ordered him beyond the walls, to a manor several miles away. It is safer that way."

"Safer from what, Roger?"

There was a gaping pause. He moved, so that the length of his body aligned to mine, our hips meeting, and he took my face between his hands. "Are you well enough to be give yourself to me? It has been weeks—I cannot bear it any longer, love. I think of you every day—what it is like to be with you, to hold you, have you." Without awaiting an answer from me, his hands were already wandering beneath my clothing, tugging at laces, lifting my skirts, peeling back any impediments to his needs, seeking out the places that often delivered me into waves of ecstasy.

"Isabeau, my love . . ." His breath quickened, mine echoing it. "I cannot live without you."

Nor I you, Roger. And I love you, though it be the end of me.

HE LOOKED DOWN AT me in that dreamy haze that follows lovemaking and kissed me softly on the lips, on my nose, above both eyes— each airy brush of his lips a promise and a memory. Then he lowered the length of his body beside mine and nuzzled his whiskered face in the warm curve between my neck and shoulder.

The moist heat of his breath curled around my neck and tickled beneath my chin as he whispered, "With all my heart, Isabella, I love you . . . only you. How I wish I could tell the world. Or better yet, that the rest of the world would just disappear. My God, there are men who madden me so, that I could kill them with my bare hands. The only way I can stop myself, sometimes, is to think of you. To be with you. And all of it . . . goes away."

"Roger, there is something . . . I must . . ." The words choked me. I could not say them. I tried again. "I m-m-must . . ."

"Out with it, my love. Tell me. If I can tell you that I have contemplated murder with those who wrong me, then we have no secrets, do we?"

How can I tell you . . . that everything we have between us . . . is in peril? How can I tell you that our love has ruined us and those around us? God mocks us, Roger. He brings us together, yet tortures us with shame and now this . . . this disgrace disguised as a blessing.

My belly tightened. My mouth was as dry as sand. My tongue stuck to the back of my teeth. I swallowed, shaped my lips into the words I loathed to say and forced the sounds of speech from the hollow depths of my throat. "I am with child."

His body stiffened like a plank. He did not move or speak or even breathe. It was as if the truth had been a boulder dropped upon him from above, crushing the air from his chest, shattering all his bones into a thousand splintered pieces, leaving him lifeless. At last, he buried his face in the pillow and mumbled, "Sweet Jesus . . . how?"

'How'? How am I to answer such a mindless thought?

He sat up straight and sudden, gulping. His breath came in ragged, angered gasps. "Were you not . . . How—how could this have . . .? I thought you could not bear any more children. My God, why now? After so long . . ."

I had known he would be shocked to hear it. Still, I had been careful. I *had* been. Except perhaps once or twice, now and again. The remedy that Patrice taught me had worked for so long. When a woman grows older, after not having conceived for so many years, after also having been told she would never bear children again . . . how was she to even think it might happen?

But what did all that matter? There was a child inside me. *Mortimer's child. Ours. Mine.*

I knew he might be angered, but what I wanted—what I needed—was for him to hold me and tell me that everything would be all right. I had not done this alone—and certainly not purpose-fully. "It is to be. We will have a child, Roger. Does it matter how or why? And we must begin to think, now, what to —"

"Isabella!" He ripped the blankets away, swung his feet over the edge of the bed and turned his bare back to me. "You will *not* have this child. Do you hear me? You cannot."

I took affront to him so readily dismissing this . . . this . . . thing that had happened to us. It was not some unwanted pup to be tied up in a sack with rocks and tossed into the Thames. It was a child, waiting to know life. Shivering terribly, I grappled for the corner of the blanket and pulled it over my hips and breast. "If God wills it . . . If I carry it to —"

"There can be no child, you stupid woman!" he shouted. The muscles of his shoulders pinched taut. He raked his fingers through the short, dark mat of his hair, and then rotated his fingertips hard into his temples, trying to massage away his angst. "Take care of it. Do what you must."

His implication was clear. He stood, drew up his braies, gathered his leggings and shoved his feet into them. With exaggerated move-ments, he yanked them to his hips, drew the cord tight, and began to wander about the room, groping in the half-darkness for his shirt, kicking at the floor in displaced vexation. Near the window, he stooped to reach for the rest of his clothing. Moonlight cascaded in silver ripples over the lean muscles in his back.

"And if I don't? It is your child, as well, Roger. You would have me murder your own blood, an innocent?"

He jerked himself upright. I heard the 'swoosh' of wadded cloth unraveling as he hurled his shirt at me. A button snapped at the corner of my eye, above my cheekbone. Instinctively, I raised my fingers to feel for torn flesh or a raised welt, but before I could,

Mortimer's thundering shadow crossed the room, seized me by the wrists and dragged me naked from the bed. He twisted my wrists hard, so that my elbows turned in and I was forced down to the floor. The impact rammed splinters into my knees. I cried out— in pain, surprise . . . in fear of him.

"It will be the death of us both, you fool!" His teeth flashed savagely. He tightened his grip, burning my flesh, cutting off the blood to my fingers until they went numb. "The pope himself . . . if not your own son . . . would have both our heads. Is that what you want? Is *that* what you want?!"

I trembled in his hold. "Roger, stop, please . . . someone will hear. They cannot find us like this."

He shoved me to the floor, away from him. I crumpled into a misshapen ball, my arms wrapped around my head, trying to protect myself from a surge of emotions washing over me like the crashing waves of the sea in a rising storm. But it was too much. Too much. Too much blackness pounding down upon my head. Too much pulling me under. I couldn't fight it. Couldn't swim from it or run. Couldn't cry out for help. Couldn't raise myself up to stand strong and dignified before Mortimer and remind him of his part.

How many times had he whispered in my ear those sweet promises of love, come to my bed without invitation, touched parts of me that others never laid eyes on, taken me in lingering rapture, spilled his seed within me and *never once* asked what if a child came of it? How easy to take his ecstasy in me, as long as there was no natural, inevitable consequence to it all.

Tears flooded my eyes, gushed down my cheeks, spilled between my cold fingers. I had not realized that I still had no clothing on, or that I was sobbing so heavily, until I felt the searing heat of his touch upon my back like a branding iron leaving its mark. He crouched beside me, trying to draw me to him as his hand slid around my waist.

"Isabeau, Isabeau . . ." The wrath in his voice had melted away. His touch was meant in comfort. "It is our circumstances that make it impossible, not that I do not love you."

Liar! You brazen, heartless liar! You shun me . . . and our child, because it inconveniences you, nothing more. I rue that I ever fawned after you, worshipped you, thought that I loved you.

On hands and knees, I crawled away from his vile hold. Snagging the tail of the bed sheet, I pulled it loose and wound it around myself as I rose to my feet.

"Bastard," I spat, conjuring even more hateful insults in my head. "Get out of here. Out! Out—damn you!!!"

He held his hands out to me, beckoning me near. "No, Isabella, we must talk . . . think this through."

"Why?" I shot back snidely. "So you can convince me that I should kill an unborn child?" I gathered the sheet into a knot between my breasts. "One sin to cover another?"

He tilted his head at me, one eyebrow arched in disbelief. "You cannot be thinking that . . ." Suddenly, he looked away. "I have a wife, Isabella. You are the widowed mother of a king. A child of ours, if . . . if allowed to live—it could never be acknowledged. *Never.* A male child, a bastard, could bring ruin upon your son's rule. Strife, contention . . . war. You know that, don't you?"

Regretfully, I did. Bastards had had their share of upstarts throughout the ages. England had even been conquered by one: William of Normandy, the Bastard King. I regretted that I had ever allowed Roger Mortimer to manipulate me in order to garner power, or to use me at his leisure for sexual pleasures. I let the sheet fall to the floor.

"Look at me, Roger. Look!" I commanded. He resisted a moment, not wanting to acknowledge the temptation that had driven him to this life of scandal. Finally, reluctantly, he turned his face to gaze at me. Only the thin, gray light of predawn separated us. "Look long and well at what you have spent your lust upon, night after night, in every bed from York to Fontainebleau, while we stifled our moans and whispered the words we yearned to cry out. Sometimes we coupled in frenzy like a sailor and his tavern whore after a year's voyage, did we not? Sometimes, you were slow and tender with me, as if I were a young, frightened virgin on my wedding night. Other times, we were like old, familiar lovers, talking and holding each other for hours afterward, sometimes not talking at all, but falling asleep in one another's arms. All this we kept from those around us, shared it only between us—as if we lived in two separate worlds: ours and everyone else's."

I stepped over the sheet, closer to him. His body twitched in response to my nearness, although he may as well have wanted to take me to bed again as to strike sense into me . . . or perhaps go from me forever. "But it is no more, Roger. We are guilty of adultery. Not once, not for only a while, but time and time again, shamelessly. You cast off your vows to Joan. I gave no regard to my son's dignity. Did we think we could sport about in bed forever and not suffer for it in the end?" I came within arm's reach of him, lowered my chin, and drew my hand softly across my belly. "Can we right a thousand sins with another, even greater one?"

He turned his head away. "No, our sins are ours—forever." Then he strode abruptly from me, picked up a loose-fitting nightshift of mine and handed it gruffly to me. "But sins can be forgiven, Isabella. A reputation, once sullied, is always stained. And power, once lost, is almost never salvageable."

Mortimer retrieved his shirt from the bed and the rest of his clothing from the floor. I kept my eyes from him as he dressed himself, the cold air from a dwindling hearth fire raising goose bumps on my flesh. I shivered, but I could not move. I only wanted him to go—away from me, forever—and let me deal with this alone, somehow.

Before leaving, he said one more thing:

"If you have the child, Isabella, I will not claim it. Someone, conveniently, will have seen another man, or perhaps several, entering and leaving your private chambers at all hours. They will call you a whore, cram you in the dungeon and let you deliver the child alone, in the darkness and filth, then rip it crying from your arms." There was a hint of smugness in his voice—a tone I had heard him use often with others, but never once before with me.

He went toward the door.

"And I will say you raped me," I threatened.

He shut the door firmly behind him. I would never have said that he had raped me—never. Not even if he levied ridiculous claims of my own lechery to foul my name and exclude himself from accusations of having fathered a child on me. I only meant to make him pause, to reconsider his ultimatum. He could not dictate what I would do with the life inside me. Such decisions did not belong to either of us, but to God.

And yet, as I stood there shivering, my knees wobbling, the sloshing bile in my stomach threatening to spew fire over my tongue, I wanted to melt into a puddle on the floor and never rise up again . . . wanted this cruel irony of a nightmare to vanish like a thinning mist in the pale light of dawn.

I did not know what to do. Did not know what was right. I only knew that so many things that I had done . . . were wrong.

By letting the child live, I would be inviting a series of calamities on Mortimer, on myself, on my son, on France and England and a hundred thousand untold souls.

Yet of all the terrible things I had done in my life, reasoning them away, I always told myself that the good in the end was worth the wrong in the moment. But this time I resisted turning down that path once more, for I did not know when it would ever end, this ugly, damning life of lies and secrets.

What I have known with you, Mortimer—a joy so intense and private it has riddled my heart with scars that will never heal—it cannot go on forever.

This stirring within me . . . if I must choose between it and you, Mortimer—this is my new beginning.

My soul drained dry, I slipped my nightshift over my head in a haze, slinked back to bed, gathering the sheets and blanket along the way, and crawled beneath their crumpled mess. I lay awake for a long, long while, wishing that I could feel something . . . anything. But it was as if I had nothing left within me—neither love, nor hatred, neither joy, nor dismay, certainty nor doubt.

Nothing but an emptiness so big that it could douse the light of day and darken all the heavens forever.

Nothing.

PATRICE PINCHED MY UPPER arm, rousing me abruptly from a hard sleep. I cracked open my eyes to blindingly bright morning light, then swiftly shut them again to close out the world.

"What time is it? Have I slept the day away?" I drawled. I did not want to rise from the warm security and solitude of my bed and set my feet upon the cold floor to pretend my way through another impossibly bleak day. "Oh, let me be, Patrice. Go away."

"Isabeau," she whispered urgently, "I must tell you something. Please, it cannot wait." She shook me so hard that it rattled the bones in my neck.

Scowling in objection, I sat up and scooted beyond her clawing reach. My own sudden movements elicited a wave of nausea, reminding me of the previous night's happenings. I sank back into my pile of pillows, wishing that they would swallow me up and spare me whatever crisis Patrice was about to deliver. With all the troubles this past year between Lancaster's insurrection, Kent's death and now . . .

Dare I ask what more could go wrong?

"Do I want to know, Patrice? Tell me good news, or tell me naught at all."

A pout tugged at her lower lip. She looked down at the floor, concern evident in the lines of her face. "Lord Roger's life is in danger."

It felt as though a knife had been punched between my ribs, letting all the air in my lungs rush out. "How so? By whom?" Brutally awake now, I scrambled to the edge of the bed to sit beside Patrice. I tried to steady myself, but my head was suddenly throbbing in whiteness, my heart accelerating to an impossible pace. I held my breath. "Lancaster?" But even as I asked it, it did not make sense. Lancaster had been subdued, the fight whipped from him. There had not been so much as a grumbling of discontent from his diminished domain of late.

Patrice shook her head. "The king."

I grabbed her by the arm. "What are you saying? What proof do you have?"

She looked at me crossly. "I would not lie about this. Lord Roger has had Arnaud follow Montagu closely. Less than an hour ago behind the Black Boar Inn, Arnaud overhead Montagu speaking to someone. He could not hear everything, but he heard enough. There was mention of arrest, a swift trial . . . and Lord Roger's name over and over and . . ." She kept shaking her head, as though she, too, wished it not to be true.

I slipped from the bed to kneel before her, clamping both my hands upon her knees. "Tell me, Patrice—who was Montagu speaking to?"

"I-I-I do not know." Tears filled her eyes. "Arnaud did not know the voice. Could not see who it was."

"Did Montagu say when?"

"No, no . . . voices, other people, were coming near. Arnaud did not want to be seen. He came to me at once, so I could tell you."

I didn't know where Mortimer was now. Likely far away. But I had to find him.

I began to stand, but my lightheadedness slowed me. I waited a moment before speaking again, seeking out the bedpost to hold myself upright. As soon as my head cleared, I swallowed back the sour taste that gushed up. "Patrice . . . how do you know the king has anything to do with this?"

She bit at her lip. The tears began to spill over the rims of her eyes. "Because Montagu said . . . that it was the king's wish . . . to stop him."

I almost asked: 'Stop him from what?', but I already knew. Young Edward had had enough of being mothered, guided, supervised . . . being told what to do.

If he believes his father is alive . . . What if he already knows . . . something? Something that even I do not?

A sharp pain flared in the lower depths of my belly. I gripped the bedpost, but my knees began to give. Then, I fell to the floor, my cheek scraping raw down the gnarled length of the carved bedpost. Patrice plunged beside me, throwing her arms around me, trying to lift me up.

"I will find him," she said.

As she began to pull away I grappled at her arm. "Please, no . . . Don't go. Send someone else for him. I need you here, with me." The pain burned hot somewhere deep inside me. "Please, don't go-o-o . . ." My words turned to a howl. Patrice slipped her arm around me. I tried hard simply to breathe, but I struggled. I captured air in gasps, guttural, uncontrollable moans escaping my throat in between, until I began to breathe more regularly. Eventually, the pain ebbed. My head began to clear. Still, something was not right.

Patrice left to seek help.

"Lord Jesus Christ . . . help me," I pleaded softly into folded hands. "If this be Your will—be swift. Do not make this child suffer for what I have done."

For I will suffer until my end.

But it is not yet time to mourn this unborn child. Not yet.

PART III:

Sweet father, here unto thy murdered ghost
I offer up the wicked traitor's head,
And let these tears, distilling from mine eyes,
Be witness of my grief and innocency.

Edward III
from Christopher Marlowe's *Edward II*

22

Isabella:

Nottingham – October, 1330

I N THE HOURS IT took to find Mortimer, my pains had ebbed and faded. I could not stay on my back like a helpless invalid. Patrice berated me for pacing from door to window and back again a hundred times, but I simply could not keep still, even as weakened as I was. He had turned from me when I needed him most; still, I could not let ill befall my gentle Mortimer. We were like two trees whose roots and branches had intertwined with the years, growing stronger as a pair. If one tree died and fell, the other would surely follow.

Love is measured not in moments, but in eternity. Not in fleeting gestures, but in sacrifices large.

THE IRON KEYS OF Nottingham Castle dangled from Mortimer's fingers. He closed the bedchamber door and held them out to me.

"Keep them with you at all times. Lock every door yourself at dusk. Then put them beneath your pillow, so that no hand may touch them but yours."

I twined the cord at my waist around my fingers. "How long have you had Montagu followed?"

His brow was sternly fixed. "Months. You see now why?"

Lifting a candle from its sconce, I lit several more—three on the center table, two on the mantel, two more in their sconces on the far wall. The more light to read his countenance by, the better. I turned away, searching out shadows. "You have kept this from me, as well?"

"'As well' as what?"

The clank of the keys made me turn back to him. He had lowered his hand.

"'As well' as what?" he repeated flatly. The terse delivery of his words indicated that time was essential and that giving me the keys was not a trifling matter.

"I don't know, Roger. Since we are full of confessions today, perhaps you could begin yours?"

He came at me so suddenly I backed into a linen chest and nearly toppled over it. But he only lifted my hand from my side, uncurled my fingers and pressed the weighty ring of keys into my reluctant grip. "Some rumors are worth listening to. They are the first hint of the truth. Rebels who had been hiding out on the continent, led by Thomas Wake, were gathering in Wales. They have been dealt with, but Lancaster denied any knowledge of their plans. Still, I do not trust his word."

The 'rebels' he referred to were those who had fled England after Edmund of Kent's execution. While I couldn't deny that we had made enemies, suspicion was overruling his sensibilities.

"Lancaster is old and blind," I said, "and no threat to either of us."

"Old and blind, yes. But not a threat? Good God, you would let your worst enemies eat at your table and dribble poison in your drink as you laughed at their jokes. I warn you, Isabella. Watch those closest to you. Watch them. Trust no one. They do not seek to whittle away at your power, but to squeeze it from you like a butcher wrings a chicken's neck. They think only of themselves, not of England's preservation."

He circled a chair by the window, but rather than sit, he braced himself against it from behind, his fingers locked on its back. "You think this is all in my head, I know. But I have spies. Excellent spies. In many places. Months ago the first rumors reached me. Or maybe it was a year? It all runs together so much. I dismissed them then, thinking myself invincible, thinking I had too many friends and allies. Too many who owed me for their good fortune. But not so. Bloody not so. The only ones truly loyal to me are those in my direct employment . . . and even them I keep a close eye on. Someone has betrayed me and I will find them out. I will.

"I sleep with a knife beneath my pillow, did you know? God help the one who wakes me from a nightmare and feels the cold slip of a blade between his ribs. Twice since coming to Nottingham, I have pricked my knife to Arnaud's throat. I would have drained the blood from him before opening my eyes had he not whispered his name to me. A curse to live so. To never sleep. I cannot help but look into someone's eyes and see malice in their hearts, even as they kiss my cheek and proclaim their loyalty. Arnaud alone do I trust. You, as well, Isabella. Two people in the entire world. Only two. Thus, I fear for you both. And that dread hangs as heavy on me as my own shadowy death." He pressed his lower ribs to the back of the chair, leaning heavily on it, his eyes darting to the door and then to the window, although there was nothing but pitch blackness to gaze upon outside. "Time to confront Edward, force this all out in the open. This whispering and plotting and conspiring to rebel—it must end."

More and more of late, Mortimer spoke as a king speaks, as if his every word and deed were law and unquestionable. That someone dared defy him or sought to shake his hold on power fed the fires of vindictiveness in him. Once, he had followed Edward of Caernarvon's orders faithfully and when he questioned his liege lord he had been punished for it. Now he sought to do that very thing to others, to be the suppressor and not the suppressed, the master and not the servant.

"How will you put an end to it? And what, precisely?" I asked bluntly, for knowing what Mortimer had kept from me in the past I had no designs on prolonging the secrecy between us. "It's the king—my son—you speak of now."

"It's your son who is planning to do away with me," Mortimer retorted with a snarl, pushing himself away from the chair to take a more offensive stance. "Should I lie down in the corner, belly up, and wait for him to trip across me and kick me until I crawl away whimpering like a small cur? *I* raised him up. *I* put him on the throne."

I wanted so much to spew out every grievance I bore with Mortimer—grievances that were mounting by the moment. Young Edward would have come to the throne with or without Mortimer eventually. Mortimer alone did not put him there. "You have forgotten that my brother Charles gave you succor when you were an outcast. You have forgotten Count William of Hainault. Without him, we would never have had the men and means to land on England's shores. Kent and Norfolk, who opened their arms to us. Lancaster, even, who did likewise. And what of Bishop Orleton, who saw that your life was spared to begin with?" *And me. What would you have ever been or done without me?* "Confront the king if you will, but take a moment to hear him out, Roger. Give him a way out of this, before it's too late."

The wry curve of his lips revealed that he was not swayed in the least. "Why? *He* doesn't seek compromise. No, I know too much already, Isabella. He wants to sever a diseased limb in its entirety: me. You, even." A full smirk twisted Mortimer's mouth. He tilted his head, almost as if he heard a voice whispering to him from somewhere. "Yes, I will 'hear him out', as you say. But *you* may not like what you hear."

YOUNG EDWARD LOPED INTO the meeting chamber with Montagu following at a respectful distance of five strides, pausing whenever the king paused, picking up pace likewise. The king threw himself into one of the two empty chairs opposite ours, slouching with one eye open and one closed. As Montagu planted himself along the wall between the king and the open door, Edward nodded once to affirm that his guard post—a pocket of shadow tucked in the corner—was well chosen.

Mortimer indicated to the guards flanking the door to close it and remain outside. There were only the four of us, eyeing each other warily. I found it a wonder, if Mortimer had been correct at all about his suspicions regarding Edward, that the king had elected to come without a formidable host of guards. Edward bore no weapons and Montagu had only the sword at his belt. Hardly the defenses of those about to be confronted by their supposed archenemy.

Young Edward let out a yawn and glanced toward one of the wide windows along the far wall. Dawn was not even a hint of gray in the distance yet. Two sputtering oil lamps threw their amber light in long, wavering streaks around the room.

"What is so dire you had to rouse me at this impossible hour?" Edward stifled a yawn before continuing. "I had not half a night's sleep and Philippa was quite aggravated to have someone banging on her door so rudely, let alone having me yanked from my bed indecent."

"Sir William, please," Mortimer said, his spine rigid against the back of his own chair, "sit."

Montagu followed Mortimer's command and slid onto the chair beside the king. I could not recall the last time I saw him take orders from anyone but the king.

Mortimer directed his comment at Edward. "There is a plot afoot to dispose of me, my lord."

"Plot?" Edward scratched at his chest and then rearranged the front of his tunic.

"Yes, a plot instigated by you."

The king rocked forward and grabbed his knees, both eyes now open wide. He cast a perplexed glance at Montagu, who hitched his shoulders in a light shrug. "Perhaps my head is a little foggy yet, but I do not understand."

"There is no need to deny it. My sources are reliable."

"I do deny it, vehemently. Dispose of you how?"

"Arrest. Trial." He did not say the rest. *Execution.* That was the presumed fate of a traitor.

"You mean in the same swift fashion that befell my poor Uncle Edmund?" Edward's upper lip twitched. The light emanating from the lamps danced erratically across his lean face, making his features much harsher and more deeply cut than their true youthful smoothness. "This is almost too preposterous to believe. I might laugh if I were not so shocked to hear it. Since you have done nothing to betray me—as far as I am aware—on what grounds would I ever pursue such action?"

"Sir William." Mortimer abruptly turned his attention on Montagu, who looked more perturbed at the ridiculousness of this scene than wary of its outcome. "You were overheard recently speaking of this very thing. To whom were you speaking?"

He returned a blank look and shook his head slowly. "What 'thing', my lord?"

"You know precisely what I'm speaking of."

"No, I do not."

"Who were you speaking to?"

"When?"

"Yesterday, early evening."

"And where was this . . ."—Montagu's ragged eyebrows folded together in grave concentration—"this conversation you say I had?"

"Behind the Boar's Head Inn. You know the place."

He leaned back and looked pensively up at the beams of the ceiling, his fingers tapping against his thigh. "I do, but only vaguely, however. The Boar's Head is best known for its prostitutes, I hear. But I was with the king and several others then, here in the castle, playing dice, I confess. A vice of mine. I shrive myself of the sin once or twice a year in confession. Shall I fetch witnesses for you? Or would you prefer to personally question the whores at the tavern, as to whether or not they saw me—or if they even know of me personally?"

A long pause ensued. The cool golden-green of Montagu's eyes resisted the smoldering heat of anger behind Mortimer's.

"Mother?" Young Edward interrupted. "Please, enough. This is baseless conjecture. Mockery without meaning, and a dangerous precedent to adopt. Explain this sham—or are you merely humoring him? If so, I should like to go back to the comfort of my own bed. Philippa will be awake until I return—and it will be me who will suffer her mood tomorrow for lack of sleep."

My son, who had come here already irascible from his rude awakening, was by now struggling to keep his virulence in rein. There was only Arnaud's word to go by. Whatever else Mortimer might have known, he had not yet revealed. I looked at Mortimer. His face was set in stone.

"Sir Roger, he is right," I said. "If you are to make accusations, you must have evidence. So if you seek some truth, some further . . . information, then lead us to it. Or let this go."

Mortimer's jaw tensed. Slowly, he turned his head to fix me with a stare so vile I could not endure it and looked away.

"Yes," Edward added, "proof. Perhaps you have a *'letter'*, in my hand, of course, accusing you of treason." He stood and nodded once to Montagu, who also rose from his chair.

Mortimer locked with the king in a stare of defiance. I closed my eyes, feeling the heat of their anger and mistrust surrounding me like a fire consuming an entire forest.

Pull your hand from the flames, Isabella! You have felt its heat for too long already.

Then . . . I opened my eyes. Fully. Finally. I saw everything as it was. Like the open blue of the sky on the first sun-bright day of spring. I saw where I stood: between them. And that I had put myself there.

They would not stop until one of them possessed absolute power—Mortimer, who felt he had earned it, and Edward, who was born to it.

I am not so brave or clever as I believe myself to be. I allow those I love and care for to use me, while I do nothing to preserve myself.

Mortimer said no more. Edward rolled his eyes, but before taking his final leave, he stooped forward before Mortimer's chair, leaning so close that his breath lifted the hair from Mortimer's forehead.

"What sickens me most, Lord Roger," Young Edward's words sliced bitterly between his teeth, "are those who profess to serve faithfully even as they grasp at the reins of power and hoard their riches. It hints of disloyalty. Had I any charges to bring against you or anyone else, I would do so openly and with infallible proof. But I suppose I should thank you for bringing this to my attention. I was quite unaware that such vicious rumors were afloat. So you may rest easy, good knight. I assure you they are unfounded. Should I discover their source, I will personally bring the perpetrators to justice."

With a tilt of his head, Edward stood up, came and gave me a cool kiss upon the cheek. "Good night, Mother. Or is it morning now? By God, I have no notion. My day is turned upside down. No matter. You look as though you need rest, though, so back to bed with you. With all of us." He gave Mortimer one more snide glance, meant in warning. "Kept up all night for nothing."

Then to me he imparted a faint smile, as if for some reason he pitied me, and left with Montagu.

I rose from my chair, went to the window and searched the sky for the first sign of day. But there was only endless darkness above and deep quiet in the streets of sleepy Nottingham far below. The chill of oncoming winter surrounded me. "Perhaps they *were* only rumors, started by your enemies on the continent, not Edward. Perhaps Arnaud did not hear correctly, or what he —"

"Perhaps," Mortimer growled, "it is your son who is lying. Who do you believe, Isabella?"

I did not turn to look at him. The bitterness between us was still too sharp. One more cut to my soul and I would bleed to death on the inside.

He stood and walked slowly toward me, then stopped close enough behind me that he could have wrapped his arms around me. But he offered nothing of his touch. No gentle hand upon my shoulder, no kiss nestled in the curve of my neck. Not even the angry clench of his strong hand upon my arm.

Slowly, he drew breath and held it long before speaking. "I ask, but I think you have already chosen who to believe."

I shook my head, implying that I had not. But it was my head that said so, not my heart. "Roger, you must offer an apology for this. Tell him you were only seeking the truth, not accusing him of betraying you. If you don't, it will only get worse between you. What you fear may very well happen then."

"What I know, I know to be true. He lies, Isabella. Your own son *lies* to you. And you, will you do nothing to save me from those lies?"

"Everyone's truth is not the same." I turned to him. "It is up to you, Roger, to save yourself. Beg his forgiveness. Lower yourself before his eyes. Vow your loyalty over and over publicly. Then prove it, day after day, year after year. And never, *ever*, put yourself above him. A kingdom can have only one king."

He recoiled from me. It was as if a stark realization was finally seeping into him—one that, even now, as brutally obvious as it was becoming, he did not want to accept. He turned halfway and uttered caustically, "What irony, coming from you." Then he looked once more at me, only briefly, and left.

Was it courage or cowardice that bade me stay silent and let him go? Even now I do not know. It was done.

FOR FIVE DAYS MORE, the mood at Nottingham was as strained as a bridge of sticks under the weight of an ox. Every word that passed between Mortimer and me was measured and forced, every response coldly polite. I looked often for Arnaud and Montagu, noting that whenever one was absent, so was the other. Young Edward, however, was always visible—sometimes walking the gardens with Philippa, other times talking to his infant son of things the babe would not be able to comprehend for decades. His routine seemed entirely undisturbed.

Parliament was set to begin in two days. Lancaster, despite his umbrage at being excluded from Nottingham, humbly restrained himself from complaint.

Mortimer wore the haggard look of one who had not slept for a fortnight. At supper, he would lean forward, elbows on the table, and hold his head in his hands as his eyes drifted shut. The sawing of a knife blade on bone far down the table or the soft treading of a servant behind him would startle him into alertness. When he was not fighting sleep, he watched Young Edward—something which began to visibly unnerve the king more and more with each passing day.

On the fifth day, supper was profoundly hushed, like a funeral awaiting mourners. Mortimer's seat sat vacant. A few hours ago, I had received word that William Montagu had fled Nottingham in the wake of Mortimer's interrogation. That would perhaps explain why Edward was so distracted, dunking his spoon in his bowl of soup repeatedly without ever taking a sip. Philippa spoke quietly with Margaret, Lord Berkeley's wife, but they, too, often fell silent, dabbing at their beef drippings with hunks of bread, nursing their wine. The side tables seemed to take their cue from the king, the ping of knives and plunk of cups barely rising above the gentle murmur of voices. Suddenly, every face in the hall turned as Mortimer tripped through the doorway.

Eyes downcast, Mortimer walked down the center of the hall, his old injury apparent in the hitch of his stride. He stopped before the king's chair and bent his knee to the floor. "I beg your forgiveness, my lord."

Edward's left eyebrow curved upward. "For what?"

Still, Mortimer kept his gaze down. "For presuming wrongly and acting upon it. I should not have." It was a feeble apology, but a humbling one nonetheless for a man as proud as Mortimer. "I owe you too much to question you thus."

"You were misled. It is forgotten. Done. Think no more upon it."

Mortimer stood, finally looking at the king as if to judge further whether or not he had truly been exonerated, but Edward had already turned his attention elsewhere. The king beckoned at a server to refresh his cup and immediately began to engage Philippa in conversation about their son.

Mortimer remained standing before the king, waiting. Edward ignored him entirely, but it was Philippa who could not ignore his brooding stare a minute more. She laid her hand over Edward's as he stabbed a slice of beef with his fork and whispered into his ear. Edward flashed a perfunctory smile at Mortimer, and then instructed one of the servers to bring Mortimer a goblet of his finest wine. Deeming the gesture adequate, the king continued his conversation with Philippa, even as she glanced toward Mortimer from time to time. But Mortimer had not yet moved, nor had he taken the wine offered to him.

I did not fully understand, at first, why Mortimer did not depart graciously. It was almost as if he were challenging the king to open the dialogue further. But the more I looked upon Mortimer, the less I saw it as an act of impudence and more a plea for pity. His once proud bearing had vanished, the shoulders slumped forward, spine slightly stooped. His meticulously trimmed beard had gone unshaven for days, so that stubble shadowed his neck and cheeks. The look in his eyes, though—it was the same morose look that Hugh Despenser had when he had been dragged before us at Hereford. The look of a man who finally realizes he is mortal. That he will die, perhaps all too soon.

Mortimer's brow began to twitch. Several times, he closed his eyes and then opened them, more slowly than a blink, like one who is trying to cleanse them of dust. I thought he was going to say something more, but whether an offering of peace and atonement or an outright, final confrontation was not revealed. For as he looked up at the king again, and then I at the king, as well, Philippa was hovering over her husband, one hand rubbing his back and the other lifting his forehead from the table.

"Are you ill, my lord?" she asked.

"My head," the king said, followed by a distinct moan. "It has not ached like this in months. The light from outside . . . it hurts to

276

look upon it. God's teeth, it feels as though someone is rapping on my skull with a mallet."

Philippa pressed the back of her small hand to his forehead and then called for a physician.

"No." Edward waved a hand at her. "I only need sleep—and darkness. See that I am not disturbed. Come morning, all will be well."

Why did I not believe that?

"DID YOU SEE THE look on his face, Patrice?" I said to my dear friend as she helped me into my night shift.

"He looked . . . hmmm, I was going to say 'sad', but that does not seem like the right word."

"Afraid, perhaps?"

Her round mouth twisted as she contemplated it. "No, I cannot imagine Lord Roger ever being afraid of anything. More like—sorrowful. Yes, like how people look when they . . . when they are burying a loved one."

"A morbid thing to say, Patrice." I sat at my bed's edge, rubbing cold feet. Patrice abated my discomfort by fetching a pair of woolen stockings. Far from flattering, but practical.

"But do you not think it is true, Isabeau? I mean, did he not look like a man in mourning? All he wanted for were the proper clothes and a grave to stand over."

His own, perhaps.

"I would not say that," I said. "All the same, though, it was strange. Beyond awkward, really. I am not certain the king ever fully trusted Lord Roger. Relied on him, needed him—maybe. But trusted him, in the way that you and I trust each other with one another's secrets? No, never. And now . . . Mortimer fears for his life." I eased back onto the bed, crossing my arms over my breasts. "Oh Patrice, I have tried everything. *Everything.*"

Patrice, who knew more than anyone when to be honest with me, also knew when things were better left unsaid. Just as she used to when we were little girls, she lay down beside me and wrapped her arm over me and held me tight, letting me know she would always be there.

"In the morning," I said, more wishful than resolute, "I will go to Edward and implore with him to show Mortimer some kindness."

But even if I did—to what end? For all that I had fought so hard to gain, for as much as I wanted to believe I could influence those around me and change the future . . .

The worst does not need to happen. Not like it did to Kent, or Young Edward's father, or even Despenser, tyrant though he was. Yet it will happen.

My wishes are but whispers against the roar of the wind. There are forces beyond my control. People whose greed and ambition consume them and those around them.

Who am I to them anymore, but a shadow upon the wall? A spring flower crushed under foot? The buzz of an insect in their ears to be swatted away?

Patrice hummed a French lullaby—one that she had sung to Young Edward when he was a babe. My hand crept downward over my belly, feeling the growing fullness there like a hot coal that would burn me from within.

23

Young Edward:

Nottingham – October, 1330

PATIENCE AND SECRECY WERE weapons as powerful as the sharpest blade, as accurate as a well-aimed arrow. I had learned that from my mother.

Isabella of France, proud daughter of the House of Capet, was a clever, clever woman—a match for any man, including myself. My father had never stood a chance against her. And now, as I neared my eighteenth birthday—the day on which I would unfetter myself of the shackles known as the regency council and rule of my own volition—she was grappling to tighten her hold on me in order to guard herself, and Mortimer, against being deprived of the power she had so stealthily gained.

It pained me to think of causing her harm, but some things simply must be done. And once done, there is no undoing them.

Her hand light upon my elbow, Philippa guided me to my bed. A servant pulled back the covers and she eased me onto the bed's edge, and then pressed a cool, damp cloth into my hands. I clamped it to my forehead, groaning.

"Leave one candle burning," I said. "Then make them go."

For days, my head had pounded, but it was not an illness that plagued me. If I did what I had to do, there would be casualties. Yet if I did nothing, England and my kingship would suffer. I could not let the guilty go unpunished.

I heard the hushed scurry of feet, smelled the smoke of candles being snuffed. Philippa pulled off my shoes, kissed me on the cheek and stepped away.

Dropping the cloth, I grabbed her wrist and firmly tugged her back to me. "No, stay awhile. Just you. I need your comfort."

And I did. Tonight more than ever. For what I was about to do. For all I might regret in years to come.

Philippa whispered to the two servants who lingered by the doorway. Heads bowed, they disappeared into the shadows beyond. The door closed with a muffled thud that echoed in my head like a boom of thunder.

"Tell me," Philippa began, turning to me with a compassionate smile, "what I can —"

With a twist, I yanked her onto the bed, pinning her body beneath mine. She gasped in surprise. Then her hands reached for me, pulling my mouth to hers. Laughter welled in my throat. I kissed her full on the lips, but she, too, was laughing by then. In defeat, I collapsed beside her, both of our bellies shaking with mirth.

She mopped away tears of merriment and smacked me on the thigh. "My husband is a shameless liar."

Jutting my lip out, I rubbed at a stinging leg. "But my head does hurt."

"Not overly much, if it indeed does."

"Very well. If I am a shameless liar, my wife is the most beautiful creature on the Isle of Britain. More beautiful than any woman in France, the Lowlands, Denmark, the Holy Roman Empire —"

"You've never been to Denmark or the Holy Roman Empire."

"Doesn't matter. I speak the truth. Not even the angels in heaven could rival you, my love, my life,"—I nudged back the veil covering her head, my fingers threading through her hair, finding the pins hidden there and pulling them loose one by one—"my reason for being. Without you, why draw breath? Why hunger or think or even bother to feel anything? But with you lying next to me, ah, the world is mine, if only for that moment."

She gazed at me dreamily, the playfulness in her eyes softening to desire. "A convincing ruse in the hall, my lord. No one will dare to knock on your door until well after sunrise. What shall we do with a whole night to ourselves?"

Her hair free of adornments, I teased the strands apart, laying it in a golden fan about her ivory face as I slid my leg over hers. "Sleep, perhaps?"

"You're being presumptuous, my lord." Philippa shoved my leg off and rolled away, swinging her feet over the edge of the bed. She stood, small hands braced on her curving hips. "I can sleep quite well in my own bed." Skirts flaring as she whirled around, she stomped away.

I sat up, disappointment crashing through my chest. She couldn't go. Not now. I *needed* her. I shot to my feet, scrambling after her. "Where are you going?"

But she reached the door long before me. And slid the bar across, locking us inside. Together. Alone.

Her arms slipped inside the loose side openings of her cyclas. In a single, seamless move, she lifted the garment over her head. It landed in a heap beside her. She kicked it away and lifted the hem of her skirt to just above her ankles. "Your help?"

I sauntered to her, bunched her skirt in my hands, and inched it upward. Dear God, how badly I wanted her. But I wanted to draw this out, make the delight of her last if only to forget what morning would bring. "Changing into your nightclothes, my sweet?"

"Hmm, eventually." She tilted her head back, letting me take command.

Layer by layer, I undressed her, until nothing separated us. We drifted closer to the bed, my clothes scattered upon the floor as we went. She slid beneath the silken sheets, holding them open for me as I joined her. I traced eager fingers over her taut nipples, and then took one in my mouth, tasting the saltiness of her flesh, licking and sucking as I held her full breast in my kneading hands.

Her breathing deepened and then caught. I leaned back, thinking I had hurt her somehow. But she pulled me close again and arched her body, pushing her breast deep into my hungry mouth. I suckled greedily. A low moan rose in her throat. Gently, I eased over her. My hand brushed the inside of her smooth, milky thigh, my fingers wandering upward until she shivered, her knees opening wide, inviting. *No, no, too soon.*

I eased back and took her in, reveling in the glory of her body and all its promises. "Are you ready for another child, so soon after the first?"

Why had I even asked? God knows I didn't want her to refuse me. If she did, I might have to follow Will to the Boar's Head and spend my pleasure elsewhere.

"If the answer to that were 'no'," she murmured, her fingertips drawing small circles at my hipbone, around my navel, lower, "do you not think I would have said so by now? I love you, Edward. I always, *always* will. Until the end of our days."

It was all I needed to hear.

FOR A LONG TIME, I watched her chest rise and fall, the blanket drawn up high about her shoulders, the beckoning curves of her body hidden deep beneath. In the steady rhythm of her breathing, I found comfort. In her presence, I knew completeness.

I wanted to stay there, with her asleep beside me, until dawn was long past. But I couldn't. Not tonight.

One last kiss upon the crown of her head. One final glimpse before the fateful dawn.

As I rose, my movements stirred a draft. The candle flame went out, cloaking me in darkness. Then slowly, my eyes adjusted to view the faint outline of Philippa's form.

"Forgive me, my love," I whispered, "for what I'm about to do. But . . . it must be done."

Then I gathered up my clothes, dressed hastily and left.

WILL LIFTED A TORCH from its sconce on the wall and handed it to me. "I was beginning to think you'd changed your mind."

"After all the lies, the secrecy? No," I said. "But I do wonder how it will all unfold."

Dampness shimmered on the stones behind him. We were in a storage cellar of Nottingham Castle. The room was stacked to its cobwebbed rafters with barrels and sacks. Somewhere, a rat scampered.

He suppressed a grin. "Ah, you asked me not to reveal anything to you until tonight, so you'd have nothing to hide. I've kept my word on that—protected your virtue *and* your good name."

"As you should, Will. Now, let's get on with it. Show the way."

While I had known for months now that I needed to take command of matters, I had struggled with how to do it. When it was announced that Parliament would convene at Nottingham, Will had proposed a plan. Until tonight, he had kept the details from me, at my request.

Will lifted a sack from a pile against the wall and placed it on the one bare spot on the floor big enough to fit it. One by one, he moved the rest, eight in all. When the last was removed, he bent down, wedged his fingers between the planks and pulled up, revealing a trap door. He peered down into it. A blast of cold, musty air wrapped around my legs.

"Give me your torch, Ned." He lowered a foot into the gaping black hole until it landed on something solid. Carefully, he turned and climbed partway down a rickety ladder, pausing when only his head was above floor level. "You can take the other torch off the wall by the outer door."

I looked over my shoulder. The door was on the other side of the now chest-high pile of grain sacks. I looked back at him.

He shrugged. "Sorry, I didn't think of that part."

"I certainly hope you've thought the rest of this out more thoroughly."

"Oh, come now. You tasked me to sort this all out months ago. Have you no faith?" He glanced down into the hole, then back at me. "There has, however, been a slight change in plans."

"What do you mean 'slight'?"

"Just that. You said you wanted Mortimer taken care of. By morning, it will be done. Now get the torch and come with me. I'll explain everything."

Handing the torch down, I jabbed a finger at him. "Wait there."

He forced a smile. "As you command, my lord. But do hurry. I think a spider just crawled up my leg."

I crammed my foot in between two sacks at knee level and hoisted myself up. As I reached for the top and lifted my left leg up, the stack began to pitch with my weight. I slipped my right foot free of my toehold, but before I could push away and drop safely to my feet, the whole thing gave way. I landed with an ungraceful 'oomph', my right arm pinned beneath me, my face shoved up against moldy sackcloth.

"Are you all right?" Will called.

"Yes . . . I think so." At least the fall had been soft. A haze of dust drifted through the torchlight. I sneezed, pushed myself up and clambered across the scattered sacks to retrieve the second torch. When I returned, I held the torch out and looked down past Will. The hole through which the ladder passed was narrow.

"Come along, then," he said, his voice disappearing with his body as he descended. "And close the door after you. We've only so much of the night left."

I clutched the torch in one hand and went down after him, pulling the trap door shut behind me. When I landed on solid ground, I turned to survey our surroundings. Will shoved his flame close, momentarily blinding me.

"A network of tunnels," he said, thrusting his arm in one direction, then another, then yet another, each time revealing a long, rough hewn passageway. "It runs beneath the castle, with just a few well-concealed entrances beyond the edges of the city."

The passageway to our right extended fifty feet, then took an abrupt turn. The one ahead went on four times as far, before ascending by a stairway. Left . . . I couldn't even see the end to that one.

"How long have these been here?" I asked. "And where do they go?"

"Beneath the castle and much of the town is a great slab of rock. A thousand years ago, they say, there were just a few caverns where the great rock had cleaved. The earliest people who settled in this area lived in those caves. Later, when the Romans came, they hid from them here." He took his knife out and scratched a mark upon the wall. "Sandstone. They carved these tunnels by hand, widening them through the centuries, adding rooms to serve as storage places for food and arms." Slipping his knife back into its sheath, he hooked a hand in the air. "This way."

I followed him for what seemed like half a mile, our path twisting, going down, and then back up. Every now and then, we paused at a fork in the tunnel, but Will hesitated only a moment before forging on. My sense of direction lost, I often wondered if he wasn't guessing.

Will ducked low to avoid hitting his head as we began up a rough set of stairs, each step irregular in depth and slant, so that we had to tread carefully. At the top, the path continued on, narrowing. A hundred feet later, it turned a corner and flared outward. The ceiling was higher here, forming a domed chamber. Two door-less 'rooms' were situated on either side of the chamber. He turned left toward the larger of them.

Before he could get beyond my reach, I grabbed his arm. "Explain 'slight change of plans' to me. You promised to take Mortimer into custody."

"And I will. Although perhaps not how we had first planned. You know he has ordered the guards doubled on all the doors and at the gates?"

"What of it? You have the castle keys, don't you?"

He raised his brows. "Ah no, it seems —"

"What?! But you said —"

He clamped a hand over my mouth. "Calm yourself, Ned. This may actually turn out for the better. When I asked William Eland for the keys earlier tonight, he said Mortimer had taken them, he thought with the intention of giving them to the queen. So, Mortimer knows something is afoot, just not when or how it will happen. But not to worry, because Eland also told me about a secret passage, for which no key is required. Now I told you to trust me. You do, don't you?"

I nodded.

"Good." Slowly, he withdrew his hand, but not before patting me on the cheek. "Follow me. I've something that will put a little hair on your chin."

Patronizing bastard.

Once inside, he leaned his torch against the wall. I did the same and soon realized the place contained several barrels. Will lifted a jug of ale and then a pair of horn mugs from behind one of them and placed them on top. He poured us each a drink.

"Have your fill," he said. "There's plenty for the two of us."

I guzzled down the ale, as much to quench a parched throat as to dull my nerves. My future—and my freedom—hinged on this one night. If things went right, I would take control of my own fate and remove that which stood in my way. Or rather—who. If they went wrong, I could lose a true friend in the attempt. Either way, my mother and I would never be on good terms again. But I knew there was no reasoning with her where Mortimer was concerned. This had to be done. When I had drained the cup, I plunked it on top of the barrel. "More."

Will filled it again. By the time I was halfway through the third cup, I felt emboldened, and more sure of what was about to happen than ever.

I leaned back against the pitted stone wall, slid down, my red shirt snagging on the protruding bumps. Gripping a loose thread end, I pulled . . . too hard. It rent in a long line from front to back. "God's rotting teeth. Philippa gave me this shirt for our wedding. Came from Flanders."

"You'll have more than just that to explain after tomorrow." Sinking to his rump, he joined me on the floor to sit cross-legged. "Or is it today, already?"

"Today, tomorrow. Tomorrow, today." I tipped my mug back, took another gulp. "My birthday is in a month. Less than that, actual-ly."

"You've told me before. Numerous times. Are you sure, though, you don't want to wait until then to —"

"No!" I shouted. Then realizing how incredibly loud I was—as

287

if I feared someone might hear us in this unending cavern of nothingness—I leaned toward him and lowered my voice. "Mortimer already suspects us. If we wait even another day, he could flee. Or turn against us. He could do anything—accuse *you* of treason, even. Then you'd end up dead, just like Kent. No, we won't wait. We can't. There's no better place than this. No better time. If we can get our men in through these tunnels without being discovered ahead of time, we'll have him." I belched, wiped my mouth and scooted closer yet. "Secret passage? I don't see how this could *not* work, do you?"

Shaking his head, Will groped for the jug. Amber liquid sloshed over the brim as he lowered it from the barrel. Then he refilled my cup, emptying the jug.

"Aren't you having more?" I offered my cup. "Here."

He waved it off. "One of us needs to keep his wits about him. Very soon, the others will join us. Eland will lead them through the postern gate at the park and bring them here."

"How many?"

"More than twenty. Enough to overwhelm whatever guards Mortimer may have posted at his door—or the queen's. Once we take Mortimer into custody, we'll leave through the passage, go down to the tunnels, out the postern gate and take him to Leicester."

"I wanted him hanged immediately, do you know? Lancaster convinced me a trial was somehow necessary. I can't say that I agree, but . . . for appearances, perhaps. When your men get here, what then?"

"Eland will escort you back to the castle. There's a door hidden in an alcove very close to the queen's apartments. I assume you know which one?"

"Yes."

"Wait there. That door leads to the passage which is connected to a tunnel not far from here. When I knock, you'll draw the bolt and let us through."

"When will that be?"

"Prime," he said. "Are you certain you don't want to make yourself known when we take him into custody?"

"No, I'll stay out of the way. It will all come out in time. It's just that . . . I don't think I could stand to see my mother's face when it happens." Feeling the pull of sleep, I rested my cheek against the barrel. "Tell me the plan again, Will. Every detail."

Just then, the murmur of voices and the faint scrape of feet on worn stone reached my ears.

"No time, Ned. They're here."

24

Isabella:

Nottingham — October, 1330

AWAKE HALF THE NIGHT, I was still waiting to hear the bells ring for prime when there came a soft rap at my door. At first, I wondered if I had heard anything at all. But when I held my breath and listened, I heard it more clearly. It was never good to be roused in the middle of the night. Even more so of late.

I jabbed Patrice in the ribs with my elbow. Mumbling, she flopped over. I shook her by the arm, whispered her name, but she slept on like the dead. The knock came again, this time more insistent. There was yet no hint of dawn between the shutter cracks. Who would call on me at this hour? Wriggling my hand beneath my feather pillow, I touched fingertips to the cold metal of the castle keys before rising from my bed. I tiptoed to the door and leaned my forehead against one of the iron straps spanning the door.

"Who's there?" I called softly.

"Roger."

At that, Patrice, who had apparently been feigning sleep, gasped. She threw off her blanket and propped herself up on one elbow, alarm flashing from the startled whites of her eyes.

I hesitated. He must have feared that I would turn him away, for his voice took on a lugubrious mewl when he spoke again.

"Please, I am . . . I am desperate to speak to you, Isabeau. It cannot wait. Hurry, *please.*"

Placing a hand over my heart, I allowed him entrance. Without a glance or greeting, he pushed through the barely opened door and darted toward the window, stealing a quick look through it. I doubted he could see anything at that dark hour, but he hung back a moment, tilting his head as if to listen for some telling sound, and then glanced jerkily again past the window's edge.

Arnaud braced himself squarely in the doorway. My personal guards both gave me a questioning look. They were aware that Mortimer had not been to see me privately in some time. When I gave no protest, they conceded to Arnaud and stepped aside, one propping himself lazily against the wall as he shoved back a yawn, the other peering at the outer door with nervous vigilance.

I ushered a groggy Patrice from my bed and told her to wait outside. She knew her role whenever someone unexpectedly showed up while Mortimer and I were alone together; although this time she hesitated to abandon me to him in his edging madness. She shuffled to the door with a scowl on her lips, fumbling to wrap the twisted blanket around her and up as high as her neck, watching Mortimer closely over her shoulder.

The moment she saw Arnaud, however, she forgot about Mortimer. Her shoulders went slack and the blanket slipped back and fell to drape loosely over her lower arms. She tossed the flowing river of her hair over her back and marched past him with an alluring sway to her hips. His eyes swept over her as his head turned to watch her.

Feet planted wide, he stiffened his spine and turned his sights back toward the outer door to emphasize his duty. His palm cupped the pommel of his sheathed sword. Patrice, however, was not so easily put off. She sidled backward to stand close beside him and gave that childlike pout that so many men had succumbed to.

"I have seen and heard so little of you of late." Her fingers wandered across his chest. "Tell me it was not that I offended you in some way."

He caught her hand and gave it a distinct squeeze. "Please, now is not the time." Then he let her hand go and stepped back.

Mortimer lurched past me, closed the door as quickly but as quietly as he could and faced me, his form so limp and unsteady he could barely stand upright.

The last time he had looked so unkempt and haggard was when he had been shut up in the Tower for years. I still remembered that image of him: the tangled hair and ragged beard, eyes squinting against the light, the threadbare clothes hanging loose on his lean frame. But then, at least, he had kept his wits about him, scheming his future with rapt diligence. There had also been a fire in his eyes. And a handsome face recognizable even behind the grime.

Now . . . death stalked him. It showed in his downcast eyes, the way he tucked his head down into his shoulders like a snail withdrawing into its shell, how he always put himself in the corner of a room so he could see every door and window. His conduct alluded to insanity, but I could not say I blamed him for succumbing. My own mood and mind were far from tranquil.

It is one thing to face your enemies on the battlefield. It is another to be surrounded by them when they call themselves 'friends'.

"Have you slept at all?" I asked in genuine concern.

"In the last five days—barely." He edged around the bed and landed himself on the side nearest to me heavily, catching his head in his hands and shoving his fingers up through his uncombed hair. At length, he pressed his chin to his shoulder. His voice was raspy, like someone who had been out in the wind and cold. "I questioned whether or not I should come to you. I would not dream of putting you in danger. Yet here I am. A moth to the flame."

We both knew the danger he spoke of. I stood before him, half-way between the door and the bed—near enough to hear him, far enough for safety. Although I had never feared harm from him, I knew his temper and I was well aware of his current instability. The two together were a dangerous coalescence.

"I am leaving tonight for Ireland," he said.

As much as I wanted to keep him near me, I knew it was not safe for him here. "Why are you here now?"

He slid to his knees on the floor, still cradling his head as if he were afraid it might roll from his body and land at my feet. "Because this is something I could not entrust to another's ears."

His hands finally drifted down. How much older and gaunter he looked than only a few months ago. How robust he had been then, even for a man whose prime had faded. I recalled the lean muscles that sloped tautly from his neck to his upper arms, the musky scent of his sweat, and the fine scars of battle beneath my fingertips as familiar as the veins on the back of my own hand. Where was that man now? What had happened to him? Did I, as well, display the sufferings of my soul as plainly as he did?

He glanced up at the ceiling, then wistfully at me. His voice was a longing whisper, like that of a child sending a prayer to the stars up in heaven so only God could hear. "Keep the child, Isabeau, my love. Go away somewhere. Bear it in secret. If it be your wish—let it live."

Utterly stunned, I went and sat down on the far side of the bed with my back to him. I needed time to think everything through, but time was something I did not have.

Slowly, he stood, then came to me and went to his knees. "Come with me. Now. This very moment." Palms up, he held his hands out

293

to me in invitation.

I clenched my fists, gathering resolve. "Roger, no, no . . . we cannot."

He grabbed at my hands, trying to unroll my fingers, but I held them tight, resisting. "Please, Isabeau," he persisted. "Come with me."

"No, no, no . . . no!" Wrenching my hands from his, I bolted beyond his reach. I could neither think clearly nor act judiciously with him so near and my emotions swirling in a maelstrom. "I cannot go with you. Anywhere. Now . . . or ever. Please, go before —"

"Do not shirk me!" he said, a hundred hurts conveyed in the strained pitch of his voice. Suddenly, he was on his feet and his arms went around my waist, just firm enough to suggest possessiveness. His roughly whiskered cheek snagged the hair at the side of my head as he pulled me toward him. I felt the hardness of his chest against my back. "Oh, Isabeau, what would our lives have ever been without each other? Some dull rehearsal of duty? The monotony of loveless marriage? No, we created a heaven together. Ours alone."

His breath curled around my ear and cheek, beckoning my lips to the warmth of his greedy mouth. I felt the moist flick of his tongue on my skin as he kissed my neck, a faint whimper escaping his throat. And then I felt the beating of his heart. My own echoing its somber rhythm. My blood hotly racing.

I began to remember—the longing conveyed in stolen glances, the bliss of eternity delivered in his touch—all the times, all the ways.

And I realized what it had brought us to. This. Fear. Panic. Despair. Mistrust.

I peeled his hands away, still holding his fingers as I twisted in his desperate embrace to face him.

"It is not enough." The knot in my throat contorted as I began to gasp. "Not enough to . . . enough to . . . It would be the end of us both, never mind the child."

294

"Shhh, shhh." He caught a tear before it trickled from the corner of my eye. "Remember, then."

I blinked at him, not understanding. Not understanding until I heard the ominous boom of a door being busted from its hinges and shouts growing louder, more vehement. The clang of metal rang out. Blade hammered on blade. A terrible groan turned into a howl, emanating from deep within a tortured belly. Then . . . the thud of a fallen body resounded.

It ended with Patrice's blood-curdling scream.

A moment of ominous silence ensued, but was quickly shattered by another burst of activity. Montagu's voice rose above the confusion.

I quivered, my blood going as cold as a frozen lake. Mortimer let go of me, stepped back, and drew his sword. He looked at me sadly one last time—and opened the door.

There, in the middle of the outer chamber, knelt Patrice. In her lap she cradled Arnaud's head, his wide eyes staring up at her lifelessly. A scarlet river of blood bubbled from his chest through his padded tunic and pooled on the floor, staining dark red the edges of Patrice's pale yellow shift.

Above him, Montagu stood, his feet braced at shoulder's width, crimson beads of blood dripping from the tip of his sword onto his right boot. The thrust had been forceful and complete. He had drawn the blade cleanly out in one swift jerk, opening up the hole in Arnaud de Mone's chest. Patrice pressed the flat of her palm over the gaping wound, as if she could stop the life from flowing out of him. But it was already gone. Overwhelmed at the start, my guards had thrown down their arms early in the scuffle. Arnaud alone had stood brave and loyal against the threat—and paid the price.

Before Mortimer could raise his sword in defense, four men surrounded him, each murderous blade aimed at his chest. He raised his weapon, and then cocked his elbow back as Montagu jostled his way past one of his men toward Mortimer.

Tears filled my eyes. "No!"

Mortimer opened his grip. His sword clattered to the floor. He knew that if he fought them, he would die, just as Arnaud had. The nearest of Montagu's accomplices rushed forward and plucked up the relinquished weapon, then snatched the knife from Mortimer's belt. Before I could cry out once more, the two men on either side of Mortimer wrenched his arms back behind him and began to shove him along as the other two fell in behind.

Mortimer twisted in their grip and stole a sorrowful glance at me. "Isabeau, my love . . ."

I tried to say his name, but my tongue could not form sounds. Sobs of despair choked me.

They yanked him forward. Tears blinding me, I stumbled, crashed to my knees. By the time I untangled myself from my skirts and stood on wobbly legs, they were hauling him out into the corridor. Montagu moved in front of me to block my way.

Shoving past him so close I scraped my arm on links of chainmail, I rushed out into the corridor after them. "Don't take him. No! Noooo! Edward? Hear me, Edward! I know you are there. Make them let him go. Let him go! Edward!"

In a distant bend of the corridor, in the exact direction that Montagu's men were dragging Mortimer toward—a shadow loomed and shifted.

"Edwaaard!!!"

After the jostle of men turned the corner with their captive, I looked again, my eyes straining against the sputtering light of a single torch along the wall, but the shadow had vanished like a puff of smoke in a gust of wind.

I shouted more after that, but what exact words they were I don't remember. Montagu reeled me back in from the corridor, even as I kicked and spat at him. Enraged, I beat my fists at his chest fecklessly, volleying every insult I had ever heard fall from the mouths of soldiers and sailors, threatening to have him arrested, emasculated and decapitated.

"I regret this, my lady," he uttered in fallow consolation, even as he wrung my wrists to restrain me. "Please, believe that."

I spat in his eyes. He flinched and rubbed his face against his shoulder to cleanse himself, then clamped his hands tighter about my wrists.

Two men slipped past us and began upturning everything in the room. One of them ripped my blankets and pillows from the bed and onto the floor. The keys slid across the tiles, then clanked against the door's bottom. I writhed, trying to free myself from Montagu's iron grasp.

A howl ripped from my chest. But he was too strong, subduing me with gruff force as I thrashed side to side. Montagu shoved me into my chamber. I tripped, skidded across the floor—hip, elbow and shoulder all at once. A blast of pain shot up my right side. I rolled onto my back. Mindless of my agony, somehow I scrambled to my feet and hobbled forward. But before I could reach the door, Montagu had plucked up the keys and torn Patrice from Arnaud's flaccid corpse, tossing her in after me.

Patrice's fingernails raked over the floorboards. Her body shook with shuddering gasps as she wept.

Beyond my door, Montagu calmly issued orders to his remaining men. The leaden scrape of boots followed as they dragged Arnaud's body from the room. Pain throbbed down my arm. Patrice lay curled on the floor at my feet, mumbling her denial in between sobs of mourning.

I clawed at the door, screeching until my voice was torn raw. By the time I crumpled down beside Patrice, both of us trembling with exhaustion, the intruding light of morning was pouring in through the window to deny us rest.

Over the hours, I undulated from a hysteria so extreme that I was akin to the madwoman who tears through the streets at midnight screaming of the devil; to a soul so steeped in a despondency of lightlessness that hope seemed to have fled from all the world; and finally to a mind so numbed and a body so drained that the only difference between me and a pile of bones beneath the earth was a barely beating heart.

My back to the door, legs outstretched, I fixed my gaze on the fluttering remnants of a partially finished spider web tucked up in a shadowed corner of the room. I wondered why its maker had not persisted. I made to rise, but Patrice was half asleep across my lap. Gently, I rolled her aside and crept on tingling feet to study the web. The threads were frail and ripped in several places. There was no sign of the spider who had laid them. More than likely, it had died waiting for a hapless fly to land on its sticky threads and offer itself up for a meal and none had ever come. If I hunted carefully enough, I could have found its withered remains curled up in some dark recess of the room. That was, I was sure, how they would one day discover me. Shut away and forgotten. Dead from lack of sustenance.

Patrice rolled herself into a ball and moaned in anguish. I went to her and knelt down. Above her ear I whispered, "I will call again for Edward. He will come. He will."

She pulled at her hair, stretching the roots from her scalp. "Can he bring back my Arnaud from the dead?"

Her outward grief struck me hard. I had been thinking only of myself—and of saving Mortimer. Not of Patrice, who herself had just lost a love as dear as mine.

"Patrice, I am so, so very sorry . . . So sorry."

I knew not what else to say. I could not assuage her sorrow. Could not make anything right in her world. It had all been ripped from her in an instant before her very eyes and she, like me, had not been able to stop it. I reached for her, thinking to lift her by the arm to help her from the floor and to bed, but the moment she felt my touch she flailed herself back toward the door. Her elbow cracked against the door, but she took no notice.

"The king cannot bring him back. You can't. No one can. He is dead! Dead! Dead because of the vile Roger Mortimer. Because of you and your shameful secrets. You think of no one but yourself and your own satisfaction." She scraped her fingernails down over her neck, leaving long red traces. "Selfish whore! Have you no care for whom you destroy?"

I told myself she only spoke through grief, that neither I nor Mortimer was responsible for Arnaud's death. But even though I should have, I had little sympathy for Patrice's problems just then. I had my own. Mortimer—I hoped and prayed—was still alive, shackled in a dungeon crawling with rats and bitten by lice, perhaps, but *still* alive.

I had to see Edward.

I ordered Patrice to move away from the door, but she persisted in cursing me, her lips drawn back in a snarl, her beautiful face contorted grotesquely. I lunged toward the door, but she clawed at me. Out of utter frustration, I kicked at her. My foot struck her so hard in the face so that her head snapped back and banged against the door. As I clutched up a pewter candlestick from the table, she whimpered in fear of me, crawled half way across the room and lay there sobbing. I raised the candlestick above my head and banged at the door.

I hammered until my whole arm and chest ached from the effort, indenting the metal straps across the door and digging splinters from the wood. A hundred times a hundred, I called for Edward, my son.

Like his father had done to me at Tynemouth, Young Edward did not come, did not answer, did not offer help.

This time there were no Scots bearing down on the road toward

299

me. No ship tossing on a stormy sea to bear me to safety. No Roger Mortimer to rescue me from the cruel neglect of a vain husband. No Charles to dress me in fine gowns or replenish my money chests or William of Hainault to spread a mighty army behind me. No Adam of Orleton to show the way to wisdom or remind me of God's grace. Not even the pope to pen an eloquent letter on my pitiful behalf.

There was only myself and the sum of my misjudgments and sins to bear—and Patrice, who wholly hated me now. Somewhere was Ida, who would chide me a thousand times over for not having a clearer head.

Was there any way to make anything right? Or should I just have asked for peace with God while my heart was still beating?

They had taken Mortimer away. Surely, I would be next.

25

Isabella:

Nottingham — October, 1330

NOT UNTIL SEVERAL HOURS later did anyone come to my door, bringing a platter of food for us. It was a girl I had not seen before. She held the platter out tentatively, as though afraid to step inside the room. Judging by her shaking hands, she had evidently heard my screams and thought me possessed by the devil. Two guards stood close at her sides.

I reached for the platter. With a thrust of my arm, it flipped over and smacked the girl squarely in the chest. I tried to lunge past her, but one of Montagu's men struck me with the butt of his sword. Overwhelmed by brute force, I raised my hands to cover my head and dropped to my knees in the doorway.

When they did not persist, I touched the tender spot on my face, probing for a lump. Already I had bruises on my shoulder and arms—and now one to my jaw. A wonder they didn't draw blood

301

from me.

The girl leaned slightly forward and in a meek, but earnest voice, asked, "Can I do something for you, my lady?"

"Send for Ida," I pled, mustering the saddest frown I could manage in order to elicit her sympathy. "I need her."

She nodded and stepped back as the guards ushered me back to my domain of solitude. The door thudded shut. Patrice had paid little heed to my riot, barely raising her chin from her chest as she sat balled up against the wall, hugging her knees tight and sniffling.

I crept to her. Her eyes flashed at me in warning. Still several feet away, I stopped. "The potion you once drank to rid yourself of Arnaud's child—what was in it?"

Narrowing her eyes at me, she dug her fingernails into her shins and shook her head so hard the tips of her curls lashed against her cheeks. "What use could you have for it? Nothing will kill a devil's spawn." She spat at me.

I blotted at my shift. "This child, Patrice . . . it cannot be. They once told me I could bear no more children. That I should not. The child could die. *I* could die."

Even if both the child and I were to survive, nothing good would come of it. Nothing but perpetual grief and tumult.

Connive as I might to keep the pregnancy a secret, the chances of it staying that way were minute. As small as a dust mote. Young Edward would find out. Joan Mortimer would hate me even more, if that were even remotely possible. All England and France would erupt in an uproar. Philip of Valois would defame me. The pope would censure me . . . Beyond disrepute. Excommunication. Did it matter that I was already damned? Not only me, but my unborn child?

How was it that a tiny, innocent child could enter the world bearing the burden of another's shame and bring such enormous ruin upon a noble house? But it would, it would. My own disgrace would be the least of it. Mortimer's life would be forfeit. And Young Edward—what extravagant price would it exact upon him?

My fingers separated the folds of my nightshift, and then pleated the wrinkles to exaggerate them. I had not changed my clothing since the night before. I did not care. I felt dirty and worn and old, and ugly to look upon, like some dog-headed monster risen up from the sewer pit coated in moss and muck. Grime seemed a suiting skin for one of my kind. I was in consort with the lowest of sinners. My soul had long since been committed to the everlasting fires of hell. Did I truly need the pope to confirm that?

My marriage to Edward of Caernarvon had been the first test of my piety and I had failed that one and every successive one afterward. I had justified my carnal indiscretions by convincing myself that my husband had committed far worse sins than I ever would. Would I still say that now? I would not. No one would ever utter my name in the same breath as the devout Margaret of Scotland, who daily fed the orphaned poor before she sat down to table herself.

The shuffle of footsteps came from the outer chamber. I keened my ears, but could hear no familiar voices. It went quiet for several minutes before, finally, the door swung open. Bent old Ida ambled in, dragging one foot, and opened her right arm to embrace me. The left had long since gone bad from a bout of apoplexy. I went to her and hugged her to my breast, crushing her limp arm between us.

"Oh, Ida." Seeing her brought a fresh spate of tears for me, but Ida would have none of it.

She thumped me between the shoulders blades and thrust herself away, tottering, to leer at me through her good eye. The creased lid on the left eye sagged so heavily she could only see from it if she tipped her head far back. "What s-s-sort of . . . t-t-trouble are you in-n-n . . . n-n-now, my queen?" she said, her syllables coming out long and irregular with immense difficulty. Since suffering the episode a few years ago, the humiliation of needing help for even the simplest of tasks had forced her to keep to herself. It had been difficult to see her change in only a day's span from a spry old mother hen to a cantankerous, withered crow, her wings broken. She rarely traveled with my retinue anymore, especially when the journey from one castle to another was far. Come November, she preferred to stay put until March, feeling the bite of sixty-seven winters in her bones. Eleanor and John made a point of paying her visits whenever they could. Even though she protested that she did not want their pity, the visits were uplifting for her.

"You have heard about Lord Roger," I said, "that Montagu took him into custody? Where did they take him?"

Ida gave Patrice a curious glance and then shrugged a shoulder. "N-n-not here."

"The Tower? Berkeley? Kenilworth, perhaps?" But I had flung out the possibilities too swiftly for Ida to respond.

She blinked in confusion, her comprehension trying to catch up with my words and sort through them. She shrugged again. The jerk of her shoulder sent her swaying and I quickly grabbed her arm and helped her to a stool, only a few feet from Patrice, who by then was leering at me less harshly.

With a grunt, Ida plopped down on her seat. A sad pout pulled at her lower lip as she studied Patrice. "So s-s-sad, child." She paused and gulped. Her tongue was thick and clumsy in her mouth. It frustrated her to speak so slowly when she used to rain words faster than a spring shower. "You loved him, y-y-yes?"

Dabbing at her wet face, Patrice sucked back a runny nose and nodded. Then Ida reached out with her crooked arm as far as she could. Patrice crawled to her and laid her head down in her lap.

With the claw of her left hand, Ida stroked Patrice's head and back. Her voice was a croaking whisper. "We cannot always help . . . who w-w-we love, can we?"

Patrice's body went still for a few moments. She raised her head to look fondly at Ida. Then she looked at me through tangles of hair that fell across her eyes in a black forest of curls. Laced through her raven locks were the first few strands of silver-gray. We were both growing older, and neither of us any wiser.

In that lingering look from her, blame and hatred were absent. I saw only the faint flicker of empathy and the careful mulling of a thought.

"Rue," Patrice said softly. "You need rue, less than what you can fit in the palm of your hand, a pinch of pennyroyal, and wild carrot— but you must get it dried this time of year and it will be very potent. It could be . . . dangerous." She bit at her lip. "Mathilda, the cook's wife—she used to know how much of each, precisely, but I don't know where to find her anymore, or if she's still alive. Even if we knew, we wouldn't have time to fetch her. It may be too late, already, to . . ." Her lip jutted out, quivered. "Oh no, you shouldn't. It's too late, Isabeau. Don't. Don't." She whipped her head back and forth, pleading with me.

Kneeling beside her, I cupped her tear-soaked face in my hands. "I must. It cannot be."

I felt the meager strength of Ida's good arm as she cuffed me. "What f-f-for? Are you . . . Mother of m-m-merciful Christ. How could you b-b-be so stupid?"

I shook my head, flushed with shame like a child who has been caught stealing pies from a window ledge. "Stupid? Yes, that and more. But I need your help, Ida. You must bring me the rue, penny-royal and wild carrot, as soon as possible. Will you?"

She gave me a condescending look and crossed her arms by holding the weak one against herself with the other. "No! N-n-n—" Vexed, she grunted at her bumbling speech and spat the rest out. "Never."

"Then I order you to. Or I will tell all sorts of stories about you. Some of them true."

"Hah. There's nothing to tell." Ida staggered to her feet and, swaying side to side like a sapling willow in the wind, she shuffled to the door, grumbling to herself. She pounded on the door with the heel of her hand.

"Out! Let m-m-me out of . . ."—Ida gasped, sapped of strength by the short walk—"here. Now!"

The servant girl helped her along while Ida squawked like a wounded jay at her. Although it was hard to tell from the slant of her bad eye, I almost thought she winked as they escorted her from the room.

"A HEADACHE REMEDY," PATRICE had explained to the quizzical-looking servant girl as she took the dried herbs and a cup of warm cider from her. "She cannot sleep."

Over and over again, Patrice apologized for her lack of knowledge, muttering that it was witchcraft to practice such arts, until I reminded her that she had been dabbling in it for years already and there was no sense in repenting now.

By the light of a single candle—for that is all they would afford us as prisoners held for an unnamed crime—Patrice crushed the herbs with the heel of one of my shoes in a wooden bowl. She measured the rue into the palm of her hand, then the pennyroyal and dumped them each in the cup. Tentatively, she pinched the wild carrot between her thumb and forefinger and sprinkled the flakes above the cup. She mixed them together with a carved ivory hair parter, clinking it against the side of the cup as she stirred vigorously. Unorthodox implements, but we had not been given so much as a spoon, let alone a knife, to eat with earlier. Nothing but coarse bread and pears on a wooden platter and some tepid stew in a wooden bowl that we had to share, scooping the vegetables up with our bare fingers after we had sipped the broth. Supper had yet to come and it was nigh on evening by then.

The very moment Patrice stopped stirring to stare down into the bowl's mystical depths, I seized it from her, splashing some over the side of the bowl. I threw my head back and gulped it down not like a poison, but an elixir. I tasted mostly the crisp tang of unripe carrots, and then something sharper, more bitter, scraping at the back of my tongue. It began to burn. I gagged and swallowed, my eyes watering hotly. I thought I would retch at the vile taste scorching my throat, but deigned to hold it in and let it work its dark magic on me.

By Our Lord God's own word, this is wrong, wrong, wrong . . . terribly, inextricably wrong—but what is one more mark upon my blighted soul? If whores and murderers can be forgiven, am I not one of them?

The first convulsion gripped me so fast and fiercely I doubled over. Bolts of pain stabbed through every length of my body. When the next spasm hit, I had already dropped to my knees, clutching my stomach hard, as if I could reach within myself and gouge out the pith of my wickedness.

Again. Again. I threw my head back, aware that some primal wail emanated from me. It was the sound that women make as they wander among broken and dismembered bodies on the battlefield, keening their dead.

I existed only within my pain. My cries, though, were not calls for help. They were a release of all my torment—every regret, every worry, all my shame.

Patrice wedged a leather belt between my clamped teeth for me to bear down on and stifle my screams.

Through the bleary veil of my lashes, I saw Patrice kneeling beside me, pressing a damp cloth to my forehead, although I could not feel it. Then, she crammed a rolled blanket between my legs . . . Why?

Wetness. Blood. Too much. Life seeping away. Out of me.

"It was too strong." She whimpered between breaths. "I will call someone to —"

Somehow I swung a hand at her to grab her forearm before she went to the door. I shook my head at her and tried to push away the leather strap with my tongue.

No, no. Let it be. What is done cannot be undone.

Had I spoken the words aloud or said them only in my own head? I do not know then if Patrice called someone for help or if she settled next to me and honored my wish. Everything went icily white.

Tides of pain pierced like a dagger being plunged into the pit of my belly and rent down toward my groin. My limbs weakened as the blood flushed from me. My core went cold. The edges of my vision darkened . . .

Silence. Floating in darkness. My body weightless upon a placid sea of black.

The pain . . . gone.

A THOUSAND YEARS FROM now, they will say Isabella of France was a wanton who abandoned her children to frolic with her lover in her brother's house. They will say that out of convenience and iniquity, she conspired in the disposal of her husband. That she opened her son's reign with scandalous infamy by defiling her marriage vows. That she hoarded her son's wealth and squandered it on her rapacious lover.

They will say that Isabella of France was a bane to England. That she was a she-wolf.

They will say what they will, or maybe I will be forgotten, a blot upon the pages of history's chronicles . . . but I know the truth—that there were injustices and evils greater than mine.

One thing, I know, they will say—that Edward III, King of England and France . . . that he was a greater king than his father and his grandfather before him and the hundred kings after him.

"ISABEAU? ISABEAU?"

I heard the familiar voice tinkling distantly, like bells from a church in a far away, unseen valley.

"Isabeau, can you hear me?"

I opened my eyes. Patrice smiled. She swept back the tangled hair from around my eyes. I tried to lift my head, but the pillow piled deep with goose down was too inviting. My neck hurt, my shoulders, lower down, lower . . . a knot of soreness between my legs. I closed my eyes again.

"Isabella? Mother?"

Is that Eleanor? Or Joanna? Has she come back from Scotland already?

"Mother?"

I opened my eyes once more. It was Philippa. When had she ever called me 'Mother'?

I turned my head toward Patrice. Pain stabbed down through my neck.

"What happened?" I said, feeling all the wind empty from of my lungs with those two words.

"You will be all right, Isabeau." Patrice stroked my arm as she donned an unconvincing smile. "You will not die."

I blinked at her. *Why would I die? Have I been ill?*

As Philippa rose to cluck orders to two bumbling servant girls, Patrice bent close and whispered, "The child is no more. But you—you will be well enough, in time. No one knows of it. Ida helped me to . . ." She bit off the rest of her words. She could not say it.

Then I remembered. I did not want to. I wanted to forget. Wanted to think it all a nightmare, vanished like the mist in the golden light of a new dawn, the world bejeweled with dew.

Let me go back to sleep. Let me dream again until Mortimer comes back. Mortimer . . .

"Roger?" I uttered, my voice quaking faintly in my own ears.

God in heaven—do I want to know? Let me go back to sleep. Let me never awaken again. Let the darkness swallow me up and wrap itself around me until I am nothing. Until I am no more.

Patrice exchanged a telling glance with Philippa.

Philippa returned and settled on the edge of my bed, her daintiness barely indenting the mattress. She dug beneath the covers for my hand and held it. Philippa was unusually sober for one of her few years, as if she had been born at the age of thirty. However temperate and diplomatic, she was not one accustomed to divulging bad news. I knew it was bad because she would not look at me.

"You have been asleep for four days," Philippa said. "Much has happened."

"Where is he?" I croaked, my throat swelling shut. My chest tightened. I gasped for air.

Still, she would not look at me. Her features were as pale as death. "He . . . Edward came to see you. He'll want to know you're getting better."

"Not him," I corrected. "Where is Roger? Where did they take him?"

For a minute or more, I received no reply. I heard only the scurrying of servants out the door and back again, the rippling of water being poured, the pinging of a spoon.

"Leicester, for now," Patrice finally told me. She patted my blankets smooth and then began rearranging my hair, although I hardly cared about those things. "Although they say he will be taken to London."

"Why? Why London? For what?" My heart began to race, stirring me to full wakefulness.

Philippa sighed long. "Parliament meets next month at Westminster. Edward means to have Lord Roger tried. Treason, I suspect. And Lord Berkeley, his son-in-law, was also taken into custody. He will be tried, as well—for the murder of Edward of Caernarvon."

"Maltravers, Ockle, Gurney," Patrice added. "They all fled before they could be arrested."

Treason. Murder. Ah. They will come for me next. When I stand before them, I will say nothing. I know the truth. God knows. They have already forged their opinions. Condemned Mortimer . . . and me. What use to battle fate? I have wearied of it.

A year ago . . . a month even, I would have fought this—written diplomatic letters, shaping every delicate twist into the proper perspective. I would have demanded to speak to my son, bargained for clemency—exile at the worst—and pled mercy with mild, sensible Philippa, who I had once believed held so much influence over her husband. But this time she was not in agreement with him. Or was it that . . . that she felt some sort of pity for my suffering?

"You spoke to Edward?" I asked. "Tried to save Mortimer?"

Philippa flinched and squeezed her eyes shut, then nodded several times before opening them. "He would not listen to me, Isabella. He went instead to Lancaster, who at least had the sense to talk him into going through the motions of a formal trial." Finally, she looked at me. "It should not be at all, but . . . his mind is made up. Better it should be done swiftly then, I suppose."

Why? Where is the charity in that? It is not even justice. It is retribution.

I had seen it looming for weeks, pretended it would not come to pass, and begged Mortimer to leave. Yet there was only one end. Only one.

I pulled my hands back beneath the blankets. My fingers wandered over my vacant belly, grinding with hunger.

"Why?" I said, to so many decisions and events that had befallen me. Why had it come to this? Had I not tried to make peace, to steer the kingdom when others sought to sink it, to be the good wife and mother, to keep my private affairs private?

"You shall have to ask Edward that," Philippa said, her gentle voice tinged with the misery of a famished child.

Edward? I do not think I wish to see Edward. Not now. Not soon. What use?

The servants propped me up to sip from a pewter cup filled with honeyed mead. Then they spooned a broth of cabbages and leeks from a bowl and fed it to me. I ate greedily until I began to cough. My stomach was filled with only a small amount of food, so much it had shrunk. Warmth and nourishment miraculously began to seep into me. My fingers, my whole body tingled with renewal. Yet my heart beat sluggishly, slow as the drums that announce an execution. My eyes began to drift shut again before they could entice me to partake of some bread and more mead.

I did not notice Philippa, being light as a bird, rise from the bed until I heard her voice from the doorway.

"When you are well enough, you will be taken to Berkhamsted," she said, her words drifting away so that I barely heard the last of them. "Away from here."

Is that to be my prison? Does it matter where they put me? I cannot raise an army now. Soon, I will have no champion. Edward will make certain of it.

It is done. Done.

26

Isabella:

Berkhamsted — November, 1330

I N THE FIRST FEW weeks that I was detained at Berkhamsted like a caged dove, I wrote letter upon letter to my son, none of which were answered. I prayed in the chapel for God's guidance, but none came to me. Time trudged forward until the day, the 13th of November—and so distraught I was that I did not remember what day it was until afterward—that King Edward III passed his eighteenth birthday.

Then everything moved forward, swiftly and mercilessly. My son, it seemed, had merely been biding his time, waiting until he could break the shackles of his minority and dissolve the regency council that he felt had stifled him so unjustly.

Two weeks later, the parliamentary session opened in Westminster with the trial of Lord Berkeley. It lasted not a day. The charges were dropped and he was set free. Again, I prayed, but I may as well have spent my breath on prayers for myself, for my hopes were short-lived. My gentle Mortimer's trial began the next day.

Fourteen crimes were cast at his feet, but Roger Mortimer, Earl of March, was not allowed to speak in his own defense. He had been gagged. He was declared guilty of them all, including the usurpation of royal powers and . . . the murder of Edward of Caernarvon.

My love was dragged on a splintered hurdle behind horses from the Tower of London to the Elms of Tyburn, some three miles away, stripped naked, lashed fourteen times, castrated while he was still conscious and then hanged to death from the gallows alongside the ghosts of common thieves. For two days, his mutilated body was left to dangle while carrion crows quarreled over his flesh and a scurrilous mob lobbed stones with wicked glee. He was finally buried, mangled though his body was, at Greyfriars in London. Later, at Joan Mortimer's request, his remains were returned to Wigmore Abbey near Ludlow.

Patrice told me. She told me because I asked. Not knowing was a sickness unto itself that devoured me from within. A pity they did not hang me with him. It would have been kinder.

Sir John Maltravers, Sir Thomas Gurney and William Ockle all fled England upon hearing of Mortimer's arrest. In doing so, they were publicly assumed guilty of taking part in the murder of Edward of Caernarvon. Parliament passed a sentence of death on them. They would never step foot on English soil again and we would never learn their accounts of what happened.

Young Edward issued magnanimous pardons, freeing Edmund of Kent's widow and restoring the inheritance of his son. Every time I heard Kent's name, I wondered why he had been so adamant that his brother was alive. There was no proof.

I gave up all my lands to Philippa. What need did I have of them? I did not see her again until I was escorted, under a sizable guard, to Windsor.

My son must have feared I would raise an army from the confines of my lavish prison and march against him with some newly infatuated lover tripping along at my side. Why would I? How could I hate the son for whom I had sacrificed all? I should have, given the pain he had inflicted on me, but in the end I had chosen him over Mortimer. My son, however, would never know that. Had I sat down with him and explained everything, I might have been able to win his love back. Or if not his love or his understanding, at least his tolerance.

Some secrets, however, are better left buried in the past. Why scrape open the wound that no longer bleeds to try to cleanse it? If it has healed, however hideous the scar, let it be.

Windsor — 1330-1331

FROM MY TOWER WINDOW at Windsor, I gazed out at the world beyond. Boats coursed up and down the Thames, but each one looked the same to me. I could not tell winter from summer, day from night. Nothing ever changed. I slept when I was tired, sat by my window when I was awake, ate when they told me to even though I never hungered. Hour after hour, I prayed. I had long since forgotten what it was I prayed for, though. It was merely habit.

I had not ventured beyond these walls in over a year. The king would not allow me. Where would I have gone, had I been able to go at all? One prison was like any other.

Sometimes, I heard Mortimer's voice, as clearly as if he were holding me in his arms, whispering in my ear: *"Isabeau, I would give my life for you."*

And he had.

"Isabeau, love . . . I cannot live without you."

Nor did I want to live without him: my gentle Mortimer. Those memories cut me to my soul and drained the blood from me. In my dreams, I would reach for him, shaping his name on my lips, and grasp nothing but cold, empty sheets to my breast. Sometimes, though, I swear I would awaken with the warm trace of his fingertips on my shoulders and back.

"With all my heart, Isabella, I love you . . . only you."

Too much so. What is any love worth? A life? Ten lives? Without life there is no love.

What does 'love' even mean? I had not known it with Edward, that was certain. Marriage to him, although I had gained four beautiful children from it, had brought me nothing but disappointment and suffering. Knowing Mortimer, loving him . . . that too had brought me pain. But in between the torture of secrecy and shattered trust, with him at least there had been ecstasy, hope and tenderness.

The world would forever see us as shameful sinners and greedy liars. Centuries from now that would be our legacy. No one would ever know who we truly were. Judged and condemned by those who had never met us. There would be no sainthood for the scheming queen. No statue in the market square for her murdering lover. Our names would forever be a stain on England's honor.

We would, however, be remembered—in ignominy.

I think I would have preferred to remain nameless.

Castle Rising — 1336

MORE THAN FIVE YEARS now since Mortimer died. His voice was growing ever more distant. I remembered the words he used to speak to me, but not their inflection. I remembered being happy, lost in the bliss of his nearness, but I no longer sensed his arms around me. My world had gone from drowning blackness to bland indifference; from the bottomless well of self-pity and mourning to the uninspired monotony of household duties and familial obligations. I could only stare out my window for so many years before madness was sure to set in.

Still, it was an effort that I forced myself to embrace. I was not there when my youngest Joanna was crowned at Scone beside her husband David, now King of Scots. Nor was I present when Philippa bore a daughter and named her Isabella. But I was there in Nijmegen when my daughter Eleanor, only twelve, wed the Duke of Gueldres. Oh, they looked so unhappily paired. I could not help but think of my own wedding so long ago in Boulogne.

I held up the tarnished mirror, tilted it to catch the light. Sunbeams illuminated my features: the widening cracks, the sagging jowls, sprigs of white hair at my temples where once I had worn a crown of golden tresses. Damsels buzzed about me, purposeful in their industry, laying out glittering jewels and silver combs and embroidered gowns of silk in every color. My mews at Castle Rising were filled with the finest hawks and falcons, my library full to bursting with every romance ever committed to parchment. I surrounded myself with things because it helped me forget the emptiness.

Philippa bounced the baby on her knee. Little Joan clapped, her gummy smile wide and pure with joy. I rose from my cushioned stool and swept her up. Her chubby arms went around my neck.

Grief crashed over me. Just weeks ago, I had awoken before dawn shivering with dread. Later that day, a messenger arrived from Scotland. Before he even spoke, I knew—John was dead. And only twenty. Far too young. As a boy, he had tried so hard to be like his older brother, wielding a stick as his sword and begging for a pony so he could learn to ride. Moments like this, holding my granddaughter, made me remember him when he was young, before dreams of becoming a soldier took hold of him.

"Thank you," I said to Philippa.

Opening one of the books stacked upon my table, she ran her

fingers along the twisting tails of ink. With her other hand, she rubbed at her stomach in slow, soothing circles. Not four months along and already it was obvious she would have a fourth child. "For what?"

"For bringing my grandchildren to visit me." The baby rested her head on my shoulder and I rocked her in my arms. Her tiny heart drummed out a rapid beat. Soon, she began to blubber and then pule like a milk-starved kitten. "Oh, I think she's hungry. Shall I fetch the wet nurse?"

"Here." Philippa took the baby and laid her down on my bed, then pulled the corner of the blanket over her, tucking it tightly around her. She stroked little Joan's fuzzy head until the baby settled. "She does that when she's tired. A mother learns their cries."

I stood for a long while, watching the baby drift off to sleep. Her chest rose and fell in a shallow, but sure rhythm, her plump cheeks puffing with each exhaled breath.

"The king," Philippa began, her tone suddenly sober, "received a letter from Sir John Maltravers in Flanders."

I had not heard his name or the others' in years. Even thinking about that time yanked me downward into a lightless place. Why did she have to tell me this now? "When was this?"

"Some time ago."

"What did the letter say?"

"He would not tell me." She placed a hand lightly on my shoulder. "But afterward, it was as if everything had changed. Like he was no longer angry."

As if everything had changed.

The time had come to banish the ghosts of my past. I wrote to Lord Thomas Berkeley and waited, my heart heavy with dread, my soul longing to be free of unspoken secrets.

Castle Rising — 1338

"THEY PROCLAIMED YOU INNOCENT, Lord Thomas," I said. "Why, when they sent my gentle Mortimer to his death so long ago?"

Previous letters to Berkeley had prompted only vague responses, but at last I had insisted on his presence. To my absolute shock, he had finally come to Castle Rising.

"Because I am not guilty of any crime, my lady."

A faint beam of evening sunlight penetrated the confines of the chapel and spilled over the floor around him. I had knelt so many hours of late before the silk-draped altar that my knees had developed calluses.

"But you knew of it?" I said.

A faint smile played at the corners of Berkeley's mouth. "I told them that I did not arrange, agree to, or aid in his death."

Within the twisting rope of words were a hundred loopholes. With Mortimer dead and Maltravers, Gurney and Ockle gone from England, Thomas Berkeley alone held both lock and key to the mystery of Edward of Caernarvon's fate now. Had he simply turned a blind eye to Edward's murder and then lied before Parliament to spare himself? Or did he guard another truth? I slumped against a column, trying to keep myself upright, but I began to slide downward.

Oh, Lord—your revenge on me will be nothing short of ironic. For keeping silent my knowledge of these sins, you will reveal them all and punish me more than twice for them—here in this world and for eternity.

Before I crumpled into a boneless heap, Berkeley caught me by the elbow. "Actually, they believed I knew nothing of the plot. Many thought me confused by too many questions—and a thousand of them they flung at me, for hours on end. At the least, they thought me too daft to be duplicitous. That . . . or mad. I told them I had been ill at the time and away from Berkeley, unable to return. When it was discovered that the king was dead, I was not there. So they let me go."

His tale was too convenient—an alibi of fishnet, with holes so big I could have stuck my fist through any of them. Berkeley had his secrets, and he had abandoned his own friends to keep them. How is it that I had ever thought him trustworthy? Had he made a pact for his soul with Mortimer long ago—a pact that, even in death, could not be broken?

"So, you absolved yourself of the sentence by pleading ignorance? Where is your loyalty, Lord Thomas? With me, whose insanity you find amusement in? With Lord Roger, defamed and dead now? With your 'friends', Maltravers, Gurney and Ockle, who ran for their lives because you spoke half-truths? What *is* the truth, Thomas? You alone, it seems, are the keeper of it. Before God, say it. If it will unfetter you, let me fetch you a gospel so we may undo our oath."

Again, the flippant smirk. "You say that you swore me to an oath that I would never —"

"Then I release you from your oath!" I screamed at him. His ambiguity served no one but himself now. "If it pleases you to hear me say it, I was wrong to demand it so rashly. I only did so because I did not want to betray myself . . . because I didn't want Roger to know I was meddling in his plan. Now I know I should have stopped him altogether. His wrath should never have been a hindrance to me doing what was right. So let us begin anew. Say that it was never agreed between us, and if we cannot reveal it to the rest of the world, then let us speak it nowhere but here, in this room, only once between us, can we? What gain is there anymore in pretending? Say it, Thomas—the truth!"

The wry smirk melted from his mouth. He sidled toward the altar, as if some refuge from my vengefulness awaited him there, and sank to his knees beside it to lean his cheek against the plain white linen cloth draped over it. "What would you have me say? That I lied? That I have concealed the truth?"

He lifted his face from the altar, bearing a look so grave that I could see the angst deep inside him. "I had *no part* in any plan to murder Edward of Caernarvon. And yes, there was such a plan. Your beloved Roger Mortimer was its devisor. The others you spoke of—they were his intended instruments, mindless puppets that he could toy with, for he would not taint his own hands with royal blood. And I . . . I was to carry the message to them, but I could not . . . could not see it followed through."

Something in his demeanor began to shift. His shoulders went slack and he slumped forward, hugging his knees hard like a hungry child left out in the cold. I moved around the altar to see him more clearly, for night was descending. The insolence had faded from his tone. The elusiveness—vanished, as if he were a base sinner bearing his darkest soul in confessional to his priest.

"Some months before Sir Edward's funeral, as you know," he continued, "Stephen Dunheved and his conspirators gained access to him at Kenilworth and tried to free him. They were thwarted before they ever got near him. They made a second attempt and succeeded. They were miles away when his pitiful cries threatened to betray them. He cursed the throne of England and said he did not want it back. That night, Sir Edward awoke in the forest where they were encamped and escaped from his liberators. He was found wandering outside a nearby village and was returned to Kenilworth. When rumors indicated the Welsh were also planning to rescue the king . . . Sir Edward, I mean," he corrected himself, "Lord Roger then decided something must be done. Gurney and Maltravers were given orders to withhold food from him, so that he would weaken and fall to some sickness of the flesh. But Sir Edward prayed, every day, and he remained strong, impervious to the deprivations forced upon him. He prayed to God to be free of the burdens of his birthright. He even prayed, my lady, that you and your 'whoring slavemaster', as

321

he called him, should be forgiven. He shirked everything that was of this earth and gave himself completely to God. In all my life, I have never seen such . . . such *utter* piety. He became more saintly than any holy man I have ever known.

"I knew him when he was king, only a little and mostly from a distance, but it was easy to see the man he was back then: vain, petty, selfish, greedy, and with an appetite for vengeance. Neither you nor I need deny how he sinned in private. His sickness was known to everyone but him. But a change came over him while he was at Berkeley. At first, he fell into silence. Not brooding, but rather contemplative—as if he were lost to our world, seeing and hearing things unknown to the rest of us. With time, he began to speak of his life and his errors, of God's way, His will, of the Scriptures . . . It was in earnest, that much I could tell.

"I took pity on him. I brought him bread and clean water—even a flask of wine, which he drank as Christ's blood. But more than pity him, I was humbled by him. I wanted to help him, to give him a way to devote himself to God wholly. To do that, there was only one way—to let him be dead to the world. Even to you.

"Your request to spare him came as a deliverance," Berkeley said with gentle reflection. "A convenience. So I played along—on all sides. And to this day, I keep my word to everyone as best as I am able."

"He lives then?"

"Still, you ask?" His voice was airy, strained nearly to breaking by the burden he had carried for so long. "Lord Roger was right, you know? Our young king's conscience would be marred if he thought his father lived. Not only that, but he would never sleep well for it. Without the crown of England, he could never hope to win that of France, could he? Lord Roger knew—and you know better than any. So perhaps it is best that Edward of Caernarvon is dead to this world—better for him, for our king, for you —"

I threw myself at him and sank my fingernails into his thin shoulders. He winced. I lightened my grip, but shook him as if I could jar loose the one morsel of information that would put all the pieces in place. "He lives—yes or no?"

"He lives."

My heart ached. Mortimer had died, not only on the premise of treason—a crime trumped up so that my son could free himself of Roger's hold on power—but also for the murder of Young Edward's father. Because of Berkeley's reticence, however, he had died for all the wrong reasons. And I was partly to blame for that.

He slipped free of my hold and stood above me, swaying with the release of his troubles.

"Did Roger know it was not Edward of Caernarvon's body that we mourned over and buried?" I asked. "Did *he* know then that he was still alive?"

Berkeley shifted on his feet to gain his balance and averted his eyes. He answered with a question. "If Lord Roger had known, beyond all doubt, that Sir Edward was dead, would he have hurried so to silence Edmund of Kent?"

No, he would not have. There would have been no reason to.

"So he did know?"

At last, Berkeley met my gaze squarely. "Yes, he knew. When Lord Roger received the news at York that another attempt to free Sir Edward had been made, he arranged with me to move him from Berkeley to Corfe Castle, but in secret. In his place at Berkeley, I put a man who looked incredibly like him, although not as tall and much thinner. The man, a monk and a halfwit, had been accused of raping and nearly strangling the daughter of the mayor of Oxford. They were going to hang him, anyway. Shortly after that, Maltravers and Gurney received word from William Ockle that Mortimer wanted Sir Edward dead. Although they discovered this other man in his cell at Berkeley, they murdered him anyway. Panicked, they hastily arranged

323

for the midwife to embalm the body."

I held my palm up to slow his stream of words. It was almost too much to absorb at once. "You mean Roger had you hide Edward at Corfe . . . but then he told Ockle to have him killed, knowing all the while that it was another man they would find there at Berkeley?"

He nodded. "He knew they would kill the man anyway, rather than be faced with the failure of having lost Sir Edward again. There would be a body, a funeral. It was all that was needed."

As swiftly as if I had been struck by lightning, I understood *everything*. Mortimer had spared Edward by entrusting him to Berkeley. Gurney and Maltravers murdered the other man to cover up their own assumed failure, and then passed him off as Sir Edward. If England believed him dead, then Young Edward's crown was secure and as long as he remained king, then Mortimer's position and power remained, as did mine.

Berkeley made to leave, but I snagged his sleeve to halt him and then leapt to my feet, blocking his path.

"But Kent," I said, "somehow learned where his brother was and threatened to reveal all, didn't he?"

"Yes. I never learned how he found out, but it was then that I decided to send Sir Edward to the continent, somewhere he could devote himself to God's service and hopefully never be found. Lord Roger never knew his whereabouts. He never asked."

"And when the king brought the charges of murder against Roger," I said, "if either of you had so much as hinted Edward was still alive . . . *I* would have been implicated, too."

"He protected you—and your son's throne—by sacrificing his own life. I once swore an oath to him that I would never reveal anything, that I, too, would protect your name and your son's crown. And I have."

I dropped his sleeve. His cloak snapped against my skirts as he swirled around.

"Wait!" I called before he could reach the door. "Where is he? Give me proof that you speak the truth."

Air gusted through the window. The candle flames on the altar bent sideways, struggled and then brightened. "The king has proof."

"What do you mean?"

"A letter from a Genoese priest named Manuel de Fieschi—ask your son about it." He hurried away.

I turned back to the altar, the rapid click of his footsteps fading away. Behind me, I thought I heard a murmur, the closing of the door, muffled footsteps, slower in cadence. I held my breath, too afraid to look. But I heard no more, saw nothing.

It was only my imagination. Or perhaps it was Mortimer's ghost, eavesdropping.

27

Young Edward:

Windsor — 1339

H ER LETTER, CURLING UPWARD at both ends, lay atop a table
overflowing with maps of France and Scotland and documents
awaiting my seal. I touched the barest fingertip to the black, swirling
words. A blot, from a fallen tear perhaps, blurred the end of her
name. Had I not known her handwriting well, I might not have
known whose name it was at all.

My Beloved Son,

*How do I begin? You will think it an old woman's senseless
prattling, desperation for a son's love. But I know not how else to win
your heart again. Let me simply begin then.*

*I have sacrificed much, sinned too often and suffered for it all a
hundred times over. I have known what it is to feel everything and nothing:
the drunkenness of power and the corruption of wealth; a husband's loathing*

and the hollow ache of loneliness; the silent cut of jealousy; the guilty ecstasy of a dishonorable love; and grief too heavy to rise up from.

I tell you these things not to shrive myself, nor to elicit your pity. Nor do I tell you to receive your gratitude for bringing you to the throne. Without me, even . . . in spite of me, perhaps, you will become one of the greatest kings England and France have ever known. To me, you will always be the small boy taking his first steps. To you, I do not know what I am anymore. I only ask that you remember more than my failings, see more than my flaws.

Whatever others may say of me as queen or woman or wife . . . those things matter not. For whatever God may deliver unto me, I shall receive with due humility. More than His judgment, however, I fear yours, for I have kept a truth from you. A truth that would put all between us right, but a truth buried in lies to protect you and others.

You have in your possession a letter from the Genoese priest Manuel de Fieschi—one whose story, I pray, will change much between us. Maybe everything. When you read his words, a man beholden to none but Our Father, the truth will be less tainted to your ears than if it came from my mouth.

Our Lord keep you and protect you.

Your devoted mother, Isabella
Castle Rising, Norfolk,

The confession clutched in my palm, I went to the window and stared out over the Thames from the heights of Windsor's ancient hill. Jagged chunks of ice clung to the river's edge in places still. Snow was falling thick and fast from an iron-gray sky.

So, she had learned of de Fieschi's revelation? But how much more did she know? When Sir John Maltravers wrote to me and confessed it was not my father he had killed, the admission had sent me on a quest for the truth that eventually led me to the continent.

Yesterday, it had snowed more lightly, the final leg of our return journey passing swiftly. Today, Philippa had risen at dawn, trying to soothe Lionel's colic. The boy could wail rather loudly for such a small louse. She was a doting mother, my Philippa. I often warned her she would spoil our youngest, but she never heeded my advice. After ten years of marriage and five children, I should have known that Philippa did what she wanted.

Philippa had accompanied me to the continent where I was made Vicar of the Holy Roman Empire and when that dull pomp was done with we had gone on to Antwerp and stayed for Lionel's birthing. It seemed she was either perpetually with child or had just had one. The pleasing curves of her youth were giving way to an un-flattering bulge of fat around her middle. The forced stint of chastity, however, always drew me back to her with renewed lust. Lionel being our fifth child, though, I did not sense it was the same for her. Each birth tired her, stretched her belly a little further, and took her mind from me more, as she adored her children immeasurably. I remember my own mother being that way.

My own mother—ah, I could not say I blamed her for running from my father. I could not even say I blamed her for falling into another man's arms, putting her husband low and shutting him up like a biting dog that deserved no better. My father had not been worthy of his crown. All of England knew that. The crown was meant for me. My father's failures simply hurried my fate along. I always knew it would come to me early, that there would be even more within my grasp. And it was Mother who sowed the seed in my head, watered it with her flowery words of ambition and shining promises of glory.

I would have conquered the world and given it to her on a plate of gold for believing in me so . . . but for him: Mortimer. She could see no evil in him. Desire blinded her.

A knock at the door rattled me from my brooding. I shoved the letter beneath a document: a request to bankers in Florence for a substantial loan to finance the war in Scotland. Parliament had soured on my father's failures before me and would extend me nothing because of that, parsimonious bastards. If need be, I would beg Flemish merchants for the money I required. They always had plenty.

"Enter," I bade, returning to the window to gaze out over the mistiness. A merchant's boat laden with faggots of iron slogged downriver, its broad belly sinking low in the silver water.

Sir William Montagu stood in the doorway, brushing snow from his shoulders. "I was told you wished to see me, my lord."

I couldn't recall how young I was when I first met Will, but he had accompanied me to France when I was sent there to pay homage to King Charles. Every king needed a good man like Will: spy, protector, companion, and mentor. I could keep the kingdom easily secure until my death with half a dozen like him and never want for merriment all the while.

Struck with a thought, I sat down on the narrow stone window-sill. Its sharp edge dug into my thigh. I scratched at my chin, feeling the stiff bristles of new growth beneath my fingernails.

"Are you up for a journey, Will?"

His lips spread into a devilish grin. "Always."

"Good. Tomorrow we ride for Castle Rising."

"So soon after your return from the continent, my lord?"

My journey to the continent had a great deal to do with why I needed to see my mother now. What I found there had indeed changed everything between us. It had even changed me. "I have matters to settle. Long overdue ones."

Oh, I knew more of my mother's secrets than she would have ever suspected. Servants can be bribed for paltry sums, traitors spied upon, and maidens will spill their secrets between the sheets to flattering lovers with barely more effort than what it takes to pry their silky legs apart.

And yet, even just a year ago, I could not have imagined how so much of what I thought I knew . . . was wrong.

What is done cannot be undone. How I wish that it could.

28

Young Edward:

Castle Rising — 1339

THE CLOUDS ABOVE THE fens were piled high and dark, driven by a howling wind that lashed at the last ripples of winter snow and lifted them to collect in scattered drifts around the spikes of yellowed marsh grass. Far behind us were the stark spires of Ely Cathedral, thrusting above the drab flatness on a sole hill of chalk like a cairn of heaven. To our left, the Great Ouse curled sluggishly toward the Wash, stinking of mud and saltwater from the last tide, although now the river huddled low between its silty banks. Then, we veered away from the Ouse and the roads leading to Lynn, to follow a more lightly traveled road to the northeast.

The cold bit at my wrist where my sleeve had fallen back. I stretched my arm and tucked my sleeve beneath the flare of my fur-lined gloves. "Even the seagulls have the sense to stay out of the wind today," I said to Will.

"The seagulls are not idiots—unlike us." He drew his lips tight across his teeth to keep the wind from stealing his breath. "Should I have come? I haven't seen her since . . ."

He left the reflection unfinished. We had never spoken of that night at Nottingham. While I had lurked in the shadows of the corridor, it was Will who had plunged his sword into the chest of Arnaud de Mone, my mother's faithful squire, and Will who had ordered Mortimer dragged from her.

"I need you for the company," I told him. In actuality, I needed him to make sure I saw this task through. Had my brother John not died two years ago at Perth, I might have confided in him and brought him with me to Castle Rising today. Once, when we were but boys, he had sworn to fight the Scots alongside me. He had done so, and bravely, but sadly it had not been enough. "Don't worry overmuch about my mother, Will. I'll speak to her alone first. Then I'll ask her to come with me to see her newest grandson."

Montagu narrowed his eyes. "And you think she'll come around that easily, Ned? She's a stubborn woman, as I recall."

I could not tell if it was merely the wind stinging at his eyes that made him squint or if he severely doubted the chances of my success.

"Time for an end to this." I could spend the rest of my days heaping guilt upon her, or she upon me, but for what—something which I had only *thought* had happened? Or for things that ought to have been said long ago that were not? It was like a dog chasing its tail. Where was the end to it?

For hours we had ridden at a steady trot, but the closer we came to our destination, the faster I pressed my mount. We rode down and then up over the short, steep incline of one of the manmade swales that helped to drain the rich fields of the fens. Rounding a small stand of woods, we saw Castle Rising, gray and bleak beneath a lowering sky. I snapped my reins, eager to reach it, and Montagu pricked his horse's flanks with his spurs, enticing me to a race.

He bent low behind his horse's neck to cut the wind. Montagu was the finest horseman I knew. He could soothe the untamable beast and in a day guide its movements with only the pressure of his knees and a lean. This time, however, he was at a disadvantage. His mount, an old favorite of his, was favoring a leg and mine, lithe and barely broken, had devilishly reckless speed.

He kicked again and closed in on me. "Tell me—what was so bloody urgent, though? What must you say to her?"

I smiled at him, the frigid air blasting between my teeth and turning my lungs into a lump of ice. Tucking my chin to my chest, I clamped my knees tighter, drew my sword from its scabbard and whacked my horse's rump with the flat of the blade twice. He stretched out his neck and flew into the wind, his mane lashing at my eyes. Trustingly, I closed my eyes as he leapt another swale. When I looked again, we were almost there and Montagu was falling behind, cursing at his lagging beast as it loped along.

I reached the castle entrance first and yanked my reins hard to the left. My horse spun madly around, clouds of steam billowing from its nostrils.

"You think that I tell you everything?" I shouted so Montagu could hear, his horse now trotting with a distinct limp. "There are some things I keep to myself—what I say to my wife in bed to seduce her into conceiving one more child, for one . . . what words pass between my mother and I, another. So ask no more, Will. I'll take this to my grave." I slammed my sword into its scabbard for emphasis.

The portcullis went up and the gates parted. Montagu drew up, panting as hard as his pitiful horse, and quick behind him the guards followed, ushering me to my decided fate.

MY MOTHER GASPED AND covered her mouth. Her hand shook so

terribly that she had to turn away to hide it. Frantically, she began to scurry about, putting away objects that had been carelessly strewn about her private chambers: an open book, an old letter, an assortment of jewels arrayed upon her small dressing table as if she were considering which to wear for the day, but had not expended the effort to make a final choice. Her hair was neatly plaited and pinned tightly back, but she wore no veil or adornments in it. Her gown was a plain, dark blue of coarse wool with an overtunic of gray—practical for guarding against the winter chill, but far from making a statement about her long, royal lineage.

"You did not write to say you were coming," she uttered, finally composed enough to face me.

"Cologne is just as dull and cold in the winter as England. Besides, Philippa wanted to come home, to be back with the other children. I have a new son. I trust you received the message?"

She barely nodded. I could tell she wanted to know more about the child—was he hale and healthy, did he have my eyes or his mother's?—but she still looked so stricken with dread that she could not even muster a simple, cordial question.

I undid the clasp on my cloak and flung the heavy garment over the back of a chair. The clasp, a pair of twining, golden snakes with jewels clenched in their fangs, had been sent as a gift from my sister Joanna, Queen of Scotland.

Dragging the chair closer to the hearth, I bade my mother to sit, while I settled down on a wobbly stool. "Enough of letters, though. Sometimes . . . sometimes it is hard to tell what the words actually mean, especially when there is no voice, no expression behind them."

Still she had not sat down beside me. Her legs quivered. Her fingers worried at the single gold band on a finger of her left hand, twisting it and tugging it until it looked as though she might yank her finger off. She gazed into the struggling fire in the hearth, as if contemplating casting herself into the flames.

"He lives," I said.

With those two words, the color—what little there was of it—drained from her face. As her knees buckled, I sprang forward, my stool clattering to the floor. I caught her just before she collapsed in shock. She was weightless in my arms—having fretted herself to a sack of bones since I left for Cologne. The lines around her mouth, on her forehead, between her brows, beneath her eyes—they were now the deep, dark trenches of declining age. Not so long ago, they were barely the graceful etchings of distinguished maturity—neither young nor old, but something in between. I felt her forehead. It was deathly cold. Her skin was pale, like one who had hidden from the light of the sun for many years. I rubbed at her fingers until finally they closed around mine. Her eyelids fluttered. She drew a long, deep breath.

I helped her up. Once she was in the chair and steady, I brought her a cup of water to moisten her cracked lips.

"I have seen him with my own eyes," I said. "'William of Wales' he calls himself. A few years ago, a papal notary named Manuel de Fieschi wrote to me and told me my father was living in Italy. I didn't believe him at first, but when Sir John Maltravers confirmed it was not my father who was embalmed and buried at Gloucester, I thought it possible. When I went to the continent, I had this 'William of Wales' brought to me. By God's eyes, it *was* him. He told me everything."

She reached one shaking, feeble hand toward the fire. "What will you do?"

"Nothing," I said.

Her eyes widened in astonishment. Water spilled over the brim of the cup and onto the floor. "But I-I-I . . . I am responsible for . . . I let Edmund die to protect . . . to protect . . ."

Mortimer. And Mortimer died to protect you.

Forlorn, she gazed into the puddle at her feet, setting the cup beside it. Was she still so heartsick that even the thought of his name made it feel to her as if his death were only yesterday?

What is done cannot be undone, I told myself. But I had come for a reason—sailed on rugged seas and traversed through dismal weather with my wife and infant son, no less: I had erred, egregiously.

"And I, Mother . . ."—I reached out, took her stone cold hand in mine—"bear the guilt of the death of another innocent man. I have not heard you speak his name for eight years now: Roger Mortimer."

I no longer hated the man. He had loved her, of that I was certain . . . and she him. Perhaps for her it was as much need of him as true love. Carnal indulgences had blinded them both to virtue. Mortimer had abandoned his wife of twenty years for her. She, as well, had forsaken her husband and turned his fate over to scoundrels. My uncle Edmund, however, had threatened everything for them. And I, not knowing any better, had failed to save his life. At the time, I knew that if he was right and my father was alive and restored to the throne, I would have lost my chance to ever become King of France. And so I let him die, rather than believe him.

Whatever the cause for all this strife and woe, I had vowed to abandon judgment—to forgive them in my heart. Did I not desire the same?

Shivering, she pulled the mantle around her shoulders. "Who have you told?"

I stoked the logs, spent to lumps of glowing charcoal, and added some kindling to revive the fire. "No one, except for Philippa."

"Not even Montagu?"

"Certainly not. Tell him and the world will know." William Montagu had been both mentor and friend to me since my boyhood. I trusted his loyalty like no other man alive, but he liked to talk, especially after several pints of ale. "It was Philippa who convinced me to come to you. I wasn't certain, when I first learned the truth, what to do really. Once I've clung to a purpose, I find it hard to let go. I've harbored anger like a battered shield . . . being the soldier I am. If set upon, I protect myself. When I am threatened, I strike. It took a wise woman to enlighten me that my anger had earned me nothing after all these years."

"Philippa *is* a good woman."

"I know." I stood to lean against the mantel and kicked little lumps of fallen ashes back into the hearth. "You saw that in her when we first went to Hainault."

"The other girls—they were prettier, but she was . . . different. Smarter."

"She is, she is. And she constantly reminds me of it. I find it humbling." I forced a smile, not so much for appreciation of Philippa, but to ease my mother's mind before broaching my reason for coming once more. "He is in good health. At peace with God."

"Does he know that I —"

"That you made Lord Berkeley swear to protect his life? That Mortimer knew he had been freed?"

Her chin tucked against her shoulder, she nodded.

"Yes," I said, "he knows."

"How?"

"Lord Berkeley told him the night he guided him to freedom."

"But I made Berkeley swear, on his life, never to tell anyone."

"Father had told Berkeley, more than once, that he did not want to be king ever again. Berkeley was keenly aware that if he let Father know *why* he was being set free, and by whom, then he would go in gratitude and live in peace, not with revenge in his soul. He was right."

Tears filled her eyes. But tears of what?

"Father has long since ceased wanting to be a part of the world that you and I know. His birthright—the crown of England—he reviled it. He was glad to be free of the burden. The life he lived, he said, was merely a test of his faith—a faith that often wavered. Truly, he is at peace now. I want you to be at peace, too, Mother. He forgave you long ago, and I came here to tell you that I forgive you, and Mortimer, for all that has been done or misunderstood between us."

I knelt before her, my head bowed. "It is me who begs your forgiveness now. Should you deny me, I'll love you no less, for I have been guilty of arrogance and presumption. Ambition blinded me. It was a trait Mortimer and I shared."

"I loved him so much." She said it so plaintively that it struck me hard and heavy.

I placed my head in her lap, as I had when I was a very small boy, begging for a story to stave off bedtime.

"Do not hold Roger as the villain in all this, my son. He was not. There was more good in him than you know. More than you know."

"Then I was wrong—about both of you."

Mother stroked my hair, winding a loose curl around one of her fingers. Her voice was husky, roughened by a sea of tears that had long since been wept dry. "I forgive you . . . for everything."

I looked up at her. It was not easy to abandon the past, to let go of an anger that was so familiar that without it, I felt as if I were bereft of both weapon and shield. But with her words, she vanquished it, for both of us. She had set us in the present, to live for today, to go forward.

"You will come to Windsor to see our newest son—Lionel?"

"I will." She encircled me in her arms and laid her head on top of mine. Then ever so faintly, I heard the murmur of a lullaby rising from her throat.

"Lionel—he has the colic. Philippa is distraught. Like you, she refuses to abandon her children entirely to nursemaids. You must tell her what you did for my brother John. I remember you saying once that he was impossible as an infant."

338

She gave a short laugh. "There was nothing I could do. It was his nature. It passed. All things do." She hummed again and I sensed myself drifting away, weary from my journey.

"Windsor," she said. "So much of your childhood spent there. Take me there, will you, and tell me more of the children on the way?"

"Tomorrow," I promised.

Today I would simply be with her. *Today*.

What is done cannot be undone, but what will be done tomorrow, has yet to be done at all.

Author's Note

For centuries, Queen Isabella has been maligned in both history and literature. One well known fictionalization of events is Christopher Marlowe's late 16th century drama: *Edward II or "The Troublesome Reign and Lamentable Death of Edward the Second, King of England, with the Tragical Fall of Proud Mortimer"*; this play may have contributed to prior beliefs regarding Isabella's involvement in the conspiracy to murder Edward II. Although I have chosen to present quotes within my story from Marlowe's play, I have strayed far from his version of events.

Readers are advised to keep in mind that, while based on extensive research and set within the framework of actual events, this novel is a work of fiction. The dialogue and internal motivations assigned to the characters are entirely my own invention. The chroniclers of Isabella's time, such as Jean le Bel, Geoffrey le Baker and later Jean Froissart, have provided us with many details of the era, but not all the answers. In 1878, the discovery of the letter from Manuel de Fieschi eventually caused scholars to re-examine events. Modern historical biographers (of Edward II, Isabella, Roger Mortimer and Edward III) have studied and written about the death of Edward II and also Isabella's relationship with Roger Mortimer. For those who wish to explore the era further, many works of non-fiction may be read for various interpretations of documented facts— although even historical accounts may contain elements of bias.

Whichever theory one chooses to believe, the thing that has always spurred my imagination is pure and simple curiosity. Did Edward indeed love his 'favorites' in a way that he could never love his own wife? There is no dispute that he both relied on Despenser and gave him his unconditional loyalty. He had lost a close and trusted friend once before with the execution of Piers de Gaveston, so it is no wonder that in the case of Despenser he would defend him even more steadfastly.

Once Isabella decided to separate from her husband and take control of matters, how much of the invasion and the deposition of her husband was her idea and how much was the machination of Roger Mortimer? I have no doubt that in some ways both Isabella and Mortimer used each other to achieve their revenge. I do believe, however, that Isabella was wholly enraptured with her lover and received from him a degree of affection that Edward was unwilling, or unable, to offer. Had she lived today, she might have sought a divorce. As a woman in the 14th century, though, she did not have that option. It has been speculated by some historians that she was, at one time, pregnant with Mortimer's child; however, no proof of such a child exists.

It would have been no stretch to think Isabella believed her son would be a better king than his father, but even that assumption generates more questions. Why did she govern so sternly in his minority and seek to increase her own wealth and that of Mortimer's? Did she foresee a split between Edward III and Mortimer? Or had her treatment at Despenser's hands hardened her to the opinions of others and fired worldly ambition in her in an age when women were discouraged from holding power outright?

Also, at what point did Edward III learn the truth of his father's whereabouts? Some accounts put that discovery at a much earlier date than what I have depicted. If such is the case, then we would have to view Edward III's actions in a vastly different light.

It was after his receipt of the de Fieschi letter and a trip to the continent that Edward III appears to have extended more liberties to his mother. During her aging years, Isabella was allowed to travel more freely and was often later in the royal household. She seems to have developed a fairly close relationship with her daughter-in-law, Queen Philippa. Isabella did live to see each one of Edward and Philippa's children born—thirteen in all.

After a prolonged illness, Isabella died at Hertford Castle in August of 1358. She was sixty-three—a respectable age for that harsh period in time. She had suffered the neglect of her husband and the ill-will of his avaricious favorite, experienced the guilt of a scandalous love affair and bore the blame that her own son heaped upon her for his father's death. Yet to pity, or despise, Isabella for all of that is to overlook her strength, much of which she wielded tacitly throughout her life.

Edward III lived to be sixty-five. History views him as one of England's greatest warrior kings—the victor of Halidon Hill in 1332 against the Scots, and ten years later against a French force four times the size of his own at Crécy, and then again along with his son Edward at Poitiers in 1356, where he took as his prisoner, King John of France. Another of Edward III's royal prisoners was his own brother-in-law David of Scotland, whom he kept under close guard in London for eleven years. During David's absence from Scotland, his nephew Robert Stewart, son of Walter Stewart and Marjorie Bruce, presided over the kingdom of Scotland and later ascended to the throne at the age of fifty-four.

Edward III is also remembered for having begun the Noble Order of the Garter, the motto of which was *"Honi soit qui mal y pense"* (Evil to him who thinks evil). But, like his father and mother before him, even this noblest of kings was not without flaw. His reign ended not with the intrigue which marked its beginning, nor the glorious triumphs that accentuated its height, but rather with disgrace. Following Philippa's death in 1369, he began to openly parade his love affair with the unsavory Alice Perrers—a mistress whom his aging wife had been painfully aware of. Even though the relationship brought him much public condemnation and the remonstrance of barons and clergy alike, he was impervious to their judgment.

Then in 1376, his beloved son and heir Edward, later known as the Black Prince, died. Edward III, some say by then bereft of his wits and most certainly sick at heart, followed in death one year later. Alice Perrers, with the king until his dying breath, stole the jewels from his dead body and fled.

Edward III was succeeded by his ten-year old grandson, Richard II, whose reign was plagued with its own troubles.

Acknowledgments

No book ever reaches the final stages without outside help. My eternal gratitude goes out to Team TKMD for their professional expertise, honesty and insight: Lance Ganey (cover artist extraordinaire), Derek and Paula Prior (for their keen editing and attention to detail), Sarah Woodbury (who reminded me to keep the creative speech tags in check), and Rebecca Lochlann (who helped me work through the pivotal scene by repeatedly posing the question 'Why?').

And to my many readers who have written and shared kind words—you are the reason I continue to tell stories. Thank you, a thousand times over.

About the Author

N. Gemini Sasson holds a M.S. in Biology from Wright State University where she ran cross country on athletic scholarship. She has worked as an aquatic toxicologist, an environmental engineer, a teacher and a cross country coach. A longtime breeder of Australian Shepherds, her articles on bobtail genetics have been translated into seven languages. She lives in rural Ohio with her husband, two nearly grown children and an ever-changing number of animals.

Isabeau, A Novel of Queen Isabella and Sir Roger Mortimer (2011 IPPY Silver Medalist in Historical Fiction) is the prequel to *The King Must Die*. Sasson is also the author of a trilogy about Robert the Bruce: *The Crown in the Heather (The Bruce Trilogy: Book I)*, *Worth Dying For (The Bruce Trilogy: Book II)* and *The Honor Due a King (The Bruce Trilogy: Book III)*.

For updates on N. Gemini Sasson's books as they happen:
www.facebook.com/NGeminiSasson

For more details about N. Gemini Sasson and her books:
www.ngeminisasson.com

CPSIA information can be obtained at www.ICGtesting.com
Printed in the USA
BVOW04s2053130314

347627BV00001B/39/P